Also by Meg M. Robinson

<u>Chloe Chadwick Series</u>

Finding Salus

Waking Salus

Remembering Salus

Saving Salus

Megaverse Series

<u>Immortal Love Series</u>

Seeking Eternity

A Fury's Heart

The Last Lemurian

Grim Favors

Dance With Death

Legacy

Meg M. Robinson

Dedication

This one is for all the book nerds who dreamed of finding a magical library.

I'm one of them!

Prologue

IT WAS JUST BEFORE midnight when four somber people found themselves sitting at a table in the kitchen. It was a modern kitchen, kept neat as a pin and painfully organized, despite the stone walls and floor around them. An older man with short salt-and-pepper hair and a scar along his jaw lifted his cup of coffee to his lips and frowned. Across from him sat a blonde woman who appeared about two decades his junior, with a similar look of worry on her face. She, too, had a cup, but used it more for something to do with her hands than out of a desire to actually drink it. To her left was a slightly older brunette woman, one who kept whatever she was feeling hidden from her features, but couldn't resist tapping a nail lightly on the table. The last member of their depressed party was a younger man with brown hair and a clenched jaw.

It was the blonde woman who spoke first. "I just can't believe Erasmus is dying. He's so young!" Tears gathered in her eyes, but she blinked rapidly to prevent them from falling.

The older man's lips twitched ever so slightly, though there was no humor in his eyes. He, too, felt grief and it showed in the tightness of his face. "Young? Catherine, he's almost nine hundred years old. That's hardly young," he replied, voice gruff.

Catherine sighed. "No, Ray, he's not actually young, but for who he is? What he is? It's young," she protested weakly. "He should have decades left, at a minimum. A century, even."

"I won't argue that he's young, but I'm still surprised it's so bad that we're saying he's dying and not sick," the other woman said, the tapping coming more rapidly. "And I'm sure as hell going to miss him."

Ray reached over to pat the woman's hand twice. "We all are, Penny. He's a good man. One of the best."

"That's for damn sure," the youngest of their group muttered as he shoved his chair back and stood. He went to the liquor cabinet and grabbed a bottle of ouzo. Half turning, he lifted the bottle and gave the other three a questioning look. Ray shook his head, but Penny nodded and, after a soft sniffle, so did Catherine. He grabbed three glasses, returned to the table, and poured.

"Thanks, Joshua," Catherine murmured before she sipped the drink. The flavor as it slid over her tongue made her grimace but didn't stop her from taking another drink. "Is it...will it happen that soon?"

Ray nodded. "A week, perhaps, though Sergei couldn't commit to him even lasting that long. But he's as stubborn as a mule, so he may surprise us." A smile ghosted across his lips. "It wouldn't be the first time."

Penny laughed softly. "No, it wouldn't. He was forever sneaking up on me, you know. I think it was—is—a game for him. He always laughs when I jumped. Laughed like a loon when he managed to scare a squeal out of me."

Not in the same mood to reminisce and use humor to mask his sorrow, Joshua looked to Ray. "I suppose we should start recalling people if it'll happen that soon?"

Ray made a sound of agreement as he took a drink. "The sooner the better. I know there aren't many who are out right now, but a few aren't exactly close by. Can't remember if they can teleport or not."

They fell silent for a minute, simply thinking of the man who lay so close by, dying all too quickly. Penny was the one to break the silence, her voice hesitant. "Should we inform Heather? And her daughter?"

The moment Heather's name was spoken, Ray's eyes closed, something about the mention of the woman making his shoulders sag. "Technically, I think we should. They are connected. It's protocol."

"But they haven't been here in what, twenty, twenty-five years?" Catherine said, her brow furrowing. "Her daughter's never been here, for that matter."

"That doesn't mean they don't have the right, the responsibility to be here," Joshua protested with a shake of his head as he refilled his glass. Like Catherine, it wasn't his favorite drink, but he barely made a face as it went down.

"He's right," Ray agreed as he opened his eyes and fixed them on Catherine. "No matter how long it's been, they're still a part of this. We should have Heather's location."

A different, deeper voice said, "We do." All four turned to watch the tall, dark-haired man stride into the kitchen. "I just left him," he explained as he grabbed a bottle of water from the fridge and guzzled nearly half of it.

"How was he? And the truth, Lucas, not the company line, not with us," Penny said, her voice respectful, but she was clearly not going to settle for a generic answer.

Lucas stared at her for a moment. "He's not doing well, but he wants them here, if they're willing. Which is why Carla and Nick are leaving within the hour. With orders to bring them back, even if they have to drag them on the plane and gain their willingness on the flight over." Despite his threat, his voice wasn't mean, just firm. If it eased the mind of a dying man, he'd see it done. He'd love to have it done instantly, but while teleporting would be faster—and preferable—Erasmus was adamant they fly. He wouldn't explain why.

Joshua twisted in his seat to face Lucas. "Where are they?"

Lucas grimaced. "America, which is why I don't want Nick and Carla wasting time trying to convince them before they're on the plane." His attention shifted to Ray. "They'll be here," he said in a quieter voice.

"Good. It's past time. Long past time."

"Yes, it is."

Chapter 1

More than half a day later, Sophia came down the stairs of the split-level house she shared with her mom while she attended grad school. Though it was Saturday, she tended to be an early riser and had already showered. Her still damp brown hair was pulled up into a ponytail as she made her way into the kitchen where Heather, her mom, was fixing breakfast. She kissed her mom on the cheek. "Morning," she said cheerfully as she moved away to pour a cup of coffee.

Heather smiled as she flipped the pancakes. "You're in an exceptionally good mood this morning. Big plans?" she teased.

"Not really," Sophia admitted as she leaned a hip against the counter. She was dressed in casual clothes; a simple pair of jeans with a well-worn and well-loved Indiana Jones tee-shirt. "Just woke up in a really good mood. Not sure why. Maybe I had an awesome dream or something. Like I won the lottery or got my doctorate."

Her mom laughed. "Winning the lottery would be nice, but I think I'd rather see my daughter as a doctor. Even though—"

"I know, I know. You wanted me to major in something else," Sophia said with a roll of her eyes, though she wasn't really upset. Though her choice in majors hadn't pleased her mom for some reason, it hadn't stopped her from supporting Sophia's choice.

"True, but I still can't wait to see that piece of paper proclaiming you as Doctor Sophia Regas."

Knowing she meant it, Sophia smiled and wrapped an arm around her mom's shoulders and gave her a quick squeeze. "I know, and I love you for it."

The doorbell rang, and they both glanced toward the sound. "I've got it, Mom. Probably just another salesman. Pancakes are much more important." She took a quick drink of coffee, then walked to the front door, humming softly to herself. She didn't bother with the peephole—she rarely did since they lived in a good neighborhood and she was too trusting by far—and simply opened the door. Two people stood there; one man, one woman. The man was tall, with chin-length brown hair and dark eyes. Attractive, if a little old for her, though he was dressed in a slightly rumpled suit. The woman, who was about the same age with slightly lighter colored hair pulled into a bun, was dressed in a pair of black cargo pants and a black tee-shirt. They certainly didn't look as though they were together, which had Sophia's greeting coming out with a hint of her confusion. "Hi. Can I help you?"

"Hello. I'm Nick and this is Carla," the man said with a small motion to his companion. "We're looking for Heather Regas or her daughter, Sophia." Though it was subtle, she was almost positive his accent was Greek.

"Can I ask why?" Sophia asked as she heard quick footsteps from behind her. She turned to see her mom, no longer smiling.

"Pancakes are on the table," she told Sophia without looking in her direction, her entire focus on the strangers. "I'll handle this."

"Wait, but—"

"I'll handle this," Heather said firmly.

It wasn't often that her mom made demands like that, so with a frown, Sophia stepped back from the door, giving the strangers a bemused smile. She did go into the kitchen, but pancakes were the last things on her mind. Instead, she stepped just out of sight and listened as well as she could.

"What are you two doing here?"

Sophia blinked in surprise. Her mom knew these people? She hadn't looked happy to see them, which was unusual. Her mom loved being around people. There were few she didn't like.

"It's nice to see you again, too, Heather," the woman said.

Heather sighed. "And under other circumstances, I might say the same, Carla, but that still doesn't explain what you two are doing here."

There was a brief silence. "Erasmus is dying," Nick said, almost too quietly to hear.

"What? How? How long does he have?" Heather asked, and though her voice was quieter, Sophia knew her mom well enough to recognize the shocked tone.

"Not long. Definitely not long enough," Carla answered, and the grief in the murmured words made Sophia's heart ache for the woman. "He wants to see you, Heather. You and Sophia."

"I..." Heather trailed off and Sophia risked peeking at the trio to see her mom rubbing her face. "No. I can't, Carla. I left for a reason."

"A completely valid reason, too," Carla agreed with a nod, "but he wants to meet his granddaughter before he dies."

Sophia's eyes widened and she gave up all pretense that she wasn't eavesdropping, walking quickly toward the others. "Granddaughter?

I have a grandfather out there? Where? Who is he?" she asked in rapid succession.

Heather's expression was one of sorrow and resignation when her gaze met Sophia's. "Yes, sweetheart, you have a grandfather. He's your dad's dad."

That explained why Sophia had never heard of him. Her mom almost never spoke of Sophia's dad, and Sophia had figured out long ago that it simply hurt her too much. She knew he had died before she was born, but not how. For a long minute, she just stared at her mom before she shifted her focus to the strangers. "He wants to meet me? He really said that?"

Nick nodded. "He did."

"Where is he?"

"Greece."

Sophia blinked at him before slowly looking at her mother, who winced slightly. "I have a grandfather living in Greece? Really?" she asked, the last word laced with sarcasm and anger.

"You do." Heather pulled the door open further and silently motioned Nick and Carla inside. They entered, skirting around Heather, but didn't move more than a few feet inside. "And just so we can get it out of the way now, he works in a...historical library and repository there. As did your father."

Sophia chewed lightly on her lip, weighing meeting another family member against upsetting the only one she currently had. "I want to meet him," she told Heather, her voice soft, but certain.

"I know," Heather said tiredly. She rubbed the spot between her eyes and closed the door before she met Sophia's gaze. "Just like I know you have a lot of questions."

Carla delicately cleared her throat. "I know this is an emotional time," she said in a careful tone, "but Erasmus really doesn't have that long. If you are coming, Sophia, then we need to leave as soon as possible. All your questions can be asked on the plane, and I promise we'll answer them to the best of our ability."

Sophia nodded. "I'll go pack. Fortunately, I have a passport. I'll be quick."

"Thank you," Nick told her.

She took the stairs two at a time, too impatient for answers to give any pretense of being ladylike. She grabbed her suitcase and backpack out of the closet and began throwing the necessities into them, which, in her mind, included her laptop and camera. If she was visiting Greece, she'd need both, no matter the reason for the trip. When she was halfway finished, Heather appeared in the doorway and clasped her hands together, a sign Sophia knew meant she was anxious. She glanced up but didn't stop packing. "I'm going," she said stubbornly.

"I know. I'm going with you."

Sophia's motions faltered and she gave her mom a wide-eyed look of shock. "I thought you didn't want to go there."

"It's complicated. Which I know you think is a cop-out excuse, but it is complicated," Heather insisted. "And before you ask, yes, I will tell you everything, just not right this second."

Sophia nodded slowly and resumed packing. "Good. Though I have to say I have a lot of questions. And I'm not happy." She zipped the suitcase up and put her hands on her hips. "I have a degree in ancient Greek history and culture. I speak two different dialects of Greek, and yet I never knew I had family in Greece."

"I know, and I'm sorry. But I do promise there's a good reason for it."

"I hope so," Sophia said as she pulled her phone out and started typing an email to her professors, telling them she had a family emergency and wouldn't be in class for a few days. "Though now I know why you weren't happy when I told you I wanted to get a Classics degree," she muttered.

Heather nodded. "I'll tell you everything," she promised before leaving to do her own packing.

Sophia took a moment, rubbing her hands over her face as she tried to process everything that had happened in the last twenty minutes. It hadn't yet sunk in, but she couldn't decide which part seemed more unreal—the part where her mom had kept secrets from her, or the fact that she was about to fly to Greece with her mom and two strangers. She shot off a few texts to friends, telling them she'd be out of town before she picked up her bags and went downstairs. Once there and alone with Nick and Carla, she suddenly felt awkward and a little shy. "So, um...you know my name, but it feels like we weren't really introduced or anything," she said, setting her bags down in a chair.

Nick grinned. "Unusual circumstances, and we have more than twelve hours on a plane to get to know each other. But if it helps, like I said, I'm Nick, and I work at the same...library...your grandfather does. Carla's my wife."

"I work there, too, though we don't call it a library," the other woman stated. "To us, it's the Athenaeum."

Sophia mouthed the word before she smiled. "I like that. Sounds cool. And it's a historical library?"

Carla nodded. "And more, yes. It's the oldest library still in existence in the world, as far as we know." She smiled, and there was something sly—but not malicious—in the expression. "And we know a lot."

"That is so cool," Sophia whispered in awe. This was right up her alley. It made her mad all over again that her mom had hidden this from her, but she pushed the negative emotions down as best she could.

Heather came down the stairs, though she was carrying more than Sophia had. In addition to the suitcase and a backpack, she also had her purse and a duffel bag. "I assume you want to leave right away?"

"We do," Nick agreed. "The sooner we get to Erasmus, the better."

"And since it's you two, I assume we're flying rather than teleporting?"

"We are," Nick confirmed.

"The usual transportation, then?" When Nick nodded, she started for the door, giving Sophia an apologetic look. "Let's go then."

"What's the usual transportation?" Sophia asked as she followed the others out, setting the alarm and locking the door behind them.

Carla laughed softly. "You'll see."

They climbed into a rented black car after placing their bags in the trunk. There was little said as they drove not to the big airport in Atlanta, but to a smaller airfield Sophia didn't know existed. Though she itched to ask what was going on, she held her tongue. She was happy she had when they pulled up near a private jet. Her eyes widened, and she looked at her mom, who only smiled and nodded. Sophia still said nothing as Nick and Carla helped them bring their things onto the plane. She had flown before, but never had she seen anything as nice as this. The seats looked comfortable, and there was also a couch, TV, and a whole compartment in the back she imagined held a bedroom and bathroom. Legs suddenly shaky, she sank down into one of the chairs and marveled at how well it cushioned her.

The others got settled, with Nick disappearing briefly into the cockpit. When he returned a moment later, he said, "We'll be taking off in a few minutes. After we're in the air, we'll answer whatever questions you have.

Sophia took a slow, deep breath and nodded. "Thank you." And she spent their take off staring out the window, wondering exactly what she was getting herself into.

Chapter 2

T HEY HAD BEEN IN the air for several minutes before Sophia felt like someone was looking at her. She turned away from the window and saw all three of the others watching her with expressions that varied from expectant to amused. "What?" she asked.

"We just expected you to be pestering us with questions the moment we were all settled, I think," Carla said, lips twitching, though she never actually smiled.

"I just don't even know where to begin," Sophia admitted. "Do I start with my grandfather? With this library, this Athenaeum? With why it was all kept secret from me?" She couldn't help but look at her mom and noticed the regret that was clear on the older woman's face.

Nick glanced between Sophia and Heather. "Why don't we start with what the Athenaeum is? It's complex, but I think it's...easiest, I suppose."

Heather nodded, never taking her eyes off her daughter. "That's probably best. That might help explain the rest."

Sophia wasn't so sure. Yes, she loved libraries and history, but even the oldest library in the world wasn't as important as her family. On the other hand, maybe knowing about one would help understand the other. "Okay. What exactly is so special about the Athenaeum?

And how do people who work for a library afford a plane like this? For that matter, you don't look like a librarian," she said, directing her last comment to Carla, not caring if she came off as rude. These three people had turned her life upside down—at least temporarily—and she was going to get some answers.

To her surprise, Carla grinned. "Better get used to that. Most of the librarians there don't look like librarians."

Seeing the confusion on Sophia's face, Nick spoke up. "The Athenaeum isn't your typical library. It's not public, for one, and it won't come up on any internet search. It's hidden. Private. It also holds a great deal more than books."

Sophia frowned. "Why the secrecy? Is this the Illuminati's library or the library of the gods or something? Does it hold political and financial secrets?" Nick grinned, and out of the corner of her eye, Sophia saw her mother crack a small smile as well. Their amusement at her total ignorance of this situation annoyed her. "Instead of laughing at me, how about you give me some answers?" she asked, trying hard to keep her temper under control.

"No, you're right," Nick said, smothering his smile. "It's just that you're not completely wrong. We're not the Illuminati, but there are a great many secrets within the Athenaeum. Most are in the form of books."

"Not just books," Heather protested.

"No, we also have scrolls, tablets...anything mortals used to store written information, really."

"Tablets? Like clay tablets? But those haven't been used in thousands of years," Sophia argued. "Even the Arcane no longer use them."

"They did fall out of fashion thanks to papyrus and other materials, but if all you have is clay, you use clay," Nick told her. "My point is, we have more than just books in the Athenaeum."

"And what sort of secrets could possibly justify all this? And give you the money for private planes?" None of this was adding up. It felt like she was in some movie about conspiracy theories and secret societies. The fact that her mother was in on all of it only made it worse.

"Why don't you just tell her what the Athenaeum is, then let her ask questions?" Heather asked as she got up and grabbed a couple bottles of water, offering one to Sophia, who gratefully took it.

It wasn't Nick who started speaking, it was Carla, which surprised Sophia. "The Athenaeum is, like Nick told you earlier, old. Like first century BC old. You've heard of the Library of Alexandria?"

Sophia blinked at Carla. "I studied ancient Greece in college. Of course I've heard of it."

Carla's brows lifted and she exchanged a curious look with Nick before she went on. "Well, the idea for the Athenaeum was sparked when that particular library was about to be destroyed. Our founder, Eugenios, did his best to rescue as many of the works in it as he could and brought them home. Scrolls and tablets primarily, but he rescued whatever he could, including relics and artifacts. He hid them, kept them safe. Over time, the collection grew, as did the number of people involved. Anytime a library was in danger of being destroyed, or during the times when people were burning books to stamp out knowledge, we saved as much as we could and took them home, protected them." Sophia started to speak, but Carla lifted a hand and continued. "The reason for the secrecy is that not all the books or relics we have in the

Athenaeum should be available to the public. Some because they hold information people would kill to keep hidden, and some because they are just dangerous in the wrong hands."

Sophia frowned and shook her head. "What do you mean, dangerous? What could possibly be in a book that's dangerous? Books help heal ignorance, which is good for everyone."

"Remember, not everything in the Athenaeum is modern," Nick reminded her. "I did say we had scrolls and tablets. Some of the information is centuries, even a millennium older than the Athenaeum. And not all the books were written by humans. Do you really think a notebook detailing how a witch created a new spell should be available to humans? Or maybe a scroll written by a god?" He leaned forward before saying, "What about a grimoire containing dangerous sorcery? Tell me, what do you think humans would do if they knew—really knew—that magic was not only real, but possible for them? How do you think that would affect the world? Affect wars?"

"Humans aren't that bad," Sophia argued, but she knew her words sounded weak.

Carla laughed softly and shook her head. "Optimism isn't a bad thing, *koukla*, but too much of it can get you hurt."

Annoyed because of the amusement in Carla's eyes, Sophia muttered, "I'm not your doll."

"No?" She shrugged. "Nick has a point. Think about it, Sophia. Wars kill more people now than they did a hundred years ago, a thousand years, because the weapons are deadlier. And now they're starting to do war by remote control. How many more people would have been killed throughout the centuries if they could use magic? If they could heal their allies and destroy entire cities? Think of how World War

II might have gone if Hitler had actually managed to get his hands on real, powerful magic like he'd hoped to find. Not only that, but think about the witch trials in America. The witch hunts in Europe. And that was when most people didn't truly believe. And if magic came out now, then think about how many people would end up in labs somewhere, being tortured for tests before they were dissected for answers that science couldn't provide." She leaned back, her spine rigid. "*That* is why we hide from the humans. It's not because the Ekklesia tells us to, it's because we have to."

A frisson of fear crept up Sophia's spine as she realized how accurate Carla's words were. She slowly nodded. "You made your point." A thought struck her. "Why hide it from the Arcane, though? We all have magic of some sort. We all know sorcery exists. A lot of us have learned sorcery, even. But you're acting like only the people in the Athenaeum know about it."

"Actually, the Athenaeum is a bit of a rumor outside of its walls. So some people have an idea it exists, but its location is a tightly guarded secret." Nick smiled tightly. "But, like you pointed out, not all humans are bad, and not all the Arcane are good. And just like the humans, we've forgotten quite a lot. There is sorcery in the Athenaeum that the outside world has forgotten about. There are relics that were supposed to have been destroyed when the gods put a limit on what relics we could create. And not all monsters are humans or demons. They are witches and elves, dryads and vampires, all who could take what we're protecting and use it to further *their* agenda."

Again, Sophia couldn't argue with his words. Evil came in many forms, often with a charming smile. "So why tell me, then? You didn't swear me to secrecy or anything before you told me about this. This isn't a one-way trip or something, is it?" She didn't think her mom would go along with something like that, but then, her mom had kept a huge secret from her for twenty-four years.

Nick blinked, then looked absolutely offended. "No! Who do you think we are? You're Erasmus's granddaughter, Greg's daughter. Of course we're not going to hurt you."

Heather gave Sophia a wounded look and shook her head. "They may be secretive, and they have no problem defending themselves, but they're not killers. And I would never have allowed you to come if I thought you'd be hurt."

"Sorry," Sophia muttered. She opened her mouth to ask more, but decided she just couldn't handle more on that topic right now. "So the plane? You never did say how a library can afford things like this."

Nick still looked annoyed, so Carla answered. "We're a very old organization. We've had some extremely smart people working in the Athenaeum and we also have people dedicated solely to investments and managing our money. We don't spend it frivolously, either. A private plane, yes, because occasionally we need to get places quickly and not everyone can teleport. Weapons, because we're not the only people out there who know relics and books about true magic exist."

"Do you guys have, like, day jobs or something?" Sophia asked, getting more and more curious.

Carla nodded. "Some of us do, and we may sometimes take outside jobs to get information or get hold of a book or relic, but a lot of us dedicate our full time to the Athenaeum."

"And it's only the Arcane who work there?"

Again, she nodded. "While Eugenios was human, that was a different time. Now, with the laws against revealing ourselves to humans, everyone is Arcane, but we're not limited to one species. Last I checked, we had at least one person from every Arcane species working there."

There was a long pause as Sophia tried to sort her thoughts out. "You still don't look like a librarian to me," she murmured as she studied Carla intently.

"Because I'm not. Not how you're thinking, anyway," Carla answered with a shrug. "I'm one of the nasaru, one of our guards. I help protect the Athenaeum or people like Nick who go out into the world to find new books or relics. And it's not like we have a dress code anyway, so I could be a 'librarian,'" she said, making air quotes with her fingers, "and have a bright blue mohawk, a bunch of facial piercings, and tattoos. No one would care as long as I did my job. Besides, blending in is useful when we leave the Athenaeum."

"That actually sounds...great," Sophia admitted. "I never got how wearing a suit and being clean cut made someone more efficient or a better person than someone who dressed like a goth or punk or whatever." Then she grinned. "Are there any librarians who look like that?"

"Actually, yes. Our tech does," Nick said with a nod.

"Just how many people work in the li—the Athenaeum?"

He paused, mentally counting. "Those who are based in the Athenaeum? Thirty, thirty-five. Somewhere in there. And sometimes family helps out or we contract outside help, though they're generally not allowed in the Athenaeum. And there are a couple hundred who don't know the location of the Athenaeum but who feed us information or provide help in other ways."

Sophia nodded as she absorbed all the information. She glanced at her mom and noticed how grim her expression was. "Why didn't you ever tell me about this? If not when I was little, then when I got more and more interested in history and ancient Greece?" she asked quietly.

It took Heather a long moment to answer, and when she did, there was a sheen of tears in her eyes. Not sad tears, angry ones. "Because the Athenaeum killed your father, sweetheart."

"No, it didn't!" Carla snapped. "A thief did. The Athenaeum didn't do that to him!"

"Yes, it did," Heather snarled. "If it weren't for that place, he'd still be alive. He would've met his daughter!"

Carla started to retort, but Nick placed a hand on her arm and shook his head. She almost ignored him but ultimately subsided, making only a low, annoyed sound.

Sophia was wide-eyed as she looked between the two women. She wanted to know exactly what had happened, but knew now wasn't the time. Not unless she wanted angry words instead of truth. When everyone else lapsed into awkward silence, she drew her legs beneath her and rested her head against the wall of the plane. Staring at nothing, she mulled over everything she'd learned.

Chapter 3

Though the flight lasted twelve hours, Sophia wasn't able to sleep much. She dozed now and again, but her mind was too full and it was well before the time she usually went to bed. The others chatted—mostly with each other but occasionally with her—and though they offered her food, she didn't think she could keep anything more than water down. Thankfully, no one pressed her, either to eat or talk. They did offer her the bedroom in the back and she gratefully took it, but it was too odd laying on a queen-sized bed thousands of feet in the air, so she just went over the information in her head.

Despite being angry at her mom for keeping this huge secret from her, Sophia was getting more and more excited the closer they got to Greece. All her life she'd only ever known one family member, and here she was about to meet a second. Added to that, she'd been in love with Greek lore and history almost all her life. It was why she'd chosen her major, even though there wasn't likely to be a lot of money in it. So to be headed for a secret, two-thousand year old library in Greece that had started with the most famous library of all time? It did a lot to help ease the worst of her resentment. It didn't eliminate it, just made it bearable. But the fact that it held relics? That threw her. While her college classes had been from a human perspective, and relics weren't things she could make, she knew of them. She also knew that the great relics were all gone. Or so she'd thought. But it sounded like the Athenaeum was stockpiling them, which made her wonder exactly what sort of people claimed allegiance to it. Were they good people who could be trusted with such things? Her mom suggested they were, but she'd also been gone for more than two decades.

And she'd blamed the Athenaeum for her father's death.

Sophia slipped into a half-conscious state as she stared out the dark window, drifting just deep enough that she didn't notice when the plane touched down. When someone's hand gave her shoulder a gentle shake, she jerked half-upright and blinked up at her mom's face.

"We've landed," Heather said quietly as she stepped back.

Sophia sat up fully and swung her legs over the edge of the bed. "I need a minute, then I'll be ready to go," she said, rubbing the heels of her hands against her eyes.

"Sure. Take your time, sweetheart." She slipped out of the bedroom and closed the door behind her.

Now that they were actually in Greece, nerves decided to make themselves known. She put her shoes on, slipped into the small bathroom, and splashed cold water on her face, letting it help wake her up a little more. She leaned on the sink and stared at her reflection in the mirror. Her ponytail was loose and her hair was a mess. Though she leaned toward pale on a normal day, given how much time she spent with books and studying, her skin almost looked translucent now. She rubbed her hands briskly over her cheeks, trying to get a little more color to her face, but it didn't do much.

Deciding it was as good as it was going to get, she left the bathroom and joined the others. Carla was nowhere in sight, but Heather and

Nick were gathering their bags. "How long will it take to reach the Athenaeum?" Sophia asked as she picked up her backpack and slipped it over her shoulders.

"About three hours," Nick told her.

Sophia nodded slightly. "And what time is it here?"

"Just after five in the morning."

She nodded again and fiddled with the handle of her suitcase.

Nick studied her for a moment, glanced at Heather, then said, "I know none of us ate much, so we were thinking of stopping for breakfast on the way." He smiled. "I'm assuming that as a Classics major you speak Greek?"

"Yeah. Attic and modern," she verified.

"Wonderful."

Carla came up the stairs and poked her head into the plane. "The car's ready whenever you are."

Sophia picked up her suitcase and followed wordlessly after Carla. They piled into a black SUV with Carla behind the wheel. Once they left the airport, Sophia felt a spark of her earlier excitement and looked eagerly out the window, looking forward to her first real life view of Greece—even if it was still dark out. To her disappointment, what she could see thanks to streetlights looked surprisingly...normal. Sure, the signs were all in Greek, and logically she knew all of Greece wasn't going to be ancient sites and ruins, but it was still a little disappointing.

"So where exactly is the Athenaeum?" she asked as she continued to stare out the window, hoping for some glimpse of the Greece she'd studied.

"Near Mount Parnassus," Nick answered with a glance back at her. "Under it, actually."

Sophia grinned. "Really? Very cool."

He chuckled and faced forward again. "I hope you think so after we get there. The road is intentionally rough to discourage visitors, and we can't drive right up to the entrance."

She frowned. "Do we have to hike or something?"

"A little, yes. We have a house near the entrance. We leave the cars there and it also means we own the land the Athenaeum is on, which helps prevent outside interference."

Unfortunately, despite taking classes in archeology, Sophia hadn't done much in the field, so hiking wasn't really her thing. Hopefully, it wasn't too bad.

"I assume there are wards and stuff, too?"

"There are," he verified. "We also have a number of gods who have provided their own protections."

Sophia had never interacted with a god, had only read about them in books, so her curiosity was piqued. "Which gods?"

"Athena, Hecate, Isis, Mimir, and Thoth have given protections." He glanced back, a small smile on his face. "And though I doubt you've heard of him, so has Seth Montgomery."

No, she hadn't heard that name, but the other five she recognized. "Very cool. So I take it there are people who worship multiple pantheons in the Athenaeum?"

"There are, and some people who focus on specific gods rather than a pantheon. Our patrons are popular, of course, since they tend to be deities of knowledge and magic."

That made sense, and Sophia nodded and looked back out the window. They really had given her too much to ponder over.

About an hour later, Carla stopped in front of a small restaurant. They went inside and talked little as they ordered and ate breakfast. She was hungry, but Sophia couldn't even finish half of her omeletta, despite it being delicious. The others tried to draw her into conversation, but she replied in one-word answers, when she replied at all. She honestly couldn't remember anything they'd said. When they got back in the SUV, they left her alone as they drove the rest of the way to Parnassus. This time she didn't doze off and was awake, though groggy, when they pulled up to a house. Small estate would be more accurate, actually. It was stone with a red roof, the land around it largely bare as there were only a few trees and shrubs nearby. It struck her as open and exposed, which made her wonder just how it helped them hide. Carla pushed a button which had the garage door opening, but when they drove in Sophia was surprised to see that it wasn't a typical garage, but rather a short tunnel which led to a large, underground parking area with half a dozen other SUVs like the one they were in and about as many sedans. She even saw a few motorcycles and ATVs.

Nick and Carla got out and moved around back to start pulling bags out, but Sophia hesitated.

"You okay, sweetheart?" Heather asked softly. "You don't have to do this."

"No, I do," Sophia murmured. "I'd never forgive myself if I tucked tail and ran, especially after flying all this way."

Understanding just how stubborn Sophia could be when she put her mind to something, Heather only nodded. "Take all the time you need. The world won't end if we get there ten minutes late."

No, it wouldn't end, but if her grandfather was really that close to death, ten minutes might be the difference between meeting him and never knowing another family member. She drew in a deep breath, then pushed her door open. "So, if we're hiking, how do we get this stuff to the front door?" she asked when she circled around to the back of the vehicle.

"We have donkeys we use when we're carrying in more than a pack," Carla answered. She looked Sophia over from head to toe. "Or when people can't make the hike."

Sophia's spine stiffened and her eyes narrowed. Clearly, Carla didn't think she could manage it. She smiled fiercely, no humor in her eyes. "Just lead the way, *koukla*," she said sweetly, emphasizing the Greek endearment.

Carla smirked and inclined her head to Sophia. "This way." All four carried the bags out of the garage and to a corral with several donkeys milling about. In less time than Sophia would have thought possible, the bags were strapped on the backs of two of the animals. To her surprise, it was Nick and her mom who led the donkeys away from the estate. They didn't go along any trail she could identify, but none of them faltered or seemed to have any issue in knowing where to go. Unfortunately, it was all uphill. Fortunately, it wasn't a steep incline, so while she was breathing heavily and her side and calves ached, she didn't have to ask them to hold up on the twenty minute hike.

When they stopped, Sophia looked around in confusion. All she saw were rocks and a short cliff, nothing that suggested an entrance to anywhere. "Why'd we stop?" she asked.

"Because we're here," Nick told her with a gentle smile. She frowned, which made him chuckle. "You didn't think it would be easily seen, did you?" he asked as they pulled the bags off the donkeys.

When they were empty of cargo, they each received a light slap on the rump, which sent them meandering back down to the house.

"Well, no…"

Carla just shook her head and walked right toward the cliff. She side-stepped a large shrub, then seemed to disappear behind it.

Sophia's eyes widened and she hurried forward, forgetting the pain in her legs. When she got around the same shrub, she saw a crack in the rock, but it didn't look like it was more than a foot or two deep. She glanced curiously at her mom and Nick. Heather smiled sadly and said, "Go ahead, sweetheart. We'll be right behind you."

Sophia bit her lip lightly but eased forward. Just when she thought she had run out of open space, the rock gave way to a good-sized chamber. Not huge, but definitely large enough for twenty people if they didn't mind being shoulder to shoulder. Her jaw dropped and she ignored Carla, who stood there waiting, a flashlight now in hand. "Was that magic or just a really lucky natural feature?"

"Both."

Nick and Heather joined them a moment later, and Heather immediately looked at the openings on the other side of the chamber, jaw tightening slightly. Nick just smiled at her and pulled out his own flashlight.

"We should get going," Carla said, but she didn't sound like she was rushing them, which Sophia appreciated. Her legs were not happy with her.

"Lead the way," Sophia told her as she walked over to the other woman.

"Stay close. The next bit is a security feature, an old one, and it's easy to get lost or hurt if you don't know what you're doing."

"By hurt, she means killed," Heather said dryly, but she didn't sound afraid, just annoyed.

"Exactly what is this security feature?" Sophia asked, more than a little apprehensive.

"It's Greece and we're underground," Carla said before she grinned impishly. "It's a labyrinth, of course," she answered before disappearing through the leftmost opening and into the dark.

"Holy shit," Sophia breathed, her apprehension increased, but now it was joined by excitement. She seriously doubted there was a minotaur roaming it, so with a guide, they should be safe...right?

"If it makes you feel better, I've been through the labyrinth dozens of times. Hundreds, maybe," Heather assured her.

Sophia nodded slowly and followed in Carla's wake. Immediately, her expectations were shattered. Rather than a man-made maze, the labyrinth looked like any tunnel in a cave. The floor was uneven and dotted by stalagmites of various sizes. The ceiling rose and fell, seemingly at random, just as the walls narrowed and widened. Other passages intersected with the one they were in, but Carla didn't hesitate as she led the way through the labyrinth.

"I don't get it," she whispered to her mom. "I thought this place was dangerous."

Heather nodded. "It is, if you don't take the correct path. From what I understand, part of the magic protecting the Athenaeum causes the labyrinth to shift regularly, and only those who belong to the Athenaeum can see the safe way through."

That was a little terrifying. Did that mean that if she wanted to leave, that she had to have an escort? Was she going to be trapped in the Athenaeum?

It took twenty minutes for them to step through a narrow arch and into a large room that was completely different from the labyrinth. The walls and floor were perfectly smooth, perfectly level, forming a long rectangle. Two rows of columns led the way to the far side of the room and the large door with a carved stone doorframe. Tall statues, each at least fifteen feet high, were placed on either side of both doors and spaced along the walls. To her delight and confusion, they resembled those she'd seen in photos of ancient temples, but it was a mix of civilizations. One statue of a woman was definitely Greek in style, but another woman clearly wore Egyptian garb. A man against the wall looked like a viking to her, while another, to her surprise, looked modern. Jeans and a tee-shirt could never be confused for a toga. When she turned to look at the opening they'd just come through, she saw two more statues, these of another Greek woman and an Egyptian man.

Torches lined the walls, bathing the room in gentle light as the flashlights were switched off. Dragging her attention from the statues, Sophia stepped to the nearest column when she realized they all had writing carved into them, and when she was closer, she saw it was a different language on each one, which thrilled her inner linguistics geek. Glancing back at the others, they seemed perfectly content to wait and let her check it out, so she took the opportunity to do just that. Wandering, she found a column she could read. Her fingers brushed over the ancient Greek words and a smile curved her lips. The words were pretty, but the intent behind them made her happy she was here, no matter what else she was dealing with.

We are the keepers of knowledge.
We will protect that which time and man seek to destroy and obscure.
We will not abuse that which we guard.
We are the Nasaru, and this is more than a library.

"That's beautiful," she murmured.

"We mean every word of it, too," Nick told her, making her jump at how close he was to her. She had been so focused on the carving, she hadn't noticed his approach.

"Does every column say the same thing?"

"Some are identical, yes, but not all. Some are warnings, some are protections laid by our patrons," he answered with a shake of his head.

Curious, she searched the columns for other languages she knew. To her disappointment, the Latin column was the same text. She found only two other columns with a recognizable language, but she didn't know enough Sanskrit to know if it was the same passage, and knew just enough Hieratic to know it was different. She made a mental note to translate them at some point.

"We should go. Your grandfather's waiting," Carla said.

Sophia gave one last look to the columns before she nodded and followed the woman to the door. The heavy stone opened with no apparent effort, allowing them into the Athenaeum itself. She couldn't wait to see what other beauty it held.

Chapter 4

Sophia's first glimpse of the Athenaeum was disappointing. It wasn't some grand room full of books and artifacts and relics. No, it was...a square, medium-sized room made of stone, with a door in the middle of each wall. All the doors were open, and there were a few columns, but these were simple columns with no writing. The closest thing to what she'd expected were the two eight-feet long sphinx statues set beside the door directly across from her. They were cool, yes, just not what she'd expected.

While Sophia had to commend the architecture that had led to such smooth, seamless walls and columns, it was odd to see something like this underground.

While the room was empty of furniture or decorations beyond the sphinxes, there were a handful of people. One of them noticed their arrival and approached them with a wide smile. He looked oddly familiar to her, though Sophia couldn't place how, since she was certain she'd never seen him before. He was about six feet, with fair skin, green eyes, and short, neatly styled brown hair that was going gray.

"Heather! I heard they were going to invite you here, but I didn't let myself believe you'd actually come," he told her mom, giving her a brief, if awkward, hug. He spoke Greek, which didn't surprise Sophia, given that they were in Greece. What did surprise her was when her mom answered in the same language. Not once had she ever heard her mom speak any language other than English, and this Greek was flawless.

"Hello, Dion," Heather murmured, returning the hug before she stepped back to stand beside Sophia, resting a hand on her daughter's shoulder. "If it weren't for Sophia, I might not have come," she admitted.

"Sophia?" Dion shifted his focus to her. He wasn't the only one and Sophia found herself shifting uncomfortably at being the target of so much attention. "Your daughter?" he asked, glancing back to Heather for a second. "How wonderful! Despite the circumstances, I mean." To Sophia's relief, he didn't try to hug her, just offered her a warm smile, one that turned sheepish. Switching to English, he added, "Oh, I didn't even think to ask if you spoke Greek, my dear."

Suddenly feeling shy, Sophia nodded. "I do," she replied quietly in Greek.

"Wonderful," he said cheerfully. "Then allow me to introduce myself. I'm Dion. We're cousins, actually."

Eyes wide, Sophia looked to her mom for confirmation. Heather nodded. "He's your grandfather's nephew," she confirmed.

"I have family," Sophia whispered in English, astonished that the number of relatives was rapidly growing. Shaking herself out of her astonishment, she changed back to Greek. "It's really nice to meet you, Dion. Sorry, I didn't sleep much on the plane so I'm a little..."

He chuckled when she trailed off and nodded understandingly. "Of course, my dear. We can talk later, when you've rested and absorbed everything. Your first visit to the Athenaeum can be overwhelming, even without everything else going on."

"Thanks. I'd like that," she told him with a smile.

Nick slipped past them. "I'll take your things to your rooms," he told them, and since he used English, that seemed to be a trigger to have everyone switching.

"Thank you, Nick," Heather told him, Sophia echoing him.

"And I'll be around," Carla said as she headed for one of the hallways leading out of the common room. Before she disappeared, she caught Sophia's eye, giving her a grin.

"And I will take you to see Erasmus," Dion said. "He asked to see you both as soon as you got here."

Nerves returned, but Sophia looked to her mom who nodded. They followed him silently as he took the same door Nick had. It led to stairs which took them down a level and into a room that was roughly the same size and shape as the one they'd left. This one, however, was full of couches, chairs, and small tables. It was also full of people.

Dion led them through the room and into another hallway. The doors here were heavy wood, which looked a little out of place to Sophia with the stone walls. They only passed a few before Dion stopped. "He was awake a few minutes ago, but he may not be entirely..." He didn't finish, just gave a mournful look toward the closed door. He cleared his throat and shook his head. "Anyway, are you ready?"

This time Heather didn't answer for them but looked to Sophia. "Whenever you're ready, sweetheart," she murmured.

Sophia swallowed, though her throat felt tight. She rubbed her hands on her jeans, trying to dry her suddenly damp palms. After a last deep breath, she nodded. "I'm ready."

Dion gave her a sympathetic smile and knocked. A weak voice told them to enter in Greek before Dion pushed the door open. Sophia was surprised once again at the large, comfortable bedroom. Tapestries and framed texts covered the walls while rugs lay on the floor, splashing color in what would otherwise be a pale, drab room. The furniture was all dark wood, from the four-poster bed to the desk to the wall full of bookshelves. There was a second door, which she assumed went to a bathroom. But the bed drew her attention almost immediately, or rather, the pale, gray-haired man who laid in the bed did. Though he looked frail, his green eyes were bright and direct. When they met hers, Sophia realized why Dion had looked familiar—Dion and Erasmus had the same eyes she did. The same color, the same shape. She'd never seen a picture of her father, but she'd wager he had the same eyes.

Without taking his eyes off her, Erasmus started trying to push himself to a reclining position. It was a struggle and everything in Sophia wanted to rush forward to help him. While she was trying to decide if it would be appropriate, Dion moved to the bed and helped the older man sit up, positioning pillows to support him.

"Heather...It's been too long," Erasmus said in a tired voice, almost too quiet to hear. He lifted a hand and weakly waved them both closer. "Come here. My voice isn't as strong as it used to be," he said with a smile.

Only when Heather's hand rested lightly on Sophia's back was she able to move, to approach the bed that held her grandfather.

"It's good to see you, Erasmus," Heather murmured.

He chuckled. "Erasmus. You used to call me Baba," he teasingly chided her.

She smiled sadly and shook her head. "As you said, it's been a long time."

"True," he agreed with a small nod. Shifting his gave to Sophia, he said, now in English, "You are more than welcome to call me Erasmus. You must be Sophia."

"I am," Sophia said with a nod. "And I think I will stick with Erasmus. Besides, it's a cool name."

"Hear that, Dion? I have a cool name," he said with a mischievous gleam in his eyes. "Does that make me cool by proxy?"

She couldn't help but grin. "It might."

Another weak chuckle escaped him. "I'd like to talk to my granddaughter alone." Though the words were polite, there was no question it was an order for both Dion and Heather. Neither looked exceptionally thrilled, and Heather gave Sophia a questioning look, but after receiving a small nod from her daughter, they both left the bedroom, closing the door behind them.

Once alone, Erasmus motioned to the chair by his bed. "Sit with me for a moment?" When she sank into the chair, he studied her face while she studied his. "You look like your father," he murmured.

She brushed the tip of a finger by the corner of her eye. "I noticed that you, Dion, and me all have the same eyes."

"Yes, but it's also the hair, the shape of the face. It makes me wonder in what other ways you take after him."

"I honestly don't know," she admitted with a sigh. "Mom almost never talks about him."

He made an understanding sound and nodded slightly. "I'm happy you're here, Sophia, and so very sorry I'm only now meeting you."

"I didn't know you existed twenty-four hours ago," she confessed. "Not until Nick and Carla came to our house."

"That's fine," he assured her. "There is no reason to mourn the past. It's to be studied, learned from, not dwelled in." He shifted slightly in an attempt to get comfortable. "I want to know about you, my only granddaughter, but I have a question first."

"Okay?" Sophia encouraged, wondering why the need for privacy.

"I assume you've been told about the Athenaeum? What it is, what we do here?"

She nodded. "They told me on the plane. It was a little...mind-boggling."

"It can be that," he agreed with a gentle smile. "The question I have for you is...do you understand the importance of the Athenaeum?"

It was knee-jerk to say yes, that preserving books and relics was important, but something told her he meant more than that. She frowned as she actually put some thought into it. Did she understand? She knew that, throughout history, knowledge had been destroyed, both by accident and with malicious intent. There were books mentioned in historical texts that few living people—if any—had ever read because they'd been lost. Given her major, she'd even heard of one. Homer hadn't just written the *Iliad* and *Odyssey*, but another story called the *Margites*, one only mentioned in other works. As someone who studied such things, it was a great loss. But what if the Athenaeum had saved it? Or other books like it? When she thought about it that way, she only had one answer for him. "I think I do, yes."

He searched her face for something. He must have found it because he gave her another smile. "Good. That's very good. Now, tell me about my beautiful granddaughter. What do you do back in America?"

She laughed softly and shook her head. "You don't have to suck up. You're my only grandfather. I already like you. But I'm a student right now."

"Oh? What do you study?"

She grinned slyly. "Greece, actually. I'm going for my Masters in Classics."

He laughed, with more energy than she would have thought possible. "Imagine that," he murmured. "Does that mean that you speak Greek?"

"Mmhmm. Attic and modern," she confirmed.

"Any other languages?"

"A couple, but I'm not fluent in most of them," she admitted.

"Wonderful, just wonderful," he said, extending one frail hand to pat hers lightly. "I'd love to talk to you more, and hope to soon, but I'm tired and do need to speak to your mother before I have to nap again. Would you get her, please?"

"Of course," she said as she stood.

"Good. And do visit me later," he said as she left and found both her mom and Dion waiting for her.

"He wants to talk to you," she told Heather, feeling more relaxed now than she'd been since Nick and Carla rang her doorbell.

"I thought he might," Heather said with a nod. "Wait here for me?"

"Sure."

Heather smiled faintly and nodded as she stepped into the bedroom. His eyes were closed, so she took the chair Sophia had just vacated and reached for a basin beside the bed. She wrung out the cloth that rested on the rim of the basin and laid it on Erasmus's forehead. When his eyes opened, not quite as alert as they had been just minutes before, she smiled sadly at him. "I missed you."

"You could have come back at any time, you know that," he told her.

"You know why I didn't. The memories...they were just too much," she murmured as she leaned back.

He caught her hand before she could go far and gave it a weak squeeze. "I know. I miss him, too. Greg was...the most amazing son a man could have."

She blinked rapidly, trying not to cry. "He was the most amazing husband, too."

He nodded and let several long moments pass. "Are you going to allow Sophia to stay?"

Heather sighed. "That's up to her. I'm her mother, not her keeper. And she's enough like her father that she'll do what she feels she should, regardless of what I say." She gave him a pointed look. "Did she tell you what she studied in college?"

"She did. I was pleased, though I imagine you weren't."

"No, I wasn't. But she loves it. She always has."

"The Athenaeum is in her blood." She frowned at that but didn't protest, so he continued. "If she does stay, will you stay, too?"

She dropped her gaze to the wedding ring she still wore and rubbed her thumb against it. "I don't know if I could. Losing Greg...he was the love of my life and it was hard. So very, very hard." Her eyes lifted to his. "But losing Sophia, losing my daughter, would *destroy* me."

Thin fingers gripped hers with more strength than Heather thought was possible. "Believe me, Heather, I understand that completely. I lost my son, after all," he told her in a quiet, hoarse voice.

When she realized his eyes were wet, she lost it. Tears spilled over and she half-collapsed onto the bed, into his arms, as she cried out her grief and anger. He simply wrapped his arms around her and held her while he grieved with her. Yes, she'd blamed Erasmus for his son's death, but they'd both lost him, and then they'd lost each other. It was past time they found each other again.

Chapter 5

NEITHER SOPHIA NOR DION spoke much as they waited for Heather to emerge from Erasmus's room. When they did speak, it was all small talk. Dion asking how the flight was. Sophia asking if he liked working at the Athenaeum. Nothing important, nothing heavy. Sophia was happy he kept it to easy subjects, because she was still reeling from everything.

When Heather did rejoin them, her eyes were a little red. Sophia started to ask what had happened, but Dion spoke up before she could. "I'm sure you're both tired. Why don't I show you to your room? I believe Nicholas put you in your old room."

Heather smiled tiredly. "Thank you, Dion, but I remember the way."

He inclined his head. "Of course. Get some rest. I'll talk to you both later," he told them before disappearing down the hallway.

"Come on. I don't know about you, but I'm definitely exhausted," Heather said as she began leading Sophia to a room not far from Erasmus's. Fortunately, unlike the labyrinth, these hallways weren't bare. There were carvings in the stone, both writing and pictures, as well as recesses in the walls that held antiques and vases with flowers. It made what could have been cold and inhospitable into something colorful and somehow homey. And fascinating. The decor was also the only way Sophia saw to differentiate one door from another.

Heather didn't hesitate until she stopped in front of a door, her hand on the knob.

"Mom?" Sophia asked, remembering what Dion had said about this being her old room. This was all hard enough for her without adding in memories of her life with Sophia's dad.

Giving Sophia a tiny smile, Heather opened the door and stepped into the room. It didn't look anything like Sophia would have imagined. Which meant it looked nothing like her mom's room back in the States. Like Erasmus's room, there were multiple shelves, a desk, armoire, and a bed. Standard, Sophia assumed, for a place like this. But instead of the warm colors and soft edges, this room was done in earthy tones, the furniture heavy wood with clean edges.

Their things had been placed by the armoire, and when Heather headed that way, Sophia thought she was grabbing something from one of her bags. Instead, she opened the armoire and her breath caught at whatever she saw inside. "Mom?" Sophia asked again.

Heather shook her head and reached in, brushing her fingers over what looked like a sleeve. "They didn't change anything," she whispered. She looked back to Sophia and gave her a watery smile. "Your father's clothes are still here."

"Oh, damn," Sophia breathed as Heather went back to touching the shirt. She closed the door and sat down on the edge of the bed, watching her mom closely. While she hesitated to cause her mom any further pain, there was a question that had been burning in the back of her mind for the last sixteen hours. "Mom...why did you say the Athenaeum killed my dad?"

Heather flinched and her shoulders hunched visibly. She sighed and closed the armoire before she joined Sophia on the bed. "There are four different groups of people in the Athenaeum. There are the aspides, who are the leaders of the Athenaeum. The current aspida is Erasmus. What he says, goes. He has the absolute final say in everything and can't be overruled, except maybe by the patrons. Then there are the curators. They're the librarians and caretakers. They basically take care of the Athenaeum, from taking care of the books to cooking to dealing with finances. The guards are pretty self-explanatory, though here they're called nasaru. It's Sumerian, I believe. They guard the Athenaeum and anyone who has to go out into the world on Athenaeum business." Her gaze shifted back to the armoire. "Which brings me to the venatores. They're in charge of leaving the Athenaeum to recover books or recruit people to work here. They go out and find the books or relics and bring them home."

Her grandfather was in charge of this amazing place? No wonder he'd seemed amused when he found out that her interests aligned so well with his. "Which one was my dad?" she asked quietly.

"He was a venator, and he was damn good at his job, too." Heather gave a short laugh. "That's actually how we met. Like you, I was interested in the ancient world, though I was studying archeology specifically, not as a minor. I was working on a dig with one of my professors in Peru. Apparently Greg had heard about it and came to see if there were any texts worth saving." She shook her head. "That's a story for another time, though. But that's what he did. When research or gossip pointed to a useful person or a unique text being located, the venatores would go try to retrieve it. One day he went to Spain to try to bring some book back. They said it should be an easy job. Just buy the book at auction and come home. But it got...complicated. Someone else wanted that book." Her eyes drifted closed, but not before a tear made its way down her cheek. "They wanted it enough to kill Greg to get it," she whispered. "If he'd just had a guard with him, someone to watch his back, he'd still be alive. He'd have seen his daughter born." She sniffled and looked at Sophia with a sad smile. "He'd have seen you grow up."

Sophia crawled across the bed until she could wrap her arms around her mom and give her a tight hug. "Oh, Mom. I'm sorry," she whispered, her face pressed against her mom's shoulder.

Heather rested her cheek against her daughter's hair and returned the hug fiercely. "You have nothing to apologize for, sweetheart. None of this is your fault."

"You're here because of me," Sophia pointed out.

"No," Heather said with a shake of her head. "I could have stayed home, but I couldn't bear not to see Erasmus once more. And I couldn't stand the idea of letting you come here by yourself, know-ing..." She shook her head again. "It's not your fault."

Sophia leaned back enough to look at her mom. Chewing on her lip, she debated what to say next. "Do you...I mean..." She smiled faintly and shook her head. "Never mind." She couldn't bring herself to tell her mom that she didn't think it was the Athenaeum's fault her dad was dead. Especially if he was the son of the guy in charge. He probably could have insisted on taking a guard with him. Erasmus didn't *seem* like a hard-ass who would just say no, anyway. "Accidents happen, I guess, but I'm still..."

Heather nodded and stroked a hand over Sophia's hair. "I know. Though I wouldn't object if you did want to leave and go home. You do have friends there."

Confused, Sophia cocked her head. "They'll still be there in a few days. Even a few weeks." Though the texts she'd received from said friends were full of worry and she felt a little guilty at having just bailed on them.

"Yes, I suppose they will," Heather murmured. It looked like she was going to say something else, but Sophia yawned, unable to help herself. "You should shower and get some rest. Though I warn you, it's going to take your body a while to adjust to the time change. You're essentially going to bed at dawn."

"Yeah, that's probably a good idea," Sophia agreed with another yawn. "I know I haven't really done anything, but I still feel kind of gross."

"Traveling will do that, especially when you're on a plane for half a day," Heather said as she stood. "I'm not quite ready to sleep, but I think I'm going to see if there's another bedroom nearby." She looked around at the room that was so familiar. "I just...can't stay in here. I'll show you to the bathroom before I go, though."

Sophia's heart ached for her mom, but she nodded. She grabbed what she'd need out of her bag and was relieved that the bathroom was just across the hall and down one door. Before she entered, she hugged her mom once more. "I love you, Mom."

"I love you, too. And don't worry, we'll get through this," Heather told her.

Though the urge to linger under the hot water was strong, Sophia was too exhausted, mentally and physically. She took the quickest shower of her life and made her way back to the bedroom. As she slid under the covers, she looked around the room, amazed that she was in the same room that had been her dad's, once upon a time. Then she wondered, if the 'normal' areas of the Athenaeum looked so cool, what must the actual library look like?

Imagining all the different possibilities, she actually fell asleep with a smile on her lips.

After leaving Sophia, Heather went to find Dion. If he wasn't able to get her a new room, he'd know who would. And out of everyone here, aside from Erasmus, she'd been closest to him. Though she'd chosen to stay away, had needed to for her mental health, she'd still missed this place and the people in it. There were new faces—that was inevitable after almost twenty-five years—but the Athenaeum did tend to attract like-minded people. She'd been on the verge of becoming one of them herself when Greg had died.

Dion wasn't in the common areas, but a question to one of the people there pointed her to his room. It was in a different wing from hers, which surprised her. She thought the curators tended to stay close to the aspides. But again, things can change in two and a half decades. She knocked on the door and after a moment Dion answered the door, still looking pressed and proper, but then, it was just a normal morning for him, even though it felt like midnight to her.

"Heather," he said with no small measure of surprise. "I thought you and Sophia would be sleeping. Is everything okay?"

"Oh, yes," she answered automatically. "Well, no. I was hoping to catch up with you, but I was also wondering who was head curator now."

Dion motioned for her to come in and pulled his desk chair out for her before he sat on his bed. She murmured a thanks as she sat. "Fortunately, you don't need to go anywhere else, as I'm head curator."

She smiled a little, happy for him, but oh so tired. "That's great, Dion. Congratulations. I know you've worked hard for it."

"Thank you. But why did you need the head curator?"

"Is there an available room? Near my old one, but not my old one?" Heather asked quietly. "Sophia's fine staying there, but I...I just can't, Dion."

"Oh, my dear. Of course," he told her, his face and voice full of sympathy. "There's one just a few rooms down from yours. I'll be happy to show you," he said, moving to rise.

She motioned for him to remain sitting. "No rush on that." She worked up another small smile. "Well, some rush, because I *am* tired, but it doesn't have to be right this second. I meant it when I said I wanted to catch up. Just because I haven't spoken to anyone here since I left doesn't mean you stopped being my family."

He smiled warmly at her. "I never stopped thinking of you as family, either. Do you remember my son?"

"I do. He was...two? Three? Somewhere around there when I left, right?"

"Three, yes," Dion confirmed with a nod. "He's officially a librarian now. He deals with all the technology for the Athenaeum," he said proudly.

"Really? That's great. I can't wait to see him again, though I know he won't remember me."

"Perhaps not, but there's nothing wrong with him getting to know you now. And he also gets the chance to meet Sophia."

"True, and I...it'll be good for her to get to know her family." She inhaled deeply. "She never seemed unhappy growing up that it was just the two of us, but it's still something she's missed out on."

"None of that," he gently chided. "She's meeting us now."

"Yes," she murmured, rubbing her chest lightly as her heart clenched. Though she'd never had a gift for prophecy, an uneasy feeling went through her. The same feeling she'd had when she'd seen Nick and Carla at her door.

Something bad was about to happen.

Chapter 6

A SOFT THUDDING WOKE Sophia, and after hearing it a few more times, she realized it was the sound of someone knocking on the heavy wooden door. She got to her feet, yawning and feeling like she could sleep another few hours, then stumbled to the door. She opened it to see a man, somewhere around her age, with a bright blue mohawk and several piercings. His appearance didn't fit in with that of the Athenaeum—except for the example Carla had given—but his warm, open smile made her like him instantly. "Hi. Can I help you?" she asked, fighting back another yawn. It only struck her after she spoke that not everyone here might speak English.

Before she could correct her error, he grinned. "Hello! And I was thinking more than I could help you. I'm Peter. Dion's son, which makes us cousins." His English was as good as hers, but there was a distinct Greek accent to it. She loved it, but it wasn't where her focus went.

She had another relative? Holy crap. That was...awesome. Although it made her wonder, and given that she was still half-asleep, her tact was at a minimum. "Do I have any other family that's going to crawl out of the woodwork here?" she blurted.

Rather than being offended, he laughed and shook his head. "Not that I know of, no. At least, the only family I know of here is you, your mom, my dad, and Uncle Erasmus."

Relieved that her tired ramblings hadn't gotten them off to the wrong foot, she leaned against the doorframe and grinned. "Good to know. I think I've had about as many surprises in the last twenty-four hours as I can stand."

The amusement faded to sympathy, and he nodded. "I can get that. I don't plan on adding to your stress, either. I just thought…Well, I wanted to get to know my cousin and see if she wanted a tour of the place." He paused and frowned. "I assume you haven't had one already?"

Sophia shook her head. "I came in, went right to Erasmus's room, then here. I'd love to see more. Though I'll admit, I think I need food first." She glanced down at her clothes, remembering that she was still in an old UGA tee-shirt and pair of sweats. Not really what she wanted to be wearing when she made a first impression on most of these people. "Just, uh, give me five?"

He grinned again, revealing a dimple in his left cheek. "Sure thing. I'll just wait out here."

"Thanks," she told him with a smile, shutting the door. She quickly changed into jeans and a tee-shirt, along with her sneakers. If she was going to be doing a lot of walking, she wanted to be comfortable. She put her hair into a ponytail and slipped her phone into her back pocket before she stepped outside to join Peter. "Do you know where my mom is, by any chance?"

He nodded and started walking. "I saw her a few minutes ago. She was catching up with people she knew when she lived here before."

That made sense. She pulled her phone out and hesitated, certain she wouldn't have a signal underground, but when she looked at her screen she was shocked to see full bars. While she knew phones could be enchanted to receive signals anywhere, she'd never had that done to hers. "How do I have signal down here?" she asked as she typed out a text to her mom, letting her know she was going for food and a tour with Peter.

Rather than answer, he just grinned impishly. As they walked, he told her whose room was whose, though she didn't recognize any of the names. Because of that, she switched the subject. "So, did you know my mom? Before, I mean?"

"Mmm. Sort of?" Peter answered. "I was little, just three, so I more have...impressions of her than real memories. But they're all good impressions."

"And my dad?" she asked, almost desperate for some real information about who her father was. She knew next to nothing from her mom. In all honesty, she'd learned more about her dad in the last day than she had the previous twenty-four years.

He gave her an apologetic look. "Pretty much the same. I remember he was fun, and I called him Geg because R's were hard for me then, but that's about it."

She smiled faintly. "That's something, anyway," she murmured.

They were quiet as he led her back through the common room and into a large kitchen. There were multiple fridges, multiple ovens, and several large cooktops, all modern despite the stone floor and walls. There was a heavy table Sophia assumed was used for preparing food rather than eating it, especially since there was a smaller table nearby. Standing at the larger table cutting up potatoes was a slender, pretty blonde woman slightly older than Sophia. At the smaller table sat Carla and two men Sophia didn't know. One looked about thirty, if she judged by human standards, with dark brown hair that was short on the top and shaved on the sides. He was muscular and had pale eyes, but from here she couldn't tell what color they were. His features were rough, but not unattractive. Quite the opposite. He was easily one of the hottest men she'd ever seen and she had to work not to stare. Despite the distance, and the table which hid half his body, she could tell he was more than fit, he was muscular. Not quite bodybuilding status, but he definitely spent time in the gym. The other man was just as beefy, though he was a little older. His black hair was cut in the same fashion as the first man, but his eyes were a bright blue. He was currently munching on what looked like trail mix.

Four sets of eyes turned in their direction, which made Sophia suddenly feel shy, but Peter just grinned and continued into the room. "Afternoon. For those of you who haven't met her yet, this is my cousin, Sophia," he told them proudly.

"Sleep well, Soph?" Carla asked as she leaned back in her chair. Her eyes were amused as she sipped at a soda.

"Yeah, though not enough. Which makes me wonder how in the hell you're so chipper," Sophia grumped, but that only made Carla grin broadly.

"Superior genes and lots of coffee," was her retort.

"Coffee," Sophia said, the single word a desperate and pitiful plea. She'd been awake all of fifteen minutes, and she'd realized when she texted her mom that she had only gotten about five hours of sleep.

The blonde laughed softly and moved to a coffee pot, pouring a cup. "We'll get you fixed up. Just have a seat. I'm Agatha, by the way. The cook."

"You are my new favorite person, Agatha," Sophia said as she sank into one of the empty chairs, putting her across from the brunette man and next to Carla.

"I hear that a lot," she admitted as she set the cup in front of Sophia, returning a moment later with a bowl of sugar and small pitcher of cream.

As Sophia added a little cream and plenty of sugar to her coffee, Peter grabbed a soda from the fridge and joined them. "Agatha? I know everyone's already had lunch, but Sophia slept right through it. She mentioned that she was hungry."

Agatha looked absolutely horrified by that. "Oh, no. That just won't do. I'll make you a sandwich. Is there anything you don't like?" she asked, hurrying around the kitchen, gathering ingredients.

"Um...I'm not a huge fan of mustard?" Sophia answered.

Agatha just nodded and went to work assembling a sandwich. In no time at all, a thick sandwich was placed in front of Sophia and the sight of it made her stomach growl. Agatha smiled and patted Sophia's shoulder. "Enjoy."

Sophia didn't hesitate to start eating, but she did glance at the two strangers, who had yet to say a word. It was the black-haired man who spoke first. "I'm Steven," he told her, his accent thicker than anyone else's she'd heard. He was definitely Greek, through and through. "I'm the fighting instructor, here."

"Fighting instructor?" It took a moment for her brain to connect the dots. "Oh, yeah. My mom said you guys have guards here. Nasaru, right? Makes sense to have someone in house to teach them to fight."

Steven inclined his head slightly. "Precisely."

Sophia's eyes shifted to the other man and, for a moment, he just met her gaze. It made her want to squirm, but she forced herself to hold his eyes and remain still. A few seconds later, one corner of his mouth turned up slightly. "I'm Lucas, head of the nasaru."

Huh. Another American. She wasn't sure why that surprised her. "Nice to meet you. All of you, actually." She took another bite, then glanced at Carla. "What's your job here, anyway? You never said. You or Nick."

"I'm a guard, he's a venator. We often work together."

"Handy," Sophia said with a nod.

Carla grinned. "Damn straight. I get to see the world with my husband and make sure he doesn't stumble into danger. It's a win-win."

"Does that happen a lot? The danger?"

Carla shrugged. "A lot?" She shook her head. "No, I wouldn't say a lot, but it does happen. That's why we have the nasaru, though."

Sophia frowned as she tried to imagine all the danger people could be in just trying to find and retrieve books and relics. Then again, that was how her dad had died. She forced her mind away from such topics though and asked the question that had occurred to her every time she met someone new. "How is it that you guys all speak English? Does everyone here speak English?"

Lucas nodded slightly. "For the most part, yes. But what you have to understand is that everyone in the Athenaeum, and I do mean everyone, is multilingual. Doesn't matter whether they're nasaru or curators or venatores."

"It's sort of necessary for all of us," Peter agreed. "The venatores and nasaru have to go to different countries and speaking the language can make or break a retrieval mission. Curators and venatores need to be able to tell if something's legitimate or not so, again, they need the multiple languages. Hell, it's good for me and I'm just the tech guy. But it means I'm often on websites in different languages, and translator programs aren't always a hundred percent accurate."

"I'm suddenly really happy that I chose the major I did," Sophia muttered, which had Carla grinning.

"What major is that?" Steven asked.

"Classics. So I learned Attic Greek and Latin. Since I wanted to visit Greece to see all the historical sites, I also learned modern Greek."

Carla smirked, but the expression was teasing more than malicious. "So you only speak four languages?"

"Fluently? Yes, for now, though I do know some of a few other languages," Sophia answered dryly. Then she smiled sweetly. "And I pick up languages quick."

A laugh poured from Carla's lips. "I like you, I really do."

Sophia's brow arched, disbelief painted over her face.

"Really? Because what I said before the hike?" Carla shook her head. "Motivation, *koukla*. I could see you were tired, and in your position, I think everyone would have been. I also figured you were as stubborn as your dad was, so the best way to get you to push yourself was to insinuate that you couldn't do it."

Eyes narrowed, Sophia glared at Carla, but the older woman looked unfazed by the attention and just took another sip while she held

Sophia's gaze. Finally, Sophia sighed and shook her head. "You really shouldn't know me that well already."

Carla smiled. "Part of the job."

"Can we go back to the part where you unintentionally picked one of the best majors for someone in the Athenaeum?" Peter asked, glancing around the table.

"It is somewhat ironic," Steven agreed.

"Maybe it's just in my blood? I mean, my dad was a venator, my grandfather is the head of this place. Even my mom said she studied archeology," Sophia said with a shrug, though the coincidence of it had been on her mind more than once.

"It is in your blood," Lucas said, no uncertainty in his voice. "Your grandfather isn't the only ancestor of yours who was the head of this place. If I recall correctly, your bloodline has one of the highest percentages of aspides. If not the highest."

"Seriously? That's..." Sophia shook her head and chose to finish her sandwich, trying to push aside the panic that threatened to push itself upward. Too much information was overloading her brain.

Peter either noticed or just had really good timing because he stood. "You ready for that tour?"

Sophia got to her feet so quickly her chair nearly toppled over. "I am. And thanks for the sandwich, Agatha. It was delicious," she said, carrying her plate toward the sink.

Before she could deal with it, it was plucked out of her fingers by the cook, who smiled. "You're welcome. Now go, enjoy your tour."

Sensing that Agatha wasn't the sort to be argued with despite being pretty and petite, Sophia smiled and nodded. She gave a wave to the others as she followed Peter out of the kitchen.

No one spoke for a minute after they were gone. To Carla's surprise, when they did speak, it wasn't about Sophia. Librarians tended toward gossip, so for them to not talk about the new kid on the block was unexpected.

"Speaking of the aspides, did you hear that Valerie thinks Dion is going to get tapped next?" Steven asked as he shifted in his chair to get more comfortable.

Agatha tsked as she dealt with Sophia's plate, then went back to preparing dinner. "That's a morbid conversation, since it all deals with Erasmus's...his passing."

"Perhaps a little, but from everything I've heard from the older members of our group, it's tradition," Steven countered.

Carla nodded. "He's right. No one goes so far into inappropriate as to wager on it, but everyone always wonders who will be chosen next." Her head tilts and she grins. "You have to have thought about it. Who do you think will be next?"

Agatha's lips pursed, but after a moment she relented. "I agree with Valerie, actually. He is well-qualified and already head curator."

Carla's nose wrinkled, but luckily no one else noticed the expression before it shifted back to a smile. "Personally, I think it's going to be Nick."

Steven chuckled and tossed a raisin at her, but she caught it in her mouth. "You're perhaps a little biased there."

"Well, who do you think it'll be?"

His wide shoulders shifted in a shrug. "I have no idea. It's not up to us anyway, and the choices are often...surprising, so not much reason to speculate."

"Spoilsport." She looked to Lucas. "What about you? You know everyone here probably as well as anyone except Erasmus."

Lucas simply shook his head, refusing to answer. But when the conversation shifted to rumors of a lost Shakespeare play, he glanced to the door and smiled a little.

Chapter 7

"So, the thing you have to know about the Athenaeum," Peter began as he led her away from the kitchen, "is that it's essentially a huge estate, just underground."

"What do you mean?" Sophia asked as she peeked into an open doorway, seeing a dining room. Dining hall would be more accurate, actually, since it was as big as a ballroom and had several long tables surrounded by chairs.

"A house has a kitchen, living room, some bedrooms and bathrooms, right? Maybe a dining room or study? Well, the Athenaeum has a couple dozen bedrooms, a dozen bathrooms, the kitchen and dining hall, of course, and a bunch of other rooms. Not including the library and repository, of course," he explained. "This level is where everyone lives and plays. Above us are the work areas, like the clinic, gym, armory, stuff like that. Most everything below us is the library and repository."

"What sort of other rooms?" It seemed safer than thinking of this place having an armory.

Peter grinned and quickened his pace. She matched him as he led her to the common room, then up a floor. "Like this. Downstairs is everything you'd find in a house, including a rec room. Up here is some of the fun stuff." He nudged open a door that wasn't latched. Though it was devoid of people, it was easy to see it was a clinic. "We've got a healer who's actually a demigod. Son of Apollo, so you know he's good. His name's Sergei. He comes off as a little icy, but he's a really good guy. Really cares about people and making them feel better."

"Good to know, though I hope I don't need a healer while I'm here," Sophia said dryly, though she was well used to being healed. As an elf, Heather was a fairly skilled healer herself. Sophia only had a touch of it, enough to deal with bumps and bruises, but she was only half elf.

He laughed. "I hope you don't, either." Further down the hall was an open doorway which led to a gym. In addition to open mats, she saw all sorts of exercise equipment. Several people were working out and two were sparring. Peter let her look for a minute before he moved along. "You're welcome to use the gym whenever you like. Steven would probably happily teach you some fighting moves, too, even if you don't plan on staying. Hell, any of the nasaru would probably be happy to help. They still talk about your dad, you know, and they all liked him."

Her heart clenched. "Thanks," she whispered.

Peter touched her arm lightly in sympathy before he pointed to a door with an electronic keypad. "Armory, and no, I can't show you that."

"How do you guys have electricity down here, by the way? I haven't seen any generators and getting power from public power companies doesn't seem like a good idea when you're trying to stay off the radar."

"No, it isn't a good idea, which is why we don't do it," he answered with a nod. "We actually use geothermal energy. There's also an underground spring further below us, which is where we get our water. Using magic for both would be a little excessive, though magic is involved in the water to make sure it's clean and safe to drink," he explained as he pointed out the workshop. "People get bored, and a lot of the people here are still old school. They like making their own stuff, or repairing it. Got a magical workshop, too, and a forge for making weapons." But he didn't seem too concerned with the workshop and moved on quickly. "And here is *my* domain," he said proudly as he opened the door to a room filled with computers. For the most part, there were just tables or desks with computers on them, but near the back was a more impressive setup that had multiple monitors and all sorts of gadgets. "That's my desk," he said, pointing to the over-the-top setup.

"Gee, I never would have guessed the IT guy had the extra monitors," she teased. "Should I even ask how you get internet down here? Since you didn't answer me about cell service."

He slowly waved his hands while wiggling his fingers and said in a low, mysterious voice, "Magic."

Sophia laughed and shook her head. "You're a dork," she said, fondness in her tone.

"True," he agreed easily. "Other than my computer, the others are available for anyone to use," he said, backing out again. "But none of this is what you wanted to see, is it?"

"Not really," she admitted. "I keep hearing how the Athenaeum saves and protects books and relics, but so far the only books I've seen were in Erasmus's room," she grumbled.

He chuckled and nodded. "To the library it is," he said, making a grand, sweeping gesture toward the common area. She rolled her eyes and started walking. He caught up to her easily and led her back down the stairs, then kept going at the landing.

"You said there were multiple levels, right?" she asked.

"Mmhmm."

"So why no elevator?"

"One, it would make it difficult to keep the whole carved into the stone aesthetic, I guess. Two, security. The Athenaeum has never been breeched, but if it does, we don't want to make it any easier than necessary to get to the relics and books."

"Oh. That makes sense," she said as they went down what felt like more than a normal flight of steps. Fortunately, they were headed down, but it made her dread when they went back upstairs. She could almost feel her calves aching in anticipation. If she ended up visiting the library a lot, she might not need the gym to stay in shape.

They passed over the next landing, where the living quarters were, then the second landing, but at the one after that, Peter placed his palm on a scanner next to a door and punched in a code on a keypad. The security made her arch a brow, but she was coming to realize they were very serious about keeping the library safe. "You ready?" he asked with a smile as the door clicked and he turned the knob.

"More than ready," she told him, eager to see what lay beyond. "Come on, I want to see!"

He chuckled. "Yes, ma'am," he said, pushing the door open wide and motioning for her to go ahead.

They were in a short hallway, with a door on either side. A glance to Peter had him inclining his head to the left. She nodded and stepped inside, the lights coming on automatically. What she saw astounded her. She'd seen plenty of impressive libraries in the movies, but this one? Nothing compared to this library. It was huge, though the ceiling wasn't much higher than a normal room. The shelves along the walls reached the top of the ceiling, and rolling ladders on tracks offered access to the upper shelves. The middle of the room was full of more shelves, each one packed with books in every possible color and size. She slowly moved further into the room until she reached the first shelf and was unable to stop herself from trailing a finger over the spine of one of the books. "I've never seen so many books in one place," she breathed, in awe of what had just become her personal happy place. "And you said there are more levels under this one? Are they as full as this one?"

"For the most part, yes," he told her, smiling indulgently at her obvious happiness. "The upper levels are the...more common books. The ones either you can go out and buy in any bookstore or the ones that aren't really hard to replace. The further down you get, the more rare or dangerous the books get."

Sophia glanced at him as she began wandering down the rows. "What do you mean, dangerous?"

He blinked at her and looked flustered. "Oh, um...well, someone else should probably explain that to you," he mumbled, scratching at the back of his head.

She stopped and frowned at him. "Why can't you? By dangerous do you mean the books on magic?" she pressed. While she couldn't wait to see the ancient books from Greece—or Rome or Egypt—she could admit she was just as eager to see the books on magic. Growing up knowing magic was real, even doing it, was different from reading ancient books on it.

He shuffled from one foot to the other, caught off guard by her question. Just as she felt he was starting to give in, that he was about to answer her question, Dion came down the stairs with a bright smile on his face. "There you are!" he said. "I heard you were getting a tour from Peter here," he said as he clapped an affectionate hand on his son's shoulder, "and figured you would end up down here. Everyone always does."

Sophia smiled at him. "I can see why. If these are the least impressive books, then I can't wait to see what's below us."

"All in good time, my dear," he assured her. "All in good time. For now, I was actually looking for you for a reason. Erasmus would like to see you."

Emotions caused a fluttering in her stomach. A happy fluttering. She didn't know how long she'd have a grandfather, so the prospect of spending as much time with him as possible was a good one. "I'll head right that way," she assured him, hurrying toward the stairs, only to stop with her foot on the first step. "Um..." She glanced over her shoulder, thinking of how the doors pretty much all looked the same. "Okay, if I try to go by myself, I'll get lost and end up wandering around for an hour."

Dion chuckled. "I'll be happy to show you the way."

Even Peter grinned and walked over to her. "Let me see your phone before you go." When she unlocked it and handed it to him, he programmed in his number. "There. If you have any questions or just want to hang out with someone more your age," he said, shooting his dad a playful look, "then you can get a hold of me."

Sophia returned his grin and tucked her phone away. "Thanks. And thanks for the tour. This place is awesome."

"You're welcome."

Dion led her back up the stairs and through the secured door. She glanced at the scanner and wondered aloud, "So anytime I want to go to the library, I'm guessing I'll need to get one of you guys to take me?"

"Mmm. For the moment, yes, but family is allowed on the upper levels without supervision. At least after they reach a certain age, which you have clearly reached," Dion began. "I don't see why we can't program you into the system. I'll tell Peter and Lucas that it's okay, but you'll need to meet up with them later."

"Why Lucas? Peter makes sense, since he's the IT guy, but what does Lucas have to do with it?" she asked curiously.

"Lucas is the head of the nasaru, which means he's also head of security," Dion explained. "I'm sure it's assumed that, as Erasmus's granddaughter, you're allowed, but there's nothing wrong with ensuring the proper protocols are observed."

"No, it sounds like the safe way to go, especially with rare books involved," Sophia agreed easily.

"Exactly," he told her with a smile. They walked for a minute before he spoke again. "I know we didn't really get a chance to talk when you got here, but I wanted to tell you that I was sorry about your father. He was an amazing man."

"Thanks. I never met him, so I don't...it's not the same as if I'd grown up with him, you know?" It was always hard for her to explain that it was hard for her to mourn someone she'd never met. It was more like she mourned the idea of him.

"True, but I'm still sorry that you never got to know him," Dion said, his voice kind. "But I am happy that you've come home and I was able to meet you. I'm just sorry that it took so long."

Part of Sophia wanted to frown at the last bit, but she just smiled at him. "I'm happy I'm here, too. Everyone's been pretty amazing, and this place is beyond interesting. Beautiful, too. I can't believe it's carved right into the earth."

"Believe me, it wasn't a quick or easy process. It began as just a natural cave and it was added to over the centuries, with both magic and manual labor. The youngest rooms are only a couple of decades old." He stopped beside a door and smiled. "And here we are. He's expecting you, so just knock. And now you have Peter's number, so if you need anything, I'm sure he won't mind if you contact him."

"I will. And thanks again, Dion."

He inclined his head. "You're welcome. Enjoy your visit," he told her with a smile before he continued down the hall.

Everyone really had been as awesome as she'd said. This was almost like a dream, but as she knocked on the door, she wondered when she was going to wake up.

Chapter 8

SOPHIA OPENED THE DOOR the moment she heard Erasmus and smiled when she saw him sitting up, a little more color in his face than he'd had yesterday. No, it had just been earlier that morning.

"Hey," she told him and, when he motioned to the chair by his bed, moved forward and sat down. "I was hoping I'd get to talk to you again," she told him warmly.

"You're welcome to come talk to me anytime you like, Sophia," Erasmus told her, and she got the sense that he wasn't just saying that, he truly meant it.

"I just don't want to…"

"To wear me out?" He shook his head. "I'm going to be tired either way. I'd rather be tired and getting to know my granddaughter."

That sounded like something she'd say, so Sophia grinned. "Won't argue with that. The only reason I agreed to come—hell, the reason I insisted I come—was because I'd heard I had a grandfather."

He chuckled and shook his head. "Stubborn, then?" he asked affectionately.

Her grin turned sheepish, but she didn't argue with his assessment.

"Yes, you're a Regas, all right. Tell me, has anyone shown you around the Athenaeum, yet?"

Sophia was a little surprised he wanted to talk about the Athenaeum and not get to know her, but all things considered, she was inclined to accommodate him. "Some, yeah. Peter was showing me around. We were in the library when Dion found us and said you wanted to see me."

"What did you think?"

"This is all…" She shook her head. "I don't even have the words. Amazing? Wonderful? Fan-freaking-tastic? I mean, even if the place was empty, just the way this place was carved is beyond awesome. Add in everything—including the library—and it's just…mind blowing. I can't wait to see the relics and take more time actually checking out the library."

He smiled, looking proud of her opinion. "I'm happy you think so. Our family has been involved with the Athenaeum since the first century. Tell me, though, did you see the lower levels of the library?"

"No, we hadn't even gone far into the library when Dion showed up. I can't wait to see the rest, though."

"You will," he said with a certainty that made her pause. "I know this is all shocking to you. Finding out you have a family, learning of what is essentially a secret society, flying halfway around the world…"

Sophia nodded slightly. "It is." There wasn't any reason to deny it. "But I think it's all a good sort of shock. Sure, it'll probably take a couple days for it all to sink in, and I might have a panic attack at some point when it hits me, but this isn't a bad thing overall."

He sighed and extended his hand, palm up. She placed hers in it and he squeezed gently. "Unfortunately, I have to add to it. I'd love to ease you into everything, but since I don't know how long I have, I can't afford to waste time."

Her brow furrowed and she shook her head. "I don't understand," she told him, a curl of dread forming in her belly.

"I know, sweet girl," he murmured. "You grew up not knowing about this place, but you know what you are, yes?"

The dread started to dissipate. "Oh, yeah. Mom never hid that from me. I'm going to guess you're an owl shifter, since I know I got the elf side from Mom?"

Some of the tension in his face eased. "Good. And yes, you did. Your father was an owl as well." He hesitated for a moment, then continued. "While we're all magic, I'm sure you're aware that doing magic for us is a little limited?"

"Sure. Mom's a good healer, but I'm only so-so. I'm better with animals, though." She grinned. "Birds, especially."

"Heather was always good at healing. Before she left, she was considering joining Sergei in the clinic as a healer."

"Sounds like her," Sophia said with a smile. "Did you know she was a nurse? Is a nurse, I mean?" Her smile faded. "Sergei hasn't been able to help you?"

Erasmus slowly shook his head. "No, and he's not the only healer who's tried. You know magic isn't infallible."

"No, it isn't," she agreed quietly.

"Don't worry about that right now. What do you know of sorcery?"

That question surprised her, but she shrugged. "The same anyone else knows, I guess. Magic anyone, even humans, can learn. You have to speak spells to use it, right?"

"Not always, but in general, yes. Words have power, whether written or spoken. Speaking them just puts them out into the world. The

Athenaeum has many, many books and scrolls on sorcery, a great deal more than what is more widely known. That's part of our job. It isn't just saving the knowledge so it isn't lost, it's protecting it from evil people."

"That's what it said in the front hallway. Protecting it, though it mentioned time and man erasing it, not protecting it from abuse."

"Actually, some of the columns do mention the abuse, but yes. That's why we're here," Erasmus confirmed. "And that's also why my position exists. The aspida is the keeper of not just the Athenaeum, but all the knowledge contained within it, especially the magic. There are books here—not just spells, either—that are reserved only for the eyes of the aspida and anyone he—or she—feels should know." He smiled a little. "Did you know the aspida is chosen by the Athenaeum? And I don't mean the people within it."

She blinked at him, the words not quite making sense to her. "The...Athenaeum...chooses?" she says slowly.

"Yes. That, I'm afraid, is part of why you and your mother were brought here. Our way is to ensure that, if possible, everyone connected to the Athenaeum is here when the aspida dies. Because any one of them might be chosen next."

Sophia shoved her chair back and stumbled a few steps from the bed, shaking her head. The earlier panic rose quickly. In the back of her head she realized she was breathing too fast, her heart was beating too rapidly, but all she could focus on was the implication that she could potentially be put in charge of this huge, amazing, confusing place. She kept shaking her head as she paced back and forth at the end of Erasmus's bed. Part of her realized he was talking to her, but she couldn't stop. Then it hit her. How egotistical was she to automatically jump to the conclusion that she'd be picked? No, she hadn't just assumed it, but the thought had occurred to her, which made her a little ashamed. There were people here who had lived their whole lives in the Athenaeum. They probably spoke dozens of languages and were terrifying with their magic. No, the Athenaeum wouldn't choose her, it would choose someone much more qualified.

With that thought, she started to calm and stopped pacing. She glanced at Erasmus, who was watching her with love and concern. "I'm sorry. I just...I'm sorry," she told him, cheeks flushing with embarrassment as she retook her seat. "I've been here less than a day. I'm not qualified to take your job. I just want to get to know you. And Dion and Peter. Having cousins is almost as awesome as having a grandfather," she said with a weak smile.

"You're fine, Sophia," he said, relief crossing his face. "There is one more thing I need to tell you if I'm to answer all your questions, but I'm concerned that I've already overwhelmed you."

Mentally steeling herself, she shook her head. "No, I'll be all right. Besides, it's like a bandaid, right? Don't ease it off, just rip it off in one go."

"If you're certain..." She nodded once, firmly, and he went on. "You asked why magic couldn't save me. Unfortunately, the answer isn't an easy one. My death isn't going to be a natural one. Someone with disturbingly impressive knowledge has poisoned me with something that apparently cannot be touched by the healing spells I and our healer, Sergei, know, or the antidotes we have access to. And we have access to powerful antidotes."

In that moment, it didn't matter that Sophia hadn't known he existed twenty-four hours ago. It didn't matter that she'd only met him a few hours ago. She was utterly and completely furious that someone could possibly poison this sweet man. "Who? Who did this to you?" she demanded, not realizing that she had leaned forward and taken his hand in her own.

"Shh," he soothed, patting her hand with his free one. "I've accepted my fate, sweet girl, and seeing how outraged you are on my behalf heals a part of my soul that deeply regretted not being in your life before now."

"But it's not right. It's not *fair*," she insisted.

"Perhaps not," he agreed serenely, "but it is what it is. Now, no one knows about this besides Sergei—"

"And the bastard who did this to you," she muttered.

He smiled indulgently. "Indeed. But it must stay this way. You cannot tell anyone, not even your mother."

Her eyes widened. "Why aren't you telling everyone this? It has to be someone here in the Athenaeum, doesn't it? You should tell people and let us figure out who did it so they can face justice for what they did."

"Which is why you can't say anything. It *is* someone here, and someone very good. Even I don't know who it is. Though I have a theory as to why."

"Why? Why would anyone do this to you? I know you're probably not perfect and have made mistakes, but you don't strike me as an asshole."

"Think about what I told you, about why you were brought here."

It took a few seconds before she let out a sound dangerously close to a growl. "They want your job? You think they're doing this to become the next aspida?" He nodded slightly. She started to go off on another rant when something he said clicked with her, which actually soothed some of her ire. "You said the Athenaeum chooses. So it's...what, sentient? Or enchanted to choose somehow?"

"Mmm. Has anyone told you about our patrons?"

"Yeah, some gods put protections in place, right?"

"Exactly. And some of those protections included the choosing of the aspida. The best way to explain it is semi-sentient because of the magic, but yes, close enough," he confirmed. "That's not all it can do, but it's the most important."

"And is this magic smart enough, is the Athenaeum smart enough, to know these things and not choose a murderer?"

He chuckled then and gave her a proud smile. "And that is why my killer's plan has already failed. Wonderfully fitting, don't you think? The act they did to get the job is the same act which will ensure they never get the job."

"That...okay, it's not quite justice, but it's definitely a start," she told him, returning his smile with a faint one of her own. "I wish I'd gotten to know you when I was a kid," she whispers.

"I wish that, too, Sophia. But while I have some time left, I can still act like a grandfather once before my end comes. And, unfortunately, it's close."

"You are," she insisted, trying not to tear up.

"Perhaps, but I can do more. I don't want my fate for you, so I'm going to teach you a spell."

Her natural curiosity warred with her sorrow for his imminent demise. Knowing how much he wanted to do this for her allowed her curiosity to win. "What sort of spell?"

"One to sense nearby threats. Unfortunately, it won't pinpoint them, or let you know whether the threat is a person or something natural like a nearby cliff, and it only lasts for a little while, but it will tell you if you need to be on your guard. Fortunately, this spell is in ancient Greek, so it shouldn't be too difficult for you."

"And what do I do? Just say the words?"

"In part. Just saying the words can be effective, but it's more effective with intent behind it. So when you say the spell, focus on wanting to know if there are any threats nearby."

Sophia drew in a breath and nodded. "Okay, I can do that. What's the spell?" she asked, trying to hide her eagerness.

He smiled and slowly spoke in ancient Greek. The syllables, to her surprise, didn't make a complete sentence, but she repeated them. When he nodded encouragingly, she closed her eyes and focused like he told her to. After getting the thoughts firmly in her head, she repeated the words again, more surely this time. The moment the last syllable was past her lips, she felt a shiver slide across her skin. It was so unexpected her eyes flew open. "What was that?"

He frowned. "What did it feel like?"

"A shiver. Like a cold breeze went down my spine at the same time someone was watching me."

His expression didn't change. "That's the spell. It means there's already a threat to you," he murmured. "If it's just a shiver, then it's not close, though. The nearer the threat, the stronger the sensation. I want you to be on your guard, Sophia. As much as I hate to say it, I want you to be careful who you trust here."

Sophia hated to hear that, but she couldn't argue with him. "I will. I promise."

He nodded and closed his eyes, suddenly looking extremely tired.

"I'm going to let you get some rest, but I promise I'll be back every day," she told him as she got to her feet.

"I'd like that. Just be careful," he repeated.

"I will," she told him again before she leaned down to kiss his cheek. "Sleep well," she whispered before she left the room, closing the door quietly behind her.

Chapter 9

Sᴏᴘʜɪᴀ ᴄʟᴏsᴇᴅ ᴛʜᴇ ᴅᴏᴏʀ quietly behind her and looked down the hallway. She thought her room was further away from the common room, but she wasn't entirely sure. Her hand went to her phone to get in touch with either her mom or Peter, but she hesitated. No, she wasn't sure where to go, but she didn't have a horrible sense of direction and, if she was going to spend any time here, she had to figure out how to get around. And honestly, what was the worst that would happen? If she went right, she'd end up in the common area and run into people. If she went left, she'd end up at her room or a dead end…Probably. Either way, she wouldn't be irrevocably lost.

Turning left, she started down the hallway. She passed several doorways and again noted how they were all identical. "Note to self…do something to make my door unique," she muttered to herself. As she passed the corners in the hallway and probably a dozen doors, she started to rethink her decision not to contact someone. Just as she'd decided to give in, she heard voices. It only took a moment for her to recognize one as her mom's. She quickened her pace and reached another corner, peeking around it. Her mother stood there with an older man with short, salt-and-pepper hair. To her shock, her mom actually laughed, which had something inside Sophia lightening.

"Hey, Mom," she said with a smile as she approached the pair.

Heather turned, her expression more relaxed than Sophia had seen since Greece had invaded their home. "Sophia. I want you to meet Ray," she said with a light touch to the man's bicep. "He's a good friend." She smiled at Ray. "He was your father's best friend, in fact," she said quietly.

Ray nodded. "And your father was my best friend as well. I'm sorry you never got to meet him," he told Sophia, offering her a hand.

She took it and smiled. "I am, too. But I've always had my mom, and now I've got a grandfather. And you."

"You do," Ray said with a firm nod. "Since your father is gone and Erasmus's health is poor, if you need anything—and I mean anything—let me know."

Sophia pulled her phone out, unlocked it, and offered it to him. "I can definitely use some help around this place, if only navigating it. If you could give me your number, I won't hesitate to let you know if I need help."

He gave a grunt she interpreted as approval as he slowly input his number, then gave her back her phone. "Good. I have to get to the gym, but you ladies have a good day."

"We will." Heather leaned up to kiss his cheek lightly. "Don't work too hard."

"It was nice meeting you," Sophia told him, watching as he left. "I'm glad I ran into you guys. All the hallways and doors look identical, so I couldn't figure out where my room was," she admitted.

Heather laughed softly and linked her arm with her daughter's. "You get used to it," she promised. "Though I'll admit that it took me about a month before I stopped opening the wrong doors," she said as she moved unerringly toward their rooms and into Sophia's. "So you met Peter and got a tour?"

Sophia kicked her shoes off and plopped down on the bed. "Yeah. A short one. He took me all around this level and showed me the first floor of the library. Which, let me say, is just..." She made a mind-blown gesture. "Wow."

Heather nodded and took a seat in the desk chair, turning it to face Sophia. "It is impressive, yes. They don't just have historical books either. Did you know that?"

Sophia shook her head. "I didn't. Well, I mean, I assumed they had language books, too, and the magic books, but I didn't think about it much beyond that."

"They have those things, too, of course, but also stories. Not just the famous ones, either. The Athenaeum is here to preserve knowledge, yes, but books more than straight knowledge. And any member of the Athenaeum is able to add a book to the collection. You can pick up a new book you've been dying for and it'll added to the library."

"That's really cool. And aggravating."

Bewildered, Heather asked, "What do you mean?"

Sophia grinned. "There's no way anyone could read all those books in one lifetime, even our lifetimes. So how do you choose which ones to read and which ones you'll never crack the cover of?"

Heather rolled her eyes but couldn't help but smile. "That would be your concern."

"It's a valid concern," Sophia argued. "I also got to talk to Erasmus again. And let me tell you, it is both extremely weird and extremely awesome to have a chat with my grandfather."

Guilt infused Heather's eyes. "I'm sorry you didn't have that growing up. I just wanted to protect you."

"I know, Mom, I do. And yeah, I'm a little mad that I didn't learn about my family until now, but I get it," Sophia promised. "Besides, I'm getting to know them now. Dion seems like a really nice guy, and Peter? I can see us becoming good friends. But Erasmus?" One corner of her mouth tipped up, but her eyes were a little sad. "He's an older version of how I always imagined Dad would be. The history and sort of serene humor and all that." The sadness disappeared when she grinned and straightened. "He taught me a spell," she said, excited all over again, though the faint shiver still tickled across her skin.

"What?" Heather exclaimed, looking almost panicked. "Sorcery? What spell? Why?"

Sophia reeled back slightly. "Whoa...calm down, Mom. It's not like he told me how to raise revenants or anything. He taught me because, A, he's my grandfather, and B, he wanted me to be safe. He taught me how to sense nearby threats. That's it, but hopefully he'll teach me more." Her stubbornness stiffened her spine and lifted her chin. "I want to learn more."

Mollified until that last adamant statement, Heather nodded. "That's a good spell for you to know. Just...be careful when learning sorcery, sweetheart. Not all sorcery is used for good, and some have become...addicted to it."

"I'm always careful," Sophia muttered, though she knew that wasn't strictly true. A fact her mom was well aware of, judging by the arched brow and stern look. "Yeah, yeah. I'll be careful."

"Good. That's all I want."

There was a knock on the door and both women looked in that direction. "Who would be knocking on my door?" Sophia asked as she got to her feet.

"You're new and Erasmus's granddaughter. You're interesting. I wouldn't be surprised if everyone made some excuse to chat with you at some point," Heather said with a shrug.

"Seriously?" She just didn't see herself as that interesting, not next to these people. She was still shaking her head when she opened the door, relieved to see a familiar face. "Peter. Hey, what's up?" she asked with a smile, one he returned.

"Dinner is, actually," he told her. When he looked around Sophia to notice Heather, he grinned. "Hi, Aunt Heather. Remember me?"

"Peter? Oh wow. You've definitely grown up," Heather said as she jumped to her feet and hurried to him for a hug. "And gotten more colorful," she teased when she leaned back and lightly ruffled his mohawk.

"I'm the tech guy. I'm supposed to be eccentric, and around here, it takes a lot to not just be a normal sort of eccentric," he told her with a feigned exasperated look.

"It works for you," Heather decided. "I, for one, am starving, but I definitely want to get a chance to talk to you soon."

"Absolutely. Sophia has my number, or I'm in the computer room most of the time," he told her. He stepped back then cocked both of his elbows out. "May I escort both of you lovely ladies to dinner?"

Sophia laughed and took one of his arms. "Certainly, kind sir."

Heather simply smiled indulgently and took his other arm.

When they reached the dining room, Sophia almost balked. There weren't just a few people there, there were almost twenty. A few she recognized, like Dion and Lucas, but most faces were of complete strangers.

Peter noticed her hesitation and bent his head to whisper to her. "Are you okay?"

"That's just...a lot of people." And most of them were staring in her direction.

"True," he said, scanning the others, "but they're just people. And you don't have to talk to any of them you don't want to. If it makes you more comfortable, I'm more than willing to sit with you at an empty table."

It was tempting, but Sophia couldn't allow herself to take the easy way. The coward's way. "No, I have to get used to these people sometime, right? And everyone's been really nice, so far." She spotted Carla at one of the tables and added, "Mostly."

"You'll do fine, sweetheart," Heather assured her.

Sophia nodded and let the others lead her to a few empty seats. She ended up sitting across from Lucas, with her mother and cousin acting as sentinels on either side of her. To Lucas's left was a muscular man with a military haircut. Despite his rugged appearance, his smile when he saw her looking was kind. "Hi. Sophia, I'm guessing?" he asked, his accent as American as her own.

"I am. And a little surprised to hear another not-Greek accent," she admitted with a little smile.

He grinned. "I'm from America. I was recruited just after I left the Marines," he explained. "I'm Jacob."

"Nice to meet you."

On Lucas's right was a petite woman, her brown hair pulled up in a ponytail. Her hazel eyes were heavily lined with black and there was a silver ring in one nostril, but she grinned brightly. "Hi. I'm Josie. Not American, though."

"That's okay. I forgive you," Sophia said solemnly, which made Josie laugh.

"Good to know. If you get tired of all the guys, come find me. I'm way more interesting than the meatheads," Josie said, giving a playful wink to Lucas and Jacob.

"Meatheads and a Marine, so I'm guessing you're a guard like Lucas?" Sophia asked Jacob, who nodded. "And what are you?" she asked, looking back to Josie. "And that sounded kind of rude, but you know what I mean, right?"

"I do," Josie said, waving her concerns away. "And I'm a venator."

Further conversation paused as several people placed dishes of food on the table. A couple large bowls of soup, trays of fresh bread, a platter of lamb, and several bowls of salad and other vegetables. At first Sophia was surprised at the amount of food until she glanced up and down the table to remind herself of just how many people were here. She watched the others and when she saw them simply transferring food to their plates or bowls, she joined them.

"Has anyone shown you around the place yet?" Josie asked, several minutes later.

Peter lifted his fork in the air. "I did."

"Some of it," Sophia corrected, but she smiled to take any sting out of her words. "I only saw the first level of the library, though."

"Hey, not my fault," Peter protested.

"I know. Not blaming you. But I'm absolutely going to make puppy eyes at someone until they show me more." Out of the corner of her eye she saw Dion, who was on the other side of Peter, lean forward and start to speak, but Lucas spoke up first.

"I'll take you."

Josie gave him a surprised look, and even Peter shifted slightly beside her, but Sophia's attention was on the head of the nasaru. He was a little intimidating. He was big, strong, and if he was the head guard, probably dangerous. Lethal even. Yet she did want to see more of the library and he was necessary to get her own access to it. "Thanks. Do you think we can do it after dinner?"

Lucas nodded. "Sure. Just let me know when you're ready," he said before seeming to dismiss her and focus on his food. Clearly, this wasn't going to be a man who was easily figured out, but Sophia did enjoy a mystery.

The rest of the dinner was more uneventful and Sophia mostly let the conversation flow around her. It made her happy to hear her mom chatting with people who had been friends years ago, and she hoped it would help her mom relax a little.

When Sophia had finally cleared her plate, she was rethinking the second tour of the library. The food had been so good she'd eaten a little more than she should have. "Where's Agatha? I have to tell her this was amazing," she groaned, rubbing her belly lightly.

"Right here," came the cheerful answer from halfway down the table.

Sophia leaned forward until she could see the smiling cook. "Stop cooking like this or I'm going to end up too big to make it through the labyrinth," she playfully reprimanded.

"Sorry, you'll just have to learn some self-control," Agatha retorted, but she looked pleased by the praise.

Sophia sat back and sipped at her water as she studied Lucas, who was done eating and now chatting with Jacob. She waited for a break in the conversation before asking, "Are you ready, Lucas?"

He turned back to her and nodded. "Sure." He pushed to his feet and moved to the end of the table, waiting for her.

Heather caught Sophia's arm before she could rise and leaned in to speak quietly. "Enjoy the library, but be careful. The saying that knowledge is power is accurate enough, but sometimes knowledge can be dangerous, okay?"

Confused, Sophia slowly nodded. "Sure. Love you, Mom." She gave her mom a quick hug before she followed after Lucas, eager to see what lay beneath the mundane books of the first level.

Chapter 10

Sophia watched Lucas curiously out of the corner of her eye as they neared the library door. "I'm a little surprised you offered to show me more of the library," she admitted.

He arched a brow and glanced at her. "Why is that?"

The real reason was he seemed more like a soldier type instead of a librarian, but she didn't want to offend him. That and he seemed more the all work and no play type. "I don't know, just seemed like you might be more...not interested in playing tour guide."

Lucas chuckled and shrugged. "I may be the head of security, but it doesn't mean I'm not friendly. I like hanging out with the others, no matter what branch of the Athenaeum they work in. And I like making new friends, too. You and your mother are the only new people here, ergo..."

Sophia grinned. "Ergo?"

"Hey, I may be a guard, but I'm still a part of the Athenaeum. Reading is a requirement," he said as they reached the door.

"Good point. By the way, I was told I needed to get you and Peter to get me my own credentials or whatever so I can get into the library," she told him as he placed his hand on the scanner, then punched in a code.

"Not a problem," he said, opening the door and motioning for her to go inside. "Find me or Peter tomorrow and we'll get that taken care of for you. Has anyone told you about the levels of the library? What's on each, I mean?"

Sophia shook her head. "Not really. Peter did say the more dangerous books were further down, but that's it. How many levels are there?"

"In the entire Athenaeum? Eleven, but only seven have books," he answered.

Seven had books? She knew one level was filled with the bedrooms and such, another with the gym and all that, but that still left two levels. Including the one above them that both Peter and Lucas had skipped. "Are two empty or something? Waiting for more books?"

He glanced at her and shook his head. "No. One is the aquifer at the lowest level, and one's has the crypts."

Her step faltered. "Crypt? You guys have a crypt in this place?"

Lucas turned toward her, the corners of his mouth tipped upward. "You studied history, right?"

"Yeah..."

"How many castles or churches or other buildings had crypts beneath them? For that matter, look at Paris. It has how many miles of crypts? They're so famous they've become a tourist attraction."

Sophia's nose wrinkled, but she nodded. "Fair point. It just caught me off guard. It's not really the way things are done in America. The closest we get is keeping Grandma's ashes on the mantle."

"Most of our crypt is filled with ashes, not skeletons, if that makes you feel better."

She thought about that for a moment. "A little. Now, what's on these levels?" she asked, eager to change the subject. Talking about crypts was too close to talking about how Erasmus was soon to be in one.

"This level and the one below it are filled with what we term common books and simple relics," he explained as he started walking again, winding his way through the rows toward the other end of the room.

Sophia nodded. "Okay, yeah. Peter mentioned that. Easy to find books or things being published now."

"Right. So if you're looking for a light read, something to just relax with, stick to the upper two levels."

Not quite directly across from the entrance was another doorway which led to another set of stairs. They went down them and she mentally groaned. Her legs were definitely going to be hating her if he was taking her to the lowest level of the library. Unsurprisingly, when they reached the bottom of the stairs he didn't hesitate, just made his way to yet another door, this one on the left wall. It wasn't until they were halfway down the stairs that he began speaking again.

"These next two levels are the semi-rare books. The fourth floor is all non-fiction books and the third is fiction—Shakespeare, Austen, Dickens, things like that."

"You can get those authors at any bookstore, though," Sophia argued.

"First editions or the original manuscripts written by hand by the author?" he challenged with a smile.

Her jaw dropped. "Are you serious?"

"I am. So be careful with those."

"Believe me, I will." And though she now wanted, desperately, to see those books, Lucas didn't stop until they were heading down to the fifth level.

"I'm not going to take you to the sixth or seventh levels—and the regular clearance for the library won't get you onto those levels, by the way—but that's all the books on magic and other books we've termed as dangerous. But the fifth level is all our rare books." He stopped just inside the doorway and she was surprised to see a pedestal with a wooden box on it. He opened it and took out a couple pairs of white cotton gloves. Offering a pair to her, he slipped the other on himself.

"I'm guessing these are mandatory?" she asked, but just the fact that they were here made her giddy for what she'd find hidden among the stacks.

"Absolutely. Some things here won't be harmed by the oils on your skin, but others can be destroyed. And before you ask, the gloves are washed daily. Just put the used ones beside the box."

"Will do." Gloves sorted, she looked around, surprised at how different this level looked. While there were shelves, this level wasn't as tightly packed as the others. More, instead of simple bookshelves, in some places there were cubbies that held scrolls, tablets, or loose pages instead of books. Her fingers itched to touch them, but she waited for Lucas.

"Your schooling was primarily about ancient Greece, right?" Lucas asked.

"Mmhmm."

"Follow me." He moved without hesitation, which proved that he spent a good deal of time down here. He stopped near the back between a row of cubbies and a set of heavy shelves that held tablets and odd-looking books. "You've read the Odyssey, I'm assuming?" he asked as he picked up one of the scrolls and undid the tie holding it closed.

"Of course. You can't very well study ancient Greece, its lore, and its culture without it."

He smiled and gently offered the scroll to her. "Have you ever seen one of the original copies of it written on a papyrus scroll?"

"Are you screwing with me?" she demanded, barely managing not to snatch the scroll from him. She unrolled it with all the caution of someone defusing a nuclear bomb, and about fainted when she saw the faded ink and familiar words. "Oh my gods," she breathed as her eyes devoured each letter. "Am I really holding a scroll that's nearly three thousand years old?"

Though she couldn't drag her gaze off the scroll, she could hear the amusement in his voice. "You really are, yes. And there are some works here that are even older."

"I don't understand...how is this still intact? Something like this should be brittle, if not absolutely destroyed," she whispered, as though even speaking too loudly would cause it to crumble in her hands.

"You did hear that there's magic, right?" he asked, grinning. "Spells have been done over and over on the library to ensure that the atmosphere is perfect for preserving the books. Add the cool, dry air of being underground, and they're as safe as they can be without being in a sealed clean room. As long as they're handled with care, they'll be fine."

Sophia slowly rolled the scroll up again, afraid that her hands were going to start shaking. "I think I love this place," she told him as she retied the ribbon around the scroll and gently replaced it in the cubby.

"I'm not at all surprised," he admitted. "I'll let you wander around and look for a bit, but two things before you fall down that rabbit hole..." He cupped her elbow and guided her to one side of the room. There was another door there with a palm scanner. "That one leads to the sixth level—dangerous books, also called the Archives—so you won't be able to get down there without Dion, myself, or Nicolas. The level beneath that is restricted to only Erasmus."

"Now that's just mean, because that made me curious. Don't tempt me with places I can't visit."

He gave her a quick smile and shrug. "I can always distract you. You know the landing we passed? The one above the first level of the library and repository?"

The one with the crypt? "Yeah..."

"You'll find three doors in that hallway, all of which are coded to everyone in the library."

Goosebumps erupted on Sophia's arms. The words were innocent enough, but something in the tone gave her a sense of foreboding. "And?"

It took Lucas a moment to answer. "The one on the left leads to the crypt. The one on the right is where the steles and ashes of all previous aspides are. And the one at the end is the room where the Athenaeum gathers when a new aspida is chosen."

"Oh."

It took a minute before either said or did anything else. Lucas smiled tightly and turned his back on it. "So, how are you liking Greece so far?" he asked as he steered her away from the doors and back to the Greek section.

"Well, I haven't actually seen much of it," she pointed out. "I haven't left the Athenaeum since I got here, remember? And it was still dark when we got here, so I didn't see all that much. I'm hoping to get to see some of the ruins, though."

Lucas nodded. "Parthenon, Temple of Zeus...places like that?"

"Yes," she sighed wistfully. "I've seen pictures, but I doubt they do the sites justice," she said as she ran a gloved finger lightly over a clay tablet.

"You can pick them up," he told her. "Just be careful." He waited until she had—giving him a bright smile—before he continued. "It would be wise to go with a guard."

Startled, she blinked at him. "A guard? Why?"

"Well, you don't know the country, and there's no need to pay money for a guide when you've got us. Besides, transportation would be tricky if you went with an outside guide since we are hiding."

All logical arguments, but something told Sophia there was something more to it than that. She wondered if he knew Erasmus had been poisoned and was just being cautious, or if it was something else. Rather than question him on that, she asked, "Any recommendations?"

One dark brow arched. "For guards or places to see?"

She smiled. "Either one."

"I have lots of recommendations for places to see, though not all of them are ancient historical sites," Lucas admitted. "As for guards?" He shrugged. "All of my guards are good at their job—and I know you just adore Carla," he said with a hint of teasing at the end. "But I will almost always recommend myself before them."

"That's kind of egotistical, isn't it?" she asked, turning away from him to replace the tablet and wander down the shelf, looking at the other millennia-old books and scrolls.

"Not really. I am the head of the nasaru. It's not like I just declared I was the best guard, you know."

She made a noncommittal sound and glanced back to him. "I'll keep that in mind, but for now I'm focused on getting to know Erasmus. The rest of you guys, too, of course, but especially him. Well, him and Dion and Peter. My family."

"Which is completely understandable," he agreed with a nod. "I take it you're not going to head back to the States soon, then?"

Sophia hesitated and dropped her hand. "I don't know. I really don't. I came here because I never knew I had a grandfather, and yeah, I've always wanted to see Greece, but I have a life back in America. I have friends, classes…"

"Here's something to consider…while you can never replace friends, you can make new ones. You have family here. And your classes…" He shrugged and tilted his head to the texts beside her. "You can learn more about ancient Greece within these four walls than you can in any university."

Judging by what she'd seen and the books she'd heard were here, she didn't really doubt that, but only said, "I'll keep that in mind." She considered going back to her room to process and adjust to the time change, but she still hadn't seen the relics. "Do you think you could show me some of the relics before I head back to my room? My internal clock is all screwy thanks to the time difference."

"Mmm. Yes, seven hours will do that," he agreed before leading her up a few levels—back to the first level of the library, she thought—and back to the hallway. Before he opened the other door, he looked to her. "Is it necessary that I warn you about playing with the relics?"

She'd never actually seen a relic in person, but Heather had ensured she wasn't ignorant. "No. I know that some of them are harmless, but I also know it's hard to tell what they do, and witches are the ones who can figure that out."

"Good." He opened the door and led her into the room. It was about the same size as the library side of the level, and the layout was surprisingly similar. The main difference was the shelves varied in height and they held objects rather than books. Also unlike the library, there were small cards in front of each object which gave a brief description of its appearance and known magic. What surprised her was the type of objects here. When she thought of relics, she'd always thought of weapons and expensive-looking jewelry. She hadn't thought of it being a simple clay pot or bland-looking quill, but she saw both on the shelves, along with tall statues and pieces of furniture. Honestly, every type of object she could think of was represented in some way.

"Feel free to look all you want, but be careful about what you touch. Nothing here should be dangerous, but it's good to make a habit of being cautious."

Since he had a point, she only nodded and curiously moved toward the quill. Her lips twitched when she saw it was definitely harmless. A quill that never ran out of ink? Really? Well, it would certainly be convenient. Or would have been back before computers or typewriters.

She wandered the rows, glancing at the cards of items that interested her, but it was clear they hadn't been kidding when they said this was the equivalent of this floor's library. Boring items. Cool, yes, because they were relics, but not what she was hoping for.

They made their way back to the stairs. By the time they had reached the floor her room was on, she wanted to cry thanks to the burning in her calves. The hike to the Athenaeum was nothing compared to climbing up seven flights of stairs, especially when they were longer than a standard flight. She half collapsed against the wall, shifting from one foot to the other to try to ease the pain. "Please tell me that there's an actual tub somewhere in this place and not just showers like the one I used earlier," she groaned.

"Of course. I'll point it out before I leave you for the night."

"Do it and earn my undying devotion," she said earnestly. To her relief, the tub wasn't far from her room so, after they parted ways, she spent a solid hour soaking in the most fantastic tub she'd ever seen. It was deep enough and long enough to actually accommodate a person who wanted to stretch out. It was absolute bliss and worked wonders on her sore muscles. When she made it to her bed was relaxed enough that it only took her a minute to slide deeply into sleep.

Chapter 11

Sophia's body had decided to rebel against the jet lag and, though she'd gone to sleep around ten, she slept until well after eight. When she woke she was groggy, and since it was her first real morning in Greece, she wondered about the breakfast situation as she shuffled to the kitchen. To her relief, they did breakfast buffet style and—thank the gods—had plenty of coffee.

She guzzled her first cup—not caring that she singed her tongue—before she learned Erasmus hadn't yet had breakfast. She begged a tray off Agatha and fixed two plates and two cups of coffee, carrying them to his room. Once there, she cursed her lack of fore-thought when she realized she had no easy way to knock, much less open the door. Awkwardly balancing the tray on one arm, she quickly knocked then put her hand back on the tray before it could tilt. When she heard Erasmus's weak voice, she shifted again to open the door, closing it with her hip.

He looked even paler than he had the day before, his eyes not quite as clear, but she made herself smile brightly. "Morning! I heard you hadn't had breakfast, so I thought...well, I was hoping..."

Erasmus tried to sit up as he smiled tremulously at her. "That we could have breakfast together? I'd love to."

Sophia quickly put the tray down and hurried to the bed to help him sit up, making sure he was supported by the pillows. Once sure he was settled, she placed the tray on his lap and took her own plate and coffee, sitting down to eat. "How are you feeling today?" she asked, careful to keep her voice cheerful.

Chuckling lightly, he began eating. "Probably a touch better than I look," he joked. "And you? I know jet lag can be brutal."

"I actually don't feel too bad," she admitted. "But then I slept something like ten hours, so that could have something to do with it."

"Indeed it could," he agreed.

"I got to see more of the library yesterday."

"Oh? How far down did you see? And what did you think?"

She fought not to watch his hands as he ate, though it was impossible for her not to notice the trembling in his arm that accompanied each bite. He was definitely doing worse today, which worried her. "Ah...I don't remember what number level it was, but everything but the dangerous books?" She shrugged lightly. "I'll admit to being curious about that level, but Lucas didn't seem like he would've taken me there even if I'd begged. And I don't beg. But the rest? I freaking loved it. Especially when he showed me the Odyssey on a scroll."

Erasmus smiled and nodded, laying his fork down and resting his arm. He'd only had a few bites, which made her want to feed him, but wasn't sure if he'd accept the offer or be offended. For now, she let it go. "I assume he also pointed out the aspida repository and choosing room?"

"Huh? He didn't mention anything called that. Not that I remember, anyway."

"He may have just said it was where new aspides are chosen," he explained.

"Oh, yeah, he pointed that out."

"Good. You'll be seeing that particular room sooner than I like."

The smile dropped off her face. "Erasmus...don't talk like that," she said softly.

"I'm sorry, *louloudi mou*. I don't mean to upset you," he told her, an apology in his dull green eyes.

Though her mood was grim, one corner of her mouth ticked up. "Your flower, huh?"

"Of course. How about we talk about what aspides do, instead?" he offered.

"Sure. I want to learn anything you want to teach me."

"Ah, if only I'd gotten to see you grow up," he said wistfully. "The aspida, as you may have heard, is the boss, so to speak, of the entire Athenaeum. Though the branches all have their superiors—Lucas as head nasaru or Dion as head curator—they all answer to the aspida. We have final say in what jobs are taken as far as retrieving books or recruiting people, and our word is, essentially, law." He shifted like he was trying to get comfortable, to avoid pain, but couldn't quite manage it. "I told you we protect the knowledge—especially magic—but we are also the primary people who teach sorcery to the rest of the Athenaeum. Yes, we're all Arcane, but sometimes our natural abilities aren't enough. There are some spells everyone knows that others can and do teach, especially to their children, but the more powerful spells come through us."

"Do aspides ever leave the lib—Athenaeum?" she asked curiously.

"Of course," he wheezed, trying not to laugh. "This isn't a prison. I've gone to retrieve books or recruit people myself. And there's a very nice restaurant not too far from here that I used to enjoy quite a bit."

"Oh, good," Sophia said, relieved. She was a little afraid it was kind of Hotel California, even if her mom had left. Her mom hadn't been a real part of the Athenaeum, though.

"Did I tell you how a new aspida is chosen?" he asked, adjusting his position again. He winced this time, so Sophia put her plate on the tray and moved it out of the way.

"How can I help you get comfortable?" she asked when she returned to the bed.

He shook his head. "I'm fine. Teaching you is more important in any case."

She disagreed but didn't argue. "Um, you said the Athenaeum chooses, right? That it's semi-sentient or whatever? You said it was enchanted by the divine patrons to choose and was smart enough not to pick the bastard who killed you."

The vehemence in her voice made him smile and he slightly lifted his hand. She shifted from the chair to sit on the edge of the bed and slid her hand into his. "I did indeed. It's actually not quite an enchantment. Or rather, I should say not solely enchanted. I told you about the divine patrons, but you also have to remember that we've been here for more than two thousand years. In that time a lot of magic has been performed here, in addition to being performed on the Athenaeum itself. The magic has seeped into the stone, into the very fabric of this place, and given it a life of sorts. It isn't enough for it to, say, protect itself, but it can do more than most structures."

"Damn. I was hoping the labyrinth would move around if someone tried to break in," she muttered, her heart swelling when he smiled at her joke.

"Actually, it does, though it's more a constant shifting than a sudden move, and that is thanks to Athena, Hecate, Isis, and Seth. But no, most of what the Athenaeum does is react to and help the aspida."

"Help how?"

Though his eyes didn't show his normal coherence or brightness, they still twinkled with mischief. "Ahh, that is a secret that only aspides are privy to."

Sophia slumped slightly and pouted at him. "Then why mention it? Not fair, Grandpa."

Despite his illness, he perked up. "Grandpa?"

"I...um...it sort of slipped out," she admitted, unsure if she'd made a faux pas.

"That's okay," he said, his frail hand squeezing hers. "I've come to realize that things that slip out are more often truth. You can call me Grandpa, if you like."

She relaxed and smiled. "I'd like that. Grandpa."

He gave her a wide smile, though it trembled and lasted only a moment. "Have you considered staying here? Becoming a part of the Athenaeum yourself?"

"I...can't say the thought hasn't occurred to me, especially with people bringing it up all the time," she said slowly. "I do have my classes, though. I'm in my last year of grad school, and I might go for my doctorate. But..." All the pros to staying ran through her head once again, and there were a lot of them.

"Just promise to think about it," he told her.

"I will. I don't think I could make myself *not* think about it," she admitted.

He started to nod but stopped mid-motion. His fingers tightened around hers with more strength than she thought he was capable of. "I want you to remember the spell I taught you, *louloudi mou*," he told her, voice strained and quiet.

Startled and uneasy, Sophia nodded. "Of course. I will," she promised.

Their conversations had so far been in English, aside from the occasional word or phrase, so when he switched to a slightly slurred Greek, her unease grew. "I know we just met, but I want you to know something," he murmured, clinging to her hand. "I am so happy you're here. I love you, my beautiful, intelligent granddaughter."

"I love you, too, Grandpa," she told him, also in Greek, fear stealing all the heat from the room. "What—"

He cut her off as his eyes slid closed. "I'm so proud of you, Sophia. So...proud..."

His words died off, his hand released hers, and for a few seconds, he was deathly still. Terrified, she checked for a pulse, momentarily relieved when she felt it beneath her fingers, though it was weak. That relief disappeared, only to be replaced by dread when he started convulsing. "Erasmus? Grandpa!" she all but begged as her hands went to his shoulders and she tried to keep him from hurting himself. Pinkish foam appeared at his mouth and a single tear of blood slipped from his right eye. "No," she breathed. Knowing her healing wouldn't be sufficient, she released him and ran to the door, flinging it open. "Help!" she screamed as loud as she could, her voice cracking. "Someone help! It's Erasmus!"

Glancing back at the bed, she saw blood was now leaking from his ears and both eyes. "Someone get here right fucking now!" she screamed one last time before she raced back to the bed. "No, no, no...Don't do this, Grandpa," she murmured as she again tried to prevent him from flailing.

The sound of several people running over stone reached her an instant before the first person reached the doorway. She looked over to see Steven's eyes widen in shock. He let out a low curse and ran to the other side of the bed to help her with Erasmus.

"My gods," Dion breathed from behind her, his voice horrified.

"You have a healer, right? We need him. Now," Sophia said in a voice that didn't allow for arguments.

"Yes," he said as he turned to leave. He hadn't even taken a step before Sergei pushed past him and into the room.

"Move," he ordered as he set a medical bag on the bed. Sophia scrambled back so he could take her place. Steven remained, helping to restrain Erasmus until he suddenly went limp.

"What's happening?" Sophia asked, fighting not to crowd Sergei.

Sergei shook his head but didn't otherwise answer as he checked Erasmus's vitals. He lowered his head to just inches from Erasmus's, but after a few seconds, he placed his hands on the older man's chest and they started to glow faintly.

"What's going on?" came a familiar voice from behind her. Sophia refused to leave the bed, but looked back to see the doorway crowded with people. The man who had spoken was pushing his way to the front, until Lucas stood in front of Dion. He let out a low, vicious curse. "Someone get Heather," he said as he moved further into the room, but stayed out of the way.

"I'm here! What's happening to Erasmus?" Heather asked, people parting to let her through. When she saw Sergei doing what he could magically, her eyes went wide and filled with tears. "No...not yet. It's too soon," she whispered. Her knees buckled and, if Dion hadn't caught her, she would have fallen. He eased her down to the ground and held her while they waited, barely breathing.

Seconds took hours to pass until Sergei sat back, head bowed. "There's nothing I can do," he whispered, his voice stoic. He twisted to look at the gathered people, meeting first Heather's eyes, then Lucas's, and finally Sophia's. Even before he spoke, the tears in this unflappable man's eyes told her all she needed to know. "He's gone."

Heather let out a wail of grief, but she wasn't the only one to start crying. Sophia stood as still as a statue, stunned and dry-eyed, while people sobbed around her.

A hand touched her shoulder and she flinched away before she realized it was Lucas. "I'm sorry," he told her quietly. "We'll give you both some time." When she could only stare at him, he squeezed her shoulder and turned to the others. She didn't hear what he told them to clear them out, and she didn't care. All she could do was stare at the blood-stained body of her grandfather. Her murdered grandfather. A man she'd known for only two days. An emotion too tame for anger began to boil within her belly and she clenched her hands so tightly that her nails bit deep into her palms.

When no one was left in the room but for her mom, she pushed aside that rage and knelt beside the weeping woman. Heather's arms wrapped tightly around her and they clung to each other. But though she mourned the loss of a man who had seemed exceptional, she couldn't cry. Not yet. Tears would come later.

Chapter 12

AFTER HEATHER HAD CRIED herself out, Sophia helped the red-eyed woman to her room and convinced her to lie down for a bit. Once she was sure that her mom would be okay, at least for a little bit, she gathered a few things and returned to Erasmus's room. To her relief, no one had found their way there in the twenty minutes she'd been gone. She wanted privacy for this.

It took some time for Sophia to manage to step further than the door and approach the bed. This wasn't the last image she wanted of the sweet, intelligent man who had told her he loved her only moments before his death. This wasn't how she wanted anyone to remember him. That was why she'd grabbed a couple of washcloths and a basin of water. True, several people had already seen him, but she couldn't help that.

"I am so sorry, Grandpa," she whispered as she carefully sat on the bed. People always talked about how the recently deceased looked as though they were sleeping rather than dead, but there was no mistaking his current state, even if she ignored the blood. She dipped a cloth in the water and started to gently wash away the signs of his malevolent death. All too quickly, the water in the basin turned pink, but she didn't stop until she'd gotten every speck of blood from his skin. She set the water aside and tenderly lifted his head, pulling the stained pillow away and replacing it with the clean one beside it.

She stroked her fingers over his hair. "This shouldn't have happened," she told him in a fierce whisper. "Not for your job, not for any reason. Whoever could do something like this to you..." She shook her head. "They're evil. Evil and greedy. But I'm going to find out who did this. I'm going to find them and make them pay. I promise." Leaning in, she brushed a light kiss over his forehead.

Someone opened the door, and she rose and turned. Two women stood there—a blonde with short hair and one with long brown hair—looking startled to see her there. Both had swollen red eyes and neither seemed to care. The blonde spoke first, in such rapid Greek Sophia had trouble keeping up. She did get enough to realize they were here to clean and prepare her grandfather's body.

"It's fine," Sophia told them in much slower Greek, gathering her things. "I..." She turned her head but couldn't quite look back at the bed. "Just be...Take good care of him," she finally told them.

"Of course," the brunette said in English. "We loved Erasmus. Everyone did."

Not everyone, but Sophia didn't say that aloud. She simply gave them a tight smile and slipped past them. Once she'd dealt with the basin and cloth, she realized she didn't want to wait to start investigating Erasmus's murder. Neither was she going to be careless about it. She closed her eyes and brought the words Erasmus had taught her to mind. It took two tries for her to correctly speak the spell, but she knew it had worked when she felt the telltale tingle against her skin. To her dismay, it felt stronger than it had the first time she'd cast it. That wasn't going to stop her, though.

Trying to remember the tour Peter had given her only the day before, she headed for the clinic. She took a wrong turn, ending at a dead end, then accidentally walked into a storage room before she finally found the clinic. The door was ajar, and she heard voices from inside. Lucas's was easy to identify, but it took her a moment to place Sergei after only having heard him speak a few words. Curious, she pressed against the wall and listened intently, thankful once more than she'd learned Greek.

"You have to have a cause of death, Sergei. Even at his age, a man doesn't just die. He certainly doesn't bleed from the eyes and ears for no reason," Lucas said firmly.

"I didn't exactly get a chance to examine him," Sergei said, his voice tired.

"No, but you're not ignorant or blind," Lucas snapped. "You're also the fucking son of Apollo. What could cause a death like that? What killed our aspida?"

Sergei said nothing for a long moment. "There are a number of things which could cause those symptoms," he hedged, and even as a stranger Sophia could tell he was holding back.

Lucas clearly thought the same. "What aren't you telling me?" he asked in a low, cold voice.

The healer sighed. "It's unlikely that his symptoms were from any...natural illness."

No, it was poison. Sophia wanted to burst in and demand Lucas find out who was responsible. Her body braced to do just that before she remembered what Erasmus had told her—to be careful who she trusted. To be careful, period.

"Then what were his symptoms a result of?"

"I don't know," Sergei answered quietly.

Lucas made a sound halfway between a growl and a huff. "Let me know if you do figure anything out."

Sophia realized his voice was getting closer and her eyes widened. She didn't want to be caught eavesdropping and looked around desperately for a place to hide. There was a door across from the clinic. Luck was on her side because it was unlocked—and empty—and she was able to dart into it and close the door before Lucas left the clinic. She listened for the sounds of his footsteps and waited until they faded before she exited what seemed to be a storage room.

The hallway was empty, so she didn't hesitate to walk into the clinic. Unlike Lucas, when she closed the door, she made sure it was latched.

Sergei was sitting at a desk, his head in his hands. He jerked up when the door clicked shut and frowned when he saw Sophia. "Can I help you?" he asked, his English tinged with a Russian accent.

Sophia pulled another chair to rest in front of him and sat down, meeting his gaze squarely. "You can tell me what you know about the poison used on my grandfather," she told him bluntly.

He blinked and shook his head. "I don't know what you're—"

She made a dismissive gesture and shook her head. "Don't bother lying to me. Erasmus told me he had been poisoned. He also told me that you were the only other person who knew. So tell me, what do you know about the poison used on him?"

Sergei leaned back in his chair and studied her intently for a full minute before he slowly nodded. "Okay. I won't lie to you, but I also don't think it's wise for you to be poking your nose into this."

"How can I not?" she argued. "My grandfather was murdered. He died right in front of me. I think the least he deserves is to have his killer brought to justice."

He shook his head. "You misunderstand me. I agree with you. Whoever killed Erasmus should be found and punished, but think of this," he said, leaning forward, his expression serious though his eyes were hot. He was just as angry at the poisoning as she was, which relieved a little of her annoyance at him trying to push her out. "Erasmus was the smartest of us all. He might have been a shapeshifter, but he had nine centuries under his belt and knew more magic than any of us. And yet someone managed to get past those things and still fatally poison him." When the color drained out of her face, he nodded once, knowingly. "Exactly. If they could get to him, then what chance do you stand, Sophia? I don't say this to be mean, but you don't know the Athenaeum, and you don't know the magic he did. You're more vulnerable."

He wasn't exactly wrong, she could admit that, but he wasn't entirely right, either. "There are two things you're forgetting about."

Sergei arched a brow. "Oh?"

"One, I'm not a man who was old even in the Arcane. I'm not saying he was weak, but things do affect someone in their twenties differently from someone in their nine hundreds, right?"

"Yes," he agreed reluctantly. "But—"

"Secondly," she continued, interrupting him, "and probably more importantly, I don't trust everyone here. I'm guessing he did. Or at least trusted the wrong person. The only people I trust here as of this very moment are myself and my mom."

He stared at her before his posture relaxed somewhat. He even almost smiled. Almost, though even that didn't reach his eyes. "Perhaps you have a point," he murmured thoughtfully. "Okay, I wasn't able to identify the poison. At first, it was just muscle weakness and his breathing became labored. It was almost...They mimicked the signs of aging, but they came on too quickly. If the symptoms had been accompanied by a disease, it might have appeared natural, but I used every spell I knew to scan for illness and came up with nothing. I tried every spell I knew to heal or reverse the effects of poisons, but nothing worked. I even tried a mythical antidote we recently got our hands on, and it didn't work. Worse, about a month ago, two of our people were poisoned. One died, and the other barely survived. I think it was the same poison."

That wasn't good. If the son of the Greek god of healing had come up with nothing, would she be able to? "What were you able to figure out?"

Huffing out a soft breath, he leaned back. "I believe it was a magical poison, but I don't know what kind. I don't believe it was ingested. You've seen how we share meals. It's not impossible that someone managed to find a way to slip it to him, but it's improbable. Inhalation also isn't likely. Gas is harder to contain, especially down here, and he was the only one who's been ill since those first two."

"So what does that leave? Did you look for needle marks or something?"

"I did," Sergei confirmed. "I found none. My best guess is it was something topical, something that could just soak into his skin and poison him from the outside in."

"That's...terrifying," she murmured.

"It is," he agreed easily.

"Tell me you're still looking," Sophia said, needing to know she wasn't alone in this. She wasn't an investigator. Figuring out where to even begin would be hard enough.

"I am," he assured her. "Erasmus was like a father to a lot of us. Certainly to me. I'm going to do everything I can to find out what killed him."

"And who." She shook her head. "Erasmus didn't want it getting out that he was poisoned. I don't know why, but he wouldn't even let me tell my mom. But...will you let me know if you figure anything out? Anything at all?"

He hesitated and she could tell he wanted to tell her no, to keep out of it.

"Please," she said quietly, prepared to beg if that's what it took to get the information.

He ran a hand through his hair, causing several strands to stick up haphazardly. "Hell. Okay, yes, I'll let you know."

"Thank you." She got to her feet and he started to speak, but she smiled tightly at him as she made her way out of the clinic. "I'll be careful. I didn't come to Greece just to die."

Then again, she hadn't come to Greece to watch her grandfather die a horrible death, either. The best laid plans...

After leaving Sergei, Lucas went to Erasmus's room. Sophia was no longer there, and he didn't disturb the two women who were readying Erasmus's body for the funeral.

He hadn't been ready. Even knowing this was coming, and soon, he hadn't been ready. Erasmus had taken him in, made him feel welcome. He'd encouraged him, pushed him, taught him sorcery he never would have known. Lucas was the man he was today because of Erasmus. And now he was dead. Murdered, likely by someone within the Athenaeum. No one else had been here in months other than that healer Suni and her man, but he truly believed them to be innocent. Not just because of his instincts, but because of Seth. The demi-turned-god had always been a friend of the Athenaeum and never would have brought murderers here.

Fuck. He needed to be informed, too. All the patrons did, but Seth was the only one with a cell phone.

Lucas stalked to his room and barely managed to keep himself from slamming the door. Alone, he called the god.

"Hello?"

Huh. Who knew gods could sound sleepy? "Seth? It's Lucas, from the Athenaeum."

"Lucas? Oh, yeah. The guard. Sorry, just woke up. What's up?"

Lucas really didn't want to be the one to tell him. Not just because he knew Seth cared about Erasmus as much as everyone else in the Athenaeum, but angering the gods rarely went well for mortals. Still, prolonging it helped no one. "Erasmus died about an hour ago."

Silence filled the line for several heartbeats. "The illness?"

He hesitated. Despite not really knowing Seth, he trusted him, but the more people who knew his suspicions, the more dangerous the Athenaeum became. But Seth would have resources no one in the Athenaeum did. "I don't think it was an illness."

"One minute." The voice was cold, but the line went dead. Lucas frowned at the phone, but a moment later, Seth appeared before him. No one could look less like a god. Yes, he was big, a good three inches taller than Lucas's six three and just as muscular, but he had a few scars, which most gods didn't, and a shaggy haircut that looked like any modern human's. The fact that he wore casual clothes rather than the regal or impressive outfits of most deities only cemented it. "What do you mean you don't think it was an illness?" he demanded, and Lucas fought not to recoil from the power radiating from the man. It was strong, but he was sure it affected him more than most. Seth was a god of mountains—of stone—and Lucas was a gargoyle. Even in his human form, he felt the pull.

"I mean Sergei all but confirmed he believes it to be murder. Said it was unlikely the symptoms were from any natural illness. And since Sergei's the son of Apollo and we have mithridate, there shouldn't have been any reason why Sergei couldn't save him."

"Do you know who could have done something like this?" Seth asked as he struggled to contain his power. He didn't entirely succeed, as Lucas could feel the stone beneath his feet vibrating.

"Until this happened, I would have said no one here would even consider something like this," he admitted. "Yes, some of us have killed, but not in cold blood."

"And now?"

Lucas blew out a breath and lifted his shoulders in a helpless shrug. "Now the only people here I can be absolutely certain of are you, me, and Erasmus's daughter-in-law and granddaughter."

Seth cocked his head. "Why are you certain they're innocent? Family drama has led to a lot of early deaths throughout history."

"First, because Heather—his daughter-in-law—isn't the sort and his granddaughter is..." He didn't have the words to accurately describe Sophia, so he went with, "Innocent. Besides, they only arrived yesterday, after he was already so ill. Sophia—the granddaughter—didn't even know about him until yesterday."

"Do they know your suspicions?"

"No. Only Sergei does."

Seth nodded slowly, his hands clenching and unclenching as he thought. "How long until the choosing?"

"The funeral pyre will be tomorrow night, and the choosing the night after."

The god nodded again. "I and the other patrons will be there, for both the pyre and choosing. We'll do our own investigating, but I want you to keep on this, and you let me know if you find the bastard who did this."

The fury in Seth's voice, and the threat in it—not for him, but the murderer—made Lucas smile. No justice he could devise would even come close to what a god could deliver. "Count on it," he promised.

Chapter 13

After leaving Sergei, Sophia wandered for a while. She had no destination in mind but just walked, trying to burn off her angry energy while she thought about her next steps. Right now she wished she'd read more mysteries and less non-fiction and historical fiction. Then maybe she'd have a better idea of how to go about solving a murder. She stopped and looked back in the direction she'd come from and thought about Sergei's words. Maybe if she could identify the poison, it would lead to the murderer. In order to do that, she needed to get into the library. Without supervision. It would suck to accidentally ask the murder to let her into the library and let them know she was aware Erasmus had been poisoned. It also wouldn't be good for her life expectancy.

Taking a moment to orient herself, she strode toward the computer room, her steps quick, purposeful. It gave her a minor thrill when she found it on the first try. Peter was there, along with a slender, elegant woman with beautiful deep brown skin and shiny black hair. Both looked up when the door opened. The woman offered Sophia a faint smile of sympathy before she went back to what she was doing. Peter, on the other hand, turned around fully and gave her a look so full of understanding that she almost turned around and walked right back out. She couldn't handle sympathy right now. Not if she wanted to keep herself from breaking.

"Sophia...How are you doing?" he asked quietly, pulling the chair out next to him and motioning for her to join him.

She shrugged and took the seat next to him, fidgeting for a moment before she sighed and slumped back in her seat. "I'm okay."

Slowly, he shook his head. "No, you're not," he said kindly, "but I'll let that go for now. Is there anything I can do to help?"

A tiny smile was all she could manage, though she was coming to like her cousin quite a bit and wanted to ease his mind. "Actually, there is. I need something to distract myself. If I stop, I'm just going to start thinking about...him."

He nodded. "I can absolutely understand that. He is—was—a great man. A wonderful uncle. We all will miss him, believe me," he murmured, turning his head as he tried to get his emotions under control. "You're welcome to the computers, of course. There are plenty of games on them. And there are the games down in the rec room, and just about every movie ever made. I'd be more than happy to play something with you or watch a movie with you."

Peter reminded her a little bit of a puppy. Friendly, sweet, eager to make people happy. "Thanks, but I'm not really an electronics girl. I only really use my computer for research and pictures. As for movies...It's too passive. My brain would wander too much, you know?"

"I can understand that, too. Is there something that would help?"

The small smile returned. "Books. I love reading. Stories and non-fiction. Your dad told me that you and Lucas could get me access to the library so I'm not constantly having to track someone down to let me in."

He brightened and nodded. "Yeah, that's easy enough," he said as he pulled out his phone, tapped on it for a moment, then set it aside. "Lucas will be here in a few."

"Why is he coming? Isn't it just scanning my palm and using the computer to..." She mimed typing on a keyboard.

"It is, but security is pretty tight. In order to add someone to the system, it requires both me doing my—" He mimicked her typing gesture. "—and Lucas clearing it in the system."

"Oh. That makes sense."

"I know it seems like it's a little...ah...overplank?"

She blinked at the strange word until it occurred to her that, while very fluent in English, it probably wasn't his native language. Mixing up words sounded like a common enough issue for multilingual people. "Overboard?"

"Yes, that. But we are here for the sole purpose of protecting those books. Normally a new family member wouldn't be getting put in the system so soon—we'd have to ensure they were trustworthy and all that—but that's more for people who marry in. With you being the...with your situation, you're already cleared for the upper levels. My dad mentioned it to me last night."

Lucas strode in, zeroed in on them, and walked over. Rather than getting right to it, he studied Sophia's face for a minute. "You okay?" he asked quietly.

She'd tried lying, downplaying it with Peter, and it hadn't worked. She knew it would be even less effective with Lucas. "No," she said bluntly. "That's why I'm here. I'm wanting to distract myself with the library. I'm not...I don't want it to sink in just yet." Even as she said the words, she knew it was true. Maybe not the whole truth, but it wasn't just an excuse to gain access to the books she needed.

He nodded sharply and looked to Peter. "Do it."

Peter nodded and swiveled back to his computer. He typed and tapped for a moment before he pointed to the glass plate that had a keypad beside it. "Lucas? Palm and PIN." He waited while Lucas laid his hand against the scanner, using the other to enter a code. Some more tapping, and Peter smiled at Sophia. "Your turn. Lay your hand on the scanner. When it turns green, you'll need to enter a PIN. It can be anything so long as it's at least six digits."

Sophia frowned as she tried to think of something not easily guessed. Then she thought of the reason she desperately wanted in. When the scanner turned green, she shifted her body to hide the keypad and entered 7-6-4-7-6-6. Poison.

"And you're all set. You'll be able to get into the library, onto any level but the sixth and seventh."

Seeing her uncertainty, Lucas clarified. "The dangerous books and aspida only levels."

"Oh. Yeah, makes sense." Though knowing her luck, the information she was looking for was only on those levels. Still, she had to try. "Thank you. Both of you."

"Of course. Anything you need," Peter insisted. "And I mean it. Losing someone isn't easy, especially when you're in an unfamiliar place."

On impulse, she leaned down and gave him a quick hug. "You're my favorite cousin, you know that?"

He blushed slightly, which was adorable, especially with his blue mohawk. "Thanks," he mumbled.

She straightened and smiled at him. "You're welcome. And now I'm going to go distract myself," she said, turning to go.

Lucas gently caught her arm. "Mind if I walk with you?"

Her brow furrowed, but she slowly nodded. She'd just have to find a way to get rid of him once she was down there. "Sure. Talk to you later, Peter," she told her cousin, who waved as she left, Lucas right behind her. He said nothing for several minutes, not until they were in the hallway leading to the library. "Did you want something?" she asked curiously.

"I know you said you weren't okay, but how are you holding up?" he asked.

Despite her grandfather's warning, and the conversation she'd overheard, she found herself opening up a little. "I'm angry," she said quietly.

"Angry?"

"Yes, angry. Totally pissed, actually." She stopped in front of the library door and turned toward him. "I've been here for two days. I've known I had a living grandfather for just over that. And I *liked* him, Lucas. I liked him a lot. He's how I always imagined a grandfather would be. And now he's just...gone. I barely got to know him. I don't know anything about him that didn't involve the Athenaeum. I don't know exactly how old he was. I don't know what happened to his wife—if he was even married to my grandmother. I don't know anything about his childhood or how he became aspida—or involved with the Athenaeum. Ten years from now when I'm remembering him, I'm afraid I won't remember him well, and I definitely won't have any stories of him. Not ones that involve me. So yeah, I'm angry. Tomorrow I might be sad, or maybe the day after, but right now I'm just angry."

"I get that," he said quietly. "It's completely understandable."

When he didn't continue, she turned toward the scanner but he again caught her arm. "You're making a habit of grabbing me, Lucas. I don't know that I like it," she told him coolly, though she had to admit he hadn't hurt her. His touch was actually very gentle.

"You should be careful, Sophia," he warned her in a low voice.

Startled, she took a step back and his hand fell away. "What?"

"You should be careful," he repeated. "You might even want to consider going back to America."

Now she was really confused. The way he hounded Sergei made it seem like he was innocent and suspected foul play, and if that was the case, then he could be genuinely concerned for her now. Or it could all be an act. She didn't know him well enough to even lean in either direction. Yet. But she was going to learn. "Why? I just got here. I'm finally meeting my family. I'm seeing where my father lived."

"But your life is back in America. And you can always email Peter if that's your concern."

"Everyone else has been suggesting I should stay. You don't agree?"

It took a minute for him to reply. "Just consider it," he insisted before he nodded to the scanner. "You should make sure the scanner works. Peter doesn't generally make mistakes, but there are always technical glitches."

They stared at each other for a moment before she placed her palm on the scanner. When it turned green with approval, she opened the door, done with Lucas's non-answers.

"Before you go," he said before she could even get through the doorway, "you should have my phone number."

She looked over her shoulder at him. "You don't think Peter can help if I need it?" she asked, brow arched.

"Depends on the help you need," he drawled, one hand extending as he waited for her phone. Yet despite his apparent threat just a minute ago, there was something more in his eyes now. A subtle heat that made her remember it had been nearly a year since she'd seriously dated. Not that she planned on dating Lucas—or anyone here in Greece, for that matter. But he was awfully nice to look at. And maybe a flirtation was just what she needed to get to know him better so she could gauge his trustworthiness. And he would be a decent distraction, too. She was going to need it after immersing herself in books on poisons. Wordlessly, she unlocked her phone and set it in his hand. He quickly added his number and held it out to her, the screen still lit up and visible. Rather than entering himself as Lucas, he was saved as Talos.

She shook her head and looked from the phone to him. "Why not Lucas? Why Talos?"

He smiled and slid his hands into his pockets. "You're the Classics major, right? You'll figure it out," he told her before he turned to stroll away.

Sophia stared after him until he disappeared down the hallway. Lucas definitely wasn't the simple guard he appeared to be. She just hoped when she figured out what he was, that she wasn't disappointed.

Chapter 14

As Sophia made her way down past the first few levels, she thought about the people she'd met since arriving. She didn't really know many of them at all, and none well. Peter was the one she knew best, and she'd still classify him as an acquaintance more than a friend. Unfortunately, even if she could identify the poison right away, she would need to learn about the people before she could figure out who would be capable of poisoning a man. Tonight at dinner she'd pay close attention. It wouldn't be much, but she had to start somewhere.

Though she was sure some of the less rare books held information on poisons, it was probably more common knowledge. Arsenic and stuff like that. Surely a skilled healer would have recognized signs of poisons like those. Even she knew what the smell of almonds meant. She stopped on the next level and, after wandering for almost half an hour without finding anything relevant, she wished she had a map that told her where to find certain topics. It wasn't that anything was mixed up—far from it, actually—but each level was just so big it took time to sort through everything. Eventually, she found the section that contained medical texts and browsed through a number of books. She spent an additional hour skimming through them, and though there were references to various poisons and toxins, they all seemed to be normal substances. She needed something magical, or at least something resistant to magic. Still, she pulled up the memo app on her phone and made a few notes for things to revisit or look up on the internet when she got back to her room. A poison called cantarella drew her interest. It was mentioned in connection with the Borgias and was relevant since it could be administered once and not actually kill the victim for weeks, or even a year.

She descended further until she reached the rare books. Fortunately, there weren't quite as many books on these levels, but they were still spread out, leaving plenty of room in each section for more books to be added. It meant that she found the medical section more quickly this time. When she found the first mention of magic in conjunction with a venom, she felt a spark of hope. She sat down with her back against the shelves and read intently. There were several things that fit one or two of the characteristics she was looking for—and they got noted in her phone—but none matched them all. It made her wonder if it wasn't a single poison or venom that was used, but a mixture. But for all she knew, mixing poisons somehow negated their lethal effects. Chemistry was like that, so why not poisons?

Frustrated, she resisted the urge to slam the book back on the shelf, instead placing it gently. She was a student of history and mythology, not toxicology. And yes, magic had been mentioned, but something told her she hadn't found the correct poison yet. She also knew it wasn't going to be easy. Erasmus and Sergei were both familiar with the library. They knew how to navigate it better than she did. If they hadn't found the answer, was she so arrogant to think she could? As she glanced to the door leading down to the next level—the off limits level—she knew she had to try, even if it was arrogant. Everyone made mistakes, even demigods and nine hundred-year-old scholars.

Sophia looked over her shoulder and listened for a moment, but heard nothing to indicate she wasn't alone. She crept slowly toward the sixth level door. Sure, Peter had told her that she wouldn't be able to get in, but Lucas said glitches happened. Maybe she'd get lucky—extremely lucky—and there would be a glitch in her favor. More likely there would be some alarm and all the guards—Lucas included—would come storming down here, aiming guns at her. But nothing ventured, nothing gained, right? She rubbed her damp palm against her jeans, hoping the moisture wouldn't affect the scanner, and hesitantly placed her hand on the plate. It flashed red and she cursed, snatching her hand from the cool glass. "Why couldn't it be that easy?" she muttered to herself.

Her stomach growled and she pulled her phone out, groaning when she realized just how long she'd been down here. Dinner was no doubt already started. Hopefully, everyone was still there. It was time to start getting to know a killer.

If only she knew which one it was.

Judging by the steady hum of conversation, dinner was far from over. Suddenly shy at walking in on it halfway through, Sophia's steps slowed, but she didn't stop. She wouldn't allow herself to.

There were more people seated at the tables than there had been the night before. Familiar faces were mixed with a larger number of strange ones. She spotted her mom sitting with Peter, Dion, and Ray, an empty seat beside her, presumably saved for Sophia herself. She walked over and sank into the chair, leaning over to give her mom a light kiss on the cheek before murmuring, "How you holding up?"

Heather gave her a weak smile, her eyes a little puffy from crying. "I'll be okay. Where have you been, though? No one's seen you for hours."

"The library. I just needed something to take my mind off...everything."

"Just don't forget that there are plenty of people outside of books who are more than willing to help," Heather said, giving Sophia's hand a squeeze. "Myself included."

"I know. I won't forget."

Conversation paused when Agatha and a few other people, Jacob and Steven included, brought out the food and set it on the table. Sophia watched people's faces as they filled their plates. The overall mood was somber, though she saw a few half smiles here and there. Though she was hungry herself, she wasn't certain she'd be able to keep anything down, so only selected a few light things. Then, wanting information but not wanting to bother her mom, she leaned toward Ray. "So who are all these people? I've only met a couple of them."

"Well, who have you met?"

Sophia's lips twitched. It was tempting to say only him and her mom, but she pointed out those she knew.

He nodded once. "Okay, the woman sitting next to Josie is her twin—which is obvious, I know. Name's Angela." Fortunately it would be easy to tell them apart, since Josie was punk while Angela was more girl-next-door. "They're both venatores. Tend to work together, since they make a really good team. The man next to Nick and Carla is Theo. He's a guard," he said, inclining his head toward a man who, even sitting, towered over everyone else. If he wasn't six and a half feet tall, Sophia would give up coffee for a week. He had dark hair that was shaved close to the head and his resting face was flat out intimidating. Hopefully, he was nicer than he looked, though his appearance probably came in handy as a guard. "That's Penny," he went on, pointing toward the end of the table and an older woman whose brown hair had started going gray. "She's one of the curators. Probably knows the library better than anyone but Dion and..." He trailed off and both their moods dipped for a moment, thinking of Erasmus. "Anyway, that," he pointed toward the other end of the table, to a leanly muscled Japanese man, "is Kaito. Though he's technically a curator, he doesn't deal much with the books."

"Then why is he a curator?" she asked, confused.

"Curator is a general term for anyone who takes care of the Athenaeum. Sergei's a curator. So are Agatha, Peter, and Steven. In Kaito's case, he's the armorer."

That wasn't what Sophia expected to hear. "An armorer? Do you...oh, yeah, that makes sense. Guards need weapons."

"Mmhmm. And we're very grateful to have a skilled man to maintain and replace weapons and body armor if we need it. Other equipment, too," Ray confirmed.

"Who's that woman next to Kaito?" she asked, pointing out the woman who had been in the computer room earlier.

"Valerie. Another curator, though she deals with finances."

"Nick did mention investments and stuff," Sophia said, picking at her food. She ate some of it but most remained on her plate. "It has to be a lot of really good investments to afford everything."

Ray shrugged. "It's not just recent investments, though. The Athenaeum has been investing—wisely, for the most part—for two thousand years. Not to mention that, well, our books are really, *really* good."

"Huh? What do books have to do with it?" Her eyes widened with horror. "You don't *sell* them, do you?"

He chuckled and shook his head. "No, but when we're looking for various books, occasionally we've come across certain...documents...that have been profitable."

Sophia still looked confused. Josie, sitting across from them, had apparently overheard and took pity on Sophia, though she did it with a half-hearted grin. "Treasure maps."

"That is so cool," Sophia whispered.

"Isn't it, though? That was before my time, though. Before the time of most anyone who's still here, for that matter," she said with a soft, wistful sigh.

While cool, Sophia realized it was also another potential motive. Yes, Erasmus thought he'd been poisoned for his job, but maybe it wasn't that. Or not just that. Maybe someone was going for the money. Her gaze slid over to Valerie. Except if that was the case, why not go after Valerie? Unless things were set up so Erasmus could have prevented the loss of money. He did say he was in charge of everything. She'd definitely have to make nice with Valerie and try to find out just how money was distributed amongst the people of the Athenaeum. Did they get a salary or allowance? Was everything just paid for by the Athenaeum? There were too many variables.

She was so lost in thought that it wasn't until Heather touched her shoulder that she realized most of the room had cleared out.

"Are you okay, sweetheart?" Heather asked.

"Yeah, just thinking," Sophia said.

"I know it's a lot." Heather took a deep, shaky breath. "Even though we came here because Erasmus was dying, it actually happening is...hard."

"I really liked him, Mom," Sophia whispered, resting her head on her mom's shoulder. "I was loving getting to know him."

"I know. He was a great man. I loved him like a father," Heather admitted.

Sophia wanted to ask more, but the room wasn't entirely empty. Another few unfamiliar faces were busy clearing plates from the table and three people—Lucas included—were just sitting down to eat. Guards taking shifts eating, she assumed. She stood, grabbed a piece of soft pita bread, and kissed her mom's cheek. "It's been a long day. I'm going to turn in."

Heather stood as well and drew Sophia off to the side. "Has anyone told you how...things...are done here?"

"Things? What things?"

There was a long pause. "Funerals."

The anger surged upward again, but she didn't blame her mom so bit her tongue. Hard. "Not in detail."

Heather guided Sophia out of the dining room and started toward their room. "Though a few people choose burials, the aspides are cremated, and a day later there's a funeral ceremony. That's...also when the next aspida is chosen."

Indignation temporarily overshadowed the anger. "They're going to give someone else his job at his own funeral?" she hissed.

Heather winced. "They consider it the old aspida passing the job onto the new one," she explained. "It's not meant to be disrespectful. Quite the opposite, really. I know you don't know these people, and I can't say I know everyone, or not well, but they loved Erasmus. They wouldn't do anything to spoil his memory."

Sophia rubbed her temple with her free hand. "Why tell me this now? It's...Mom, I don't know how much more I can handle."

"I know," Heather murmured, rubbing Sophia's back. "But the cremation is tomorrow. There will be a funeral pyre at the estate just before dusk. I just figured you'd want to know."

"I do. I'll be there." She wrapped her arms around her mom and hugged her tight. "I'm sorry. I've...I've never seen anyone die before," she whispered.

"I know," Heather repeated. "I didn't take it personally." She drew back and cupped Sophia's cheek lightly. "Go sleep. I can't say it'll help, but it might. And if you need me, you know where I am."

"I do. Love you, Mom."

"I love you, too, sweetheart."

They parted ways at Sophia's room, but rather than getting ready for bed, she got her laptop out, along with a flash drive. As she nibbled on the bread, she transferred the notes from her phone to a file on the flash drive. Someone who would kill a man wouldn't think twice about hacking into a computer—if they knew how, anyway. She also made notes of everyone she'd met so far. Nothing she'd learned was damning, which meant Lucas's conversation with Sergei and his insistence she go home were the most suspicious things so far.

She didn't get too far with her observations. Her brain was simply turning to mush. Worse, she still felt numb aside from the anger. She'd break, she knew it, and hoped it would be soon. The longer her mind resisted mourning, the harder it would hit her. And while sleep could potentially be a sweet oblivion for a little while, she was afraid she'd see Erasmus's death again in her dreams.

To stave off that moment as long as possible, she decided to do one more thing before bed and searched for Talos. The name had sounded familiar, and when the first search result came up, she knew why. In Greek lore, Talos was a bronze giant created by the god Hephaestus. According to the story, he'd been given to Europa to act as a protector for her.

As she closed her laptop, she wondered exactly what Lucas had meant by the nickname. Was she Europa? Or was she the thing Europa was protected from?

Chapter 15

THERE WERE SOME TIMES when being right was the worst thing possible. The early hours of the morning, when Sophia thrashed in her bed until the sheets became a tight, uncomfortable cocoon, was one of those times. As she'd predicted, she dreamed of Erasmus's death. That would have been bad enough, but the pre-dawn nightmare emphasized and exaggerated all the worst parts of his dying moments. The convulsions were strong enough to break bones. The blood that had dripped from his body flowed like a river. And through it all, his red-stained eyes had stared at her pleadingly. Just before she woke, she felt moisture drip down her cheeks. She touched her fingers to it, horrified when they came away crimson.

She woke with her mouth open in a silent scream, her heart beating a rapid tattoo against her ribs. Her hands lifted to her face, shocked when she found her cheeks bone dry. No blood, not even tears. Though she mourned, though she dreamed, she still couldn't shed a tear for the man she'd become so attached to so quickly. It made her even angrier, but this time the anger was directed inward, not just at Erasmus's murderer. Because of that, her movements were jerky as she got up and dressed.

Her stomach rebelled at the thought of eating, but given how little she'd eaten the day before, she decided to go to breakfast, anyway. There weren't many people there, which made her think that people wandered in and out for the first meal rather than gathering like they did for dinner. Agatha, her face pale, her eyes red, accommodated her need for something light and fixed her some buttered toast. Sophia thanked her and wandered back out. Still rattled by the nightmare, she wasn't quite up for scouring the library or getting to know potential murderers. Instead, she began to wander. Getting more familiar with the layout of the upper levels of the Athenaeum was still useful—and she was getting tired of wrong turns.

As she wandered, she pushed the idea of losing her way out of her mind. She had no destination, so she couldn't get lost. Really, she just wanted to not think. Not think about the murder. Not think about the cremation that was going to occur later that day. She'd never been to a funeral for anyone before, and she wasn't looking forward to this one.

When she reached the gym, she watched for a moment as several of the guards—and a few others, like Josie and Kaito—worked out and sparred. It sparked her interest, but she'd never taken a self-defense class in her life. Probably because she wasn't exactly the most graceful person in the world. Still, it might not be a bad idea to see if Steven or one of the other guards would give her some instruction.

She found a number of rooms that were either empty or used for storage. A couple looked like labs of some sort, but without going in and investigating, she couldn't identify for what. Since people were in them, she moved on.

Sophia opened another nondescript door—identical to the hundred other nondescript doors here—and stepped forward to peek inside. Her foot caught on a rough part of the floor and she tripped. She proved her lack of grace when she stumbled several steps forward, but managed to catch herself before she landed face down on the stone. Before she'd fully gotten her feet back under her, the door slammed shut behind her.

"Hey!" she shouted as she turned and blindly walked toward the door. Unlike every other room she'd been in, this one didn't automatically light with a soft glow upon entry and, without windows, it was pitch black. Her hands smacked into the heavy wood of the door and she felt around for the knob. She turned it and pushed but, while it moved a little, it didn't open, not even enough to allow a sliver of light to penetrate the darkness. As she tried again, her heart rate began to accelerate. She shifted and shoved her shoulder against the door, but even that didn't budge it.

Panic started to build before she remembered the phone in her back pocket. Dimly she noted her hands were shaking a little as she pulled it out and, after a few taps, a weak beam of light dispelled the worst of the darkness. Being able to see helped soothe the worst of the growing alarm. With her back to the door, she slowly slid the phone's flashlight around the room. It was one of the storage rooms, this one for linens.

After she'd assured herself that she wasn't in any immediate danger, she turned her attention back to her phone. Her mom would be able to find her and was, for now, the only person here Sophia trusted. Except the phone simply rang over and over until the voicemail picked up. "Damn," she whispered. Her mom was notorious for forgetting her phone, but she'd hoped today would be different. There were only a few other numbers she could call, but for all she knew, one of them had locked her in this room. She lightly banged her head against the door and sighed. Lucas would probably be the best choice for someone to build a rapport with. As head of the nasaru, he was in charge of security, after all, and with Erasmus gone, he was the natural choice for temporary boss.

"Hello?"

Sophia closed her eyes, entirely too relieved just to hear someone else's voice, which annoyed her. She'd been in this closet for all of a minute, not days. "Lucas."

"Sophia? Is everything okay?"

She laughed weakly. "Define okay?"

His voice shifted to cautious, ready. "What's wrong?"

"Um...I seem to be locked in a linen closet." Silence met that pronouncement. "Lucas?"

Lucas's words were carefully spaced and made her wonder if he was trying to keep a hold of his temper. "Was this an accident?"

"Well...the door could have jammed?" She winced at how untrue that sounded, even to her. "You know, after the wind blew the door shut behind me," she added, and a deaf man could have heard the sarcasm in the statement.

A slew of angry Greek curses followed her pronouncement. Oddly, they made her feel better. If he was responsible for her being locked in here he wouldn't be so upset, right? "Where are you? I'll come let you out."

"Um...I'm not exactly sure," she admitted. "I was just wandering around, getting to know the place. I'm near the gym, though."

"And you said you're in a linen closet?"

"Yeah."

"I think I know where you are. Just hold on."

"I will. And Lucas?"

"Hmm?"

"Thanks."

Sophia hung up but kept the flashlight on, not willing to go back to the limbo that an utterly lightless room reminded her of. A minute later, the door against her back moved and she fell backward, right into Lucas.

"Whoa...Are you okay?" Lucas asked, not immediately releasing her. Instead he looked her over, searching, she assumed, for injuries.

"Um...Yeah," she said as she straightened and pulled away from him, sure her cheeks were bright red with embarrassment. "I was just leaning against the door when you opened it," she explained as she turned the flashlight off and put her phone away. "So was the door just jammed?" she asked hopefully.

His face went dark, his eyes hard, and he lifted his hand and the oddly shaped rock that rested in his palm. "This was wedged just right in the door. Acted like a doorstop and kept it from opening."

Embarrassment forgotten, she took the rock from him, studying it. It looked so harmless. "So it wasn't an accident," she murmured.

"No, it wasn't," he said, his voice low and angry.

Her eyes lifted from the rock and fixed on his. "What kind of people do you have here who would do this? Especially to someone whose grandfather literally just died?" she demanded, her voice trembling as her anger rose up. Being pissed off wasn't fun, but it was better than being scared.

"We have good people here," he told her, but she noticed his hands were curled into tight fists, his knuckles white. He wasn't any happier with the situation than she was. "Come on, I'll walk you back down to the common room." Since Sophia wanted far away from the linen closet, she nodded and fell into step beside him. When they made it down the stairs and the common room was in view, he paused and gave her a once over. "Are you all right?"

"You keep asking me that. But yeah, I'm fine. Go do guard things. I'm going to stay away from closets for a little while." And wonder if the person who had locked her in a closet was the same person who had killed Erasmus. Even if it was, she couldn't figure out why. It wasn't like she could have died in that room. Even if she hadn't been carrying her phone, someone would have noticed she was missing and come looking for her. The Athenaeum was big, but it wasn't impossibly big.

Lucas hesitated, but ultimately nodded once and walked off, still angry.

To her relief, she found Peter and Josie in the common room watching a movie.

"Sophia! Come join us," Peter said, waving her over.

She schooled her face, determined not to show anyone she was upset. Especially since both Peter and Josie looked like they were suffering. Which made sense. They'd known Erasmus better than she had, and he was Peter's relative, too. "What are you watching?" Sophia asked as she dropped down on the couch between them.

"I have no idea," Josie admitted with a shrug, offering popcorn.

Sophia's lips twitched and she took a handful of popcorn. She was down for watching absolutely nothing, so she half-focused on the screen and tried to relax and enjoy the company of potential friends.

They made it through the first movie—which had turned out to be one of the Marvel movies—and halfway through a second before Dion stepped in front of the TV, his expression somber.

"I'm sorry to interrupt," he told them before focusing on Sophia. He cleared his throat before continuing. "The funeral pyre is set up. We'll be carrying his...him down soon. I thought you might want a few minutes with him before that."

"Yes," Sophia said without hesitation, shoving the bowl of popcorn that had gravitated to her lap at Peter before she scrambled to her feet.

"Your mom is with him now in his room," he told her.

"Thanks." She took off, relieved to find it on the first try. Opening the door, she saw her mom sitting on the bed, holding Erasmus's hand.

Heather turned, showing the tears sliding down her cheeks. "Sophia," she whispered, voice choked.

"Mom." She wrapped an arm around the older woman who leaned into her, both of them looking down at the peaceful expression on Erasmus's face. For some reason, that made her angry again. He hadn't died peacefully, not like he should have. He'd died in pain, probably panicking. It seemed somehow insulting to her for his expression not to show that somehow.

"I shouldn't have left," Heather whispered. "You should have grown up here, or at least near here. You should have known him your whole life, not just the last two days of his."

"It's okay, Mom," Sophia murmured, though she couldn't really argue with the words. She wished she'd grown up here, with family and the truth of her heritage. Wished she'd gotten decades to get to know him instead of days.

"No, it's really not," her mom said with a shake of her head. "But I can't change the past. No one can. What I can do is support you and stop letting my fear and anger get in the way." She tipped her head back so she could look up at Sophia. "I know you've been asked if you're going to stay. I have, too. I think...even if you choose to go back to the States, I'm going to stay. Aside from watching you grow up, the best years of my life were spent here. I loved the Athenaeum, almost as much as I loved your father." She looked back to the body on the bed. "And Erasmus. My own father died when I was young. Erasmus was the father I only could have hoped for." Her eyes closed and fresh tears joined the dampness on her cheeks.

"I haven't decided what I'm going to do. I've thought about it, but there's just...a lot."

"There is," Heather agreed. "And I won't pressure you either way, though if you want to talk about it, you know I'm here for you, sweetheart."

"I know, Mom." And she did. It had always been the two of them against the world. Even knowing that her mom had lied to her for years didn't change that.

The door opened. Heather didn't look away from Erasmus, but Sophia did, seeing a stoic Valerie and a red-eyed Angela.

"We're sorry to interrupt," Valerie told them, her voice tight as her gaze flicked to Erasmus, then back to Sophia, "but we need to prepare him."

Heather sniffled and nodded before she got to her feet. "Of course." She drew Sophia away from the bed. "We'll be outside." Once she'd drawn her daughter outside, she leaned heavily against the wall. "They'll wrap him, then we'll carry him down to the pyre," she explained. "It's ceremonial, but not the actual funeral. You don't have to go…"

"No," Sophia said instantly. "I'm going. It's the least I can do for him." And in addition to the respect she wanted to pay him, she wanted to watch the reactions of the others. The last gesture of respect she could give him would be finding his killer.

Chapter 16

A WOOD AND CANVAS litter was brought in and the wrapped body placed reverently on it. Lucas, Jacob, Ray, Dion, Peter, and Carla gently lifted it and carried it out of the room. Sophia and Heather followed, other people following in their wake. Everyone was silent as they carried it through the labyrinth and down the non-existent path down to the back yard of the estate.

The sun was beginning to set and Sophia stopped for a moment and stared at the sky. It was impossible to miss how it looked as though it were on fire, a strange mirror to the literal fire they were about to set. She shook her head and continued walking, keeping her gaze firmly on the wrapped body of her grandfather.

The litter was set with utmost care upon the wooden pyre while the gathered people formed a loose circle around it. Sophia noted that not everyone was here, but rather than being offended on Erasmus's behalf, she understood. Everyone reacted to death differently, and watching a loved one burn wasn't going to be easy.

A flash of light distracted her, and she frowned at the group of six people who had appeared. One of the men—tall and muscled—wore a modern suit, but he was the exception. Of the other five, there were three women and two men, and all wore what she thought of as ancient garb. Two women looked Greek, the third woman and one of the men looked Egyptian, and the other she couldn't quite place. All six radiated power in a way that Sophia had never before felt. And while they looked familiar, she couldn't place why.

"Who are they?" she murmured to her mom.

"Athena, Hecate, Thoth, Isis, Mimir, and...I'm not sure. He looks more modern than most gods, but I guess they can change with the times as well."

The man next to her—someone she hadn't been introduced to yet—overheard and answered. "That's Seth Montgomery. He's the newest patron, but we're not sure how. He used to be a demi."

That explained why they looked familiar—she'd seen their statues. Sophia nodded slowly, but even this wasn't enough to truly take her mind off what they were doing.

Heather's hand twined with hers as the sun dipped further in the sky. When it had just touched the horizon, Dion approached her, holding a freshly lit torch. "As his closest living relative, it's your right to light the pyre," he explained in a low voice, one nearly drowned out by the soft crackling of the small fire. "If you're not up to it that's fine, I can do it," he added kindly when she hesitated.

Sophia glanced at her mom, who just gave her hand a squeeze, letting her decide. Shaking her head, she turned back to Dion. "No, I'll do it."

She took the torch from him and stepped away from the security of her mom's presence. Stopping just in front of the wood, she gave one last, long look to Erasmus. "Goodbye, Grandpa," she whispered before she touched the torch to the tinder at the base of the pyre. In seconds it caught, flames licking higher and higher, enveloping the wood beneath the man who had been so loving to her. It wasn't until the heat became uncomfortable that she stepped back. Someone took the torch from her, but she didn't bother to see who it was. It didn't matter. All that mattered was that the flames had reached the soft white linen that covered Erasmus. Around her, she heard the sounds of people sniffling and sobbing, but she still couldn't take her eyes off the pyre.

The fire grew, turning wood and cloth to ash, scorching flesh, and people began to leave. Some paused to say things to her—probably kind words about Erasmus—but it was nothing but white noise to her. Even when her mom told her something, kissed her cheek, then left, Sophia didn't move. Her entire existence was centered on the pyre.

It wasn't until hours later, when the fire had died to the smallest of flames that her focused changed.

Her eyes closed and finally the first tear escaped her and slipped down her cheek. It was quickly followed by a second, a third. Her legs gave out and she collapsed. Only strong arms kept her from hitting the ground hard. They eased her down as she began to sob, all the grief and anger culminating in an intense breakdown. When the arms around her started to loosen, she grabbed blindly for the person and clung to them. To her relief, those arms slid around her once more and gently rocked her as she purged her emotions through tears. She found her head pressed gently against a chest, felt the fading heat of the fire against her face. The person holding her began to hum softly, the tune not one she recognized, but it was soothing, nonetheless.

The fire was nothing more than embers when she opened her eyes again. They were tender, and she had no doubt her eyes were swollen and red, her face blotchy, but she didn't care. What mattered was that the shape of Erasmus had disappeared. There was only ash and coals now. Sniffling, she eased back and looked up to see who had held her during one of the worst moments of her life. It was Lucas. She hadn't expected that, even with the Talos nickname. Protecting was part of his job, comforting a near hysterical woman wasn't. Still, she appreciated it.

"He's gone," Sophia whispered, her throat sore, voice hoarse.

Lucas nodded and loosened his hold on her but didn't release her. "He is," he agreed softly.

"He's never entirely gone," Carla said from Sophia's right, her voice surprisingly close. Sophia turned in her direction and saw the most compassionate look on the guard's face that she'd ever seen. Gone was the snark and hard-ass routine. She knelt a mere foot from where Lucas held Sophia and reached out to brush some of the moisture from Sophia's cheek. "I know it's something most people say, but it's especially true in this case," she explained quietly. "His ashes will remain forever in the Athenaeum. His wisdom will remain in the journals he penned. His compassion and intelligence will live on in each and every person he taught, which in this case means every person in the Athenaeum." She worked up a smile, but it was watery. "And he lives on in you, his granddaughter."

"Maybe," Sophia said, drawing away from Lucas, though she didn't really want to leave the comfort of his strong arms, "but I can't speak to him anymore. I can't learn all the little things about him you only learn after years of interacting with someone."

"No, you can't," Lucas agreed as he pushed to his feet and offered his hands to her. "But you can learn about him from those of us who did have those years," he pointed out.

Still sitting on the ground, Sophia mulled over their words. They weren't wrong. It wasn't the same, no, but they weren't wrong. She placed her hands in Lucas's, letting him pull her up effortlessly. "Maybe tomorrow I'll agree with you, I might even appreciate it, but right now?" She shook her head as her gaze drifted back to the embers. "Right now, I'm just trying not to lose it again."

"I'll take her back. I'll send someone to..." Lucas glanced meaningfully at the remains, but it was enough for Carla to understand his meaning.

"I'll stay here until they're done," Carla told him.

Sophia didn't protest as Lucas led her back up to the Athenaeum. Her legs did, but they were a minor irritant at the moment, nothing more. In the common room, he left her long enough to speak quietly with one of the other guards before he walked her to her door. She opened it and stepped inside, only to pause.

"Will you be all right?" Lucas asked. "I can stay with you for a while if you want," he offered. He looked a little uncomfortable making that suggestion, but he also wasn't taking it back. "Or if there's something else you need..."

Suddenly Sophia realized one thing that could potentially make her forget, at least for a little while. It might not make anything better—it might do the opposite, actually—but she needed something right now. "Please," she asked, taking a few more steps into the room so he could join her. "If I'm alone right now, if I stop, I'm just going to break, not just crack." When he'd shut the door behind him, she stepped close and smoothed her hands down the front of his shirt.

He grabbed her hands, pinning them to his chest so they were still. "What are you doing?"

"I would think that's pretty obvious," she murmured as she leaned up and pressed her lips to his. For a terrifying couple of seconds he didn't react, but then he let go of her hands and sank his fingers into her hair as he deepened the kiss. Breathless, wanting more, wanting the oblivion only ecstasy could provide, she whimpered when he broke the kiss only a minute later. "Why'd you stop?"

"I want you to be sure," he murmured huskily as his lips trailed across her jaw and brushed her ear when he continued, making her shiver. "Tell me you want me, and not just anybody who's available."

"Trust me, I want you," she promised him. She'd wanted him since the moment she'd seen him. And while she couldn't be sure he wasn't involved with Erasmus's death, she wasn't sure she cared at the moment. There was something about him that drew her to him. She wanted to forget, yes, but she wanted to forget with *him*. With this gorgeous, dedicated, tough man who had been there for her when no one else had.

He took her at her word and nodded, turning to press her against the stone wall. Either he was a mind reader or had first-hand experience with guilt, because he didn't speak and wasn't gentle or timid. She didn't want either one. She needed to be overwhelmed.

Lucas wasn't sure this was a good idea, but he also couldn't deny either her or the instant attraction he'd felt when he'd first seen her. And he understood what was driving her, because the same thing was driving him. Death had a way of making people want to prove they were still alive. This was likely to be one night, so he would make it good for both of them. He'd make sure they could both forget.

One of his hands grabbed her ponytail, tilting her head back. He took her mouth fiercely, not just daring her to respond in kind, but compelling her to. She moaned and her hands grabbed his belt, tugging him closer, and he hissed as his stiff cock pressed against her belly. With his free hand, he worked her jeans open and started working them over her hips. After only a second, she released him to help. She wiggled against him as she tried to kick them off, forgetting about her shoes. Making a sound of frustration, she shifted to get them off so she could step out of the denim. He dragged his fingers over her soft skin and he felt himself throb with the need to be inside her.

He wasn't a virgin and hadn't been in decades, but he couldn't recall ever being with a woman who was so passionate. She didn't just let him know what she wanted, she was taking it. And while he didn't mind letting his partner take control in the bedroom, he didn't think that was actually what she wanted, not tonight. So when her hands went to undo his pants, he released her hair and grabbed both of her wrists, lifting them above her head. Pinning them both there with one hand, he nipped at her lower lip.

"What's your rush?" he asked, though when she ground her hips against him in both invitation and demand, he almost growled and gave in.

"Don't tease me," she shot back, testing his grip, but his hold was damn near unbreakable.

"I will," he promised, tilting his head to run his lips along her throat, "but you'll love it," he promised before biting, just enough to sting. She moaned, causing his lips to curl against her skin. The hand not holding her wrists slid down her arm, fingers light enough to almost tickle. His fingers made their way over her breast and down her belly until they could ease beneath her shirt. Her muscles twitched, and it was tempting to simply play with her for a while, but he knew neither of them had the patience for that. Instead, his hand moved lower, fingers sliding beneath her panties until he reached her core. When he found her just as ready as he was, he groaned.

In a movement faster than most would have thought him capable of, he released her wrists, then yanked her panties down. It didn't matter that she still had her shirt on, or that he was fully clothed. Tonight wasn't the night for sensual explorations or tender touches. Tonight, what he wanted was to lose himself in her, and he had a feeling she wanted to do the same with him.

This time, when she reached for his pants, he let her. She hurried, too, unbuttoning and unzipping his pants before she yanked them open. When her hand slipped inside and closed around him, he hissed and rocked against her palm.

She went up on her toes so she could kiss him hard, drawing his cock free of his pants. "Don't tease me," she repeated before giving him a squeeze that was just shy of too tight.

Lucas slid his arms around her, then down, cupping her ass. When he lifted, she wrapped her legs around his hips, so he settled between her thighs, hard flesh nestled perfectly against soft. One of her arms wrapped around his neck, while the other, still holding him, positioned him so the head of his cock was pressed against her entrance. That was all he needed, and his hips snapped forward, sheathing him inside her in one motion.

She moaned, but he needed a moment before he had the air to make a sound. This was supposed to be a quick fuck, something to ground them both and take their minds off the funeral they'd just attended. He hadn't expected her to feel this good, or match him so perfectly. And feeling her surrounding him, feeling her legs gripping him as her nails dug into his shoulder through his shirt, was enough to make his mind empty of everything but the need to move.

He rocked into her, the motions hard and deep. For the first few, her hand slid up his chest, almost lazily, but when he picked up the pace, that hand curled, clinging to him. A few more thrusts and she was whimpering, her shoulders braced against the wall so she could match his movements better. It let him go deeper and he clenched his teeth as he fought his body's need to come.

Yet while they were frantic, panting with exertion as they moved like they were one, he found he couldn't stop watching her. It wasn't anything he normally did—he was hardly the type to stare longingly into someone else's eyes—but he didn't feel the need to break her gaze, to kiss her, or bury his face against her throat. The fact that she was watching him in return, her pretty green eyes dark and heavy, made him feel entranced by her. If he didn't know better, he'd think she was a vampire or snake shifter. But no, it was all her. Maybe the moment, the events that had led to this desperate need.

Lucas shifted her slightly, positioning her body so every time he drove into her he was also brushing against her clit. The soft, surprised cry she gave him was beautiful and went straight to his cock. "Let go," he demanded, jaw clenched as he tried to hold on just a little longer. She didn't misunderstand him, her arms tightening as her sex started to flutter around him as her orgasm built. "Let go," he repeated, quickening his strokes, his hands now gripping her ass so tightly he wondered if he would leave finger-shaped bruises.

She gave a low, long groan and bucked against him as the pleasure broke within her. He could feel her nails clearly despite the fabric of his shirt, but it didn't hurt, not with her body clenching around him as she climaxed. Only then did she break his gaze, her eyes closing as her head fell forward to rest against his shoulder.

His own eyes slid closed as he grit his teeth, but as much as he wanted to keep going, to push her to another orgasm, his body had other ideas. It was less than a minute later when her body dragged him to his own orgasm and he groaned, pushing deep into her as he gave in and spilled inside her.

Only his weight leaning into her, and toward the wall, kept them upright, as his legs were far from steady. Slowly, once he was sure he wouldn't fall over, he drew out of her and lowered her until she was on her feet.

Sophia blinked up at him, a lazy little smile playing over her lips. She looked like she could easily curl up and go to sleep. He probably could, too, but his mind was starting to work again, and he hadn't yet had his fill of her.

He took a minute to catch his breath before he grinned. "I'm not done with you yet," he warned before he scooped her into his arms and carried her to the bed. He wanted another round, but wasn't sure he was up for anything quite as athletic as round one. Not yet.

She laughed softly and her teeth closed on his ear, giving a playful tug. "Sounds good to me," she said, her voice lower and full of satisfaction and promises.

He didn't just go for round two, but several more after that, this time learning every nuance of her body. When they finally exhausted each other, it was the wee hours of the morning. He slept on his back while she was half-draped over him, too exhausted to move. But though she dozed, sleep did nothing more than tease at her until nearly dawn.

Chapter 17

Her pillow was moving.

Confused, Sophia cracked an eye open to try to figure out what was going on. It took a minute for her eyes to focus enough to recognize that her 'pillow' was really a chest. That brought the previous evening back to the front of her mind. Half of her expected to feel shame at having used sex to combat grief, but she couldn't bring herself to regret what had happened between her and Lucas. Not unless he did turn out to be the murderer, anyway. It was a possibility she couldn't dismiss, no matter how much she'd enjoyed spending the night with him.

She eased out of bed, careful not to disturb him, but she was still a little surprised that he didn't wake. Shouldn't the guards be the sort who would wake if someone breathed wrong? For now she didn't question it, just got dressed and slipped out of the room. Only then did she look at the time, groaning when she saw it wasn't even eight yet. Hopefully, that meant there wouldn't be too many people up and about. The risk of being smothered in sympathy wasn't enough to discourage her from going to the kitchen, though. Her stomach was all too keen to remind her that she hadn't eaten since the popcorn yesterday. There was no one in the hallways, but Agatha and a man she didn't recognize were busy preparing breakfast in the kitchen.

"Oh, you're a bit early," Agatha told her, sounding distressed. "I won't have anything made for another few minutes."

Sophia shook her head. "That's okay. I'm hungry, but I don't think I could handle anything too heavy right now. But I'll definitely take some of that coffee."

"Tsk. No, coffee alone won't do," Agatha said with a sharp shake of her head. "You'll at least have a croissant. And the eggs will be done by the time you fix your coffee."

Sophia started to protest but recognized the determined glint in the cook's eyes. She wasn't going to get out of here with anything less than the croissant. "Okay, I'll have the croissant. But to go," she insisted.

"If you must, but at least you'll be eating." And Agatha wasn't wrong. By the time Sophia had poured her coffee into a travel mug and doctored it to perfection, the strong-willed blonde had a croissant filled with fluffy eggs and was placing it on a plate. "You come by anytime if this isn't enough," she demanded.

"Yes, ma'am," Sophia told her obediently as she took the plate and left.

When she got to the library, she went down to the second level and found a table to sit at and eat while she planned what to look for today. What she really wanted to do was get to level six, but that wasn't happening without outside help. She might be able to talk someone into taking her, but she might have to explain why, and she really didn't want to get into that. Or lie. She was a terrible liar.

She didn't get the chance to decide right away. Penny came down the stairs and headed right for Sophia. It didn't look as though she'd slept much more than Sophia, and her eyes were rimmed in red, but she still managed a smile.

"Hello. I'm sorry we haven't met sooner. I'm Penny," she offered.

"I don't guess I need to tell you my name, huh? But it's nice to meet you."

"You don't, no." She cocked her head. "You love the library, hmm? Your grandfather was the same way," Penny told her.

"I suppose it's in my blood, then. Though I do wish it was easier to navigate." That was an easier topic to focus on right now.

Penny brightened. "I can help you with that."

"You can?"

"Of course. Did no one tell you about the computers?"

Sophia frowned. "What computers? I saw the computer room..."

Penny shook her head and beckoned for Sophia to follow her and, curious, she did. "Those computers are all connected to the internet, so we don't put anything about the Athenaeum on them. Even Peter doesn't and he can do things with those computers that may as well be magic. No, we have a closed computer network that only exists here in the library and in the repository. No internet access, no wireless connections. It's how we keep track of what texts and relics we have and where they're located."

"I am so going to kick some asses later," Sophia muttered. "I've had two people show me the library, and neither mentioned the computers. For that matter, I haven't seen any computers down here."

"Oh, they're pretty discreet. Books are king down here," Penny said, waving that observation away. She was nearly at the stairs when she stopped and lifted the lid on what Sophia now saw was a laptop. Made to blend in and resemble a book. No wonder Sophia hadn't noticed it. "There's only a couple of programs on them, like this database. It has everything you could want. Title, author, what format it's in, what edition it is, keywords...All searchable, too. And you can see what's on any particular level. With a map. It won't show an exact location, like whether it's on the third shelf, fifth from the right, but it'll get you in a pretty close area."

This would have saved her so much time and trouble. She was going to threaten to shave Peter's mohawk when she saw him. Lucas...well, she'd have to think of a good threat. Although she had to wonder if it saved searches. It didn't look like there was a login, so it might not be able to say who searched for what, but if the murderer noticed someone searching for poisons, it might show her hand too soon. "This is great, Penny. Thank you. Sometimes I like wandering, just seeing what's there, but this will save a lot of time."

"You're welcome. I'm sorry no one mentioned it sooner."

Sophia waved a hand dismissively. "Not your fault. And I won't keep you any longer. I'm going to do the wandering thing for a while."

"Of course. I'm going to be going through some books on level three, so let me know if you need more help, all right?"

"I will."

They went down to the next level, then parted ways, Penny dealing with her books, Sophia going deeper into the library.

With others in the library, Sophia decided to be more careful and didn't go straight for the books on poisons. Instead, she started to look for books on magic. Sure, everyone had said the real books were on levels six and seven, but maybe there were some that didn't have spells in them, to help her understand the whole concept of sorcery better.

She'd never had a need to study sorcery before, but it sounded like it would be necessary here.

Half an hour later, she was still looking when her mother poked her head around a corner, relief flooding her features. "I was hoping I'd find you somewhere down here."

"What's wrong?" Sophia asked, closing the book she'd been skimming.

"Everything's okay. I was just worried about you," Heather admitted, her gaze moving over Sophia's face.

"Oh. Yeah, I'm okay, Mom," she assured the other woman. "Yesterday was just…I'm sticking with what's familiar, which is research and history."

Her mom nodded understandingly. Ever since Sophia was little, she'd retreated into books when she was upset, so this wasn't anything out of the ordinary. "Have you eaten anything?"

Sophia gave her a half smile. "When I went to get coffee, Agatha wouldn't let me leave without taking at least a croissant. With eggs. So yes, I've eaten. You can stop worrying, Mom. Besides, you knew him better than I did."

"Mmm. True, but I can see how that might be harder for you."

The book was set haphazardly on the shelf and Sophia crossed the short distance to Heather, wrapping her in a hug. She loved just how well her mom knew her. "Thanks, Mom."

"You're welcome, sweetheart," Heather murmured. "I'll get out of your hair, but—"

"Let you know if I need anything?" Her mom nodded and Sophia smiled. "I'm hearing that a lot. But you might want to keep your phone on you if you want me to be able to get a hold of you," she teased.

Her mom gave her a sheepish look and nodded. "I'll get it as soon as I get back upstairs." She kissed Sophia's cheek, then left her to the books.

Not ten minutes later, Dion found her and she fought not to sigh. Had someone sent out a memo that everyone should check on her at some point today? "Hi, Dion. Come to make sure I'm okay?" she asked, forcing cheerfulness into her voice instead of the exasperation she really felt.

"Guilty," he admitted. "I heard you were very upset last night, and when someone said you were awake already..." He shook his head and clasped his hands behind his back. "I couldn't not check on you. Just as you have very little family left, the same can be said for myself. I have only you, Peter, and your mother."

That thought hadn't occurred to her, and now she felt a little guilty for being annoyed at the interruption. "Of course. But I'm as okay as I can be in the situation. I didn't know him that well."

He nodded knowingly. "Mourning the possibilities, though, that is almost as bad, isn't it?"

"Yes, it is," she murmured. "But seriously, I'll be okay. And Agatha even made me eat."

His lips curved. "She looks like a sweet, delicate woman, but when it comes to feeding the people she cares about—which is the entire Athenaeum—she's more ferocious than a lioness. But since you are okay—and have told multiple people that, I'm assuming—I won't keep you. Enjoy the books."

"I will, thanks," Sophia told him and watched him leave. Just how many more people were going to come check on her? Hopefully none, but she doubted she'd be that lucky. At least three was her guess.

She had almost fifteen minutes of peace before the next one arrived. Or two, actually, since Peter and Ray showed up together. They hadn't even gotten a word out before she pointed at them and spoke. "You two are the fifth and sixth people who have made sure I'm okay since I got up. The fourth and fifth to actually come down into the library to check on me." The tone was accusing, but more playful than serious.

Ray arched a brow but didn't otherwise react. Peter, on the other hand, gave her a quick grin. "It wasn't planned, if that helps any?"

"Would it help you if you were constantly getting interrupted when you were just trying to distract yourself?"

"Not really," he had to admit.

"I would have come down here even if I'd known about the others," Ray admitted without any hint of guilt. "You're Greg's daughter. I'm going to make sure you're okay, even if it irritates you. Besides, doesn't irritation give a distraction, too?"

Sophia glared at him, but it lacked any heat. "I don't like that you're right. But irritation is also a very temporary distraction," she pointed out, and he inclined his head, conceding the point to her.

"We really were just worried," Peter chimed in, and that concern showed on his face. "I know this isn't how anyone wants to be introduced to the Athenaeum. But I'll leave you alone. For now," he said, emphasizing those two words.

"I'd be sad if you left me alone entirely. Favorite cousin, remember?"

Because of that, he was smiling as he left. Ray gave her one last look, nodded like he was satisfied with something, then left on Peter's heels. If she was lucky, they'd spread the word that she was okay and annoyed with all the interruptions.

For a while, it seemed as though she'd gotten her wish. She was able to flip through dozens of books, reading numerous passages about magic, but none of them actually referred to real magic, just magic in lore or rumors that were unsubstantiated. The human 'magic' books, basically. When she'd been left alone for a few hours, she went deeper and resumed her search for information on poisons. One was written in the sixteen hundreds and detailed a number of poisons throughout history. It was interesting enough that she'd just sat down where she was at and started reading.

Sophia was fully immersed in the book when she caught a scent that didn't belong. It was so out of place it pulled her out of the pages. She drew in a deep breath and placed it almost instantly. Smoke? Why would it smell smoky in the library? She lifted her head and gasped as the flicker of flames immediately caught her attention. A shelf of books was on fire, and the flames were quickly spreading. "Shit!" She dropped the book she was reading and jumped to her feet. She looked around but didn't see any sign of a fire extinguisher, and unfortunately, none of her magic involved putting out fires. In the thirty seconds it took her to verify there was nothing here for her to use to put the fire, it had jumped to another shelf and threatened the books on either side of it. Worse, the smoke was filling the area, causing her to cough and her eyes to water.

Seeing no other option, she ducked and awkwardly ran until she was free of the smoke, only to straighten and run full out toward the stairs. She grabbed her phone, but it was hard to hit the right buttons when she was moving so quickly, so her first attempt to call her mom failed. Just as she was going to make a second attempt, she saw movement ahead of her. Her head whipped up and she abruptly stopped. Lucas was coming down the stairs, a plate covered by a napkin in one hand. He saw the look on her face, dropped the plate which shattered on the stone stairs, and ran toward her. "What is it? What's wrong?"

"Fire," she told him, throat raw from the smoke.

He turned and went to the first shelf inside the room and grabbed a fire extinguisher she hadn't noticed before. "Show me," he told her as his skin went gray.

Was he a gargoyle? She'd never met one, but that would have to wait for later.

Sophia nodded and led him back toward the fire, but was quickly confused. The smoke had been spreading even faster than the fire, but now there wasn't even a whiff of it. Her steps faltered as she reached the row she'd been reading on. No smoke, no fire. Not even a single flame.

After she stopped, it only took an instant for Lucas to reach her side. He took in the area, then looked at her with an expectant look on his face. "Where is it?"

"I don't understand," she murmured, slowly walking down the row. She bent and picked up the book that she'd dropped, proof that she had, in fact, been here. "I was sitting right here, looked up, and this shelf was on fire," she told him. When she turned back to him, she saw a skeptical look on his face. "I'm serious! I could feel the heat, smell the smoke. It burned my throat!"

Lucas approached her slowly, like one might approach a wounded animal, as his normal skin tone returned. "I believe you," he said in a tone that made her think he was just humoring her. "How much did you sleep last night?" he asked, his voice surprisingly gentle.

"Not much since you kept me up half the night, but what does—" She broke off and thought about it. Stress, not eating right, a lack of sleep...could she have just hallucinated it all? It wasn't out of the realm of possibility, she supposed, though coupled with the closet and Erasmus's poisoning, she wondered if it could have been something more insidious. Lucas could even be responsible. He was around for both incidents, after all. She rubbed her face and tried to settle herself. "Not much," she repeated in a much calmer tone, though she felt anything but calm.

"You should lie down for a bit," he told her, taking the book from her and setting it on the shelf before he wrapped an arm around her. He used that to guide her through the shelves, not letting go until they'd reached her bedroom door. Even then, he only shifted to rest a hand on her lower back as he opened the door and led her to the bed. He urged her to sit on the bed and pulled her shoes off before encouraging her to get under the covers. "Just sleep for a while," he told her, brushing a hand lightly over her hair.

Sophia nodded and rolled onto her side, curling in on herself and cuddling a pillow to her chest. Though she doubted sleep would come, she closed her eyes and let herself drift. She was out before Lucas had even closed the door behind him.

Lucas returned to the library after leaving Sophia. He passed the remains of the lunch he'd planned on bringing to her and retraced his steps until he found the book he'd put on the shelf as a way of marking the location. Without her there he was free to search for signs of fire, but everything looked pristine. If Sophia hadn't claimed there was a fire here, he'd never have suspected anything. And while he'd insinuated that she was hallucinating due to stress, he didn't really believe it. He'd seen no signs of mental instability in her.

He searched the nearby area, looking for anything out of place within a fifty-foot radius, but found nothing. Still, it was likely she hadn't been as alone as she'd thought. He returned to the site of the supposed fire and closed his eyes. Magic didn't come as easily to him as it did for some of the others—he just didn't have the patience to memorize all the spells in the dozens of languages they could be in—but as the head of the nasaru there were a few spells he'd made the effort to learn. One such spell worked perfectly for this situation.

As his lips moved, forming the words of a language that had been considered dead for centuries, a pressure settled over his skin. Slowly, he moved along the row and down the next one, paying attention to how the pressure increased and decreased. It was strongest just two rows over from where she'd been, but there was no sign of anyone having been there. Still, he was convinced. Someone had used magic to make Sophia think the library was on fire. The only question was why.

Chapter 18

Waking alone was a relief. Sophia wasn't sure she could handle dealing with anyone first thing. For that matter, it took her some time before she could even manage to pull herself out of bed. She thought she'd dreamed something weird because she woke with an odd, antsy feeling. It felt like something bad was about to happen. Given the closet and the fire that wasn't a fire, it could just be paranoia, but she didn't think so. To be on the safe side, she cast her threat-sensing spell and wished Erasmus had been able to teach her more before succumbing to the poison. Now more than ever since the sensation of the spell was a little stronger than it had been the other times she'd used it.

Her steps were sluggish as she made her way to the kitchen, but anxiety had her stomach churning too much for her to eat more than a few bites. At Agatha's urging, she took a sandwich as she left the kitchen and made her way to the common room. Safety in numbers was an often-said saying for a reason, and she felt more comfortable with others around. If nothing else, she'd have a witness if something else like the fire occurred. As expected, people wandered in and out. Some stayed for a while to play games or watch the TV, while a few stopped to speak with her for a few minutes before moving on.

Sophia's nap hadn't been restful, and Lucas really had kept her up the night before, so she found herself dozing here and there as the sounds of life flowed around her. It was during one of this brief naps when Heather found her.

"Sweetheart? I'd love to let you sleep, but you need to wake up."

She jerked upright and blinked before rubbing at her eyes. "What? Why? Huh?"

Heather laughed softly, but even to Sophia's drowsy brain it sounded forced. "It's almost time for the funeral."

"What? Now? Crap." Sophia got up and half-ran toward her room, leaving her mom behind. Though she'd known from day one that she'd be attending a funeral at some point, the thought of dressing for said funeral hadn't occurred to her. She hadn't brought a single black dress. For that matter, the only things she brought that were black were a pair of socks, jeans, and a hoodie. It wasn't until she shoved her door open that she stopped and realized a very important fact. In Greece, at least ancient Greece, black wasn't the color of mourning, white was. Unfortunately, she hadn't brought any dresses since she wasn't really a dress sort of girl. She did, however, have a nice white button-down shirt. Coupled with the black jeans, it wouldn't be the nicest outfit ever, but it was the best she could do. Hopefully Erasmus would have understood.

Not knowing just how close the funeral was, she dressed with record speed and pulled her hair down from her ponytail, brushing it out. She even took the time to use some of her meager makeup supply to apply a bit of eyeliner and some sheer lip gloss. The end result wasn't entirely pleasing, but given what she had with her, it was the nicest she could look on short notice.

A knock on the door was followed by Heather poking her head in without waiting for an answer. "Sophia? Oh good, you're ready," she said as she moved into the room.

"As ready as I'll ever be, yeah," Sophia murmured, turning away from the mirror. Her mom had come a little more prepared as she was in an ankle-length white dress. "Is it wrong to say you look beautiful?" she asked, forcing a faint smile to her lips.

"It's never wrong to compliment your poor old mother," her mom said as she moved to Sophia and wrapped her arms around her. "Just like it's never wrong to tell my daughter that she's beautiful and has grown up entirely too fast for my liking," she murmured.

"Mom," she complained, drawing the word out until it was three syllables. When they drew apart, Sophia took in the strain on her mom's face. "Is it time?"

Heather nodded and brushed a strand of hair behind Sophia's ear. "It's time," she confirmed.

Sophia took a deep breath and nodded. "Let's go, then. I don't want anyone to have to wait on us."

"It's okay if they do. Besides—" She cut off as someone else knocked at the door. "That's probably Dion," she murmured as she went to the door and opened it. She didn't say anything, just opened the door further so Dion and Sophia could see one another. Lucas and Nick stood behind Dion, all of them solemn.

Dion held a ceramic urn painted in the style used in ancient Greece. Under any other circumstances Sophia might find it beautiful and interesting, but knowing that the urn contained Erasmus's ashes simply made her sad.

"Sophia," he said, his voice thick with emotion, "as Erasmus's next of kin, it's your right to carry him to his resting place in the crypt."

Sophia swallowed. It wasn't that she didn't want to honor her grandfather, but carrying his urn put her right in the center of everything, and she wasn't sure she was up for that kind of attention. Still, it was the last thing she could do for him.

Sensing her hesitation, Dion added, "You don't have to. If you're uncomfortable—"

"No," Sophia said with a shake of her head. "No, I'll do it," she said quietly. She crossed the room and reverently took the urn from him, mildly surprised by the weight of it. Actually holding it had her closing her eyes for a moment as she got her emotions under control. Like every other day since his death, she didn't feel only grief, but the anger that was becoming so familiar.

"Are you ready?" Dion asked gently. When she nodded, he backed out of the bedroom and led the way toward the next level down, his steps slow. Lucas and Nick fell into step behind her, with her mother just behind them, but Sophia noticed that as they made their trek to the stairs and down them, more and more people joined their procession. And yet, even when everyone in the Athenaeum was following them, no one made a sound but for the occasional scuffing of feet against the stone floor.

Dion opened the door leading to the crypt Lucas had told her about and continued to lead the way inside then through a second door. Sophia wasn't sure what she'd expected, but this wasn't it. They passed through a hallway with pedestals lining both the long walls. It had to be at least as long as a football field, and she wouldn't be surprised if it was longer. The first thirty or so pedestals were empty while the ones further on held urns very similar to the one in her hands. Behind each urn was a metal plaque. She was sure they were steles, though even with their slow pace she wasn't able to read much of the writing on any of them. It was obvious that people's names were listed at the top and she assumed the smaller writing—various forms of ancient Greek, of course—detailed information about the aspida on the pedestal.

When they reached the end of the hallway, Dion pushed the heavy stone door open. It was one of the few doors she'd seen that was stone rather than wood. A useless fact, really, but focusing on it helped her not to dwell on what she carried in her hands.

The next room was circular and more than large enough to fit everyone who had joined them, even if their numbers had been tripled. There was writing in multiple languages carved into every inch of the walls and ceiling, but that was almost overshadowed by the rest of the room. Along the perimeter of the room were statues; twelve of them that alternated between the divine patrons and sphinxes. In the middle of the room was one more pedestal, this one larger than the ones they'd just passed. And where the others had been smooth and bare of writing, this one was covered in it like the rest of the room. Sophia wished that she'd thought to ask for details about the funeral, because this was unlike anything she'd ever seen or read about.

As she gawked at the place, the others filed in and spread out around the edges of the room, leaving an empty space around the pedestal and at the far end of the room. She squinted at the nearest markings on the high ceiling but wasn't quite able to make them out. And like the stone door, it really didn't matter at the moment. Or so she hoped.

There was a flash and the same six people from the night before appeared in the gap across from her. The divine patrons. It made sense that they'd be here, but it made her nervous to be in the same room with six gods. Something she seemed to share with several others, judging by the wide berth the others gave the deities.

Dion lightly touched her arm and spoke quietly. "Would you place the urn on the pedestal, please?"

Sophia took in a slow breath and fought not to look back at her mom for reassurance. Instead, she stepped away from the crowd, feeling dozens of eyes on her as she walked to the pedestal and set Erasmus's ashes carefully atop it. The moment she was sure it wasn't going anywhere, she turned and walked back toward her mom, her steps a bit quicker now that she wasn't burdened with the responsibility of carrying the urn. Once she had faded back into the crowd, Dion stepped forward. It was only a few feet, but it was enough to make him stand out. When he spoke, his voice was deeper and carried farther than it had when they'd talked before. It surprised her a little, but she more worried if her mom could understand him, since he was speaking an older form of the Greek tongue. It wasn't the dialect she was used to, but she was able to follow along.

"We are here, my dearest friends, my dearest family, to lay to rest the man who watched over us all. The man who acted as father, brother, grandfather to each of us. The man who was caretaker of this glorious sanctum of knowledge. We ask that the gods and the universe watch over Erasmus Regas and guide him gently to the next life. Though part of his spirit will remain here with the knowledge he loved so deeply, we ask that his spirit find peace in Elysium."

The words were said solemnly and with damp eyes. His were not the only ones that filled with tears either. Around the room, Sophia could see people wiping their cheeks out of the corner of her eye, hear the sniffling as people fought back sobs. It struck her as a little odd, though. Sure, it was ceremonial, but where were the words about loving Erasmus? Missing him? Did whoever had written this ceremony not care about emotions? Because when Erasmus had died in front of her, Sophia hadn't cared about the books, just about the man.

When the last echo of Dion's speech had been absorbed by the stone, the gods each raised a hand toward the pedestal and a brilliant light appeared from over the urn, encasing it and the pedestal. Sophia was the only one who gasped in surprise. There hadn't been any sort of spotlight there. That shouldn't surprise her given that the lights elsewhere in the Athenaeum seemed to come from the stone itself, but like all new forms of magic, it took her a moment to process. Which was why it took seconds for her to realize that everyone around her seemed to be holding their breath, vibrating with anticipation. She frowned in confusion and was about to dare a whisper to her mom when Dion began speaking again.

"Though our aspida is gone, his body returned to the ether, every sanctum needs a guard, every family needs a head, every circle needs a center. We ask that the Athenaeum choose a successor for the beloved Erasmus. Show us who will protect us next," he beseeched.

All eyes became fixed on the near blinding light in the center of the room. Part of it separated and shifted away from the pedestal. It moved sluggishly across the room, heading toward the door, toward Sophia and those she stood with. She automatically tried to step to one side, but someone's strong hand wrapped around her bicep and held her in place. While the grip was tight, it wasn't painful. The same couldn't be said for the light as it grew nearer, hurting her eyes. Then it enveloped her and softened, bathing the room in a gentle glow.

Around her, Sophia could hear soft gasps and murmurs as people put distance between themselves and her. She started to panic and turned, wide eyes searching for her mom, who had moved back along with the rest, leaving her standing alone in the light. "What's going on? What is this?" she demanded, her voice half an octave higher than normal.

At first, no one answered her. Her eyes shifted from person to person, seeing a mixture of reactions—happiness, shock, resignation. That last expression being on her mother's face was what really ramped her anxiety up a notch. "Mom? What's with the light?" she asked, getting closer to a full on anxiety attack. She'd never had one before coming to the Athenaeum, but since arriving, there was so much that had freaked her out.

Once again, it was Dion who spoke next, though even he kept his distance from her. "You have been chosen as Erasmus's successor, Sophia. This is how the Athenaeum tells us its choice."

She stared at him in disbelief. "I'm...the new aspida?" she whispered, not willing to believe she'd heard him correctly.

"You are," he confirmed.

No longer caring what anyone else thought of her, she dropped into a crouch, lowering her head between her knees as she did her best to control her breathing. This wasn't why she'd come to Greece. She'd just wanted to meet her grandfather. She didn't know the first thing about running a place like this. For that matter, she still didn't understand the Athenaeum, not entirely. It was all too overwhelming.

Her eyes squeezed shut so she didn't notice when the light faded. It wasn't until gentle arms wrapped around her shoulders that she opened her eyes to find the room had returned to its original level of brightness. She turned her head slightly and saw her mom's face close to hers, concern painted on every feature. Silently, Heather urged her back to her feet. Not quite steady, she leaned against her mom, only then realizing Lucas stood on her other side. He didn't touch her but was close, his expression stoic.

"I know this is a lot, but you need to be strong until you're out of here," he whispered to her. Though she wanted to run and hide or immediately abdicate, she saw the wisdom in his words and lifted her chin slightly. She was teetering on the edge, but she was determined to hold herself together. She wouldn't shame herself, her mom, or her grandfather's memory.

To her relief, people started to file out. Some inclined their heads to her and offered her a reassuring smile. Others gave her a considering look, like they were wondering if she'd live up to her grandfather's legacy. Luckily, none gave her any flat out hateful looks or snubbed her. Peter started to head for her, but Josie and Angela each hooked an arm through one of his and drew him out, whispering to him. Josie mouthed, "We'll give you time," before they left. The last ones to go were the patrons, though each one caught her gaze before they disappeared. The modern-looking man inclined his head to her before he joined them. Eventually, she was left alone with Dion, her mom, Nick, Lucas, and Penny. The latter approached slowly and gave her a comforting smile. "I'll leave you to adjust. I just wanted to let you know that the aspida's room is ready for you to move into whenever you're ready."

She turned to leave, so she missed the look of horror that spread across Sophia's face.

Chapter 19

Heather continued to speak calming words to Sophia for several more minutes until they all started for the door by some unknown signal. Though they all kept close, no one spoke. It was both a blessing and a curse for Sophia. On one hand, she would love the distraction. On the other, any conversation they had was likely to revolve around her new promotion.

When they reached Erasmus's room Dion and Nick stopped, but Sophia continued on. After a moment, they followed. When she opened the door to her room and took a step inside, all four moved to join her. "Um...I'd like just a few minutes by myself," she said, giving her mom an apologetic look.

Heather just smiled and nodded. "Of course, sweetheart."

No one else said a word as she hurried into her room and shut the door firmly behind her. She had intended to use the solitude to get control of her emotions, but reality went the opposite direction. Her breathing and heart rate quickened, and she felt like she was going to pass out. Panicking, she crossed the room with rapid, stumbling steps. When she reached the corner, she leaned against the wall and sank down to the floor, wrapping her arms around her knees. She tried to focus on breathing, relaxing, but her mind just kept replaying that odd light and the words Dion had spoken.

You have been chosen as Erasmus's successor, Sophia.

This wasn't how it was supposed to happen. Sure, she'd been considering staying, but as a curator or maybe a venator, not the boss. She was only twenty-four! There was no way she was ready for this level of responsibility.

Her thoughts made her spiral further and further from calm until her breathing was too rapid and she was truly on the verge of passing out.

"Oh, Sophia."

The soft voice, so full of worry, broke through the frenzy building inside her. She fought to lift her head, to see who had spoken, but even when she managed it, her eyes were so full of tears that she could only see blurred colors.

A gentle hand carefully wiped the tears from her cheeks and drew her away from the wall and into a warm embrace. "Sweetheart...this isn't the end of the world," her mom whispered.

Sophia slid her arms around her mom, taking strength in her presence. "I'm not the right person for the job, Mom."

Heather bent her head, resting her cheek against Sophia's hair. "I wish I could agree with you. I wish I could tell you that this place is bad for you, but I can't. You loved your classes, but I think you'll love it here even more. And the Athenaeum..." She sighed and closed her eyes as she held her daughter a little tighter. "As much as I wanted to blame it for your dad's death, the Athenaeum doesn't make mistakes. The people in it do sometimes, but the Athenaeum doesn't. The patrons don't. You are who it chose, which means you're the right person for the job."

"No," Sophia said, shaking her head. "It made a mistake this time. A twenty-four year old who just learned about this place shouldn't be running it," she insisted. "I can't do this, Mom. I just...can't."

The door opened and she wanted to snap at whoever it was to leave her alone, that she couldn't handle dealing with people on top of everything else. Lucas didn't give her the chance.

He stalked over to her, knelt, and met her gaze directly. If she had expected him to be gentle like her mom, she was very wrong. His voice was stern, almost harsh. "Stop acting like a selfish child."

Sophia reeled back as though slapped. "Excuse me?" This was the man she'd slept with? Sure, sex didn't always come with the expectation of affection, but she thought they were at least becoming friends.

"You heard me," he said, not backing down one bit. "I get it. You weren't expecting this. Tough. Other people weren't expecting this either, and there are more than a few people disappointed it wasn't them. But like it or not, you're now our leader. You need to act like it." He stood and looked down at her with the same unyielding expression. "Now, I'm going to give you five minutes to clean your face and get yourself together, then I and the other heads are coming in here to explain things to you." He didn't wait for a response, just strode to the door and out.

His speech had accomplished what her mom's sweet words hadn't—she wasn't freaking out any longer. Panic had been replaced by a familiar anger. It lived in her almost constantly the last few days, but now it surged.

"How dare he?" she whispered, pushing away from her mom and the floor to stand. "Doesn't he know what I'm dealing with? And he called me selfish?" she demanded as she paced.

Heather's lips curved and she glanced from the door to her daughter. "I think he knows exactly what he's dealing with," she said calmly as she got to her feet as well. She found a cloth and dampened it with a bottle of water, offering it to Sophia. "I think that's exactly why he said what he did."

Sophia had to fight not to snatch the washcloth from her mom. She wasn't mad at her, just the arrogant guard. "I don't get it. What do you mean?" she asked as she ran the cloth over her face in brisk strokes that turned her skin a light shade of pink.

"Well," Heather said as she sat down and crossed her legs, "being comforting and supportive wasn't helping to calm you down, sweetheart. He comes in here and says a few words and you're not freaking out anymore. You're angry, sure, but you were barely conscious when I came in."

The truth of Heather's words sunk in and Sophia's hand stilled mid-stroke. The anger shriveled within her before she narrowed her eyes at the door. "Why that manipulative little..." She huffed softly and resumed washing her face, much more gently than before. "I don't know how I feel about him knowing me that well," she muttered.

Her mom's lips twitched a little and she arched a brow. "Are you ready for the heads to come in? The sooner they explain things to you, the sooner they can leave and you can take the rest of the night to adjust."

Sophia sighed and set the cloth on her nightstand as she dropped down onto the bed. "Yeah, I guess." She knew she was acting like a sulky child, but part of her didn't care. She was entitled to be upset. Her entire life had just changed.

Heather opened the door. "She's ready," she told the others who filed in and spread out through the room.

Lucas met Sophia's glare and half smiled for an instant.

"We're sure you have a lot of questions," Dion began, "and while we will be happy to answer them, we thought it might be simpler if we explained things first."

Sophia nodded. "Sure, but I do have one question first."

Nick cocked his head curiously. "Of course."

"Can I abdicate or step down or anything? Pass the job onto someone else?" she asked, trying to keep the desperation out of her voice.

He slowly shook his head, an apologetic look in his eyes. "I'm sorry, but no. The Athenaeum simply will not choose a new aspida until the ashes of the previous one are placed on the pedestal."

She blanched and shuddered at the idea of her body turned to ash and put into a pot, however pretty it was. "Right, no stepping down," she muttered. "Okay, explain away."

Nick and Dion exchanged a look before Nick nodded to Dion. Apparently, it was a signal that Dion should begin since he started talking. "I'm sure it has been mentioned, but you are now in charge of the entire Athenaeum. However, most aspides—including your grandfather—do tend to delegate quite a bit. That's actually what Nicholas, Lucas, and I are here for."

Sophia cocked her head. "How so?" she asked curiously. If she focused on details, maybe she wouldn't be so overwhelmed by the big picture.

"Keep in mind that you can overrule anything we decide," Lucas said, "but the three of us tend to take care of the day to day business within our respective branches. So I tell the nasaru where to go, when to train, what venator to go with, etcetera. Dion is in charge of all the curators and Nick is in charge of the venatores."

"For the most part," Nick said with a small shake of his head.

"What part are you not in charge of?" Sophia asked.

"It's not so much we're not in charge, and it's mostly for Dion's people," Nick said, inclining his head to said man. "I'm sure you've heard people referred to by a title other than curator, venator, or nasaru? Such as Peter being our tech, Sergei our healer, things like that. While we can recommend people for those positions, the choice is ultimately yours."

Her nose wrinkled. "I don't have to do any of that right now, right? They can all just keep their jobs?"

"Absolutely. Unless you chose to replace them, of course."

She shook her head. "I don't see any reason for that. Erasmus seemed like a really smart guy, and if he signed off on everyone being where they are, then I'm good. But I don't get it. If you guys are handling everything, am I just here as a sort of...I don't know, overseer? Figurehead? To veto anything I think is way too wonky?"

Dion chuckled softly and shook his head. "No, the role of aspida is more active than that. I'm sure in the beginning, before the Athenaeum chose, that some aspides did operate that way. Part of your job is, yes, being an overseer, as you called it, but you're also the primary one to do research on level six, and the only one allowed on seven. You're the one to approve any guests or recruits, and the one to teach the basics of sorcery, as well as the major spells."

Sophia instantly shook her head. "No, I can't do that. I don't know sorcery! How am I supposed to teach what I don't know?"

"Relax," Lucas said, his conversational tone replaced by the stern tone from before. And like before, it helped ground her. But if he thought he was going to boss her around regularly, he had another thing coming. "One, you won't be teaching each and every spell. You wouldn't have any free time if that was the case. Second, again, you have us. I can't say that we know every spell in existence—even Erasmus couldn't make that claim—but we can get you started until you're ready to delve into the books reserved for you and you alone."

"Oh. That doesn't sound too bad." It really didn't. She had enjoyed learning the spell from Erasmus. Learning more would be just as enjoyable, or so she hoped. She looked back to Dion. "What did you mean by research?"

"As I'm sure you have guessed, not all books or relics are easy to find. It's not always a matter of finding a collector who's willing to sell their relic or copy of some book or scroll," Dion answered. "Sometimes it takes a great deal of research in order to locate where a book *might* be."

"What he means is it's a treasure hunt," Lucas said bluntly.

"Wait, like Indiana Jones?" she asked, warming up to her role.

Nick grinned. "Similar, but with fewer whips. Usually. So don't take the movies as gospel, no matter how much you might like them."

Sophia was surprised by his words until she remembered that she'd been wearing an Indiana Jones shirt when she'd first met him. Then she grinned. "So I can't expect one of you venatores to walk around in a fedora?" she teased.

He chuckled and shook his head. "Not likely, no. Sorry to disappoint."

She gave a heavy sigh, feigning disappointment. "I suppose I'll survive," she muttered. "Wait, you said guests. There are outsiders here in the Athenaeum?"

"Not usually," Dion disagreed. "And we don't really see family as outsiders," he said with a smile to Heather, who returned it. "But we might, on occasion, bring in an expert, or someone who has earned our friendship and is proved to be trustworthy. And there are a handful of people who locate things for us but who aren't actually part of the Athenaeum. Seth Montgomery used to be one of those."

"But you don't have to worry about any of that right now," Lucas said as soon as Dion was done. "Even if you'd grown up in the Athenaeum, protocol is that you get a few days to adjust to your new role. Unless there's an emergency, you can take the time to just get more familiar with the Athenaeum and its people. I'm sure there are several you haven't met yet."

"Judging by the people who were down there in the crypt? Yeah, I haven't actually met even half the people here."

"Then take the time to adjust and meet people. And if you do have questions in the mean time, just let one of us know."

"I can do that."

Lucas nodded and didn't say anything else as he strode out the door.

Nick gave her a reassuring smile. "Just take it easy on yourself, okay?"

"I will," Sophia promised him as he followed Lucas.

Dion was the last to go, and he smiled and patted her shoulder comfortingly. "Everything will be all right, Sophia. Things always turn out as they're meant to."

She smiled faintly. "I hope so. Thanks, Dion."

Another pat and then he left as well.

Heather sat next to Sophia and rubbed her back gently. "Nick and Dion were right, you know? You should take it easy on yourself and relax."

"Are you going to leave? Go back home?" Until she asked the question, Sophia hadn't realized that the fear had been lingering in the back of her head since she'd realized what that bright light had meant. The fact that her mom had said she was likely going to stay even if Sophia didn't slipped her mind with everything else going on.

"Oh, sweetheart," Heather murmured, sliding her arms around Sophia. "No, I'm not. This is where you're going to be, which means it's where I'm going to be."

Some of the tension Sophia had been carrying drained out of her. "Thanks, Mom."

"Of course. Now, I might go back to the States just to see about packing things up, having them shipped here, but I won't stay there."

"Oh gods. I need to get a hold of my school and withdraw." Yet the thought of not getting her masters degree didn't scare her like she thought it would have.

"Give yourself a few days for that, too," Heather suggested. "You've been through a lot in a very short time."

"Yeah, that's probably a good idea," she said, the last word garbled as a yawn hit her.

Heather laughed softly and kissed Sophia's forehead. "Get some rest. We can talk more later."

Sophia stretched out as Heather got up, yawning again when her head hit the pillow. "Okay," she murmured, her last thought that she hoped she wouldn't dream.

Chapter 20

EVERYONE IN THE ATHENAEUM seemed to realize that Sophia need-ed some time to herself, time to process, because there was only one knock on her door for the rest of the night. It had startled her from sleep, so by the time she got up to answer, no one was there. A tray with covered plates of still hot food was. Groggy, she picked up the tray and set it on her nightstand. She stared at the food for a moment and decided it was probably her mom who had left it for her. It was a sweet thought, but she wanted to sleep more than to eat.

She slept off and on for the rest of the night, though her periods of unconsciousness were fitful. Occasionally she woke herself up by thrashing in the bed, but more often it was a result of nightmares. Though Erasmus featured heavily in most, he wasn't the star. In-stead, her subconscious had dreamed up dozens of scenarios where she caused the downfall of the Athenaeum.

After a particularly bad nightmare where half the Athenaeum was dead and half shunned her, she gave up on the idea of going back to sleep. She showered and changed into a pair of yoga pants and a tee-shirt. At first she hesitated in the choice of clothing, given her new status, but ultimately decided not to care. If Peter could be a tech guy with a blue mohawk and gods knew how many piercings, she could be the aspida in comfy clothes.

Sophia was mostly alert when she walked into the kitchen. Agatha gave her a smile and automatically started to pour a cup of coffee, but everyone else started watching her like she was an oddity. Which she was, she supposed, but it didn't make the staring and whispers any easier.

She took her coffee and sat down, unsurprised when Agatha placed an omeletta in front of her. She gave the petite woman a quick smile and focused on her coffee. Not wanting to offend Agatha, she did try to eat, but stress had wiped her appetite out of existence. The watchful eyes surrounding her didn't help, either.

By the time her cup was empty, she was about to snap. To avoid lashing out at people who probably didn't mean any harm, she dealt with her cup and plate, murmuring a thank you to Agatha before she left.

Hoping to find someone who would treat her normally, she decided to track down Peter or Josie. Given that she didn't know where Josie's room was—or have the other woman's number—she headed for the computer room. When she arrived and found Peter there, she smiled for the first time since the funeral the day before. He was in his computer chair, feet propped up on the edge of his desk. He was also out cold, his head tilted back, mouth slightly open, a tiny snore echoing softly against the stone. It was adorable.

Silently she crept across the room, nearly giggling when he didn't wake up. She bent down until her mouth was close to his ear and let out a quick, sharp whistle. He shot awake, trying to stand up so quickly he nearly fell out of his chair.

"Ti?" he demanded as he looked around and tried to get his bearings.

Sophia cracked up and leaned against the wall as she took in his bewildered gaze and limp mohawk. "You always wake up asking what?" she teased.

He blinked at her for a moment as he sank back down into his chair. "Only when people startle me awake," he said in a sleep-roughened voice, running his hand over his hair.

"Sorry," Sophia said, only half meaning it. "I just couldn't resist. Besides, I needed a giggle," she told him, giving him her best big, sad eyes.

He glared at her but it was obvious he didn't mean it. "Fine. I'll forgive you this once. But only this once."

"Thanks," she told him as she drew a chair over to his desk and sat. "Do you always sleep in here?"

The sheepish look he gave her answered her before he even spoke. "Not always...But I do tend to fall asleep at my desk, yeah."

"That can't be good for your back. Or neck. Or the rest of your body."

"Eh, I'll stop when I hit three hundred," he told her with a quick grin. "What brings you to my domain, though?"

Just like that, her mood took a dip. "Wanted some company that wouldn't stare at me like I had grown a second head, mostly."

Understanding showed in his eyes and he nodded. "I've never witnessed a new aspida being chosen, but my guess is that they're just...surprised...that someone so new to the Athenaeum got the job. It'll die off soon," he promised.

"I hope so. My nerves were bad enough before everyone started staring." She shook her head. "I figured I'd hang out with you or Josie." She smiled faintly. "Considering I know you better, don't have her number, and have no idea where to find her, you won."

"Oh, I can take care of that." He held his hand out, wiggling his fingers in a gimme gesture. When she unlocked her phone and passed it over, he programmed in Josie's number and handed it back. "There. Now you can get either of us anytime you need us."

"Thanks," she told him, slipping the phone back in her pocket.

"And speaking of your new position...I wanted to tell you congratulations...and I'm sorry."

Surprised, her eyes widened. "You're sorry?"

"Mmhmm. I know this isn't what you wanted, and I know you're not ready. So while I think this could be good for you, and that you have the potential to do a great job at it, I'm sorry."

The simple understanding made tears well. It meant more to her than she could express, so she simply said, "Thank you."

"You're welcome. Now, you said you were mostly wanting company, but that implies you wanted something else. What was it?"

"It really was mostly the company. I don't want you thinking I need an ulterior motive to come see you," Sophia insisted. "Favorite cousin, remember?"

He smiled. "Yeah, I know. And I didn't think that." He puffed up his chest and lifted his chin until it was comical. "I am a very useful man, you know. Many skills. Everyone needs my help sometimes."

Peter deflated when she poked him in the side, twitching like it tickled. "I know you're useful. And I was wondering...I know I'm supposed to be allowed in the whole library now, but I'm guessing you have to make a tweak or something in the computer for it to actually happen."

"Oh, that's easy," he said with a smile. "Lucas found me last night and we took care of it. You're good."

She didn't know why it surprised her that Lucas would think of that, but it did. Next time she saw him, she was going to have to thank him. "Thanks," she murmured. "I've been pretty curious about the sixth level," she admitted.

"I've heard it's amazing. But I would suggest that you allow one of the heads to take you the first time," Peter suggested.

Sophia cocked her head. "Why?"

"You know the dangerous books are down there. Dangerous isn't an exaggeration."

"Yeah, but I'm sure there are signs or warnings or something..."

Peter shrugged. "No idea. I've never been down there. But I really would feel better if you let someone show you around for your first visit." When she would have resisted, he hurried on. "Please, Sophia. Promise me."

Seeing the earnest look in his eyes, Sophia sighed and gave in. "Fine, I'll see if I can find one of them."

Relief caused his shoulders to relax. "Thank you."

She leaned over and ruffled his already messy mohawk until he batted at her hands. "You're welcome," she told him with a short grin. "I think I'm going to go track one of them down, but later? I'm going to hunt down you and Josie and we're going to do something fun and not at all aspida-like. Okay?"

"Sounds good to me."

Sophia stood. "Awesome. I'll see you later."

She hadn't even made it to the door when it opened and Dion strode in. "Ah! Sophia, I was actually coming to ask Peter if he knew where you were."

That news didn't relieve her. Though she'd been told they were going to give her a few days, she was afraid he was coming to foist some head librarian business on her. "You were?" she asked suspiciously.

"Of course! I know you enjoy the library and, now that you're permitted on level six, I thought you might like a tour of it." Her mood improved at that and she exchanged a grin with Peter. Dion saw and looked between them, his brow furrowed. "Why is that funny?"

"Because we were just talking about that," Sophia answered.

Peter added, "And I was telling her she should get one of you to take her for her first visit."

"Ah! So I've arrived at just the right moment. Assuming, of course, you were on your way to find one of us?" Dion asked with a bright smile.

"Pretty much," Sophia confirmed.

"Then I would be happy to take you and answer any questions you might have about it."

"Sounds good to me." She turned back to Peter. "There, I'm keeping my promise," she teased.

"Good. Then maybe you'll stay out of trouble," he told her, feigning a stern look. He even wagged a chiding finger at her which brought another smile to her lips.

"Not likely. Bye, Peter."

"Good bye, Peter," Dion added.

"Bye," Peter said, waving at them before he turned back to his computer and dove into his world of zeroes and ones.

Sophia just smiled and went with Dion, excited about the tour to come.

Chapter 21

Dion stopped when they reached the door leading down to the deepest level of the library. She was all but vibrating with eagerness, wanting to see not only the books on sorcery, but itching to find the right book on the right poison. When Dion hesitated, she drew her attention away from the door and cocked her head. "Is something wrong?"

He offered her a smile and shook his head. "No, not wrong, but before we go in here, I want to ensure you're aware of a few things."

If one more person warned her about level six, she was going to scream. As it was, part of her was terrified about stepping through that door, almost afraid the books were going to jump off shelves and attack her. Unrealistic, she knew, and she'd even been told they weren't sentient or anything, but so many warnings led to her imagination running wild. Still, she summoned her patience and asked, "What things?"

"First, I'm not sure you're aware, but you are now one of only four people who have the security access to even get through this door."

Sophia nodded. "The heads of the three factions and aspida, right?"

"Precisely," he agreed. "And you're the only one who can get to the eighth level. You should also be very careful when you're entering your passcode. Since we take security very seriously here, we've implemented a few measures that are considered overkill or unnecessary in most systems. The most relevant being that if you enter your passcode incorrectly twice, an alarm will sound through the entire Athenaeum and the library will lock down."

Her eyes widened. "Oh wow. Yeah, most places would consider that overkill, but I get it for this place." And it made her very happy that she'd given up after only a single try when she was down here before. Being locked in the library and putting the Athenaeum on red alert would have been embarrassing, not to mention difficult to explain.

"Our first priority is preserving the texts and knowledge within the library, which means nothing is overkill," he explained. "Lastly, though I'm sure you've been told that this level holds dangerous books, I need to know that you've taken those warnings seriously."

"I've heard they were dangerous," Sophia said slowly, "but I'll admit, no one's said how other than some of the information being dangerous if it gets out. I mean, I was told they weren't sentient, but...are they going to attack me or something?"

He smiled. "No, they aren't sentient," he confirmed, "but some contain spells that are dangerous to use and others, well, are spelled."

She frowned. "What do you mean, spelled?"

"Touching them incorrectly...Actually, your previous question about them attacking you would be fairly accurate. The books themselves won't attack you, but the spells placed on them will."

"Okay...And how do I know which ones are dangerous to touch?" Finding the poison that killed Erasmus was going to be a hell of a lot harder if she couldn't touch the books.

He patted her shoulder lightly. "Don't worry, it's obvious. They're either marked as spelled or kept within protective boxes to prevent accidental contact," he assured her.

"Oh, well, good." She drew in a deep breath. "Shall we?" she asked, equal parts apprehensive and excited.

"Of course. Would you care to do the honors?" he asked, motioning to the palm plate.

Silently, she stepped up and placed her palm on the screen before entering her PIN, discreetly making sure the keypad wasn't visible. It wasn't that she didn't trust Dion specifically, just that she wasn't letting herself trust anyone. Unlike the previous attempt, this time it flashed green and a soft click told her the door had unlocked. She smiled brightly at him, which caused him to chuckle and gesture her to go in.

There was no surprise when she saw yet another set of stairs. She was on level five and trying to get to level six, after all. At this rate, her legs were going to end up looking amazing. When she got to the bottom of the stairs, she stopped and stared. This level didn't resemble the others except on a superficial level. There were shelves, yes, but they weren't jammed as closely together, nor were they as full. She wandered a few steps further into the room and, on the second row of shelves, saw an ornate wooden box, covered in black lacquer and gold-painted words, but not in a language she knew. She pointed to it as she glanced back to Dion. "Is this...?"

"One of the books we were just talking about? Yes, it is," he said. "None of the boxes are identical, but be assured that a box means to handle carefully. They have instructions on how to safely handle the contents written on them."

That explained the paint, but also meant she was going to have to start studying new languages, and quickly. It was doubtful anyone here would find that unusual, either, which meant she could ask for help. But that could wait for later.

"Not all the books down here are spelled or speak of sorcery and forgotten magics," Dion said as he led her through the room. "Some simply hold information that others have tried to bury. Truths that would change the course of history or upset things that are widely believed to be fact. Both in the human world and the Arcane."

"I'm almost afraid to ask what sort of things," she murmured as she looked at one of the books as they passed by. It was gorgeous. Large, no doubt heavy, it was bound in leather that was well-worn on the edges, the gilded words only partially legible as the gold had flaked in places.

"You'll learn about them in time," he promised, "but for now, just look around, familiarize yourself with things."

Sophia was certainly going to familiarize herself, but not when she had company. Still, this was a treasure trove to a history buff or bibliophile, and she was both. She stopped at a shelf full of books that had familiar names on them. "Anne Boleyn? Rasputin? What are..." The question died off as she caught sight of another name. Though her specialty was Greece, especially ancient Greece, she loved myths and folklore—whether based on truth or not—and pretty much everyone had heard of this woman. "Morgana Le Fay? Like *the* Morgana Le Fay?" she asked. Her hands lifted and moved toward the book, only to stop short as she wondered if it was dangerous to touch.

Dion chuckled. "Yes, as in King Arthur. That's her journal. And yes, she was a witch. All of the books on that shelf are journals of the Arcane," he answered as he led her to a new section, this one heavy on

Greek writing. "These should be to your liking. Greek histories. The *real* Greek histories," he said, resting his elbow lightly on the shelf. He smiled encouragingly. "Why don't you take a look at one of them?"

It might not be a part of her grand plan, but her interest was definitely piqued. All too excited, she reached out for the closest book to her, thrilled when she saw the words 'Trojan War' on the cover. When her fingers closed on the worn leather cover, pain shot through her. As the book slipped from her fingers and a scream tore from her throat, she realized she hadn't used her threat spell that morning. It was her last thought before the pain faded and everything went black.

Sophia was aware of soft voices nearby and a gentle warmth surrounding her, yet her body felt heavy. Her head was pounding and she tried to lift a hand to her temple, but her arm barely twitched. Mind fuzzy, it took her a minute to crack her eyes open. It took another minute for them to focus. She was surrounded by three concerned faces—Heather, Sergei, and Peter—and a single angry one—Lucas. The voices stopped as she blinked at them and tried to figure out what they were all doing in her room.

"Sophia? Are you okay?" her mom asked, but the words sounded like she was underwater.

"Mmm...Head hurts," she mumbled, her tongue thick, her mouth dry. "Did I drink too much last night?" Sergei and Lucas exchanged a look which had her frowning. "What?" Keeping her eyes open took too much effort, so she let them slide shut.

Hands rested on her hand and shoulder and she heard someone whispering in some form of Greek she couldn't quite make out. The gentle warmth returned, beginning at the hands and spreading outward. Her headache eased up some and she was able to open her eyes once more. This time she was able to recognize that she wasn't in her bedroom, but in the clinic. More, she realized just how dry her mouth was. "Water," she whispered.

Peter stepped away while her mom took her free hand. When her cousin returned, he placed a straw at her lips. She sipped greedily, but Peter took it away entirely too soon. "I don't want you getting sick," he explained when she made a soft sound of protest.

"What happened? Why am I in the clinic?"

"What's the last thing you remember?" Lucas asked, his voice surprisingly gentle.

Sophia stopped to consider. She remembered the funeral and being tapped to replace Erasmus. She remembered being angry at how everyone was staring at her. She remembered visiting Peter and Dion joining them. After that, everything was a little fuzzy. "Going to see Peter. His dad coming in, offering to show me level seven. But what happened?" No one answered for a minute, which had her heartbeat quickening. "Guys? Someone tell me what happened."

"You were in level six and touched a spelled book," Sergei said slowly. "It hit you with a blast of magic, which is why you feel like you do, though you were actually very lucky."

Her jaw dropped. "I did what? How? And how am I lucky?"

"You're lucky because Dion got you help as quickly as possible down on that level. You're lucky because..." He trailed off, not quite meeting her gaze.

"Because that book has killed people," Lucas said flatly. "What in the hell were you thinking? You have to be careful on level six. We've all warned you that it's dangerous. Did you think we were joking?" he demanded.

Sophia's eyes widened at his outburst. "Wait a minute, you're blaming *me*? I'm not the one who has books that kill people!"

"Technically, you are," he said, folding his arms over his chest.

She started to shoot back a retort before she realized that he was right. As aspida, she was responsible for all the books in the Athenaeum, including the dangerous ones. "Maybe, but I'm sure there's a good reason why I touched that book," she told him, the headache making her more surly than usual, so the words came out snappish.

Lucas clenched his jaw but said nothing else.

"Sweetheart...let's just focus on you for now," Heather said, glancing briefly at Lucas before she focused on her daughter. "How are you feeling right now?"

"My head hurts and my body feels like it's being weighed down. I also have the world's worst cottonmouth," Sophia admitted.

Peter stepped forward again and offered her more water. She drank until he took it away and offered her a faint smile. "I'm glad you're okay," he told her quietly.

She returned the smile, though it was more a twitch of her lips. "Me too." She closed her eyes and took several deep breaths before opening them and focusing on Sergei. "I am okay, right?"

Sergei scratched at the scruff on his chin as he studied her intently. "I'd like to do one more round of healing, but then you can go so long as you get plenty of rest, drink plenty of fluids, and have a good meal in the next hour or so. I'm good, but I'm honestly shocked you made it to me."

"The way I feel, I'm not going to be doing anything but getting plenty of rest," she muttered.

He smiled faintly and moved back to her side. "Just relax," he told her as he again placed his hands on her arm and shoulder and began pouring healing magic into her again. When the warmth came again, she felt her headache ease further, almost disappearing. By the time he was done, she felt like she could move, too, though she wouldn't be running any sprints. "How do you feel now?"

"I think you are currently my favorite person in the world," she told him sincerely. She flashed a quick smile at first her mom, then Peter. "Sorry."

Peter just rolled his eyes and grinned while Heather laughed softly and shook her head. "No need. I'm still your favorite mom."

"Yes, yes you are." She looked back to Sergei. "So I can go now?"

"Sure can. Though if you start feeling bad again, or have any new symptoms, I want you to let me know as soon as possible," Sergei said.

Sophia frowned and patted at her pockets, relieved to feel her phone and the flash drive she'd been carrying, too paranoid to leave it in her room, even hidden. When the phone was undamaged, she felt even better. She unlocked it and handed it to him. "Add your number? I'm getting quite the collection."

"I can get you a list of everyone's numbers," Peter offered. "You really should have them, anyway."

"Oh. Yeah, I guess that's true," Sophia said, though she wasn't entirely comfortable with the reminder of her new duties. "Tomorrow, though?" she asked as she accepted her phone back from Sergei.

"Sure thing."

Sophia pushed herself slowly upright, surprised when Lucas pushed his way forward to help get her vertical. After his tirade, she figured he was going to leave her to fend for herself. "Thanks," she mumbled, confused. She wasn't quite steady on her feet, but Heather wrapped an arm around her to help stabilize her.

"I'll help you back to your room," her mom offered.

"I think I'm going to need it."

"I'll go grab some food and some water for you," Peter offered. "I could hang out, too, unless you wanted to sleep."

"I'll probably do that sooner rather than later, but hanging out sounds good," Sophia told him as she slowly made her way out of the room. Peter slipped past them and beelined for the kitchen, but she couldn't resist looking over her shoulder at Lucas. He was still watching her, but rather than anger, she saw a flash of concern on his face. It was gone as soon as he noticed her attention, replaced by his stoic expression.

It took at least twice as long as it should have for them to make it back to her room and, once there, Heather insisted on fussing and helping Sophia into bed. She bore it all with a kind of amused resignation. Her mom was worried about her, even though she wasn't a child anymore. It was a nice feeling, even if the fussing wasn't necessary. Soon she was settled and Peter had joined them, the pair ensuring she ate while they talked, deliberately keeping to easy topics. After a little while, Josie joined them, remaining until exhaustion won the battle and pulled Sophia into sleep.

Chapter 22

Since Sophia went to sleep early, it didn't surprise her when she woke several hours before dawn. Fortunately, she felt rested and mostly recovered from the day before. She took a shower and was back in her room before anyone else started to stir. After dressing, she snuck into the kitchen, pleased to see it was even too early for Agatha to be up and about. Making a pot of coffee seemed to take forever, and she mentally tried to hurry it along. One day, she just wanted one day where she didn't get odd looks. She wasn't likely to get what she wanted, though, especially after the events of the day before.

When the coffee was finally brewed, she found the largest travel mug she could and filled it before she went down to the library. She didn't even pause in the first few levels, nor did she relax until she'd opened the door down to the sixth level and was halfway down the stairs. Now there were only three people who could get to her. Hopefully, no one would realize she wasn't still sleeping for a while, giving her time to search freely. But things weren't going to be quite that simple for her.

The coffee was halfway to her lips when she reached the bottom step and got a look at the level she'd seen for the first time only the day before. A level she hadn't remembered thanks to the spell on the book she'd touched. That veil on her memory lifted abruptly, so she suddenly remembered everything. She remembered how Dion had led her here, warned her about the boxes, suggested she pick up a book. She remembered the pain, more intense than anything she'd ever experienced before.

Sophia set her cup down on the first available surface and hurried through the shelves. She found the journals she'd first been intrigued by, but continued moving until she found the Greek section. She saw the books that had been near the one she'd touched, but she didn't see anything that had Trojan War on the cover. Fueled by a desire, a *need*, to figure out what had happened, she started looking at the boxes. Unwilling to have a repeat of the day before, she was careful when she cracked open the lids of box after box, just enough to see the covers within. It took time and more than a dozen boxes before the right words stared back at her.

Cautiously, she lifted the lid a little more, getting a better look at the book that had, quite literally, attacked her. This definitely wasn't where this book had been before. It wasn't even in the same section. A quick glance at the visible words on surrounding books and tablets told her this section wasn't historical, but dealt with what she decided to call spells of mass destruction. So why was a book on the Trojan War here? It made sense to ensure a dangerous book was in a box, safe from accidental handling, sure, but to move it to a new section? Was someone just too lazy to move this box to the correct location, or was someone trying to hide it? None of the people with access to this room struck her as particularly lazy, but neither did she know them very well. Still, the thought that this was done deliberately terrified her, especially after Erasmus's horrible death.

She closed the box and walked robotically back to where she'd left her coffee. She sat on the stairs and sipped while she thought. Only three people besides herself had access to this room—as far as she knew, anyway—which made her suspect list very short. Though Dion had been with her, she had a hard time imagining her cousin, as understanding and nice as he was, orchestrating any of this. And Nick? She hadn't spent much time with him since they'd arrived at the Athenaeum, but it hadn't seemed like he had a mean bone in his body. Lucas...he ran hot and cold so much she didn't know what was going on in his head, but he had been nearby for both the linen closet and fire incidents. She didn't want to believe he could be responsible, but there was no way she could rule him out. She couldn't rule any of them out.

"Screw this," she muttered, taking another drink before she pushed to her feet. Sitting here mulling over things without all the facts wasn't going to get her anywhere. Besides, she was here for a purpose. Determined, she moved through the shelves, fingers itching to pick up some of the books she saw, but she wasn't going to let herself get distracted. She was here to figure out what had killed Erasmus so she could find his murderer. She wasn't going to be selfish. Unfortunately, there wasn't a book called *Ye Olde Poisons,* so it wasn't an easy hunt. The fact that she only spoke a few of the languages that these books were written in didn't help matters, either.

There were a few books which looked promising, and a couple even mentioned poisons, but none fit everything she knew about what had been used on Erasmus. One would take a while to kill, another would cause bleeding from beneath the nails, but none mentioned magic. Still, her search wasn't a total loss. She came across a spell in one of the books that looked like it could come in handy. So far, no one had actually attacked her directly, but if her luck continued as it was, someone would eventually come after her. If and when that happened, knowing how to create a magical shield could potentially save her life. Though she wasn't sure how she was going to practice it without letting someone else know she had learned it. She started to take a picture of the spell before she remembered what Penny had said about the computers. Nothing connected to the internet or outside world had anything about the Athenaeum on it, which probably included sorcery, too. Making a mental note to start carrying a small notebook with her, she sat down and worked on memorizing the Latin.

Sophia had been so focused on her tasks that she didn't realize how much time had passed until her stomach growled loudly. She pulled out her phone to check the time, only to receive a text from her mom asking if she was going to join them for dinner. After sending back an affirmative answer, she replaced the book she'd been studying and started for the stairs. Before she could step on the first one, she decided to cast the threat sensing spell. It was almost a relief to feel the now familiar tingle against her skin and not something worse.

Unfortunately, that relief was short-lived. As she got closer to the dining room, the sensations from the spell grew stronger. By the time she actually reached the room, it felt like her skin was crawling. It wasn't painful, but it was the most awkward and uncomfortable sensation she'd ever experienced. She fought not to shudder or rub her arms, especially when several pairs of eyes turned in her direction. She forced a smile, made a mental note of who was there, and started for the chair next to her mom. Dion intercepted her, his expression worried. "Sophia...are you okay? Sergei told me he'd released you, but I wanted to check for myself."

"I'm fine," Sophia assured him. "A little tired, but Sergei's healing was awesome."

"Oh, good. I was so worried when you touched that book," Dion said, sighing in relief. "I'm so sorry you were hurt. I don't know how that happened," he said with such sincerity it was hard not to believe him.

"Seriously, Dion, I'm okay," she told him again, her voice softer.

He nodded and patted her shoulder gently. "Good, good. I'll let you eat now. I just wanted to check on you."

"Thanks," she said before she joined her mom.

"You okay, sweetheart?" Heather asked quietly.

"Yeah, I'm fine," Sophia told her. Her mom gave her a questioning look, no doubt wanting to know what Sophia had been doing all day, but Sophia didn't want to worry her. Yes, she could trust her mom, absolutely, but she also had entirely too much going on. Sophia did too, but that couldn't be helped at this point.

Realizing Sophia wasn't going to say anything more, Heather motioned to the people across the table from them. "Have you met?"

Two women and one man sat there. One of the women looked to be in her thirties with blonde hair. The other was a little younger, with dark hair and eyes. The man was dark complected with short brown hair. All were strangers to Sophia. She'd seen them around, but that was it. She shook her head and offered them a quick smile. "Not yet."

"This is Catherine. She's a venator. Morgan and Joshua are both guards," Heather told her, motioning to each person in turn.

"Hi. Nice to meet all of you," Sophia said, aware that this was her first time meeting new people as their boss, at least technically.

They all smiled and offered friendly greetings, with Morgan asking, "How are you liking the Athenaeum so far?"

Sophia tried hard not to laugh. "It's definitely interesting, though my introduction to it hasn't been exactly...smooth," she admitted.

"No, I suppose it hasn't. Things will settle down soon though," Morgan promised.

"I hope so," Sophia murmured. "I do want to get to actually know everyone at some point, too. Like more than just names."

"You'll get there," Joshua said with a shrug. "You've been here less than a week and your attention has been focused on your grandfather. No one blames you for that."

It made her feel better for him to say that. They ate with only casual conversations for a while before Nick walked up to her, accompanied by two young girls. Twins, about four or five, she assumed, but she was horrible with judging ages of kids. They were cute kids, though, with silky blonde hair, big blue eyes, and shy smiles.

"Sophia...My girls wanted to meet you," Nick told her with a smile, hands resting on the girl's shoulders. "This is Emily and Marley." And from his tone, the way he looked at them, he was completely in love with his daughters.

Sophia, on the other hand, was a little scared of kids. The younger they were, the more terrified they made her. Still, she couldn't not return their smiles. "Hi Emily, hi Marley."

Speaking almost in unison, they softly told her hello. She was a little surprised they spoke English until she realized they'd probably been raised speaking at least two languages. It was common enough in many countries, and in a place like the Athenaeum, it was almost guaranteed.

"They live here, too?" Sophia asked Nick, surprised.

He nodded. "They do, half the time, anyway. We don't want them growing up entirely underground, so half the time they—and Carla and I—stay at the estate. It's fairly normal for children of the Athenaeum."

"Huh. Makes sense." And it made her realize she hadn't seen the sun since she first boarded the plane to Greece. She was going to need to go topside pretty soon. Maybe she'd take Lucas up on his offer and do double duty by also trying to feel out whether he was guilty.

"It's time for these two to get a bath before bed, so we'll get out of your hair," Nick told her.

"Okay. Bye guys," Sophia said, waving to the twins.

"Bye," they responded, again in unison, in their sweet little voices as their father led them away.

The rest of dinner passed uneventfully, and Sophia stayed until everyone had cleared out but for her mom. She had tried to pay attention to the threat spell, but it was hard to tell just when it had lessened to a manageable level. Or rather, who had left just before it did.

"I'm going to go," Sophia said, kissing her mom's cheek before she got to her feet.

"Me too," Heather said. "Ray wanted to spend a little more time catching up."

Something in her mom's tone made her grin. "Catching up, huh?" she teased, but Heather only rolled her eyes.

"Friends, Sophia," Heather chided. "Ray has always been a good friend, and no one will ever replace your father."

As Sophia walked away, she thought about how sad and simultaneously sweet that was. Because of that, she didn't know whether she wished for a love like the one Heather and Greg had shared, or wished to never experience it.

Both ways could be agony.

Chapter 23

It wasn't late enough to turn in, and Sophia hadn't accomplished nearly as much as she would have liked, so she decided to keep working. She didn't head back down to the library, but made her way to the clinic. Sergei hadn't been at dinner, and no one would think twice about her going to see him after the incident the day before.

His door was open, but she still rapped on the wood as she stuck her head in. "Sergei? You have a minute?"

"Sophia. Yes, of course. Come in. Are you feeling okay?" he asked, turning toward her from where he sat at his desk.

She didn't answer right away, but shut the door and leaned against the exam table. The one she'd just laid on the day before. "I'm actually feeling pretty good for someone who's lucky to be alive," she joked.

Concern faded to relief. "Good. I'm glad I could help. But if you're feeling okay, what can I do for you?"

"I...The poison. I was wanting to know if you'd found anything."

That relief shifted to failure as Sergei shook his head. "Unfortunately not. I've looked through every medical and toxicology book I have access to and haven't been able to find anything. I promise, though, I've been trying."

"I know," she assured him. "I am well aware that people here knew him much longer than I did, and that you loved him, too. I've been looking myself, especially since I was granted access to level six. Have you looked there?"

He shook his head again. "As you know, I'm not allowed access without an escort, and once we realized it was poison, Erasmus wasn't in any condition to take me."

"Damn. I assumed that was the case, but I wanted to make sure. I've been looking for the…the things that happened to him as he died, but is there something else I should be looking for?"

"That's actually a good start," Sergei told her with a quick smile. "Also focus on slow-acting poisons. He started getting sick about a month before he actually died. It was gradual, too. At first he—we, actually—thought it was just the natural signs of aging, but soon we realized it wasn't anything that simple. When I realized it was poison, we tried an antidote called mithridate that supposedly can cure almost any poison." He grimaced. "Or it was supposed to. Not long before Erasmus got sick, another man was poisoned, and that antidote wasn't able to save him. Though, to be fair, a woman was poisoned at the same time and we were able to save her, but it took the antidote, my magic, and the magic of a powerful healing witch."

Sophia nodded slowly. "I'll keep that in mind." She straightened. "I'll let you know if I find anything."

"And I'll do the same," he promised as she opened the door and slipped outside.

She didn't get far, nearly running face-first into Lucas. "Holy crap," she said as she caught herself by planting both hands on his chest. Once she'd regained her balance, she took a step back and glared at him. She was still annoyed with him after the way he'd treated her in the clinic yesterday, so this wasn't exactly a welcome interlude. "What the hell, Lucas? Lurk much?"

"We need to talk," he said, looking unaffected by her ire.

"Well, I have things I need to do, so talk and walk," Sophia said, skirting around him and striding down the hallway.

Though he fell into step beside her, Lucas didn't say a word as they went down the stairs, passed through the common room, down another hallway, and into her room. She was a little surprised he'd actually followed her into her bedroom, but it wasn't like he hadn't been there before. Hell, he'd seen her naked in her bedroom. More, it didn't seem like he really had the social limits most people did.

"What do you want, Lucas?" Sophia asked as she grabbed her suitcase and tossed it on the bed. After opening it, she started to shove her clothes inside.

Lucas closed the door and turned toward her, arms crossed over his chest. "I heard what you said to Sergei. You—" He paused and frowned. "Why are you packing?"

Hoping she could distract him from the conversation with Sergei, she shrugged and continued what she was doing. "Why does anyone pack? To move from one location to another."

"And what location are you moving to?" he asked suspiciously.

"This isn't my room anymore, now is it?" Sophia asked sarcastically. "Aren't I supposed to be moving into the aspida's room?"

She glanced at him in time to see his obvious surprise. "You are...but are you sure you're ready?"

His tone was gentle, which she hated. She never knew what he was thinking, and she didn't want to let him in. She stopped and turned toward him, mirroring his pose. "Why do you care if I'm ready or not? I'm just a stupid girl who touched a dangerous book, right?"

He flinched at that. Actually flinched. Sophia barely managed to hide her surprise at the reaction. "That was out of line," he admitted.

She snorted softly and went back to packing. It wasn't like she'd brought much, so she was almost done. "You think?"

"You almost died, Sophia. I'm supposed to make sure that people are safe in the Athenaeum. I don't take it well when I fail."

She frowned and shook her head as she tossed the last of her clothes into her bag. "You weren't there, and isn't it the curators who deal with the books, not you?"

"Mostly, but that's not the point."

"Mmm." She slung her backpack over one shoulder and reached for her suitcase. Lucas moved quicker than she would have thought a man of his size could move and picked it up. She arched a brow at him, but he simply walked to the door, opened it, and started out. "Hey, where are you going?" she asked indignantly, since he had her clothes.

"To your room," he said without looking back. He didn't stop until he reached the room that had been Erasmus's only days before. To her surprise, he waited for her to catch up before he pushed the door open, motioning for her to go inside.

Sophia hesitated for a moment before she forced her feet to move forward. The room looked identical to the last time she'd seen it, other than the bedding being different. She stared at the bed as Lucas followed her in and closed the door. Though she'd decided to take her rightful place in this room, she wasn't sure how she was going to be able to sleep in the same bed he'd died in.

"Are you okay?" Lucas asked as she set the suitcase down.

"I...is there any way to get the mattress changed or something?" she whispered.

"It's already been taken care of."

Her head jerked around and she looked at him in shock. "What?"

He shrugged and walked to the desk chair, sinking down into it. "I thought that you'd have an easier time of it if the entire bed was replaced."

"Oh. Thanks." That made it easier for her to cross to the bed and sit down, the backpack beside her.

Rather than acknowledging the gratitude, Lucas cocked his head and studied her. He let a full minute pass before he said, "As I said before...I heard what you said to Sergei."

Damn. She'd hoped he'd be too distracted to remember that. "Yeah? And?"

"And what do you know about it? How do you know your grandfather was poisoned?" he demanded. It was clear he was trying to temper his mood, but felt too strongly to hide it entirely.

"Why in the hell should I trust you, Lucas?" Sophia shot back. "Why should I trust anyone here other than my mom?"

He got to his feet and started toward her with slow steps. "One, I'm the head of security here. If someone is poisoning anyone—especially our aspides—then I need to know so I can investigate. Second, you don't strike me as the sort of person to sleep with people you don't feel *something* for, regardless of the circumstances. Third, I've been doing my best to keep you safe, Sophia. I let you out of that linen closet. I went back to find the fire you said started in the library. I was there when you woke up after touching that book," he said, coming to a stop just a foot from her, close enough to touch. "What in the hell have I done to make you think you can't trust me, at least a little?"

Rather than remain on the bed with him looking down at her, Sophia stood. She almost rethought the action when it put them chest to chest. Mostly. He did have almost a foot on her. "First, liking someone, thinking they're attractive, doesn't mean I trust them. Second, none of those actually clear you. As head of security, you could get around some security features others couldn't, I'm sure. And yeah, you were there during all those incidents, but that doesn't mean you were innocent. Maybe you were just trying to manipulate me or the situation. How in the hell am I supposed to know? I've known you for all of a *week*. I don't know shit about you but your name and position."

Lucas let out a low growl of frustration. "Look, there's a spell I can teach you. It helps to identify threats."

"Yeah, I know it." And it only just occurred to her that it had faded. That or there were zero threats to her, which she doubted.

That caught him aback. "You do? How?"

She glanced back to the bed. "Erasmus taught me," she murmured.

"Well, good. Then cast it. You'll see I'm no danger to you. Sophia...I want to find out who poisoned the best man I've ever known," he said quietly. "That and keep you safe."

For some reason she believed him, but she wasn't going to take chances with her life. She kept her gaze on his as she cast the spell. Only the slightest tingle came in response, but she'd felt that when alone with Erasmus, and he had been no threat to anyone. But just because he wasn't currently a threat didn't necessarily mean she could trust him. "And I still don't know anything about you," she reminded him.

He sighed, frustration in every inch of his body. "Lucas Tennant. Forty-six. Former Marine, recruited just days after I left the service. Gargoyle. Been head of the nasaru for almost three years."

So she'd been right about him being a gargoyle. Cool. "Wait, Marine? But you sound Greek." And he was also the second ex-Marine. But it did make sense that they might recruit from the military or police.

He gave an easy shrug. "I've been living here for the last twenty-two years. I soaked up the accent."

She nodded and studied his face, his body language. Between his words and the effects of the spell, she decided to give him the benefit of the doubt.

"You can't say anything," she warned him. "Not to anyone. I mean it. When Erasmus told me what had happened to him, he told me not to tell anyone, not even my mom. Only four people in the Athenaeum know he was poisoned. Sergei, you, me...and the one who poisoned him."

"And what exactly is it you know?"

Sophia sighed sadly and sank back down to the bed. "I don't know much more than that. Sergei thinks it was some sort of topical poison, something mixed with magic because it wasn't affected by any of his healing spells or some mythical antidote. He hasn't been able to find the poison, though, but he didn't have access to level six or seven, either."

"No, but I do," Lucas said, stepping back to retake the chair. "Why didn't he ask me to see what I could find?"

"Because he didn't know who to trust, Lucas. If it was something only found on level six, then there are only three suspects," she pointed out.

He cursed and his hands clenched into fists, his knuckles turning stark white. "That's logical," he finally said, "but what if it's not on level six?"

"It's a magical poison. Where else would it be?"

"Okay, fair point, to an extent. And just because someone can't get down there on their own doesn't mean they weren't down there. They could have had an escort," he pointed out.

"True," she allowed. "And I've been thinking about all of that. I've also started searching level six. So far I've found some poisons that match some of the qualities, but none that match them all. I intend to keep looking, too."

"Good. I'll help."

"Lucas—"

"I'll help," he said in a tone that allowed no argument. "He was your grandfather, I get that, but Sophia...he was my best friend, even if he was old enough to be my grandfather, too."

Sophia couldn't help but soften, then cave. "Okay, but we have to be careful."

"I agree. And the fewer people who know we're looking, the better. Right now, the murderer probably thinks he or she got away with it." A slow smile curved Sophia's lips, which had him frowning in confusion. "Why are you smiling?"

"Something Erasmus and I talked about. He thought the murderer killed him for his job."

It took a beat before Lucas began to smile, too. "Well, that failed, now didn't it?"

"It definitely did." And for the first time since the ceremony that had named her as the aspida, she was happy for that fact. "Okay, we keep it between us and update Sergei when necessary. I've also got a flash drive I'm making notes on. I'm going to disable the wi-fi on my laptop, too, so we have a safe computer to use."

"Good. We should also make notes if and when anyone does anything that seems suspicious to us."

"That's going to be more you than me. I don't know anyone here well enough to know if someone's acting off or not."

"Good point."

"Also, I found a spell when I was looking for the poison earlier. It should come in handy, but in order to practice it I sort of need help, so it's actually kind of a good thing that we're on the same page now."

"What spell is that?"

"A shielding spell. The murderer may have gone with poison the first time, but I've already been locked in a linen closet, had someone somehow make me think I was seeing a fire and..."

"And?" Lucas prompted when she fell silent.

"I don't think it was an accident that I touched that book," she admitted.

He leaned forward and frowned. "What do you mean?"

"I went back down there today, and I remembered going down there with Dion. The book I touched was sitting out on a shelf. It wasn't in a box, there weren't any warnings, nothing. But this morning? It was in a different place and in a box. At first I thought, okay, someone wanted to make sure no one else got hurt by this book, but then I started thinking, and now..."

"Now it seems like someone tried to hide it," Lucas said with a nod. "At first glance, it would look like Dion's guilty, but what if that's what someone wanted us to think?"

"Damn," Sophia whispered, running a hand over her face. "I hadn't considered that. I'd wondered if it was Dion, but I hadn't gone into real conspiracy theory stuff."

"We'll figure it out," he promised. "But as to the spell, I'll help, if you'll agree to a few conditions."

Suspiciously, she eyed him. "What conditions?"

His lips twitched. "First, we practice safely."

"Oh, agreed, without question," she said with a nod. "I don't want either of us hurt, and I've never done sorcery before, other than the threat spell."

"Good. Second...well, I assume you're a halfling? Elf and owl?"

"Yeah, which is why I need all the practice I can get. Shapeshifting and some minor healing ability doesn't really give me experience with practicing magic. And I don't think being able to sense the emotions of birds is going to save me, either."

He nodded. "That's the second thing. I want to teach you a few more spells. You're entitled to learn any spell you want, but there are a couple I think should be priorities."

"Don't gargoyles have even less active magic than elves, though?"

"Yeah," he confirmed, "but I'm also nasaru. I've made sure to learn spells that can keep myself and my charges alive. And I want to teach you some of them."

"I can also agree to that. I'm liking this spell stuff. Though I do need to start working hardcore on learning some new languages."

"Talk to Peter. He's got lists of just about everything. Who knows what language, who's been in what country, who knows what weapons, who has what skills."

"That makes sense. And will be good for me to get, anyway. I need to get to know these people."

"You do. Just don't put too much pressure on yourself. It'll come."

"I hope so." Because right now she was still worried that she wasn't qualified for this job. " Any other conditions?"

The smile he gave her worried her. "Just one. You start training in the gym."

"Excuse me?" Sophia asked, instantly offended. "Are you trying to say something? Because you didn't seem to have any complaints the other night."

He chuckled and shook his head. "No, no complaints." His gaze roamed over her, masculine approval naked in his eyes. "No complaints at all," he murmured. Shaking himself out of it, he added, "Fight training. Because you're right. If someone does want you gone, too, they aren't going to repeat themselves. They would have the entire Athenaeum hunting for them if two aspides were killed by poison. It's already tricky enough that we had a death and a near death by poison."

Her nose wrinkled. "Fighting? I'm not really..." She sighed and fell back on the bed. "Yeah, okay. It's a good idea. I don't like the idea of fighting, but I like the idea of dying even less. But do you think those other poisonings were the same one used on Erasmus?"

"That isn't going to happen," he all but growled. "And I'm not sure. Poisons aren't my forte, but it's possible. They could have been testing it. And with all that in mind, I only want you learning from myself or Steven."

"You trust him?"

"With my life. But I don't fully trust him with yours, so say nothing about the poisoning."

"I hate lying, but...okay."

"I should get going, but before I do, there's one other thing you should know."

Sophia lifted her head so she could see him. "If you have to," she grumbled. She was getting tired of revelations.

"After I left you in your room after the fire incident, I went back to the library."

She scrambled to a sitting position. "And?"

"There weren't any signs of fire, which you knew. No smoke, no char, but there were traces of magic."

"What sort of magic?"

"I couldn't tell that from the spell I used, but my best guess? It was an illusion spell."

"Someone intentionally did that to me? Seriously? Someone here is a major asshole."

"They are," he agreed, "but we'll find them." To her surprise, he walked over to her and touched her cheek lightly. "Just be safe for now."

"I will," she murmured as he left the room. Too bad keeping safe was looking like an impossible task.

Chapter 24

After Lucas had gone, Sophia looked around the room that was now hers. No one had removed the personal touches Erasmus had added, and she found she had mixed feelings on that. It made her wonder why all the aspides were required to take the same bedroom. It felt a little wrong. Maybe it would be different if the previous occupant hadn't been her grandfather—and murdered—but she felt a little like she was intruding.

She got up and moved to the wardrobe, happy to see that his clothes had been taken out, at least. She spent all of five minutes putting her clothes away and setting her laptop on the desk. Before she forgot, she opened it and turned the wi-fi off. She still felt paranoid, but it was the best she could do without help.

Peeking through the other door, she discovered she had been right, it was a bathroom. Even better, it had a huge tub. The one she'd used the other day was nice, but this one was deep enough and long enough that she could truly stretch out and get comfortable. There was a shower, too, nicer than the one she'd had back in the States. It was tempting, very tempting, to make use of the tub, but she was honestly so tired she was afraid she'd fall asleep and drown. Instead, she changed and got ready for bed before returning to the bedroom. Except once there, looking at the bed, she wasn't sure she was ready for sleep. Even if the entire bed had been changed, it still felt weird. Instead, she roamed the edge of the room, looking at the various books and wall hangings.

Erasmus had some very interesting books in his room. Personal favorites, she was guessing. A few were modern, or close to it, but a few were old. They all dealt with language, history, and magic, though, except for a copy of a Stephen King book. That one surprised her. She wouldn't have guessed Erasmus was into horror novels.

She moved past the bookshelf and to a framed map of the ancient world. As she did, she heard a soft grinding sound. She jumped back and her eyes widened as she saw that part of the wall had shifted to reveal a small alcove carved right into the stone. "Holy shit," she whispered, staring and hoping that nothing was going to jump out at her. True, it wasn't a large space, no bigger than a microwave, but there were all sorts of dangerous things that were small. The fact that it had opened apparently on its own only made it that much alarming.

Once her heart rate had begun to slow, she realized that the alcove wasn't empty. There was a book sitting in it. She crept closer, noting that it was leather bound and worn. Cautiously, she reached inside and drew the book out, letting out a sigh of relief when nothing happened. Curious now, she undid the leather thong that held the book closed and opened the cover. In the center of the first page, she saw her grandfather's name. On the second, she saw Greek words in what must have been his handwriting. This was his journal.

Sniffling, Sophia took the journal back to the bed and crawled onto it, her eyes devouring the words. The first entry was written in 1780. While Erasmus might have had other journals in his lifetime, this one was begun on the day he was selected as aspida. Instantly absorbed, she forgot all about the troubles in the Athenaeum. For the next few hours, she did nothing but read. She devoured the words detailing his surprise at being chosen as aspida, but how he wanted to do justice to the title and his ancestors who had also held the title. How he wanted to ensure he did the best he could for the other people in the Athenaeum. She read about the changes he made, such as cataloging the contents of the library on computers when they'd been invented. About some of the missions he'd sent people on—or went on himself—to retrieve important books or relics.

It wasn't until she reached a page dated almost twenty-four years ago that she surfaced, however briefly. He hadn't written about the mission her father was going on, not until it was done and his son was dead. She wiped the back of her hand over her cheeks to clear them of tears as her eyes slid over the physical proof of his grief. A grief that was heightened when her mom had decided to leave not just the Athenaeum, but the country. A soft sob broke free as he wrote of his anguish when he realized he wouldn't get to meet his grandchild. It was painfully clear that Erasmus had loved not just his son, but Heather as well. He'd even loved Sophia herself, despite never meeting her. It made her wish yet again that she'd had more time with him. Not so he could teach her magic or about the Athenaeum, but so he could teach her about himself.

After that, she had to take several minutes to compose herself so she could go on. Gradually the grief faded, but it didn't disappear. Her parents were mentioned now and again. So was she. He'd made sure he'd known where they had ended up. But most of the entries revolved around the goings on in the Athenaeum. The last few pages were the most concerning. He wrote about feeling poorly. At first he'd feared that age was simply catching up with him, but he'd performed several spells on himself and had Sergei do the same, until they'd realized it was poison. Sophia focused more intently on the words, hoping to glean some small clue that he hadn't gotten a chance to share with her. Unfortunately, there wasn't anything more than he'd told her.

Sophia flipped the page and her breath caught. This wasn't a journal entry. It was a letter, in English, addressed to her, and dated the day before he died. The handwriting wasn't as neat as the previous writing, nor was it as strong, which made sense. He'd barely been able to lift his hand. It did make her wonder how he was able to retrieve the journal and hide it again. She set the journal aside and went into the bathroom, splashing cold water on her face. She needed a moment before she read the letter, but she couldn't force herself to wait longer than that before reading what he'd left for her. After climbing back on the bed, she curled up against the pillows and picked the journal up once more.

Sophia,

I know it may take you a bit to find this journal, but I have no doubt that you will. I have a feeling that it will be you the Athenaeum chooses, though I'm sure others would wager on different names. If I'm correct, that means that you are now in danger. If I guessed right, and I was killed for my position, then being aspida now puts the target on your back. I want you to be careful, my flower. Before being poisoned, I would have said you could trust every person here without question, but now I don't know who can be trusted. Unfortunately, if you're going to be safe, you must discover who has done this to me, and why.

I would love to pass on all my secrets, but I must operate on the assumption that someone else could find this letter, so I cannot be straightforward. However, there is a place in the Athenaeum which could help you. This is an old place, my dear, ancient, and it holds many secrets. Some, as you surely know by now, are known to all who belong to the Athenaeum. A few are reserved only for those of us with the greatest responsibility on our shoulders. A responsibility that many of our ancestors have carried as well.

Part of me regrets that you have to deal with this now. You weren't prepared for any of it. Another part can be nothing but proud that the legacy of the Athenaeum will continue with my granddaughter. With that in mind, I will give you this advice. Be strong, be smart. You are a leader now. Take the time you need to adjust and learn, but you will need to step up. Ask questions, about the Athenaeum, about what you once believed was truth. Be firm, but fair. And remember that fair isn't the same as nice. Punishing a crime isn't nice to the criminal, but it is necessary. Above all, stand up for yourself, stand up for what is right.

Remember that I will always belong to the Athenaeum, and I will forever be proud to be your grandfather.

With all my love and best wishes for the future,
Erasmus

Sophia closed the journal and let the tears stream down her face. Weakened, literally at death's door, he'd taken the time and effort to write this to her. It meant more than she'd realized when she'd first seen the letter, and not just because he'd tried to help her in her new role. For several minutes, she allowed herself to simply cry for all the things she'd never get to say to him.

When she got control of herself again, she reopened the journal and traced her fingers lightly over the page. She frowned. He'd mentioned a place that held secrets, but he hadn't said where it was. Unfortunately, after the day she'd had, her brain was mush. If she was going to figure out where it was, it wasn't going to be tonight.

Suddenly drained, she got up and walked over to the alcove. Not wanting Erasmus's journal to get into anyone else's hands, she placed it back in its hiding place. After a moment, she retrieved the flash drive and set it on top of the journal. She lightly chewed on her lip as she tried to figure out how to get it to close again. Saying 'close' in either form of Greek did nothing, nor did Latin. She waved her hand in front of it like it had some way to detect motion. Nothing. She stepped back and frowned at it. She sighed and put her hands on her hips when the alcove suddenly slid shut once more. "Seriously? Now how the hell did I make it close? And how do I get it open again?" she muttered as she shuffled back to the bed and climbed under the covers.

Though exhaustion pulled at her, it took an hour before her mind finally quieted enough to allow her to slip into sleep. Even then, she was plagued by dreams that had her tossing and turning all night, but come morning, she didn't remember a single one.

Lucas was on a mission. Worse, he was pissed. There was a major problem in the Athenaeum. He may not be the boss, but since he was head of the nasaru and it was a security matter, it still all landed on him. So the fact that someone—or several someones—was killing and attacking people in the Athenaeum? He took it personally. He took it *very* personally.

Especially since they were threatening Sophia.

He was relieved when he didn't pass a single soul as he entered the library and went down to the sixth level. While he didn't doubt Sophia's recollection of what had happened with the book, he still had to look into it. This wasn't her area of expertise. She may know a spell or two, but she wasn't comfortable with magic and she wasn't an investigator. It was entirely possible that she missed something. Not that he was going to make that suggestion unless he had to. She seemed the sort who didn't like being viewed as less than capable. And she was probably very capable when it came to things she actually had time to learn about.

Once on the sixth level, he quickly moved through the room, en-suring he was alone. To be extra safe, he cast a quick spell which re-vealed nearby life. Nothing. The closest person was several levels above him. Reassured that there was no one to witness his search, he followed

Sophia's directions and found the box and the book she'd touched. He opened the box and narrowed his eyes. This wasn't a book he'd seen before, but since he wasn't a curator, that wasn't unheard of. And since he wasn't, he chose not to examine the book too closely at the moment. He considered taking it—box and book both—to his room until he could safely examine it, but opted against it. For one, if this had been an attack on Sophia, the absence of the book might let the culprit know someone was onto him. For another, he didn't want to risk someone finding it in his room and either touching the book or seeing him as guilty.

Unfortunately, there wasn't anything near the box to point to someone having messed with it, so he backtracked to where Sophia had said she'd originally seen the book. Here he got a little luckier. Normally, the books in this section—whether boxed or not—were spaced fairly equally. It wasn't exact, no one brought out a ruler or anything, but they kept things neat and orderly. However, in this section, they weren't quite right. It looked more like someone had hastily rearranged the books so they'd look properly placed at first glance. Lucas moved a little closer and peered carefully at the shelf. It wasn't wood like most of the levels above him, but stone. Sandstone, to be specific, which was a relatively soft rock. And this one? It had a small scratch, like one of the metal stands some of the books rested on had been moved quickly and without care.

Not satisfied despite finding proof of Sophia's claim, he went back upstairs, finding the first available computer in the library. He pulled up the security log and entered his credentials to see who had accessed the sixth level since Sophia's accident. He saw four, including his own just now and Sophia's from before she'd touched the book. Unfortunately, that meant that both the other heads had been in the sixth level, which didn't rule anyone out or point the finger at anyone.

Curious, he looked at older attempts and saw a failed attempt for a few days before. After a moment, his lips curved as he realized it was most likely Sophia. Everyone else knew that they couldn't get in, and if it had been a bad scan from one of the other heads, they would have tried again.

He closed the log and went back to his room, mulling the facts over in his head. Logically, he knew it could only be one of two people—assuming that the same person had killed Erasmus and they weren't dealing with multiple people, anyway. But Peter couldn't be ruled out, either. The blue-haired man was extremely good with computers, and if anyone was going to hack the system, he was the most likely candidate. Unless one of the witches had technology-based powers. It was possible, even likely. Still, at this point, they couldn't truly accuse anyone.

When he reached the door to his bedroom, he looked at Sophia's door, hoping that she was managing to get some rest. Not willing to disturb her if she was, he went into his room to find some sleep.

Chapter 25

WHEN SOPHIA WOKE, SHE felt expectant. She couldn't have said whether it was anticipation or dread, but it felt like something was going to happen today. It was probably silly. Just because she knew some magic didn't mean she had the ability to see the future. She was no Cassandra to be spouting prophecy. And sure, she was part owl, but stereotypes called them wise, not all-knowing.

Though part of her wanted to pull the covers over her head and stay put, she wasn't going to accomplish anything hiding in her room. So she dragged herself up and headed to the bathroom for a quick shower, unable to resist glancing at the now hidden alcove. As she showered, she replayed the words from Erasmus's journal, both the sentimental ones and the cryptic riddles. But she was no closer to figuring them out by the time she was dressed, had retrieved her flash drive, and was heading for the kitchen.

Pushing it aside when she saw the group of people gathered for breakfast, she forced a friendly smile on her lips. She knew everyone present but for one man who was standing and talking to Angela. He was about six two, leanly muscled, with bright red hair and eyes so blue she could tell the color from across the room. It was a striking combination. He wasn't her priority, though. Coffee and something light in her stomach had to come first. Fortunately, Agatha had anticipated her. Before Sophia could reach for a mug, a full cup of coffee was being pressed into her hands.

"I know you probably won't eat much, but I made you an omelet, anyway," Agatha told her with a warm smile and gentle tone. "Eat what you can, please."

Some people were so nice, so genuine, that telling them no was akin to kicking a puppy. Agatha was one of those people. Sophia didn't even try to resist, just nodded and took the offered plate along with the coffee. "I will. Thanks, Agatha."

The cook beamed at her. "You're very welcome. Enjoy." She didn't stick around to make sure Sophia ate, but instead went back to preparing food for others.

There were a couple of empty seats at the table, but none away from people, so Sophia sat beside Lucas and did her best to ignore him while she ate. She wasn't very successful, especially when she felt his eyes on her, but it was the only way she could manage to get the fluffy omelet down. Focusing on him reminded her of their conversation the night before. That and the night he'd spent in her bed. Definitely their night together. But if she allowed herself to focus on the way he'd felt inside her, the way he'd kissed her, she'd never get anything done.

Unfortunately, ignoring him only worked long enough for her to eat half her breakfast and down the entire cup of coffee. That was when he leaned in close enough for her to feel his breath against her ear as he whispered, "Are you planning on ignoring me all day, or are you just not very social in the morning?"

Sophia fought the urge to either draw away or lean closer and just stiffened her back. "Neither. I just haven't been eating much the last few days and wanted to focus on my breakfast." A half truth, at best, but he seemed to buy it.

"After you eat, we'll start your training."

She grimaced faintly, but understood the necessity. "What sort of training?" she asked, aware that the eyes of half the room were on them.

Rather than answer, Lucas inclined his head toward the redhead. "Have you met Lachlan yet?"

Her gaze shifted to the man and she shook her head. "I haven't, no. And I'm sorry about that, Lachlan," she told the man with a faint smile. "I really do need to make an effort to meet everyone. Sooner rather than later."

Lachlan grinned at her and shook his head. "It's okay. Everyone is well aware that you've been through quite a lot," he said, startling her with a Scottish accent. It really shouldn't have surprised her, given his hair and name, but with the melting pot that was the Athenaeum, there really wasn't a good way of judging someone's origins without getting to know them.

"True, but I *should* be making more of an attempt to meet people," she argued. "I'd want to do that even if I wasn't top dog."

"You'll get there," he assured her as he stood. "I need to get to work, but I'm sure we'll talk again soon."

"I'm sure we will." When he was gone, she turned back to Lucas and arched a brow questioningly.

"What?" he asked before sipping his coffee.

"What sort of training are we doing?"

"You'll see."

Sophia ground her teeth but knew better than to argue with him. In public, anyway. "Fine." She shoved her chair back and started to take her plate to the sink, but Agatha intercepted her and plucked the plate from her fingers. "Thanks, Agatha," she called to the woman, not bothering to sigh. Sophia may be aspida, but in this room, Agatha ruled. She turned back to Lucas. "Let's go."

Lucas took his time standing and taking his mug to the sink. Surprisingly, Agatha allowed him to rinse it and put it in the dishwasher. Nor did she stop him when he went to the fridge and grabbed a covered bowl. He motioned for Sophia to follow as he left the kitchen. Rather than heading for the gym, he turned to head toward the hallway that housed her own room. In fact, he stopped in front of her door, though rather than open it, he opened the one across the hall and waved her inside.

Curious, Sophia stepped inside, unsurprised to see another bedroom. It was masculine and, while it had a shelf with a couple dozen books, there weren't really any personal touches. She looked around until Lucas closed the door behind them. "Is this your room?"

"It is," he said, setting the bowl down on the nightstand before he sat on the bed.

"Why are we in your bedroom for training?" she asked suspiciously. It wasn't that she was against another round in the sheets with him—he was too skilled a lover for that—but sex was far from her top priority. It couldn't be.

"We're not going to be practicing fighting or weaponry today. You mentioned a shield spell, and wanting my help practicing it."

Sophia's interest was piqued. "And how are we going to do that in your bedroom?"

Lucas uncovered the bowl and reached inside, withdrawing a grape held between his forefinger and thumb. "With these," he told her, before he launched it at her.

She wasn't expecting that, so it hit her right between the eyes. Startled, she jerked back and blinked at him. For an instant she wanted to be angry he'd just thrown food at her, but then she realized how brilliant his idea was and grinned at him. "Nice. Even if the spell doesn't work, testing it won't hurt me."

He shook his head and popped a grape into his mouth. "Testing it *today* won't hurt you, but if you can get comfortable with the spell when grapes are the projectile, then we'll upgrade it, so to speak."

Deflating a little, she leaned back against the door. "That makes sense, though I'm not looking forward to something coming at me that can actually hurt me."

"Which is why we're starting with grapes. We won't step things up until you're ready for it," he promised.

Which all made sense. What good was a shield spell if all it would block was something as harmless as grapes? "Okay, let's do this."

Lucas transferred the bowl to his lap and sat a little straighter. "Cast the spell and let me know when you're ready."

She nodded and closed her eyes, bringing the words she'd worked so hard to memorize to mind. Slowly she spoke the Latin, struck once more how real spells didn't actually make any sense. Nothing seemed to happen and she cracked an eye open, half expecting to see some sort of shimmer in the air around her, but there was nothing. "Did it work?" she asked, opening both eyes.

Rather than reply, Lucas threw another grape at her. This one splatted against her cheek. "I would say not."

Sophia huffed softly and said the words again. Still nothing. "Try again?" she suggested, before quickly adding, "And don't aim at my face this time."

His lips ticked upward in a grin before he threw another. This one hit her left breast.

She glared at him and rested her hands on her hips. "Not funny."

"I thought it was funny," he disagreed. "When you say the spell, are you just saying it, or are you focusing on your intention?"

Erasmus had told her intention was important with magic, and she automatically thought about wanting to sense danger when she cast the threat spell. It wasn't habit, though, and she had forgotten when casting a new spell. "Of course I am," she mumbled before closing her eyes again. This time, she mentally pictured an invisible bubble around her as she said the words. This time, she felt something. It wasn't as obvious as with the threat spell and it took her a moment to realize it. There was a slight charge in the air, similar to how it felt just before a lightning storm. She opened her eyes and grinned at Lucas. "Try again."

He cocked a brow at her sudden change in demeanor, but complied. The grape still hit her—just below her right breast this time—but when it got about a foot from her it seemed to slow a little.

"Yes!" she said, jerking her fist down in victory.

"You seem entirely too happy when the grape still hit you."

"Yeah, it hit me, but did you see how it slowed? Like it was moving through water instead of air?"

He tilted his head. "I can't say I noticed that." Which was probably why he threat another fruit at her, carefully watching as it flew through the air, slowed, then hit her belly. "You're right," he murmured.

For the next hour, they continued to work on the spell. There were a few other mishaps where the shield didn't hold, but they were early on. Eventually, every grape Lucas tossed at her was slowed by the shield. At the end of the hour, the spell began stopping them entirely. Lucas called a stop when her shield had successfully stopped a dozen in a row.

Sophia was elated, despite being drained and surrounded by grapes. She grinned tiredly and took a step back to slump against the door. "It works. Finally."

"It does," Lucas agreed as he set the remainder of the grapes aside and stood. He crossed the room and scooped her up, causing her to let out a surprised squeak and grab hold of his shirt.

"What are you doing?"

"You're exhausted. You're going to lie down for a minute until you're not in danger of collapsing," he said as he gently placed her on the bed.

She started to argue, but she *was* tired. Not that she could figure out why. "I got plenty of sleep last night," she murmured as she rolled onto her side and cuddled against his pillow.

Lucas began cleaning up the grapes. "And you've been performing the same spell, over and over, for the last hour. Of course you're tired," he said matter-of-factly.

"I don't get it. How could sorcery make me tired? Shapeshifting and stuff doesn't."

He paused and glanced at her, brows arched. "You're a student. Are you telling me that sitting and studying for an hour straight doesn't leave you tired?"

"Well, no, but—"

"In addition to the cramming, you were doing *sorcery*. You know that magic isn't just about repeating the right words, don't you?"

"Yeah," she agreed with a tiny nod as her eyes drifted closed without her permission. "Erasmus said intention played a part, too."

"It does. Think of performing magic as both a mental and physical exercise, in that doing it can leave you physically and mentally drained." With the last grape cleaned up, he sat on the bed beside her. "With that in mind, we're going to alternate in your training. Magic one day, physical the next."

"Mmhmm. Sounds good," she mumbled, already half asleep.

His lips twitched. "You nap for a bit, but I'm teaching you two more spells today."

"Mmhmm. Sounds good," she repeated.

Just before she drifted off, she could have sworn she felt something warm and soft brush her forehead.

Chapter 26

Someone was shaking her.

Sophia grumbled and rolled over, turning her back on the intruder.

"Sophia, you've been asleep almost two hours. We still have work to do."

It took her a moment to recognize the speaker as Lucas. "Don't wanna," she mumbled.

"Maybe not, but you need to," he said, giving her shoulder a squeeze.

She sighed and flopped onto her back, forcing her eyes open. Immediately she saw his pale green ones, close to her own. She blinked and he eased back. "You never said what spells you were going to teach me," she said as she fought off a yawn and pushed herself upright.

"There are several that you should learn, but the two I decided were most immediately useful are one that allows you to detect when magic has been used recently, and one that allows you to see through illusions," he explained as he offered her a glass of water. "Even once we've cleared the...bad seed...from the Athenaeum, they'll be useful. Especially for our aspida."

Sophia nodded before taking several swallows of the water and setting the glass aside so she could stand. "I can see how they would be." She frowned. "The fire I saw in the library...you're sure it was an illusion?"

"I think so, yes," Lucas confirmed. "Unfortunately, I can't confirm it, but it's the only thing that really fits the situation."

"Yeah," she murmured, "but what's the point? I wasn't aspida then, and it's not like anyone could have predicted I would be." Except Erasmus had. Maybe he hadn't been a hundred percent certain, but he'd been sure enough to write it down.

"I really don't know," he admitted with a shrug. "We likely won't figure that out until we find out who's been doing all this." He hesitated a moment before he added, "Assuming that the person who killed your grandfather is the same one who cast the fire illusion."

"Don't forget the linen closet," she reminded him bitterly.

"I'm not," he said.

She glanced to him and saw his expression was dark. He really wasn't any happier about the situation than she was. Somehow, she didn't think it was all because someone was doing this under his nose. After studying his face for a long moment, she rolled her shoulders and straightened her back. "Okay. Let's do this. Teach me some magic."

He almost cracked a smile and nodded. "It's not like the shield spell," he began. "It's more like the threat spell, though neither one lasts as long as that one. The one to sense recent magic lasts only a moment, long enough to tell whether something was there or not. The illusion spell generally lasts a couple of minutes and...well, it's sort of a cross between the threat spell and shield."

"How so?"

"You know how intention determines how strong the shield is?" When she nodded he continued. "With the illusion spell, intention and strength of will determine how strong an illusion you can see through."

"That makes sense. Which one first?"

"Sensing magic. Do you know Sumerian?"

Sophia's face fell. "No, though I'd love to learn."

"It's fine. As long as you can memorize the words, you'll be fine."

"Maybe, but I'm still going to get the list from Peter so I can start learning more languages." She shook her head. "It feels wrong that the head of this place only knows four languages fluently," she told him with a wry smile.

"You'll learn." He waited a beat, then slowly spoke the Sumerian.

It was just gibberish to her, so she had him repeat it a few times before she carefully said the words. It took her a couple of tries before she got the unfamiliar syllables correct. Pressure settled against her. It was subtle, no more than the feel of a light blanket covering her, but it was noticeable. "Should it feel like something pressing against me?"

"Exactly. The stronger the pressure, the closer or stronger the magic. Since I've only done one small spell, there's not much for you to sense."

She nodded and mouthed the words to herself several more times to commit them to memory.

"The illusion spell will be harder," Lucas warned. "Since there's no illusion here to see through, all I can do is teach you the words."

"Couldn't you just cast an illusion?"

His mouth turned downward. "No," he said bluntly.

Her brows lifted in surprise at his tone, but she decided to pick her battles. "Okay, teach me the words, then."

This time the language was one she knew, and one she knew almost as well as English—Attic Greek. It took her considerably less time to learn that spell.

"You learn quickly," he said with a small smile.

"That's one thing I've always been good at. Being a good student, I mean," she told him with a shrug. "Was there anymore training you wanted to do today, though?"

Lucas shook his head. "No, you've done quite a lot for someone unused to magic. Why?"

"I wanted to go to level six. Finding the poison might not stick a big red arrow on the murderer, but it might help. I'd like you to come with me."

"I agree about pinpointing what poison was used, but you already almost died down there, Sophia," Lucas argued. "We can't lose another aspida."

It stung a little that he was worried about losing another boss and not *her*, but she let it go for now. "That's why I want you to come with me. You may not be a curator, but you know more than I do about this place." He still looked unconvinced, so she added, "You are my head guard, right?"

He sighed and folded his arms over his chest. "Fine. But if I tell you to do something down there, you do it," he told her, his tone and face telling her clearly that he wouldn't budge on that condition.

Smiling, she nodded. "Fair enough. Let's go."

They only passed a few people as they made their way to the library and down through the many levels. None of them did more than smile or offer a quick greeting. By the time they'd reached level six, Sophia's calves were starting to complain at her, so she sat down on the bottom stair and shook her head. "If I'd have known that I'd end up going up and down so many damn flights of stairs, I would've started working out a long time ago," she complained.

Lucas only chuckled and stepped around her. "You'll get used to it. You've only been here a week," he pointed out as he started browsing the books.

"At this rate, I'll have the best legs in the world in another week." She stood, not wanting her muscles to stiffen up, and moved to a different shelf than Lucas to start looking. "So, I'm thinking we can go through the books we can read for now, and if we need to, bring down translation dictionaries later for the ones we can't?"

"That sounds reasonable."

For half an hour, they searched in silence. Sophia hadn't found anything about poisons, though she had found a number of books that she'd like to spend a lot more time with at a later date. She really could spend years doing nothing but reading the books on this level alone. And while she normally enjoyed quiet, was all too happy to hide away and read or study, the lack of noise, of conversation, was pressing on her now. Lucas had taken a seat on the floor and was carefully flipping through a book. She selected a book nearby and broke the silence.

"Who was head nasaru before you? Are they still here?"

"Yeah. Steven used to have my job. He got hurt on the job, something Sergei couldn't fully heal, which is why he teaches now, instead."

Sophia slowly nodded and focused on the book for a couple of minutes. There were still plenty of questions she still wanted to ask, and most of them didn't actually involve Lucas directly.

"Are there any other parts of the Athenaeum that I haven't seen?" she asked. "I mean, the first day Peter said he couldn't show me the armory, which made sense, but other than that?"

"Depends. Do you mean actually seen, or places that you haven't been told about?" he asked without looking up.

She considered for a moment. "Places I haven't been told about," she decided.

"Possibly," he said, glancing at her. "I'm sure you've noticed there's another panel on this level?" When she nodded, he continued. "I've never been down there, and I'm not sure if I told you about it. It's the books and relics reserved only for aspida access, or those they personally take down there. The seventh level."

Sophia thought another level had been mentioned, but with what she'd experienced in the last few days, it scared her as much as excited her. "There are books more dangerous than the ones here?" she asked, eyes widening. If a book here had nearly killed her, what did it take to earn an even more dangerous and restricted level?

"No idea if they're more dangerous or just more sensitive," he admitted. "But as far as I know, that's the only thing that you couldn't have come across. Well, and the aquifer, but that's just our water source."

Relieved, Sophia nodded and shifted her focus back to the book. She soon became engrossed in the hunt for the weapon that had killed her grandfather. An hour later, she let out a gasp and scrambled to her feet, staring at the ancient language on the tissue thin pages in front of her. "Lucas! I think I found something."

He didn't quite run, but it was close. "What is it?"

"I found a poison that might just be the one we're looking for," she said excitedly. She offered the book to him. "It has all the symptoms—the bleeding from the eyes, the weakness, taking a while to…" She cleared her voice and went on. "I'm not sure what this bit says," she told him, pointing to a passage that was in what looked like cuneiform to her, "but it does mention magic being necessary."

"That part's Old Persian," he murmured, his eyes tracking across the symbols that were nonsense to her. "It says that without the magic, the ingredients won't bind. They're dangerous, since most of them are toxins in their own right, but they're not quite as deadly." His gaze lifted to meet hers. "It also says that it's one of the few poisons that's resistant to magical healing."

"Do you see what they called it?" she asked as she stood shoulder to shoulder with him, pointing to a word. "Achlys. Isn't that the Greek goddess of poison?"

"It is," he said, his voice somber.

The sudden shift in his tone startled her. "What's wrong? This is good. We found what was used to kill Erasmus."

"Yes, but we found it too late."

Sophia took a step back and frowned. "What do you mean, too late?"

His eyes closed, his expression pained. "Magic can't be used to counteract its effects…not alone. But there is an antidote," he said quietly.

That was the last thing she'd expected him to say, and it hit her harder than a punch to the gut. "No," she whispered, shaking her head in horror. "You're wrong. You have to be. Because otherwise, if he'd just shared the fact that he was being poisoned with you, he might still be alive."

Lucas gently set the book on a shelf and wrapped his arms around her. She remained stiff against him, fighting against tears. "Not necessarily. This book may have been hidden until after his death, to avoid anyone from saving him. And I don't know how easily the ingredients for the antidote are to get," he murmured against her hair.

"But we could have tried," she insisted.

"And we would have, but there's still no guarantee, Sophia. And you can't focus on what ifs or what might have been. All we can do is deal with what is truth *now*," he told her, rubbing his hand up and down her back.

Slowly, she relaxed against him, her eyes closing as tears escaped. "Maybe," she whispered. "I just hate thinking that he could still be alive. That I could still have my grandfather."

"I know. I don't like it either. I loved him, too."

She pressed her face against his shoulder and let her grief flow, though the tears weren't accompanied by sobs this time. When she was drained, she stepped back and wiped her eyes. "We still don't know who killed him, but at least the number of people who could get down here is limited. If it wasn't you—and I believe it wasn't—then it had to be either Dion or Nick."

He studied her for a long moment. "Not necessarily. We like to think our security is foolproof, but I don't think anything is impenetrable." He closed the book, took a look at the cover, then placed it back on the shelf. "Come on, I want to check something."

Curious, she grabbed the book, then followed him up to the next level.

"Why'd you bring the book?" he asked.

"I'm going to show it to Sergei. Since he's the healer, he should know about it."

"That makes sense." He gave her a tight smile. "Do you realize you just made your first aspida decision?"

She flushed as she realized he was right, in a way. Maybe after she'd made a few more decisions she'd stop feeling so much like an impostor. They stopped at the first computer they passed, but when he started to type the title of the book into the search bar, she got concerned. "Are searches not logged? Do we really want that being out there for anyone to find?"

"They are logged, but not everyone has access to it. And, as head nasaru and aspida, we can wipe the search from the history."

That made her uncomfortable. Not only did it mean that history could be deleted, but it triggered her impostor syndrome. She shouldn't have that sort of responsibility. "Who all can wipe the history like that?"

"As far as I know, only you and Peter could do it by yourself, but I'll admit that I'm not fantastic with computers," he admitted.

She filed that away and decided to try to figure out if he was right. "Wait, a second...does that say what I think it says?" she asked when the result page popped up.

"Yes. It was supposed to be on this level, not on level six."

"But why? It has a magically resistant poison in it," she protested.

"Yes, but that was the only thing in it that could be considered dangerous. And like I said, it did have an antidote."

"Then why move it down to level six?"

Lucas cleared the search, which meant she had to enter her PIN to approve it. "My only guess is to ensure that the poison couldn't be identified without risking the book being found in the culprit's room."

Sophia's mood plummeted as they slowly made their way back upstairs. They may have identified the poison, but it brought them no closer to identifying the killer.

Chapter 27

WHEN THEY'D PARTED WAYS, with Sophia promising to keep the book out of sight, she realized there were still several hours until dinner. She spent only a few minutes in her room before she decided to continue acting like the aspida and went to the clinic. To keep her promise, she hid the book that spoke of Achlys in a small stack of 'safe' books. Holding them so the title of the dangerous book was hidden, she walked with purpose through the increasingly familiar hallways until she reached the clinic. To her relief, Sergei was there and alone.

"Hey, you got a minute?" she asked, poking her head through the open door.

He looked up and gave her a nod. "I do." He swiveled his chair around and watched as she came inside and shut the door behind her, even going so far as to flip the lock. "It's to be one of those conversations, hmm?"

She said nothing as she fished the book out of the stack and sat in front of him. "I found it."

"Found what?" he asked, confused at first, but the Athenaeum's healer was quick. "The poison?" he breathed.

Sophia nodded and flipped through the fragile pages until she found the appropriate one, then she turned the book around and held it out to him. "I'm ninety-nine percent sure this is it. Everything matches. It's called Achlys."

Sergei took the book from her and frowned down at it. "Achlys," he murmured as he skimmed the words. "This I know," he motioned to the Greek, then continued as he pointed to the Old Persian, "but I don't understand whatever this is."

This was the part she wasn't looking forward to, but the part he truly needed to know. "It's Old Persian. You should get a book so you can translate it properly, but the short story? It...Achlys has an antidote, Sergei," she said quietly.

His head whipped up and she saw the same anger and disbelief she felt flashing on his normally stoic features. "Are you sure? This...Erasmus..."

"I know." She leaned forward and rested one of her hands over his, feeling how tense he was. Despite that, he was careful not to damage the book in his hands. "Believe me, I know. But that's why I brought you this book. You need to be familiar with this poison, and with how to make the antidote. Hopefully, neither of us will ever see Achlys again, but if we do..."

He grunted softly and looked back to the book. "It was on level six?"

"Yes...but it wasn't supposed to be. It was moved there, from level five." Outrage sparked within her once more as she added, "It must have been moved so no one could save Erasmus."

"That means that Nick, Dion, or Lucas—"

Sophia cut him off with a shake of her head. "No, not necessarily. Yes, they're the only ones who could get down there without an escort, at least through normal channels. And even if they are the only ones who could have gotten down there alone, who's to say that someone couldn't have gotten one of them to take them down there and snuck the book in? Or maybe one of the top dogs found the book and mistakenly thought it belonged on level six." She shook her head again. "Right now, there's no way of knowing who was responsible. But we're going to find out."

He didn't calm, not exactly, but her words seemed to focus him. Better, he actually listened. A minute ago she had been half afraid he was going to go beat answers out of the heads of the Athenaeum's factions. Now he looked like he was using his brain. Slowly, he nodded, pried his fingers from the book, and set it gently on his desk. "You're right. This isn't conclusive. I can't help but still be suspicious of those three."

She hesitated for a moment, unsure if she should tell him about Lucas, but if there were only three of them working on this, they couldn't hold back. "Lucas is clean."

Sergei's expression was torn between relief and skepticism. "Are you sure?"

"I am. He's helped me out a couple of times since I've gotten here, and I used a threat spell Erasmus taught me. He's no danger to me."

That didn't seem to truly settle the conflict. "I know that spell. It's not absolutely foolproof..."

"No, but I *do* know what it feels like when there's a nearby threat. When I'm standing next to him, I feel as much danger as I did with Erasmus. And let's face it, Sergei. Neither of us are detectives. We need the help."

He mulled over that for a moment. "What do you mean he's helped you out?"

"It actually started before Erasmus..." She pressed her lips tightly together until the fresh wave of grief passed. "Someone locked me in a linen closet. I couldn't get a hold of my mom, so I called Lucas and he let me out. Then, when I was in the library, someone created an illusion of fire. I ran into Lucas. He took care of me and used a spell to check for recent magic. Unfortunately, he found it."

Sergei cursed under his breath in Russian. It sounded cool, so she made a note to ask him to teach her a few choice words later. "It's good he was able to help you, but I don't like that you were being targeted before you were chosen as aspida."

"Believe me, I don't like it either," Sophia said with a sigh. "Hell, I'm not sure *why* they were targeting me. It's not like the choice can be rigged, right?"

He shook his head. "Not as far as I know. The Athenaeum chooses, period. At this point, the magic is likely so deeply embedded in every stone of this place that I don't know that a single person could affect it. The patrons, probably, but none of us."

"Mmm. Well, then yeah, it doesn't make sense. No one could have known that I would become everyone's boss, so what possible point could there be in scaring me away from here?"

His head cocked slightly. "You assume that is why they did those things, but perhaps there was another reason?"

Skeptical, she asked, "Like what?"

A tiny smile appeared. "That I cannot answer. But I want you to be careful, Sophia."

"I know. It would be bad for two aspides to die so close together," she mumbled.

"There is that," he agreed, "but it would be bad for *you* to die, even if you weren't aspida."

"Oh." She let out a small, awkward laugh. "Yeah, I can't say I'd be too happy to be dead. You should be careful, too, though." She inclined her head toward the book. "Keep that hidden, too. Someone used it to kill Erasmus. I don't think he, she, or they would hesitate to kill someone else."

Sergei gently closed the book and stood, placing it in one of the cabinets and locking it. "I won't leave it there indefinitely, but for now it will work. And I will ensure a copy of the information about Achlys and its antidote is made."

Sophia nodded her approval of that plan. "Make a couple. I'll keep one and give one to Lucas." She grinned. "Maybe you should consider writing a book of your own."

He frowned in confusion. "A book?"

"Mmhmm. Rare or magical poisons...and their antidotes."

His expression smoothed and was replaced by amusement. "That isn't a bad idea. I've actually gathered quite a bit of information, so it wouldn't be too hard to put together. And I can get in touch with Erasmus's friend, the healer. She made sure he passed it on, since we're both healers."

"Good. It's not like it'll be published, either, so you don't have to worry about being literary or anything, just factual."

"That is an even better idea. I'm a good healer, but a writer?" He shook his head. "Not so much."

"I have faith," she told him as she got to her feet. "I need to take care of a couple other things before dinner, but I'm going to text you so you have my number. Don't hesitate if there's something I need to know. And if you can't find me, find Lucas," she told him as she sent him a quick text.

For a second, Sergei's natural suspicion of everyone in the Athenaeum surfaced, but he shoved it down and nodded. "I will. Be safe, Sophia."

She smiled. "I will," she told him as she slipped out of the clinic.

Sophia's next stop was the computer room. To her surprise, Peter wasn't there. Deflated, she leaned against the wall and frowned at her cousin's darkened monitors. Intellectually, she knew he didn't live in this room, but she'd always found him here, so had just expected to find him here now. She sent him a quick text, telling him she was looking for him. A notification that he'd received the text popped up, but he didn't respond. Just as she was starting to wonder why, he walked into the room with a grin and a bottle of soda.

"Sorry. A man can't live on zeroes and ones alone," he joked, bumping her shoulder with his as he passed her to get to his computer. A slight jostle of his mouse had the multiple monitors lighting up. "Is everything okay?"

"Yeah, it just threw me off that you weren't here," she told him sheepishly as she dropped into a chair.

He laughed and shrugged. "Ninety percent of my time is spent here, so it's a reasonable expectation. What can I do for you, Soph?"

"Unfortunately, not just hang out with me," she said apologetically.

Unfazed, he shrugged. "You're aspida, now. It's to be expected that you'll need to talk to people in a more...uh...professional capacity. Besides, there's plenty of time to just hang out when work is done."

"True." And she was relieved he felt that way. It was weird going from just being friends or family to being people's boss. "Thanks. Okay. I figured, first order of business, I need to know who I'm working with. Like, I don't know, a list of everyone in the Athenaeum? Their role here, what languages they know, phone numbers...stuff like that, you know?"

He perked up and spun his chair so he faced his monitors, once more reminding her of a hyperactive puppy. "Oh! That's easy. We have files on everyone. They've got everything. Or almost everything. What faction they're in, what their specific role is, what languages they know, what country they're from, what weapons they're proficient in...And their phone numbers, of course," he said, alternating between maneuvering the mouse and tapping on the keyboard. A moment later, the printer whirred to life and started popping out sheet after sheet.

"Really? Do you have one on me?" she asked, leaning forward and peering at the screen. To her disappointment, it didn't hold information on anyone, but looked more like search results.

"Of course," Peter said, giving her a cheeky grin. "It's not complete, but everyone in the Athenaeum, whether official or family, has a dossier."

"That's kind of...creepy. Handy though, I guess."

"I don't know about creepy," Peter said, shrugging as he went to a different screen. Something—it could have been a map or blueprints—flashed on the monitor for a second before it went to a print screen. "We need to know all sorts of things, though, especially about the nasaru and venatores. We're not going to send someone to, say, China, if they don't speak Mandarin or know the customs, you know? Or send someone who's all about negotiating to a tomb instead of someone who has field experience."

"Makes sense," she admitted. "It sure can't hurt me in trying to figure out who is who. And I know eventually I'll have to start making decisions about people and trips and stuff."

"Exactly," he said cheerfully. "I'm also printing out a map for you."

"Of what?"

"The Athenaeum."

She stared at him, more than a bit miffed. "There's a map of the place I've been getting lost in for a week? Really?" she asked dryly.

He had the grace to look sheepish. "I'm sorry, Soph. I didn't realize you were getting lost." He gave her a hopeful smile. "But now you won't get lost anymore!"

Sophia huffed out a laugh. "I've got the hang of it for the most part, now." Though it was entirely possible that there were still places she hadn't seen. In fact, she knew there were. They just weren't going to be on his map.

"Sorry," Peter said again.

He both looked and sounded so dejected that she had to take pity on him, giving him a warm smile. "It's okay, Peter. Getting lost wasn't so bad. You learn more by doing anyway, right? And I've got the map now."

A smile gradually slid into being. "That is true," he agreed. The printer went silent and he rolled over to it. He grabbed the freshly printed pages, straightened them with a tap, placed them in a folder, and offered it to her with both hands. "Here you go! Information on everyone in the Athenaeum and your very own map."

She grinned and took the folder. "Thanks." She considered, then asked, "Can you write the wi-fi password on there before I leave?"

"Absolutely." He took the folder and, in neat block writing, wrote the password down before handing it back to her.

"Thanks," she repeated. "I want to go take a peek at these before dinner, but I'll talk to you later."

"Sure thing! Let me know if there's anything else you need."

"Will do," she told him as she left, wishing he could give her what she most needed. Answers.

Chapter 28

IT WASN'T UNTIL SOPHIA was safely within her room that she opened the folder. Sitting down at her desk, she flipped through until she found the map and skimmed over it. To her disappointment, it didn't actually show anything that was out of the ordinary. Plenty of bedrooms, storage rooms, and the like that she hadn't seen were listed, and she saw some earmarked as offices for various people such as the heads and Valerie, the finance curator. Nothing unusual there, though, even the office that was now hers. But then, some secret area for aspides wouldn't really be secret if it was public knowledge within the Athenaeum. What was useful was how the bedrooms and offices all had names on them or were listed as unassigned, so it would be easy to track people down in the future. Again, kind of creepy, but it would definitely come in handy.

That was set aside so she could focus on the other papers in the folder. It made her a little uncomfortable to see her file on top. A quick scan of the other pages told her they were loosely ordered by hierarchy. After her were the three heads, the curators, nasaru, and finally, the venatores. Going back to her file, she looked through it, unsurprised to see that it listed her education, birthday, and family. In the spots for skills, languages, and weapon proficiencies, it simply said

'Unknown.' Her lips twitched a little, entirely too pleased to see proof that the Athenaeum wasn't all-knowing. Perhaps it shouldn't satisfy her so much since this was now her organization, but it didn't set well to have someone knowing everything about her before meeting her. The section for notes only listed how she had grown up away from the Athenaeum. Below that was a section labeled 'Sorcery,' which threw her off at first, despite how it, too, said 'Unknown.' Did they really keep track of every spell they knew? Or was it just for spells that could serve a specific purpose, such as healing?

Dion's was next. She started to look over it before she realized she should be making notes. Doing it on the files wouldn't be smart, just in case someone found them, so she pulled the flash drive from her pocket and plugged it into the computer.

For the next hour, she read through the files, put numbers in her phone, and made notes in a document on her drive. Though she was extremely impressed by almost everyone, nothing jumped out of her as being overly suspicious. Yes, Dion spoke Old Persian fluently and one of the guards named Kirk was an expert in poisons, but neither were the only ones with either skill in their file. Nor was either fact incriminating on its own. No, the worst thing she discovered after she finished her first read-through of the files was that she was woefully inadequate for her job compared to some of these people. Most had grown up in the Athenaeum. More than half spoke at least ten languages fluently. Almost all the curators and venatores had dozens of useful skills and sorcery spells listed. To her relief, it did seem like only spells that could be utilized in some manner were listed. If there were frivolous spells, she found none on any of the files. Still, she had to wonder why the Athenaeum chosen her when there were all these people with way more experience and skills than her. It didn't make any sense. What about her was special enough to set her apart? Unless Sergei was wrong, and it was possible to rig the decision. But even then, why would another—even her grandfather—have chosen her?

Sophia closed the folder and rubbed her temples, only now aware that a headache had developed while she'd been learning about all the people she was now—reluctantly—in charge of. People she barely knew. Hell, there were a good dozen whose names she'd never heard yet. That had to change, even if not all of them lived in the Athenaeum.

Unwilling to sit and stew in her room, she removed the flash drive and closed down her computer. After changing into a pair of yoga pants and a snug tank top—and hiding the flash drive in the hidey-hole with Erasmus's journal—she made her way to the gym. She'd never been the sort to enjoy running—or exercise of any sort, for that matter—but perhaps some physical exertion could help her now. She'd work out some stress and get to know some of her new extended family. Most importantly, she could work on her legs so they didn't cry after a day of going up and down the stairs of the library.

She wasn't sure if she was relieved or resigned when she found almost a dozen people in the gym. Almost as one, they paused what they were doing and looked at her. Since she wasn't used to being the center of attention, she nearly did a one-eighty and left right then. But she was the boss now. She'd have to get used to these people, and to occasionally having all eyes on her. Squaring her shoulders, she offered a light smile. "Afternoon," she told the room in general as she crossed to a treadmill—the only piece of equipment in here she recognized aside from the weight bench.

A few voices echoed her greeting, a few heads nodded in her direction, before most went back to what they were doing. It was a relief when the vast majority left her to do her own thing, even if eyes did flick toward her curiously more than once. Her intention had been to talk to some of these people, but this might work just as well. People were watching her, so she'd watch them right back.

After programming the treadmill, she started an easy jog and studied the room. A handful of people were strangers. Guards, she assumed, judging by their builds, though they could also be curators, she supposed. A book alone wasn't heavy, but a box of books? She could see needing to work out in order to move large numbers of them if they didn't have the magic to do it. It wasn't all that different than her working on her legs to help with the stairs. Then again, if the venatores did go traipsing around old temples and the like, they had to be in shape, too, which meant there was no way of guessing who was what.

She was studying a group that included Theo and Nick when a voice came from her other side.

"Didn't expect to see you in here."

Surprised, she stumbled, which was the last thing she wanted to do on a treadmill. She flailed and grabbed hold of the treadmill with one hand, while the other was caught in Steven's firm grip. He continued to hold on to her until she'd regained her balance and stabbed the off button. "Christ, Steven. Warn a girl, will you?" she asked, pushing a damp strand of hair behind her ear.

He grinned, completely unrepentant. "I'm not exactly a stealthy man, Sophia. You must have been lost in your own head."

Since he was absolutely right, she said nothing and cocked her head. "What's up?"

"You looked a little...overwhelmed when you came in. I thought I'd see if I could help."

"Oh." She looked around at the various pieces of unfamiliar equipment. "Yeah, sort of. I want to get in better shape—especially my legs because of all the damn stairs—but I don't know how to use anything but this," she told him with a pat to the treadmill's display. "I figured this at least would help."

He nodded. "It will. Variety would be good, too, though, but not today."

"Why not?"

Steven smiled. "I've officially only been the trainer here for a few years, but I helped with training before that. I can tell when someone's exhausted, and you are definitely on the verge."

Again, he was right. "Good point. Does that mean that if I come in here when I'm not about to fall on my face that you'll help me?"

"That's my job. Beyond that, I like you, Sophia, and I have a feeling you're trying to figure out how in the hell to prove yourself to everyone in the Athenaeum. If I can make that a little easier on you by helping you in here, then I absolutely will. But can I give you a piece of advice that has nothing to do with fitness or muscle?"

Intrigued, she nodded as she stepped off the treadmill. "Of course."

"I can't say that people aren't going to watch you and judge the job you're doing, because they're absolutely going to. It's human nature, even if none of us are actually human."

"Gee, thanks," she said dryly. "As if I wasn't nervous enough already."

He chuckled and shook his head. "You already knew that. My advice is to not get caught up in what you *think* you should be doing or saying. Yes, there are specific duties you'll have to perform as aspida, but you're still you. You're not going to perform those duties the way Erasmus did, nor should you. You're your own person, Sophia. You have your own thoughts and experiences that will shape the decisions you make. Since you're the one the Athenaeum chose for the role, I think it means it wants you to be you, not the title."

"So your advice is just to be myself?"

"Exactly."

Sophia thought about that, and oddly, it made her feel better. He was right. She was the one picked, not someone who would be stuffy or someone who didn't know how to bend. She smiled up at him. "Thanks, Steven. I think that out of everything everyone has said to me about becoming aspida, that's the one thing that has actually made me feel like I could do this job."

"I'm not just brawn," he teased with a quick grin. "I'm glad I could help, though."

"I don't think anyone here is just brawn. They may be nasaru," she said, motioning to the others in the gym, "but this is still the Athenaeum. I don't see anyone dumb being a librarian."

"Exactly," he said again. "I'll see you soon, but be prepared to work when you're in here."

"Trust me, I'm going to be working hard no matter what room I'm in," she told him as left the gym.

Sophia swung by her room and grabbed a quick shower. After casting the threat spell, she headed to the dining room. She was one of the first ones there, so she got a chance to watch people as they came in...at least at first. Then people started coming up to her to chat and it became impossible for her to monitor the multiple entrances into the dining room. By the time everyone was sitting down to eat—and with Josie talking in one ear and Peter the other—she had no idea who had caused the threat spell to change from mild tingling to full-blown bugs crawling over her. At that point, it took all her focus to just respond coherently while fighting the urge to scratch at her skin.

Dinner felt like it took forever. She'd intended to linger and meet more people, but the spell was still active, so she smiled tightly and hurried out of the dining room. She was almost to her room when the intense sensations subsided and her steps slowed. Her hand was on the knob of her door when she heard steps behind her. Tensing, she glanced over, relieved to see it was her mom.

"Sophia? Is everything okay?" Heather asked.

Swallowing a slightly hysterical laugh, Sophia opened the door and wiggled her hand in a 'sort of' gesture. "It's been a long week."

Heather followed her inside, shut the door, then cupped Sophia's face, studying it closely. "It has," she agreed, releasing Sophia just long enough to reposition her arms and give the younger woman a warm hug. "How are you handling everything? I haven't seen much of you since the funeral."

Guilt leapt above paranoia as Sophia's dominant emotion. She had been neglecting her mom. Sighing, she pressed her face against her mom's shoulder. "I know, and I'm sorry. I know this is hard for you, too."

"It is," Heather agreed easily, "but I didn't have as much dumped on me all at once. I can't even imagine how it would feel to find out about an organization a week before ending up running it."

Sophia's head jerked up and she flung her arms out. "Exactly! Thank you! I'm glad someone gets that," she muttered. Walking over to the bed, she turned and dropped back onto it, her arms spread. "I'm getting a little more okay with that, though. I just hope everyone can be patient while I figure out how to do the job."

"I'm sure they will. These are good people," Heather assured her as she sat on the bed. "But I'm not asking about the job, sweetie. I want to know how you're doing."

She blew out a breath and stared up at the ceiling. "Stressing," she admitted. "Part of me—a small part—wants to run back to Georgia. The bigger part is excited to be here, but freaking out, still." She turned her head to look at her mom. "I love this place. The library? It's beyond anything I could imagine. I got to see an original copy of the Odyssey, Mom. They've got journals of people I've studied in school. I mean, sure, when I decided what I wanted to do I had dreams of finding things—artifacts, tablets, that sort of thing—but these books? They're freaking amazing. And I'm so freaking glad that being aspida doesn't mean I'm chained here."

Heather smiled. "No, you're really not. I know Erasmus went on several missions as aspida. Not necessarily special or tricky ones, either." The smile trembled. "I really should have let you grow up here."

Sophia propped herself on her elbows and shook her head. "No, Mom. No more of that. We can't change the past. Besides that, I'm still here. So we're good. Promise."

"I'm glad. I'll probably be leaving sometime in the next few days, though."

"What? I thought you said you were staying!" On one hand, if her mom left, she'd be safe from the killer. On the other, Sophia really wanted to have someone familiar around.

Heather laughed. "I am, but I also told you I'd need to pack up and take care of things. Selling the house, sending our stuff here, selling what we don't want to keep. Easier to do it in person."

"Oh." She remembered that now and felt silly for her outburst. "Yeah, that makes sense."

"Don't worry, I'll let you know before I leave," Heather teased. She leaned over and kissed Sophia's forehead. "I'll get out of your hair. Try to relax and get some sleep, okay?"

"I will," Sophia promised. Once she was alone, she decided to go ahead and deal with withdrawing from school, then flopped back down and sighed as she thought about her mom's last words and her answer. If only it was a promise she wasn't almost guaranteed to break.

Chapter 29

The next morning, after a dreamless night, Sophia went to breakfast, only to run into Lucas as he was leaving.

"When you're done eating, report to the gym. We're going to start on your combat training," he told her, already starting to take off in the direction of the gym.

His abrupt command—because it wasn't anything but a command—had her gaping at him for a few seconds. "Only if someone helps me with the labyrinth when we're done!" she called after him. "I haven't seen the sun in a damn week," she added on a grumble as she walked into the kitchen. She also hadn't shifted since Nick and Carla had shown up at her front door, and she missed the feel of wind in her wings. This was honestly the longest she'd gone without shifting in decades.

Since she was probably about to have her ass handed to her—not to mention do more physical activity than she normally did in a month—she decided to keep breakfast relatively light. She'd recover the calories later. Agatha wouldn't let her escape with anything less than a breakfast sandwich, but it was quick and she scarfed it down along with a cup of coffee. She grabbed a couple bottles of water, returned to her room to change into another pair of yoga pants and a tank top, then made her way to the gym.

There were more people there today than she'd seen the day before. Instead of just working out, she saw multiple people sparring. What was really jarring was that a couple of them were sparring not with fists, but with weapons. Her first instinct when she saw Morgan swinging at Theo with a sword was to scream. She barely managed to bite back the sound to a small squeak, her eyes wide with shock. It helped that Theo blocked it with a sword of his own before they both stopped to chat.

"Not what you were expecting?" Lucas asked as he walked over to her.

"No, though I guess I should have," Sophia murmured as she watched the sparring. "Well, not the swords, maybe. I didn't think anyone used swords anymore outside of exhibitions and movies, you know? I figured you guys were all fists and guns. Maybe knives." Which was silly, because she knew the Arcane rarely used guns.

He nodded. "I can understand that, but there are times when a sword is a better choice than other weapons. Guns are noisy, fists and feet don't have the...stopping power or reach, and knives have limited reach, too. Swords are less commonly used, but I insist that all the guards have a thorough knowledge of a wide range of weapons, just because you never know what you'll need and what's available."

"We're not going to start with the swords for me, right?" she asked. The thought of using a sword was kind of cool, but also terrifying. Not being the most graceful of people, she'd be more likely to lop off her own foot than actually hit someone else. Sure, it could be healed, but that wouldn't keep it from hurting like hell.

Lucas chuckled and shook his head. "No. First, have you ever done any form of fighting? With fists or weapons?" When she shook her head he asked, "How about guns?" Another shake of her head. "Then we're going to start with hand to hand. It'll help when we do eventually move to weapons."

Sophia blew out a long breath and nodded. "Okay, but I've never been super graceful," she warned. "I don't trip over my own feet all the time or anything, but I'm a book nerd, not an athlete or fighter."

He shrugged, unconcerned. "No one is until they are. And no one here is expecting you to go from pacifist to ninja in one day."

She let out a short laugh. "That's good, because I'm a lot of things, and could be a lot more, but ninja? It's not even close to one of them."

"Maybe not, but you might surprise yourself." He arched a brow, a smile playing on his lips as he gave her a challenging look. "Unless you think I'm a bad teacher?"

"I don't know. Are you planning on throwing anything at me this time?" she shot back.

He laughed and shrugged. "It wasn't on my to do list, but things can always change. How well do you think you could dodge a knife?"

The idea made Sophia shudder and she shook her head. "Let's not find out today. So what first?"

"First? We stretch." He guided her through a series of stretches that made her realize just how inflexible she was. At the end of the fifteen minutes, she already felt like she'd started a workout, but she had to admit she felt looser than she had in ages. "Do you know what the key to fighting well is?" he asked when they were both standing in relaxed poses once more.

"Don't get hit?"

Lucas grinned. "That doesn't hurt, but no. It's muscle memory. You practice the motions so often that you can react before you can even think about what to do." He paused then added, "Muscle memory and adaptability, but we'll get to that part later."

"Okay, that makes sense. So what you're telling me is I'm going to be doing the same thing over and over until I'm sick of it?"

"Yes," he answered with no hint of joking. His actions proved just how truthful he was being. For the next hour Sophia practiced the same two punches, though for some variety he allowed her to practice them with her left hand after a while. He wasn't an easy teacher, either, but he was unfailingly patient. Each error in her form was corrected—repeatedly in some cases—but he did it in a way that was helpful rather than making her feel stupid or inadequate. Who knew that tucking her thumb under her fingers when she punched wasn't a way of protecting said digit, but a good way to break it? It was definitely a useful lesson, but at the end of the hour her arms felt like jello and her shirt was damp with sweat.

"That's enough for today," he told her, and she gratefully slumped down to the mat, leaning back against the wall. "I promise it'll get easier. Every practice session will strengthen those muscles, and the ones we'll be working out later on. The gun practice won't be quite as grueling, either."

"That'll be a great relief to me when I can lift my arms again," she said, too tired to work up any annoyance at having to do this again.

He grinned and reached down to haul her to her feet. "Go take a hot shower. You'll feel better." He leaned in and sniffed her neck before teasingly adding, "Smell better, too."

Sophia glared at him, but it lacked its usual punch. "If I could move my arms, I'd practice what you just taught me. On you," she warned.

Her words didn't scare him in the least. He just repeated, "Go shower," before striding across the gym to talk to Steven.

Grumbling to herself, Sophia slowly made her way to her room. It took twice as long as normal to get the shower going, but when she stepped under the steamy water, she let out a low moan of pleasure. The heat felt so good on her abused muscles it took nearly ten minutes before she actually started to wash. She was in there so long she was shocked the water hadn't gotten cold, but she was grateful for it.

After getting dressed, she glanced at the time, unsurprised to see it was already noon. She was halfway to the kitchen when she was waylaid by a grinning Josie and Peter. Stopping, she eyed them suspiciously. "What are you two up to?"

"Nothing bad," Josie said as she linked her arm with Sophia's. "We heard you were wanting to get outside, and we thought we'd help you out with that."

Hunger warred with a desire to see the sun. "That sounds great, really, but I was just heading to the kitchen—"

Peter drew his hand from behind his back, revealing a picnic basket. "That's already been handled," he told her cheerfully.

Since she didn't have to choose, Sophia beamed at them. "Sounds great. Can you guys teach me how to navigate the labyrinth while we're at it?"

"Of course," Peter said as they fell into step together, heading for the entrance. "Though you shouldn't have a problem now that you're officially part of the Athenaeum."

"What do you mean? Because I really don't want to risk the death by labyrinth Carla mentioned when I first got here."

Josie laughed. "I'd like to say she was exaggerating...but she really wasn't."

Sophia wrinkled her nose. "Fun."

"But yeah," Peter continued, "if you belong to the Athenaeum, it sort of shows you the way. It's not like a line appears on the floor or anything, but you can 'see' the correct path and traps."

"What counts as belonging to the Athenaeum? Like do Nick's kids see it?"

Peter shook his head. "Family members have to have an escort, just like you and Heather did when you got here."

"Oh." Sophia frowned as she thought back to when she'd followed Carla through the labyrinth. She'd have to pay attention and see what looked different now.

They passed the entrance hall and she once again marveled at the statues and carved columns, but all too soon they were into the natural-looking tunnels that made up the labyrinth. Peter and Josie both pulled out flashlights, but stopped as soon as they reached an intersection.

"You see what we mean?" Josie asked.

Uncertain, Sophia squinted at the circle of illuminated stone and dirt. Peter was right. There wasn't anything overt, but there was something different about the left-hand passage. At first glance, it looked the same, just a cave tunnel full of dust and dirt. The more she paid attention, the more off it looked. There wasn't anything she could have picked out, nothing she could have described, but she *knew* that it was the way they needed to go to reach the outside.

"I...do. That's really weird," she admitted.

They both grinned and Peter nodded. "It is, but since it keeps us from gruesome deaths, I won't complain."

"Me either," Sophia agreed.

They continued on with Sophia paying close attention, easily identifying the correct path now that she knew what to look for. Peter even helpfully veered off to point out a trap so she could spot that as well. Then, finally, they emerged into the sunlight.

Unable to help herself, Sophia closed her eyes and tipped her face upward, basking in the feel of the warmth on her skin. "I will never again take this for granted," she murmured after several minutes, smiling at Josie and Peter.

"It is easy to forget how long you've been underground," Josie agreed as she started walking. They'd clearly planned this in advance, because there was already a blanket nearby, a rock sitting on each corner to ensure it didn't blow away while they were gone. "Some people don't mind, especially since we've got sunlamps to help with the vitamin D thing, not to mention Sergei, but most of us make a point of getting out once or twice a week. Go shopping, get lunch, just walk around, whatever. Venatores and nasaru probably have it easiest since they get out of the Athenaeum more often than the curators."

"That makes sense. I hadn't even thought about the vitamin D thing. That can mess with your moods, can't it?"

Peter nodded. "It can."

"Wonder if all my mood issues the past couple of days is really all...everything...or if the lack of sunlight has something to do with it."

"Probably a mix of both, but that's just my guess. Either way, getting outside is nice."

Sophia smiled at him. "It is."

What was even nicer was how they stayed out there, chatting and munching, until the sun had started to set, turning the sky a dozen shades of purple and orange. Though Sophia wished she had her camera, she didn't hesitate to pull out her phone and, smiling, snap her first picture of the Greek scenery.

When the sun had dipped below the horizon, she gave in to her instincts and shifted, getting a literal bird's-eye view of the surrounding land. As good as the sun had felt, it was nothing compared to the way it felt to soar. This was almost a merging with the sky, something that always left her feeling lighter, mentally and physically.

Maybe things could turn around. Maybe her time in Greece wasn't going to be all bad. The only way she could get through it all was to hold on to that thought.

Chapter 30

With the full day she'd had, Sophia expected to fall asleep as soon as her head hit her pillow. Yet two hours after she'd climbed into bed she was still wide awake. She checked her phone and groaned when she saw it was almost three in the morning. Not willing to simply lay in bed staring at the ceiling all night, she put on her slippers, covered her sleep shorts and tank top with a robe, and left her room to explore. At first she did nothing more than wander, wishing she'd brought the map Peter had given her.

It was a little weird to see the Athenaeum so empty and dark. There was a light on in the common room, and another in the kitchen, but the lights in the hallways and other public areas were dimmed. Even the computer room was dark when she peeked in, proving that Peter had actually abandoned his precious computer for the night. A few guards were in the common room playing some video game, but other than that, she didn't see a single person.

Not finding anything interesting, she headed down to the library. As she made her way down flight after flight of stairs, she thought back to Erasmus's note. He'd mentioned a place in the Athenaeum that could help her. He hadn't included detailed directions or a map, which meant she had to figure out where such a place could be from his infuriatingly vague letter. As she descended the stairs to the sixth level, she brought to mind the rest of the letter, desperate to glean any sort of clue from it. Mostly he'd just talked about how she was in danger as aspida and how he'd always be a part of the Athenaeum.

Sophia stopped in the middle of the library, hands on her hips, as she tried to decide where to look first. "Why couldn't I have been born a necromancer so I could summon ghosts?" she muttered, wishing she could ask him. Then, on a whim, she hurried back up the stairs to the crypt. She passed the pedestals and urns, making her way toward the round room at the end where her life had changed. When she entered, she stumbled to a stop, frowning. Erasmus's urn wasn't there. It took a minute for her tired brain to catch up and stop worrying about what had happened to it. There was no reason to leave it there indefinitely, after all. It was probably out with the others.

Spinning on her heel, she went back to the long hallway, searching for her grandfather's remains. Fortunately, they seemed to be placed chronologically, which meant the last urn, the one without a plaque, had to be his. Her chest grew tight as she looked at the small container that held the remains of a wonderful man. She sighed and ran a finger over the intricate paint. "Oh, Grandpa...why did you have to go so soon?" she whispered. "It's bad enough that I didn't get enough time to know you, but now you've left me with all these secrets to figure out. And if you couldn't figure it all out after a lifetime here, how am I supposed to figure it out after just a week?" Her hands rested on the pedestal as she lowered her head, eyes closed. "I can't even find this secret place that's supposed to help me."

She pushed away from the pedestal and turned, tucking her hands into her robe pockets and walking slowly down the row of the dead.

Her eyes skimmed over the plaques, barely paying attention to the words engraved on them. A few carried her last name, reminding her that she'd been told several of her ancestors had been aspida before Erasmus. As she moved to the earlier plaques, the surnames disappeared, and she wondered just how many of these were her family.

The first urn, the oldest, also had the longest plaque. Eugenios, the very first aspida, the one who'd started this whole thing. "I could blame you for the situation I'm in right now," she grumbled, even as she marveled at being in the presence of so much history. So many historical figures, even if most of the world had never heard of them. She leaned her shoulder against the wall next to the urn, thinking. If magic was used for the labyrinth, maybe magic was used to find this secret place? The only question was, did she have the right magic to find it? It could be sorcery with a magic word, but which one? "Open sesame," she said dryly, her lips twitching when—predictably—nothing happened. "Abracadabra. Alakazam. Hocus pocus." She blew out a breath and folded her arms over her chest. "Okay, seriously. There needs to be some sort of instruction manual to being aspida, since you never know who will be the next."

Tired, frustrated, and mourning, she straightened and glared at the urn in front of her. "What good is me being appointed aspida if none of you guys are around to help me?" she demanded, her voice echoing quietly against the stone walls.

She let out a girly squeak when the wall holding Eugenios's plaque slid back and to the side, revealing a room behind it. "I wish this place would stop doing that," she hissed at the urn, knowing it was unreasonable to blame ceramic and ashes for scaring her. After glancing toward the exit and ensuring she was alone, she stepped around the pedestal and peeked into the room. "Holy shit," she breathed.

Her feet carried her forward before she fully registered what she was doing. This place looked like some sort of stereotypical witch's study. There was a heavy wooden desk against one wall, and every other inch of the walls was covered in shelves. Most predictably held books, scrolls, and tablets, while others contained jars, small boxes, and bottles. She couldn't even begin to guess what they might contain.

The moment she was past the opening in the wall, it slid shut again. She spun around and pressed her hands against it, pushing, but it didn't move. "Not cool! Don't lock me in here!" The door opened again and she frowned. Was the doorway responding to her commands? The cubby in her room hadn't responded to her voice, but maybe this was a different sort of magic? "O-okay...as long as I can get back out, you can close again. I don't want anyone finding this place." She barely jumped when the door closed again, though she was relieved when the room remained illuminated. She'd had enough of being locked in the dark.

Reassured that she was relatively safe here, she slowly walked around the room, looking at the contents of the shelves. Some of the books were in languages she didn't know, but the ones she could decipher all seemed to be about magic in some way. Closer to the desk, she found one that seemed to be about the history of the Athenaeum. Her fingers itched to pick that one up, but she pushed that desire aside for later. Recent history was more pressing at the moment. She did have to pick up one called *Magic of the Athenaeum*, excited when she saw it listed the spells that had been cast on the Athenaeum itself. Most of it was Greek to her—metaphorically, anyway—and would take a lot of time to go through. It was tempting to dive into it now, but closed it instead. She didn't put it back, but held onto it, knowing she'd want to read it sooner rather than later. Just as soon as she found Erasmus's killer.

When she finally reached the desk, she found two books sitting on it. Both were large and obviously very old. She set *Magic of the Athenaeum* down beside them, then drew the chair out. It, too, looked old, and she was hesitant to use it, but after a quick check, it seemed sturdy enough. Still, she sank down onto it carefully, testing it before she set her full weight against the wood. It creaked slightly but held, and she released a breath she hadn't realized she'd been holding.

Sophia pushed *Magic of the Athenaeum* off to the side, then gently opened the cover of the thinner of the two books in front of her. Unsurprisingly, the writing on the first page was Greek. Very, very old Greek, which wasn't a problem, but it did take her much longer to translate, as it was a dialect she wasn't familiar with. Some of the words were easy enough as they were similar to what she was familiar with, but not all. Which meant it took several minutes for her to get through the first page, which was almost enough to make her slam the book closed. Instead, she gulped, closed her eyes, took a few deep breaths, then reread the warning.

There is a cost for all knowledge, a cost which cannot be thwarted. Be warned, the spells within this tome are powerful, but using them comes at great cost. They pose a great danger, to both the wielder and the world. Because of this, these spells cannot be allowed to exist anywhere but on these pages, even the ones that, at first glance, appear harmless.

Aspides that come after me, I beseech you to share the contents of this book with no one else. I beseech you to hide similar spells within these pages and destroy all other mention of them. I know this seems to go against the basic principles of the Athenaeum, but we are meant to protect knowledge, and some knowledge is best served by documenting it and keeping it from those who would misuse it. It pains me to think that any member of the Athenaeum could potentially use these spells for ill, but I have personally seen how good people can be corrupted by the promise of power. How they can be fooled into believing they are doing good when they truly are serving evil.

As aspida you are entitled to the knowledge of these spells, but be wary of using them except in dire need.

"Great. Now I'm going to have nightmares about world-ending spells," Sophia muttered. Still, she was curious and couldn't help but carefully flip through the pages, skimming a few. What she saw made her understand the warning. There was a spell to cause large earthquakes, another to raise the dead en masse. She stopped there, afraid of what else she'd see if she continued looking.

Gently, she closed the book and pushed it aside, pulling the thicker book to her and opening it. This one had no warning, which relieved her. Instead, it was a journal. Unlike the one she'd found in her room, this one had entries from a number of aspides. For all she knew, it had entries from all of them. While they were all written in Greek, they weren't all in the same dialect. It was fascinating to watch how the language evolved throughout the years and from aspida to aspida. Some of the entries just detailed major events that had occurred during their tenure—wars and natural disasters as well as internal events such as betrayal of a curator or nasaru. Or a visit from one of the gods who helped protect the Athenaeum. Others mentioned when they upgraded the Athenaeum in some way, whether it was adding a level to the complex or a layer of magic. A few even got more personal, writing about their issues as aspida, or their hopes, both professional and personal. She only skimmed through it, but it was enough to both pique her interest and terrify her.

That book was closed, before Sophia folded her arms on the desk and dropped her head onto them. Being aspida was so much bigger than anyone—even Erasmus—had led her to believe. And the responsibility? It was now her duty to make sure no one got a hold of these spells or misused the Athenaeum. The thought of someone raising the dead and causing the zombie apocalypse freaked her out. Especially since if they did, it would be *her* fault for allowing that spell to get out.

"Erasmus looked just as stressed the last time I saw him."

The male voice from behind her scared her enough that her throat tightened so she couldn't even scream. She quickly stood, knocking the chair over in her haste to turn and face whoever had managed to not just find this room, but enter it. When she saw the modern-looking god from the days before, confusion short-circuited her brain. "What?"

The man was about a foot taller than her, and at least as muscular as Lucas. Unlike Lucas, he had a gentle smile on his face. And unlike the last two times she saw him, he wasn't in a suit, but jeans and a long-sleeved tee-shirt. "Your grandfather. He looked as stressed as you do. Which I get," he said, leaning against the wall and folding his arms over his chest. The easy tone and pose had her relaxing some, but not completely.

"Who are you?" She knew she'd been told his name, but she couldn't bring it to mind at the moment.

"They didn't tell you?" He sighed deeply and shook his head. "If I'd been a god for more than a year, I might be upset about that. But a year ago, I was actually less powerful than you. I'm Seth. Lemurian though, not Egyptian."

"The patron," she said, nodding to show she was following along, but inside, she was freaking out. She'd never met a god before, and hadn't really wanted to. On the other hand, he was one of six gods protecting the Athenaeum, which meant he was an ally. Right?

"Now, yes," he confirmed. "Prior to becoming a god, though, I was just an archaeologist who shipped magical stuff here when I found it."

That statement took most of the rest of her nerves. "You were an archaeologist? I bet you've seen so many cool sites."

He grinned and nodded. "I have. But it's funny that that's what caught your attention and not me telling you I'm a Lemurian god."

That had escaped her noticed, but the word wasn't one she was familiar with. "I don't know what that means. The Lemurian part, I mean."

He grimaced. "Right. Most people haven't heard of Lemuria. No time now, so just know that it's like Atlantis, but in the Pacific ocean. And it's not completely gone, it's just hidden. For our protection. Which means you can't share anything about it with anyone." He paused, made a soft noise, then corrected, "The three heads know, but Erasmus kept it from the rest of the Athenaeum. They know I'm a god now, but no details beyond that."

Sophia really, really wanted to ask more about Lemuria, but there was a more pressing question. "Why are you here? If it was standard practice for the patrons to visit a new aspida, then all six of you would be here."

"Actually, I think it is, but not until the new aspida has had time to settle in and figure a few things out."

"Then why are you here by yourself?"

Seth sighed and scratched at his jaw. "Because I know that Erasmus didn't die of natural causes. That he was poisoned by something not even mithridate could counteract. That there is something evil in this place, and it needs to be destroyed."

"You knew? If you knew, why didn't you save him? Why didn't one of the others? Hell, isn't Hecate a goddess of poisonous plants? Why didn't she do something? Why didn't Isis? Isn't she a healing goddess?"

Several expressions moved over his face; regret, grief, frustration. "Because even the gods aren't all-powerful, Sophia. Not even we can always circumvent what's meant to be. And we're definitely not all-knowing. Even we have to accept consequences. Believe me, I consider Erasmus to be one of the best friends I've ever had. I've never met anyone else like him, and I'm not likely to."

"Then why are you here? If you know he was murdered but didn't—couldn't—do anything about it, why come to me? I definitely can't do anything to prevent it, since it's already happened!" She'd started off speaking in a low voice—pissed, yes, but low—yet by the time she finished, she was yelling at him. Not really her wisest move, but she couldn't stop herself.

"Because I made Erasmus a promise. He loved you. He might have only met you a couple of days ago, but he loved you. He used the Athenaeum's resources to keep track of you and your mom, making sure you had what you needed to be safe and happy. And he wanted you to stay safe, even after he was gone."

Voice weary now, she asked, "Do you know who poisoned him? I know what they used, but not who."

"If I did, they'd be dead," he said flatly. "Like I said, even the gods aren't all-knowing, and there's something evil here keeping me—and the rest of the patrons—in the dark."

"Then how can you protect me? I can't leave. That was made clear to me. An aspida can't just resign. They stay or they die."

He smiled and pushed away from the wall until he stood just a few feet in front of her. "I said the gods aren't all-powerful, but we're still powerful. And I might be here alone, but I'm not here without the knowledge of the other patrons. It was just thought that—as the youngest god—I might be the easiest for you to deal with."

Sophia shook her head. "I don't understand."

Seth held out his hand, palm up. "Isis is a goddess of magic and healing. Hecate is a goddess of witchcraft and poisonous plants. Athena, Mimir, and Thoth are all gods of wisdom. We're not all-powerful, but we still have gifts we can give you. You only have to accept them."

She considered his hand for a long moment, but decided that she should trust him, at least in this. If a god wanted her dead, he wouldn't need to trick her. Slowly, she placed her hand in his, then gasped as what felt like warm lightning poured through her body. It didn't hurt, not at all, but the power was beyond anything she'd felt before. After only a few seconds, Seth drew his hand back. "That's the protection we can give you, Sophia. Wisdom, to see through deceptions and plan your next move. Healing, to help you recover from anything that might be done to you. Magic, to help boost your own abilities. And Hecate's skill with poisonous plants to give you some protection from them."

Her legs didn't want to support her and she stumbled back, wishing she hadn't knocked over the chair. Seth noticed, setting it upright and helping her into it. "Why? I mean, you, yeah. If you made him a promise, but why would the other gods help me?"

"We're the patrons of the Athenaeum, Sophia. It's not just a pretty title. All of us want to see it not just survive, but thrive. There are books and relics in this place that would have been destroyed centuries ago if it weren't for this place. And one day, this place may be all that stands between Earth and its destruction. You are the leader of it now, and given what happened to Erasmus, we want to make sure we don't lose another."

It made sense. She wasn't sure that was the whole truth, but she believed he hadn't lied. "How do I get in touch with you—any of you—if I need to?" It was the easiest thing for her to focus on.

He smiled and pulled a cell phone out of his pocket. A moment later, her own phone signaled a text. Drawing it out and looking at it, she saw he'd sent her a text that was just his name and a smiley face. "Call or text me. The other gods don't have cell phones, but I was Arcane too long to give it up." He rested his hand on her shoulder. "I need to get going, but be everything Erasmus thought you were, Sophia. And above all, stay safe," he told her before he disappeared.

This night had not gone anything like she'd expected it to. Her mind had been whirling even before Seth's visit, but now it was too full.

"Nope. Nuh uh. Not going to worry about this right now," she muttered as she pushed out of her chair and to her feet. She stomped over to the still closed wall and put her hands on her hips, glaring at the stone. "I want out now." The door slid open and she stalked through it, unsurprised this time when it closed behind her with the slightest of noises.

Chilled by what she'd discovered and been told, she wrapped her robe snugly around her and made her way back to her room. Though sleep didn't elude her this time, the nightmares that followed made her wish it had.

Chapter 31

Sophia dragged herself to breakfast the next morning, knowing she looked like hell. It was only fitting because she felt like hell, too. Unfortunately, even Agatha's superior cooking and a large cup of coffee did little to dispel the bone-deep exhaustion. She didn't even have it in her to argue when Lucas showed up and told her that they were going to do her spellwork in an empty room. She didn't even ask why they were doing it there instead of his bedroom. She just followed him, too tired to complain.

"You're going to learn how to throw a punch today," he told her the moment the door was shut.

She frowned in confusion. "We did that yesterday, though. And I thought we were going to do magic today?"

His lips twitched. "We did, and we are. You're going to throw punches...with your mind."

That perked her up. "Seriously? I didn't know sorcery could do that."

"Of course. There's not much that isn't possible with sorcery. This is a little trickier than the other spells, since you have to learn how to say the right words with the right motions, but it's not too bad."

Learning how to defend herself with magic was intriguing, but she had doubts as to how well she'd absorb the lesson in her current state. Still, she had to try. She wasn't the sort of person who'd give up without even trying. Steeling herself, forcing herself to stand straight though her exhaustion wanted her to lean and hunch, she nodded. "Okay. What do I do?"

"The two parts are pretty simple, it's the timing that can be difficult to get the hang of." He spoke a word in a language she didn't know, which made her happy it was a single syllable. He waited until she'd repeated it several times and gotten it right. "The word alone won't do anything." He paused. "Or at least it shouldn't. I've never tried putting any intention behind it, but let's not try it."

That, of course, had images of the spell gone wrong flashing into her head. The worst was one of a shock wave exploding out of her. She grimaced and nodded. "Yeah, let's not," she agreed.

"Good. The motion is really easy, though. You just need to make a throwing motion. A punch or kick would work, too, though it's not necessary to mimic an actual attack." And he demonstrating, flinging his arm out sharply. It looked more like he was about to flick a playing card than, say, throw a baseball, but she got the impression. "To actually strike someone, you have to say the spell at the same time you're ending the motion. And yes, aim definitely counts, though you don't have to be exact. It's like the difference between shooting a pistol and shooting a shotgun filled with buckshot."

That didn't really make sense to her as she wasn't familiar with guns, so Sophia focused on making a few testing throws—her lips sealed, of course—before she frowned. "You want me to practice this in here? If aim is such a big deal, aren't you worried about me hurting you or anything?"

The grin he flashed at her surprised her. "Why do you think we're in an empty room? I'll stand behind you, and since that wall is stone, I think it can stand up to your attacks."

She doubted that was true. Unless the telekinetic power was weaker than she thought it was, it *could* damage a stone wall. However, Lucas was a stubborn sort, so she knew arguing wasn't going to do any good. Instead, she gave him a resigned nod. "Okay, so fling my arm out and say the word, that's it?"

"Don't forget the intention. Like this." He gave the same flinging motion as he spoke the surprisingly smooth syllable. She'd expected to see something—a ripple in the air, maybe—but she saw nothing until the magic hit the stone, but even then it was just a faint puff of dust. The area was smaller than she'd pictured, too, no bigger than a softball. "Your turn."

She took a deep breath and focused on the wall. The first throw, her timing was off and nothing happened, but on the second, she hit the wall. Not where she'd intended, unfortunately, but two feet lower and one to the left. Her nose wrinkled even as he nodded.

"Good job. Try it again."

So she did. Again and again, until her arm was starting to hurt, but her aim improved a minuscule amount with each throw, until she was hitting basically where she was aiming. It was enough, though. She wasn't in good enough shape to do these things for hours after hours. She stepped back and slumped against the wall, letting her arm fall limp at her side. "That's enough for one day. Besides, as much as it still sort of freaks me out, I should be trying to figure out the whole aspida thing."

Lucas studied her face for a moment before he nodded. "True. There's not really much for you to do with the guards, at least. You could micromanage—if you wanted—and decide which guard goes out with which venator each time, but you don't seem like the micromanaging type."

"I'm really not," she confirmed. "Besides, you know your guards better than I do. It'd be stupid and egotistical for me to think I know better than you just because I've got the job title. I'm a lot of things, and have a lot of flaws, but I try to avoid arrogance."

He smiled. "A good thing to avoid. Confidence is attractive, arrogance is not. Still, let me know if there's anything I can do to help."

"Trust me, everyone is going to know if there's something they can do to help. Thanks for the training, by the way," she told him as she pushed away from the wall and moved to the door.

"You're welcome."

Once in the hallway, Sophia paused. She'd spoken of doing aspida duties, and she'd meant it, but now she wasn't quite sure where to begin. After glancing back to the doorway, she decided to start with the faction heads. She returned to her room and grabbed the map before searching out Nick's office. His door was halfway open when she got there. She rapped on the wood while she peeked in the gap. "Nick? You got a minute?"

He looked up and she was surprised to see glasses perched on his nose. "Of course," he told her, taking those very glasses off and setting them beside his keyboard. "What can I do for you, Sophia?"

She stepped inside, not bothering to close the door. The office was large enough for half a dozen people, despite the tall filing cabinets lining three of the walls. The fourth held the desk Nick was sitting at, and two monitors sat on it. In front of it were four chairs. She sank into one as she blurted out, "I didn't know you wore glasses. I mean, I figured Sergei could fix vision problems."

He smiled. "He can, but even his magic can't prevent eyestrain, and since I tend to spend a lot of time staring at tiny words or computer monitors, the glasses help prevent me from getting headaches."

"Oh. Makes sense. So, I decided it was time I started acting like I was aspida. Figured the best place to start was by talking to you, Lucas, and Dion. You know, figure out exactly what you three do and what I can do to help."

"Ah." He nodded approvingly. "It's definitely a good place to start. I won't get into what Dion and Lucas do, but I basically research and organize. Probably a little more organizing." Motioning to the monitors—one of which held a map, the other some sort of spreadsheet—he said, "Some of the curators—and you—help with the research. Finding out where certain books or tablets are. We figure out the risk involved in obtaining the relic or volume, what it will cost—either to buy or in supplies, travel, that sort of thing—and how rare the volume or relic is. Then I have to decide which ones we should send people to obtain, and who is the best venator to do it. That might be speaking the language, having the skills required to reach it, or the contacts to get close to it."

Trying to process all the work that went into doing Nick's job made Sophia's head spin. She'd always considered herself organized, but that was a lot just to get one book into the Athenaeum. "Oh...wow. So how do you decide all those things?"

He chuckled. "It's not as complicated as it sounds, I promise. Not the way I do it, anyway. I assign each book or whatever ratings. How rare it is, how costly it is, and how dangerous it is to get it."

"Wouldn't the rarer books come first?"

"If possible, yes," he agreed. "But even if we heard about a book that held all of the universe's secrets, if it would bankrupt the Athenaeum or be so dangerous that we were guaranteed to lose a dozen people to get it?" He shook his head. "We revere knowledge and books, but we revere our people, too." She started to relax and smile but he added, "However, that being said, we do sometimes have nasaru or venatores who are...passionate...about a particular book. Even if I've deemed it too risky, even if the aspida agrees, they may volunteer to attempt to retrieve a book anyway."

"That...I love books, I really do, and I'd love to solve some of history's mysteries, but I don't know if I could see myself risking death to find the answers," she admitted.

"Most don't, but you also have to remember that most of the people here? We grew up in the Athenaeum. This is our life. Sometimes, it's worth it. And wouldn't you risk one person if it meant you could, say, find a book that held the cure for cancer or something else equally valuable?"

She blew out a soft breath and nodded. She could understand being so passionate about something it became indistinguishable from obsession. "Fair enough. But what's my role in all that?"

"Day to day? Not much. I will be sending each mission to you for final approval before the team goes out, but it tends to be fairly routine. Aspides generally also do their own research and can send a mission to me to organize, or even organize it themselves. And occasionally go on their own missions."

"That...sounds easy enough." She grinned crookedly. "Though I'm probably going to be rubber stamping things at first. You know what you're doing more than I do."

He laughed and shrugged. "And that's fine. Unless we get something major that's time sensitive, I was planning on keeping things fairly low-key for a while. Not just because we have a new aspida," he assured her, "but because everyone needs to recover from losing Erasmus."

All traces of humor fled as she nodded understandingly. "So no one's gone out since he..."

He shook his head. "No. I'm planning on sending a team out in two days, though. You'll get the details emailed to you." He paused, frowned. "Has Peter set your Athenaeum email up yet?"

"Uh...I have no idea. But he's also on my list of people to talk to." Or he was now.

"Good. Any other questions I can help you with?"

She considered that as she studied his face. She wanted to ask him if he had been the one to poison Erasmus, but since she couldn't, she just tried to read his expression. Unfortunately, she didn't know him well enough to know if he was hiding anything from her or not. Finally, she just smiled, shook her head, and rose. "Not right now, no. But after I talk to Peter, I'll send you my email."

"Appreciated. Have a good day, Sophia."

"You too."

After leaving Nick's office, Sophia referred to her map and started toward Dion's office. She couldn't say she was starting to get the hang of being aspida, but at least she was beginning to understand the inner workings of the Athenaeum. It made her feel good. This was the first step in her long journey. Sure, she'd had a pretty crappy start, but she could do this.

She was smiling as she neared the corner that led to the first floor common area. Dion's office was just past that, in the hallway to the left. Before she got there, she heard her name and paused. What surprised her was the fact that they weren't speaking English. Aside from Dion when she'd first arrived, and Erasmus during one of their conversations, everyone had spoken English, at least around her. It was fortunate that these people had chosen Greek so she could understand.

"Look, I'm sure Sophia's a nice enough person. That's not the issue. My issue is that someone who didn't even know we existed two weeks ago is now running everything."

The male voice wasn't one Sophia recognized right off, and she didn't dare peek around the corner to see if she knew the person. It was clear the conversation wasn't meant to be overheard, given how they were speaking in hushed tones.

Part of her told her that eavesdropping wasn't a pleasant habit, that she should just leave, but she couldn't bring herself to walk away. Not only did she not exactly disagree with the sentiment, she also had to know what the people she was now in charge of thought of her.

"I'm not saying it makes sense—to us, anyway—but has the Athenaeum ever made a mistake in choosing the aspida?" a woman asked.

"There's a first time for everything, isn't there?" the man retorted.

"Erasmus was a good aspida, no one's questioning that, but I think the Athenaeum made a mistake this time," a second man said. "That girl might do well as a curator, maybe even a venator, but there's no way she's going to be able to run this place. I heard she was just a student. You know what that means, right?" His companions murmured denials. "No experience. She's going to get us all killed or expose this place. Mark my words, having her as aspida is going to doom us."

Sophia couldn't bear to listen to anymore. Since she couldn't argue with any of his points, she couldn't even get mad. Tears stung her eyes as she went back the way she'd come before checking the map. There wasn't a way to get to Dion's office without going through the common area. Instead of trying to sneak past, she found a bathroom and locked herself in. She splashed cold water on her face as she tried to push the hurtful words out of her mind. It didn't work. They were on repeat. Instead, she waited until she was calmer and wasn't on the verge of crying. Hoping there had been enough time for the trio to disperse, she resumed her walk to Dion's, albeit at a slower pace than before.

They may not believe she could do the job—*she* may not fully believe it, yet—but she was going to try her damnedest.

Chapter 32

DESPITE SOPHIA'S DETERMINATION NOT to prove the naysayers right, her mood was still in the toilet when she reached Dion's door. It was closed, but she didn't knock right away. Not only did she want to try to talk herself into a better mood, she'd remembered how he was currently the prime suspect. Well, him and Nick, but Dion edged him out just a little, due to the incident with the booby-trapped book. Unfortunately, she wasn't a spy, and wasn't sure how to go about trying to get anything out of him about Erasmus's murder without letting on that she knew it was a murder. Rather than give herself a migraine trying to plan out something that was so far out of her skill set, she knocked.

Dion answered the door with a polite smile, though it warmed when he saw her. "Sophia! I was expecting you," he told her, sweeping the door open and motioning her inside.

She blinked at him before she stepped inside. "You were?" His office was surprisingly similar to Nick's. The main differences were that he had a third monitor on his desk, and a picture of him, what she assumed was a young Peter, and a woman she could only assume was Peter's mother. A woman she hadn't heard anything about, but she decided not to pry.

"Of course," he told her as he sat down and gestured for her to do the same. "Not at this exact moment, of course, but I had a feeling you'd be making your rounds today or tomorrow." He beamed proudly, at having been right, she guessed.

"I didn't even know," she protested as she dropped into a chair.

He waved a hand dismissively, never losing his smile. "I know how stubborn members of our family can be. You wouldn't have allowed yourself to put off doing your job for any longer than another day. I assume you want to hear about what I and the other curators do?"

"Yeah. I know the basics, of course, but your faction seems to be the most...I don't know, diverse?"

He nodded. "It is and it isn't. Curators take care of the Athenaeum, period. Top to bottom. But that means we take care of everything, from the people to the books to everything else. Just think of it that way and it isn't too complicated."

"No, it isn't, but it does sound like it makes your job more complicated."

"True, it can," he agreed. "Everyone has a skill, though, or a burning desire to do something specific to take care of this place. Like Agatha. Yes, she loves books, she loves the Athenaeum, but cooking, feeding the people she cares about, that's her passion. Peter? He'd rather read something on his computer than go traipsing all over the world looking for books."

"So people just get assigned where they want? And does no one just deal with the actual library? The books?" That was the part that had been bugging her. No one, as far as she'd seen, had just been assigned to keep the library in order, though she'd been told it was a curator's job.

He chuckled. "To answer your first question, yes, to an extent. We don't need two techs at the moment, so if someone else wanted to do that, I'd have to deny them the request. But if a position is open and they have the desire and aptitude to do it? Absolutely. As for the second question, we do have several people whose sole job is to care for the library. They ensure the books are all in order, input new books into the system when we get them, and mark books for repair."

"Let me guess, there's someone whose sole job is to repair books?" she asked, lips twitching.

"Of course. Our conservator, Ellie. Very nice woman."

"Huh. I should pay more attention to the information Peter gave me."

He cocked his head. "Information?"

"He gave me print outs of everyone, so I could familiarize myself with them. I haven't had a chance to look through them in any depth, though. Are there any other curators who have jobs I probably wouldn't have understood, like the conservator?"

He grinned and shook his head. "I think you'll do fine with everything else."

"Oh good. I've got enough new knowledge crammed in my head." His laughter made her helpless not to smile. "What can I do? Or what role does the aspida have for your faction?"

"When someone is assigned to a new position—or reassigned—you are the one who ultimately makes the decision there. And historically, the aspida normally deals with ensuring the most dangerous books are safely stored so no one is hurt." His smile drooped and his eyes filled with remorse. "Like you were," he said quietly. "I am so sorry about that, Sophia. I have no idea what that book was doing out in the open."

He sounded so sincere her suspicion of him dimmed, just a little. "It's okay, Dion. Accidents happen, and I'm all right."

"You are, but..." He drew in a deep breath and shook his head. "I'll work with you once you're ready. Show you how to make the protective boxes and handle the books safely."

"I'd like that. Even though only a few people are allowed down there, it's best not to take chances."

"Absolutely right, my dear. And while we're asking what we can do...is there anything I can do to help you settle into your new role?"

"No, I think I just need time to adjust and learn and meet everyone, but if I think of anything, I'll let you know."

"Please do," he told her earnestly.

She rose to her feet, unsurprised when he did the same. "I'll let you get back to work, but let me know if there is anything I need to be doing, okay?"

"I will. You'll do just fine, Sophia, so try not to worry yourself too much."

"I'll do my best," she told him, unable to promise anything else. As she walked out and closed the door behind her, she had to wonder if he was truly as innocent as he appeared, or if he was just a fantastic actor.

She mulled over that on her way to the computer room. At the very least, she wanted to check in with Peter and Valerie, the finance curator, before dinner. That would give her the five biggest priorities out of the way—aside from the books, of course. Hopefully, doing something productive would help her shake off the funk the overheard conversation had put her in. If not, then hanging out with Peter for a bit couldn't hurt. After a week, it was easy to see that no one could be bummed for long around the enthusiastic geek.

Peter was alone in the computer room, his mohawk partially crushed by the headphones he was wearing. Judging by the way his head bobbed, he was listening to something with a good beat, completely absorbed by the music and the words streaming by on his monitors. It was tempting to sneak up on him, but it wouldn't be professional. Since she was here—at least partially—as aspida, she should at least try to act like it.

She came at him from the side, his body language shifting just before she tapped his shoulder, telling her that he'd noticed her.

He slid the headphones off, glanced up, and grinned broadly. "Boss lady!"

Sophia groaned as she collapsed into a chair, just hard enough that the rolling chair slid back a foot. She let out a soft squeak of surprise, which made Peter visibly bite back a laugh. "Don't call me that," she grumbled and inched the chair back to where it had started.

"Why not? You are the boss. I think it's fitting. And it suits you." His grin softened to a comforting smile. "You'll get used to being the boss, Soph. Just give yourself time."

She grumbled wordlessly as her arms crossed over her chest. Pouting wasn't really her thing, but she took a moment to do just that, until Peter's intense look and steady smile had her lips twitching. "Okay, okay. Fine. Besides, I'm here as said boss."

"Ooh, now I'm curious," he told her as he straightened. "What can I do for you?"

"First, I'm told there's email just for the Athenaeum and I need my address."

"Oh! Yeah, I've got that all set up for you." He spun back to face his computer and did some tapping on the keyboard. After grabbing a sticky note, he neatly printed an email and series of letters and random symbols. Tearing the top sheet off, he handed it to her. "Here's your login information. The first time you log on, it will let you change your password, of course."

Sophia took the note, skimmed it, then gave him a wry smile. "And where exactly do I access my email from?"

Peter's cheeks flushed and he opened one of his desk drawers, pulling out a paper and handing it to her. "Sorry. This tells you how to get the program—and app—and set everything up. But let me know if you have any problems."

She frowned as she looked over the section on the app. "I can check it on my phone?" she asked, uneasy.

His frown matched hers. "Yes? Why wouldn't you be able to?"

"You said that there was nothing about the Athenaeum on any computer connected to the outside world, and phones definitely are."

His expression cleared. "Oh, I get what you mean. And I did say that, but it was a...what's the word...oversimplifying?"

"Oversimplification?"

"Yes, that," he agreed with a nod. "There is technically one thing on every librarian's phone that's Athenaeum-related. It's an app for our email and the group texts that we use for mass messages. It's not a hundred percent foolproof, so we are still careful what we say, but we secure our phones so the risk is minimal."

Pulling her phone out, she wiggled it. "Not secured, Peter. Just an ordinary cell phone." She sighed softly. "And I'm going to have to get it switched over anyway, since it's with an American carrier."

Peter plucked it from her hand, frowned, and held it back out to her. "Finger." After she had unlocked it, he started tapping on it. "I'll take care of the carrier thing for you," he said, distracted by his task. A couple of minutes later, during which she'd just watched him silently, he handed it back to her. "All secured. Give me a couple of days on the other thing. But you can now deal with the group messages and email without worrying."

"Thanks," she said, poking about on her phone. She expected to find something different, but if she hadn't just watched him play with her phone, she never would have known anything had been done to it. Until she found a single icon with an envelope and silhouettes of several people. "What's this for?"

He glanced briefly at it. "That's a shortcut for the email and group messages, both receiving and sending."

"Ah. Gotcha." Opening the app, she shot off a message with her email address to Nick, Dion, and Lucas, so they'd be able to send her stuff. While she had her phone out, she took a moment to peek at the time and sighed. "I should get going, but before I do, is there anything else I need to know about the tech side of the Athenaeum?"

"Not really. Since it's been set up, it's basically just maintaining it. Though I always welcome feedback, both for bugs and suggestions for new features," he said, cheerfully enough that she guessed he'd welcome something to do.

"Will do. I'm good at breaking technology, so I'm sure there will be something," she said playfully as she got to her feet.

"Why off so soon?"

"Need to meet with Valerie before dinner. I told you, I'm playing boss today."

He shook his head. "You're not playing, Soph. You *are* boss."

"Yeah," she sighed. "I'm just acting like it today. Or trying to. I'll see you at dinner."

Valerie was easy to track down and, while not as friendly and warm as the others she'd spoken to, very helpful. Most of what she said went over Sophia's head. Her idea of finances to that point had been keeping track of what was in her single bank account. An account which never went above four digits and rarely went higher than three.

What she did take away from the meeting was that the Athenaeum had a *lot* of money. Not the most money she'd ever heard of someone having, but enough to temporarily stop Sophia's heart. Especially when she learned that she had access to literally all of it. Then Valerie had to make it worse by showing Sophia a list of all the property and things that the Athenaeum owned—all secretly, of course. The jet and estate that served as their cover were only the beginning. There were houses and apartments all over the world, dozens of cars, two more jets, not to mention multiple businesses. Not all of the properties were for business, either. Apparently, working for the Athenaeum had its perks, and one of them was some prime vacation homes.

At the end of the meeting, Valerie told her that Sophia's two cards would be there in a few days. One was for business, the other for the account that everyone in the Athenaeum had, where their salary was directly deposited into every month. A very generous salary, considering not all of them had to pay for rent, utilities, or meals.

Sophia was overwhelmed with information, so couldn't think of a single question to ask when Valerie was done. Instead, she just smiled, thanked Valerie for her time, and left, trying to process it all.

Chapter 33

Sophia was in a daze as she left the finance office, gripping the pages she'd gotten from Valerie and Peter without realizing she was still holding them. Before she knew it, she was in front of one of the few rooms she hadn't been in. The armory. Wanting a distraction from the money, she unlocked the door and stepped inside. The moment she did, her jaw dropped. The room was split into three sections. The first, nearest the door, held modern weapons and armor. Which meant she was staring at more guns and military-looking knives than she'd ever seen in her life. Kevlar vests and helmets were lined up neatly as well, in a variety of sizes. The next section was all older style weapons. Swords, whips, spears, and quite a few she had no name for. Some looked as though they were actually old, but a few looked newly made. The last section was a workshop. A forge, she supposed, but since she had no idea what went into making weapons, she could only guess.

At second glance, she saw that some of the weapons had small cards near them. Curious, she stepped closer, only to be interrupted by an annoyed voice. The words were rapid and not in English or Greek—she thought it was a language from east Asia—so she had no idea what the man had said. Turning, she saw a man only a few inches taller than her. By the tone of his skin and his facial features, she knew she'd been right on the language region. He had short black hair, not quite a military cut, and a lean, muscular build. She also recognized him as someone who had been pointed out to her, but couldn't place his name.

"Sorry, I don't speak that language," Sophia told him, choosing Greek for her own words. Though she knew most people in the Athenaeum spoke English, it was arrogant to assume everyone would.

The man frowned at her. "What are you doing here?" he asked in the same language.

"Uh...just looking around? Don't worry, I wasn't planning on touching anything." Given how little she knew about weapons, even just picking something up could be dangerous.

"Why?"

The blunt question made her blink. "Because it's one of the few rooms I hadn't seen and I was curious?"

The man huffed and folded his arms over his chest. "Do you have any questions, then?"

"To start, who are you?" she asked, finding his abrupt manner almost amusing. She fought not to smile at his discomfort at having what his space invaded—or what he clearly seemed to view as his.

"Kaito."

Now she remembered. He was the armorer. "Nice to meet you, Kaito. I'm—"

"Sophia. The new aspida. Yes, I know." He cocked his head but didn't otherwise move. There was no fidgeting, no shifting of his weight. He did, however, switch to English. "I was not aware you were interested in weapons."

Though she loved Greek, was fluent in it, English was still easier, so she was relieved to speak her native tongue once more. "I'm not, not really. But it seemed like I should at least take a look."

"That is wise. You should always know everything you can about what you are in charge of. Before you ask, I am in charge of this room and nothing else. I'm the armorer."

"I'm guessing that doesn't just mean you take care of the weapons. Ray said something about repairing and making weapons. That would be your job?"

He gave one short nod. "It would. I maintain everything in here, including the spelled weapons and armor."

That caught her interest. "There are spells on some things in here? Like what?"

"Like that," he said, motioning to the Kevlar vest with a note card she'd spotted just before he'd arrived. "Like that. Normal bulletproof vest, but it has more stopping power than anything you can purchase, even for the military. And that," he pointed to a sword on a different aisle, "will never need sharpening, will never break. Not unless it is attacked by magic, anyway."

"That is so cool." The casual use of magic in the Athenaeum would probably stop shocking her one day, but for now, every day was as special as Christmas. She was so used to having to hide her own powers, given that she lived in a place mostly populated by humans. "Why so much, though? There aren't enough guards for all this."

"People other than the nasaru are trained to use weapons and armors, and often venatores will go on missions armed. And while the Athenaeum has never been invaded, that is because we are careful and prepare for as many scenarios as possible. One of those scenarios is an invasion, which would mean as many people as possible would need to have access to the items in this room. Not only that, but you have to account for weapons breaking, getting lost, or being stolen."

Sophia didn't have to have grown up in the Athenaeum for the idea of it being invaded to chill her blood. Rather than dwell on it, she wandered closer to the workshop area. "Would it be okay if I watched sometime? You making a weapon, I mean?"

He scowled, still unmoving as he considered her request.

"Please? I mean, I do need to understand all aspects of the Athenaeum, right? How can I make good decisions without knowing how things work?"

That did it. He sighed and let his arms drop. "Fine. But you have to stay back. Blacksmithing can be dangerous if you are distracted."

There was no way she was getting close to red-hot metal, so she grinned at him. "I can do that. Thanks, Kaito. I'll get out of your hair for now." She left before he could change his mind. Checking her phone, she detoured to her room. Following the instructions Peter had given her, she got her email set up and checked it. Nothing yet, but the heads had replied to her earlier message, confirming they'd received it.

That done, she headed to the dining room. She was one of the last ones there and took a seat between Lucas and Josie, since her mom was surrounded by Dion and Ray. They were just across from Sophia, though, so conversation was still possible. Heather offered her a smile and questioning look, which Sophia returned with a smile of her own. Surprisingly, it wasn't even forced. Sure, she had a lot to do, but the various meetings that day had helped.

It was a relief when dinner was normal. There were a few looks sent her way, but nothing that lingered overlong. After the conversation she'd overheard, it would have been too much. Especially since she'd finally gotten her good mood back. She wasn't the sort to mope, so was determined to stay upbeat as much as she could.

Conversations flowed around her, but she wasn't excluded. She ended up chatting about movies, favorite books, language, not to mention joking around. For the first time since she'd arrived in the Athenaeum, she didn't feel like an outsider. She may not feel like the boss, not just yet, but this was definitely a good start.

One set of eyes fixed on her halfway through the meal. She wasn't sure who it was, though he didn't look like a guard. While his gaze wasn't antagonistic, it still made her smile dim. It almost looked like he was trying to figure her out. Not that she could blame him. She was a stranger to these people. Only a handful knew her well enough to even consider her an acquaintance, really.

"I should set up a meeting or something," she murmured to herself as she poked at her food with her fork.

"What was that?" Heather asked.

Sophia glanced up and shrugged. "I just thought maybe I should set up a meeting, so everyone can meet me and ask questions and stuff. Most of them don't know me, or have only said hi."

"That's easy enough to do," Dion told her with a gentle smile. "I could set it for tomorrow afternoon, if that suits you."

Though it had been her idea, she was suddenly nervous at the thought of actually going through with it. Still, it was a good idea, a smart idea, so she drew in a calming breath and nodded. "That works. Let me know what time and where."

"Of course," he assured her.

"That's a good idea," Josie told her, bumping Sophia's shoulder with her own. "And don't be nervous. These are all good people. Change can just be hard sometimes."

Sophia nodded absently, but Josie's words actually made her nerves worse rather than better. Most of those here may be good people, but there was at least one who wasn't. One who would love to see her in an urn right next to her grandfather's.

Scenarios ran through Sophia's mind as she tried to sleep. In each one, the meeting went beyond badly. People yelling at her, trying to throw her out, even attacking her. Shortly after one, she gave up and made her way through the Athenaeum and to the hidden room. The room that, supposedly, no other living person was aware of besides the divine patrons. Given the sheer number of texts in the room, it would take her a couple of centuries to read through it all and learn the spells, but learning them wasn't her intention. There were some things that shouldn't be learned, power that should never be held. Power she didn't want. She was no saint, she had no illusions about that, but she liked to think she was a good person. Raising the dead? It definitely wasn't for her.

Still, ignorance wasn't for her either, so she did flip through the grimoire. She made a note of spells she thought could be useful, as well as languages she recognized but couldn't read. If she was going to do this job justice, she was going to have to start working on learning more languages quickly. Given how thick the book was, it took quite some time, even just flipping through. Unfortunately, her brain was still too full of pessimistic scenes that she opted to remain where she was and, rather than go back to bed, grabbed the book on the Athenaeum. It would be good to know more about how the Athenaeum had come to be what it was now, but she hesitated, as it wasn't really top priority. It didn't matter how much of the Athenaeum's history she knew if she ended up the next victim of the resident murderer. Then again, wasn't she entitled to a little bit of downtime?

Curiosity warred with responsibility and she glanced at her phone, groaning when she saw the time. Almost three. She knew Lucas was going to insist on more training in the morning, not to mention she had the meeting. Sleep wasn't optional, not tonight, so she dragged herself back to her room. It took time, but eventually, sleep found her.

Chapter 34

After breakfast—waffles and bacon, made especially for her—Sophia checked her email, signing off on the mission Nick had sent her. It didn't seem like anything major, just attending an auction in Paris, though it did have a rather large budget, at least in her opinion. That done, she joined Steven and Lucas in the gym for more hand to hand training. They built upon what she'd learned before and, though they claimed she was making progress, she still felt as clumsy as she had a week ago. She was definitely just as tired and sore afterward as she'd been the last lesson, but they had graduated from punches to a few kicks, so that wasn't surprising. But the physical exertion did a damn good job of distracting her from thinking about Seth's visit.

Midway through the lesson, when she had been 'graciously' given five minutes to rest and get some water, Dion showed up.

"Ah, good. I was told you would be here," he told her with a gentle smile.

"Unfortunately," she grumbled, shooting both Steven and Lucas glares. "These slave drivers are doing their best to torture me," she said, her tone good-natured despite the words.

Dion chuckled. "Perhaps they are, but they are the very best at what they do."

"Told you," Lucas said with a faint smirk.

Sophia rolled her eyes and gave Dion her attention once more. "What's up?"

"The meeting is set for one this afternoon in the lower common area. Everyone will be there. I just wanted to tell you in person," Dion answered.

Her mood hadn't been great to begin with, but that brought the nerves back. She gulped down more water to keep from having to answer right away, but it only allowed her to delay for a few seconds. "Okay. I'll be there." She glanced down at her sweat-stained shirt and flicked a damp strand of hair behind her ear. "After a shower," she muttered to herself, but the others heard, based on their quiet laughter.

"I have no doubt you will. What's more, I know you will be just fine, Sophia," he assured her, resting a comforting hand on her shoulder.

His encouragement and demeanor soothed her, then immediately made her feel antsy. He was their best suspect, but it was so hard to imagine him as a murderer. Then again, it was hard to imagine anyone in the Athenaeum as a murderer. She worked up a smile but could tell it looked forced. "I'm going to do my best."

"That is all anyone can ask for," he said before smiling at her and her instructors, then walking out of the gym.

Sophia closed her eyes and tried to put her nerves and suspicion away.

"Break's over," Lucas told her, plucking the water bottle from her hand before he nudged her toward Steven, just hard enough that she stumbled once.

She scowled at him but shifted her focus back to Steven and the training. He worked her hard for the last hour, stopping just before noon. By that point, Sophia's limbs trembled with fatigue, but she did feel marginally more comfortable with the movements. A long shower eased the worst of it, so by the time she was dressed and heading for the common area, she felt mostly like a person again. That was when her nerves returned. She'd dressed in her nicest jeans and had borrowed an amethyst blouse from her mom, so she at least looked like she knew what she was doing. Sort of.

Her already slow steps lagged even more when she heard the low murmur of voices from the common area. At ten till one she'd expected to be one of the first ones there, but others had beaten her to it. A full dozen, she realized when she reached the designated meeting place. Multiple pairs of eyes turned in her direction and part of her wanted to bolt back to her room. Public speaking had really never been her thing. The only things that kept her from doing just that were a desire to do her job justice, and the warmth and faith in her mom's eyes when they met her own. Rather than join her mom and gain comfort from her presence, Sophia gave her a small smile and made her way across the room, pausing when she heard greetings. There weren't many, but it was enough to bolster her confidence, especially when Lucas winked at her. The boost was more a result of her shock in seeing Lucas, of all people, wink, but the effect was the same.

It didn't hurt that he'd started to get under her skin. They'd only slept together once, but it was enough to make her want more. It was unfortunate that circumstances kept it from being as easy as knocking on his door. Though she might give that a try. To lose herself in his arms, if only for an hour or so, would be wonderful, even if it was nothing but entertaining sex for him.

She wasn't sure what it was for her.

Ten minutes later, the common area was teeming with people. Dion made his way to her and spoke, voice low. "Everyone is here, except for the children, of course, so you can begin whenever you're ready."

"Thanks," she told him, moving to the front of the room. The voices silenced, one by one, until she could have heard a pin drop. Her gaze slid around the room, moving over both the familiar and unfamiliar faces. The expressions varied from supportive to curious to bored. She tried to ignore the latter and took a slow breath, steeling herself and forcing a smile to her lips.

"Hi everyone. I'm sure you know who am I, since I'm the only new person here, but just in case, I'm Sophia." She paused for a moment but there was no reaction, not even a rustle of clothing as anyone shift-ed. "I've met quite a few of you, but I know I haven't met everyone. I want to fix that as soon as possible. I'll be trying to at least introduce myself and have a proper conversation with all of you, but my door is open to anyone who wants that conversation sooner rather than later. Metaphorically, anyway, since I'm still trying to figure everything out and get settled in." She looked around again, slightly reassured by the warm smile on her mom's face and the nod Lucas gave her. Some of the bored expressions had grown mildly irritated, and she knew she needed to address the elephant in the room.

"I know that's an issue for some people, the fact that I'm new and haven't been a part of the Athenaeum long. I'm sure that a lot of you expected someone else—maybe yourselves or friends—to become aspida when my grandfather died. You're wondering what in the hell qualifies me to fill his shoes." She shook her head and shrugged. "Nothing." She saw some surprise at that statement, but Heather just smiled wider. "I didn't know him long, but no one is ever going to be just like Erasmus. No one is going to do the job the same way he did. I'm not even going to try. And no, I didn't grow up in the Athenaeum, I haven't been here for years, learning the ins and outs, but I'm not dumb, and I've actually been working toward being here my whole life, even without having any idea this place existed." Her head inclined to her mom. "You all know my mom, right? She can tell you I've been interested in ancient history and languages my whole life. When I was told there was an ancient library filled with lost books and relics? It was like a dream come true." That got her a couple of chuckles and loosened some of the pressure in her chest. "I'm going to make mistakes. Everyone does. I'm also going to learn just as fast as I can. About the Athenaeum, what we do, and I'm definitely going to learn more languages so I can do my job properly."

"Are you saying you only speak English?" a voice with a Greek accent called out. Sophia recognized it as one of the ones who hadn't been sure of her being the boss. She looked over to see a man with lightly tanned skin, dark brown hair, and green eyes.

She shook her head and switched to Greek. "No, I'm not saying that. I also speak Greek—Attic and modern, obviously—and Latin, and I'm conversational in a few other languages. Like I said, I'm going to be learning more as fast as I can. Hopefully everyone can be patient and help me. Including you..." She trailed off, hoping he'd take the hint and give her his name. Oddly, having him speak up, and being able to answer him, helped settle her nerves some.

The man said nothing for a long moment before he nodded. He didn't look entirely relieved, but he accepted her answer. Fortunately, he took the hint. "I'm sure everyone will do their part. And I'm Jericho."

"Nice to meet you, Jericho. And like I said, my door is always open. If any of you want to talk to me, about anything, I'm not hard to find. You all know where my room is, and several people have my phone number and email address."

"The phone carrier thing was taken care of, too," Peter called.

She grinned at him. "Thanks. Now, I won't keep you guys too long as I know we all have things to do, but if anyone wants to ask me something, you're more than welcome to do that now, just like Jericho," she said, waving a hand toward said man. Before anyone could speak up, she added, "And if I haven't already met you, getting your name would be good, too."

A handsome man who looked like he came from somewhere on the Arabian Peninsula and had just a touch of gray at his temples was the first to say anything. "I'm Farid, one of the guards. Are you planning on changing anything?"

"Hi, Farid. And I don't know," Sophia admitted. "Right now? No. The Athenaeum seems to be running just fine as is, and, as I said, I haven't been here long enough to be comfortable making any big changes. Now, that doesn't mean I'm not going to make changes in the future, but I know enough to know that I need to listen to advice. Which means if there's something you guys feel needs changing? Let me know."

"That's fair," he said, giving her a short nod.

"Does the lack of changes include letting everyone keep their jobs?" Jericho asked.

"It does," she assured him with a nod. "Erasmus was okay with everyone being where they were. So were the faction heads. They all know you guys better than I do. I'm not egotistical enough to think I know better than everyone else, especially not after a week and a half."

A few more people called out questions, but they were all simple questions and, surprisingly, more about her than her job. It made sense. People wanted to know who they were working for. By the time everyone started filing out, she'd put more faces with names. A pretty goth girl was named Ellie and she was responsible for all the book repairs. The tall blonde woman was Melissa, a guard. The almost painfully average looking man with skin the color of mahogany and a smooth British accent was Manny, who was one of the venatores.

Even with her being more relaxed, it was still draining to have been the center of so much attention for almost an hour. All she wanted was a nap or a long soak in the tub. Before she could make her escape, Lucas walked up to her.

"I know how hard that was for you," he told her, too quietly to be overheard, "so how would you like to get out of here for a while?"

Sophia frowned. "Out of here? To where?"

A slow smile formed. "It's your first time in Greece and you've seen nothing but this place. Shouldn't you be wanting to change that?"

"I saw a restaurant, too," she corrected automatically before the rest of his words sank in. "Wait, sight-seeing? You want to take me sight-seeing?" she asked, exhaustion evaporating under her instant excitement. "Yes! Absolutely! When can we go?"

He laughed. "As soon as you're ready."

"Can we take a couple of people, too? Make it an outing?"

"Sure. Invite who you want. I'll be waiting at the entrance to the labyrinth when you're ready."

Sophia practically skipped over to where her mom was talking to Josie. "I'm going sight-seeing! You guys want to come with?"

"You seem awfully excited to be playing tourist," Josie teased.

"I've studied Greek history all my life and have never seen a single historical sight," Sophia replied.

"Oh. Well, I can't miss that. Give me five?"

"Sure. Lucas is going, too. We're going to meet over there," she said, pointing to where he was leaning against the wall, browsing something on his phone while he waited.

"Okay," Josie said before leaving.

"What about you, Mom?"

Heather smiled. "I'm going to pass, but you have fun," she said, giving Sophia a hug. "You did great, by the way. You'll win the doubters over."

"I hope so. Okay, gotta go see if Peter wants to come with then grab my camera. Love you!"

She went hunting for her cousin with her mom's soft laughter trailing behind her. She caught up to him halfway to the computer room. "Peter!" When he turned, she grinned at him. "Want to join me, Josie, and Lucas in sight-seeing?"

He cocked his head. "Sight-seeing?"

"Yeah! I've always wanted to see all the important old places in Greece. And we're right by Delphi. I'm dying to see the Temple of Apollo."

Peter grinned and shook his head. "It sounds like fun, even if I'm only watching your reactions, but I've got a lot of work to do. Enjoy yourself, though."

Pouting, she asked, "You sure?"

"Sorry, but yes, I'm sure. Take lots of pictures, though, and you can show me later?"

"That works. See ya!" She hurried back to her room, exchanging the blouse for a comfortable tee-shirt, and the short boots for a pair of sneakers. After checking to make sure her camera battery was full and the memory card empty, she slung the camera case and her purse across her chest and rushed back to the entrance, finding not just Lucas and Josie there, but also Carla.

"I invited myself," Carla said with a tiny, smug smirk. "Can't have our aspida wandering around with just a single guard."

Sophia groaned. "Nothing's going to happen, but I know it'll make you guys feel better. Can we go now?" she asked, fighting not to bounce with anticipation.

Lucas laughed and nodded. "We can," he said, and she grinned the entire way to the SUV.

Chapter 35

Sophia was so thrilled at the thought of seeing the places she'd studied that the hike down to the estate felt like it took only a minute. She claimed shotgun as soon as they reached the SUV and grinned during the entire ride to Delphi. The others playfully teased her about her enthusiasm, but she brushed it off. She just didn't care. For the first time, she was going to see all the things she'd studied for most of her life.

The other three had already been to Delphi—several times, in fact—so Sophia was more than happy to allow them to play tour guide. Carla and Josie more than Lucas, who was in guard mode, watching the people rather than the sights. Still, he smirked more than once at her reactions as they took her to the various structures. She grinned like a fool at the treasury, marveled at the Tholos, and just stared in awe at the theater. Actually, she stared so long that Carla laughed and had to jab her in the side gently to get her attention.

"Huh? What?"

"Do you realize that you've been staring for the last twenty minutes?" Carla asked, highly amused.

"No, I haven't," Sophia answered automatically. "Wait, have I really?"

"Yes," Lucas answered, at the same time Josie nodded and said, "You really have."

Sophia felt her cheeks heat as she turned her attention back to the ancient stone rows. "Sorry," she said, only half meaning it. "It's just..." She blew out a soft breath and shook her head, trying to find the words to explain what the sight in front of her meant. "I live—lived—in the States. Old there is a few hundred years. But this? This is *thousands* of years old, guys. It was constructed before they had electricity, cars, the printing press, steam power...Hell, before they had paper. It's even older than most anyone who's alive. And it's still here. Maybe not entirely intact, but it's still here and it's absolutely freaking beautiful."

Her voice was soft and filled with awe, she knew it, but she also couldn't bring herself to be embarrassed at the display of emotion. The others seemed to understand, too, because Josie just smiled, wrapped an arm around Sophia's shoulders, and said, "Come on, you have to see the temple, too."

"Trust me, you'd have to drag me away from here if you tried to leave before we saw that," Sophia said with a grin. As they made their way down the path to the temple, her stomach growled. "How long have we been here, anyway?"

"A little over two hours," Carla answered.

"Seriously? It feels like ten minutes, tops." She glanced at Lucas and some of her eagerness slipped away at his posture and the expression on his face. "Lucas?" She waited until he looked at her. "Everything okay?"

"Not sure," he admitted. "Something feels off."

Carla immediately closed in, moving to Sophia's side opposite Lucas. "Off how?"

Sophia didn't bother asking, just murmured the threat spell under her breath. She expected to feel the normal low-level tingling, but it was stronger than usual. Not as bad as it had been the night she felt like she wanted to scratch her skin off, but still unpleasant. "There's a threat somewhere," she said quietly to them. "Not right on top of us, but it's close."

"Tourist day is over. Back to the car," Lucas said, his voice stern. Automatically, all three formed a triangle around her and began ushering her back the way they'd come. They'd only gotten a few steps before Lucas jerked and fire sliced across Sophia's shoulder. Even as she gasped, she heard the gunshot, but it didn't click right away that both she and Lucas had been shot. Lucas and Carla moved closer, trying to shield her with their own bodies. Both had pistols in their hands, and Lucas's once white shirt was stained with red—and the stain was growing.

Everything in Sophia told her now was the time to freak out. She'd never been around guns, and now she'd been shot. Worse, she wasn't the only one. All she'd wanted to do was see the ancient sites of Greece, dammit. She shoved the panic down and closed her eyes, trusting that the guards would keep her safe. There was no need to whisper this time as she recited the words she'd practiced more than a hundred times while Lucas threw grapes at her. It was hard to focus, especially when more shots rang out, but she didn't dare even open her eyes to see if anyone else had been shot. It took three tries before the invisible barrier came into being, and just in time, too. Sophia opened her eyes as a bullet was stopped just inches from Carla's head. To her horror, she saw that there was a second red spot on Lucas—through his shoulder this time—and Carla had taken a shot in the arm.

"Can you hold that while we move?" Lucas asked, his voice strained.

"I can try," she told him, not at all sure. She'd only practiced it while stationary, and even then not enough to truly call herself proficient.

"Try hard," Carla suggested before they started ushering her at a run toward the car.

Sophia glanced back to see Josie was on their heels, looking calmer than she was, but not by much. "Stay close, this shield doesn't extend far," she half-yelled and Josie nodded to show she heard.

The SUV seemed forever to get to, though the shots stopped after another two were fired at them. Though Lucas had driven there, he wasn't going to be able to drive back. Carla dug the keys out of his pocket, unlocked the vehicle, and tossed them to Josie. "Drive."

They scrambled in, with Lucas and Sophia in the back seat. Josie quickly started the SUV, driving just a little too fast, but Sophia couldn't complain. Carla kept her gun close and watched the landscape carefully. After a few minutes and no activity, she dared to pull her phone out and make a call. "We're on our way back. We were attacked. No, Sophia's fine. She got grazed, but nothing serious. We need Sergei standing by for Lucas, though. Yeah, two, one in the shoulder, one in the side. I've got one in my arm, but it seems minor. It was a sniper. Lucas and Sophia took the first shot before we heard it." She paused to glance back to Sophia. "We'd be dead if Lucas hadn't noticed something was off and Sophia hadn't put up a rather impressive shield. Just be ready. We'll be back as soon as we can."

Now that no one was shooting at them, Sophia was edging closer to panic. "What do I do?" she asked as she stared at the growing amount of blood on Lucas. Yes, being part elf meant she had some healing powers, but nothing like her mom had. She was better at paper cuts and headaches than bullet wounds. She'd also never seen this much blood before, and the fact that it was her lover's blood made it twice as bad. She couldn't rely entirely on her healing, not if she wanted Lucas to live.

"Put pressure on the bullet holes. There should be a blanket in the back. It'll help," Carla said without looking back.

Sophia found the blanket and pressed it against the wound in his shoulder, since it seemed to be bleeding more heavily. Doing so caused her own pain to come rushing back, but she just winced and kept the pressure on Lucas. "I'm sorry," she whispered to him as she sent what magic she had into him. If only he'd been able to shift his skin to stone, the bullet never would have been able to hurt him, but in public like they'd been, it could have been a death sentence. The only law that applied to all Arcane was not to reveal themselves to humans.

"W-why?" he asked, his eyes drifting closed. Before she could answer him, his body went slack.

"Lucas? Lucas!"

"Relax," Carla said without looking back. "Check his pulse. If it's good, he's just passed out. He's strong, but blood loss affects everyone."

Sophia tried to ignore the blood on her fingers as she fumbled at his neck for his pulse. When she felt it beneath her fingers, her head dropped. "He's just out." Or she thought, but she still pushed her healing abilities to the limit, hoping they'd at least slow the bleeding.

Carla nodded once. "It's probably for the best. Unconscious, he's not in pain. Just keep pressure on and let him be."

Nothing more was said until they pulled up to the estate. Sophia's arm was starting to scream, but she didn't dare relax the pressure.

Sergei was waiting in the garage, along with Heather, Dion, Nick, Angela, Peter, and a few others Sophia couldn't immediately put a name to. They were at the SUV before Josie had even shut off the engine, doors being opened before the occupants could move.

Nick got there first, opening Carla's door and dragging her out and into a fierce hug. He murmured something to her before drawing her further away from the SUV and looking at her arm.

Sergei was next, opening Sophia's door while Heather, Dion, and Peter tried not to crowd him. "How badly are you hurt?" he asked, his accent stronger than usual.

Sophia shook her head. "It hurts, but it can wait. Help Lucas first." It looked like he was going to argue, and she fixed him with a hard look. "He took those bullets for me. He's unconscious. Help. Him. First." This wasn't something she was going to back down on, and if her position as aspida meant anything, she'd make sure this was an order they followed.

Sergei gave in and, with the help of Dion and Peter, got Lucas out of the SUV. Someone, she wasn't sure who, levitated him, which made getting him up to the Athenaeum relatively easy. Later she might be concerned about someone seeing the obvious display of magic, but right now she was just happy it meant he was getting there quicker. She moved to follow, but her mom caught her first, catching her in a hug as tight as the one Nick had given Carla.

"I heard you'd been shot and I just..." Heather shook her head. "You're not allowed to get shot."

"Trust me, it's not an experience I want to repeat," Sophia assured her as she returned the hug with one arm. "I know I scared you, but I need to go with him," she said as she drew back.

"That's fine, but don't expect me to let you out of my sight for a while," Heather said as they followed the others.

Josie was obviously shaken, but Angela was with her. Peter fell into step beside Sophia, looked at her arm, then frowned, all but wringing his hands in concern. "Are you sure you're okay?"

"I will be. Lucas really is hurt the worst. Both him and Carla shielded me with their bodies." And that guilt was going to keep her up at night. She got why they did it, but she didn't feel like she deserved it. Other people were more useful, more important to the Athenaeum. It didn't stop Heather and Peter from sticking to her until they were in the clinic, watching as Sergei cleaned the wounds, then grimaced and began to search, supposedly for a bullet that hadn't exited Lucas's body. Unfortunately, the guard in question started to wake up before Sergei was finished. He moaned and started moving on the table, making Sergei frown.

"Hold him, he needs to stay still," the healer said before resuming his search. Peter, Nick, and a tall, muscular man moved forward to help. Sophia watched as the bullet was found and discarded, then the wound in Lucas's knit closed, fresh, pink skin replacing the hole the bullet had left. "Damn. Another bullet's still in, too." He grabbed a tray of medical tools and glanced up to Sophia. "You may want to wait outside."

Heather started to draw Sophia out of the clinic, but Sophia shook her head. "He took that bullet to protect me. The least I can do is be here for him." Instead of leaving, she stepped forward and took

Lucas's bloodied hand in hers. His fingers tightened weakly around hers, but she could tell he still wasn't fully awake. Rather than watch what Sergei was doing, she kept her eyes on Lucas's face. It was the only way she could make herself stay instead of running away to throw up. She'd never had a problem with blood before, but her prior experience was all with small cuts and scrapes, not bullet wounds.

It felt like hours later when Sophia heard the soft clink of the second bullet being dropped in a metal dish and Sergei resuming his healing. It wasn't until he stopped that she dared to look at Lucas's side, relieved to see it, too, was closed. It was still shiny and pink with new growth, but it was a vast improvement. As was the fact that Lucas's eyes were now open and no longer clouded by pain.

"How do you feel?" she asked Lucas, giving his hand a careful squeeze.

"Better. Getting shot is never fun, but Sergei knows what he's doing," Lucas told her as he started to sit up.

Sergei stopped him with a hand in the middle of his chest, pushing him gently—but firmly—back down. "Not just yet. The wounds are closed, but you lost a lot of blood. You'll need a few days to rest before you resume your normal activity." Lucas grumbled, but complied. When he had, Sergei focused on Sophia. "Now to look at your—"

Sophia shook her head and cut him off. "Not yet. Carla was hurt worse than me, too. And she's a guard. She needs use of her arm. Fix her, then I promise I'll let you look at me." She just hoped it wouldn't take him too long. The graze was throbbing and—unused to the pain as she was—she felt a little shaky. But considering that they'd both protected her, she just couldn't allow her relatively minor injury to get treated before theirs.

Sergei looked like he wanted to argue, but she glared at him until he gave in and treated Carla. Unlike Lucas, Carla was done in just a minute and only told to take it easy for a day or two. Once she had left—with Nick stuck to her side, of course—Sergei led her to a chair and delicately pushed her into it. "No more excuses. You're getting healed. Now," he told her sternly.

It was hard, but Sophia managed not to smile. "I wasn't going to argue. Anymore."

He narrowed his eyes at her before he nodded sharply and examined the graze. It had stopped bleeding, but it felt like the pain increased with every beat of her heart. She was also very much afraid that if the pain didn't abate soon that she'd do something embarrassing—like throw up or pass out. Possibly both. To her relief, Sergei started working his magic after a moment, and a moment after that, the ache began to diminish rather than grow. Before long it was gone and she could breathe her first easy breath since Lucas had noticed something amiss at Delphi. The sudden change made her feel light-headed.

"Don't try to get up right away," Sergei told her gently as he stepped away, returning with a damp cloth. He didn't clean the blood from her arm like she expected, but folded it and put it on the back of her neck. The shock of cool against her skin had her jumping a little, but it also brought instant relief, helping her settle more quickly.

"Thanks," she murmured as she held the cloth in place. She glanced to Lucas, who was watching her. "Maybe sight-seeing isn't for me," she told him, her joke falling flat.

"You should go. Shower and sleep," Lucas told her.

"I'll shower, but I'm coming back here."

He frowned. "Why?"

"Because you got shot protecting me. The least I can do is make sure you're not alone. I trust Sergei," she said, giving the healer a quick smile, "but after Erasmus…"

Sergei looked between them for a moment before he said, "I'll have a cot brought in for you." He didn't wait for either of them to respond before he quickly left the room.

"You should sleep in your own bed," Lucas told her after the door had closed.

Feeling more herself, Sophia stood and walked to the bed, taking his hand. "So should you. Since you can't, neither will I."

He scowled but didn't argue with her.

She smiled and gave his hand a squeeze. "I'll be back once I'm clean. Sleep if you can." She hoped he could, because she was very much afraid any sleep she managed would be plagued with even more nightmares.

Chapter 36

THE NEXT MORNING, SOPHIA woke before Lucas. Part of that was due to his injuries, as his body was trying to recover. A larger part was due to how uncomfortable the cot Sergei had given her was. She went to grab breakfast for them, running into Nick on her way back. Fortunately, he didn't keep her long, just telling her the groups that had planned to leave that day were being delayed while the shooting was investigated. Though she only thanked him and continued toward the clinic, she was torn about the decision. On one hand, it was good the shooting was being taken seriously—they might even find who was responsible—and one of the venatores or nasaru who had been scheduled to leave might be the guilty party, but if they were all innocent, leaving would have meant being out of the line of fire. Two people had already been hurt because of her. She didn't want another added to the list. Sure, logically she knew it was the killer's fault, not hers, but emotions and guilt rarely paid attention to logic.

When she got back to the clinic, Lucas was still sleeping. Sergei was awake, though, and was checking to make sure Lucas's injuries still looked good. He glanced up when she entered. "How are you feeling?"

Sophia shrugged and set Lucas's tray down, sitting cross-legged on the cot to eat her own breakfast. "Stiff. Have you ever tried sleeping on this thing?" she asked dryly.

He chuckled quietly and nodded. "I have, more than once. I can't say you're incorrect."

She smiled faintly at that and began eating while she watched him, not wanting to interrupt his examination. Only when he'd sat at his desk did she speak again. "Sergei? Why are you the only healer? Hell, why aren't there more people who know any sort of healing magic? There have got to be witches and elves here."

Sergei blew out a breath and slumped in his chair. "A few people know a little, though it's usually very minor magic. Some know more, but they choose other jobs. Maybe it's because we don't often need it here in the Athenaeum. And since they don't, why not focus on things they will use more often? I really don't know. I won't say that I wouldn't welcome the help, though. Normally it's quiet, but there have been times when a second set of hands would have been handy."

"That doesn't make sense." No longer hungry, she set the tray aside and leaned forward. "You said it's not needed here, but the venatores and guards aren't always here. They leave. Sometimes they're on the other damn side of the planet. So why don't they learn it, even if the curators don't?"

He shook his head. "I really couldn't tell you, Sophia."

She tapped a finger on her knee as she mulled over that puzzle. "Well, that's going to change," she decided, giving him a sharp nod.

One brow arched, he said, "Oh?"

"Mmhmm. I know I just said yesterday how I wasn't going to be making changes and all that, and I don't like breaking my word or lying—even inadvertently—but this is too important to ask the opinion of everyone in the Athenaeum."

"And what, exactly, are you planning to change?" His expression didn't change, but there was definitely a hint of interest in his tone.

"The lack of healing in this place," she told him with a bright smile. "How do you feel about helping those who can heal refine their powers, and teaching first aid to the nasaru and venatores?"

For the first time, Sophia saw him smile. It was small, just the corners of his mouth tipping slightly upward, but it was a smile. "I have positive feelings," he admitted. "Who are you planning to send to me for instruction?"

"If I have my way? Everyone who regularly leaves the library, all the guards, and someone who can be your assistant." She paused, then added, "And me."

"Ambitious."

"Maybe, but in the two weeks I've been here, my grandfather was poisoned, and three people, including myself, were shot. If I hadn't come across a shielding spell and practiced it, I'm pretty damn sure I'd be dead. I don't like it, so if my being ambitious can save even one life? Then you bet your ass I'm going to be ambitious."

Sergei studied her face before he slowly nodded. "I can't argue with your reasoning. Like I said, I would be happy to teach what I do to others, and I don't just mean the magic side of it."

"Excellent." Though, when she thought about how to actually go about doing this, she was happy she had others to help. "I'll talk to Dion, see how we can get this all set up. Classes, probably, rather than one on one, but that's up to you. I have some weak healing magic and know some very basic first aid thanks to my mom, but I'm hardly an expert in how to teach any of this to others."

"No, classes would be preferable, at least for the basics. When I find an assistant, that will be one on one. I'll ask around for that, see who would be willing and who has the aptitude for it."

"Oh good. And thanks. I don't want to come off as one of those high-handed leaders who just expect people to jump when they say jump, but this is important."

"No, it is. It's also a good idea, Sophia, and definitely important. I'm only one man, and even with divine blood I might not live forever."

Sophia shook her head before he finished speaking. "Uh uh. Nope. No talking like that, not now," she said, waving her hands in a 'stop' motion. "Not after Erasmus and my own close call."

"I understand. Sorry."

"It's okay." She picked up her coffee, draining it before she stood. "I'll talk to Dion, see what we can do and when we can get it rolling." She glanced at the still sleeping Lucas, concern on her face. "Is he okay? I was under the impression he was an early riser."

"He is," Sergei verified, "except when he's under a sleeping spell so his body can recover."

She blinked at him before she laughed softly and shook her head. "Right. I'm so used to hiding magic outside of the house that it's not that commonplace for me. But don't let him sleep too long or his food will get cold."

"I won't," Sergei promised as she left the room.

She'd only taken a few steps when her mom turned the corner, her face shifting from concern to relief as she saw Sophia. "Oh, good. You're okay."

Sophia had been caught in a hug before she could respond. "Of course I am. You saw me last night," she said as she squeezed her mom in return.

"I know," Heather said as she stepped back, "but I'm still allowed to worry. It's what moms do." She studied Sophia's face for a long moment. "Are you sure you're okay? I don't mean physically. I know Sergei did a good job healing you."

"I'm..." 'Okay' wanted to roll off her tongue, but Sophia couldn't bring herself to give her mom the easy answer. Instead, she sighed and started walking slowly, Heather falling into step beside her. "I'm upset. Not so much about me being shot—though that wasn't fun. I'm more upset that Carla and Lucas got hurt protecting me. Because of me."

"Protecting you? Yes. Because of you?" Heather shook her head. "No, because of whoever shot at you. You can't be blamed for the actions of some psycho."

She could when said psycho was going after aspides, but she wasn't going to put that worry onto her mom. She just changed the subject. "I just talked to Sergei. We're going to try to get him an assistant healer, and teach more people first aid and how to develop any healing abilities they have. The fact that no one here is really good at it besides Sergei is insane, especially with so many people being away from here so often."

"That's a good idea," Heather said with a smile. "Even if the assistant doesn't really do much with major injuries, just having someone to help take some of the load off Sergei will be a good thing." She went silent for a moment. "I know I told you I was going to stay here in Greece. I don't just want to live here, though. I want to do what I didn't do last time I was here."

"What's that?"

"Join the Athenaeum."

Sophia stopped and blinked. "You're going to become one of us? Seriously?"

"Seriously," Heather said, stopping and rubbing Sophia's arm. "I've just been trying to figure out where I want to go. I'm not cut out to be a guard and wouldn't be even if I was your age again. I've also done my share of traipsing around the world, so I was thinking curator of some sort."

"And healer is a curator, and you're a nurse who also happens to be an elf," Sophia said, showing she was following her mom's train of thought. "You'd be perfect to be Sergei's assistant! Holy crap, Mom, this works out just perfect, doesn't it?"

"It does seem to, yes."

Sophia laughed. "Okay, let's go find Dion. I was going to talk to him about healing classes anyway, and now we can find out what needs done to get you made an official curator. Then we'll talk to Sergei and make sure he's cool with all this." They started toward Dion's office, steps a bit quicker than before. "He is one hundred percent going to be your boss, by the way, because being my mom's boss would be way too freaking weird."

Dion was in his office, the door open. Fortunately, he was all too happy for an interruption and listened as Sophia explained why they were there. He agreed whole-heartedly with the need for more healers and said he'd set up classes as soon as possible. When she asked about the process for someone becoming a part of the Athenaeum, he perked up, thrilled when he heard she was talking about Heather. To her delight, the process was simple. Family members were always thoroughly vetted before they're allowed in the Athenaeum, so all that was needed was to make it official. That process was easy, too. Heather just needed to declare her faction, the head of that faction approves it, and unless the aspida overrules it, it's all done but for the announcement. Dion, of course, was happy to give his approval, pending Sergei's acceptance.

Too excited to remember how Dion had felt off to her, Sophia gave him a quick hug, grabbed her mom's hand, and started dragging her out of the office, promising to let him know what Sergei said.

Lucas was still asleep when they reached the clinic, but Sergei looked as though he was about to wake the guard. "I didn't expect you back so soon. I promise, Lucas is okay," he told her.

"No, it's not that. I believe you. I just talked to Dion and he's going to set up the lessons, but best of all..." She released Heather's hand and gestured grandly at her mother. "I've found you an assistant!"

Sergei didn't look like he was sure how to react at first. "Heather? You want to be a healer?"

Heather smiled. "After I left the Athenaeum, I became a nurse. And you know I'm an elf. So while I'm a little rusty with the major magical healing, I won't be starting from nothing."

His thick brows lifted. "You're a nurse? And you really want to be my assistant?" When she nodded he grinned broadly. "That's wonderful. When do you want to start?"

"As soon as I get back. I need to go back to the States to put the house on the market and get our things. I'm going to try to leave tomorrow," she said, glancing at Sophia.

That was a huge relief, knowing her mom would be out of the way of danger, so Sophia only smiled.

"That's fine," Sergei said without hesitation. "I'd rather have to wait a few days—or weeks—than give up an assistant who knows at least some about medicine and healing. And I know moving here was a surprise to both of you."

"That's an understatement," Sophia muttered.

"I'll try to be back as soon as possible. I don't want to be gone too long, anyway. But I'll keep you updated," Heather promised.

"Wonderful. Thank you. I do need the help," Sergei answered.

"I'm going to go let Dion know, then I'll be back to see Lucas," Sophia told them with a smile before she slipped out. Dion was happy to hear that Heather would be staying as a healer and encouraged Sophia to make the announcement. Luckily, he walked her through how to do it using the app, and soon everyone in the Athenaeum knew Heather Regas was the newest curator. Because of that, even with the shooting, Sophia had a smile on her face as she headed back to the clinic.

Chapter 37

Despite all that had happened, Sophia was smiling as she walked back to the clinic. She was starting to get the hang of this aspida thing, and best of all, her mom was going to be out of the line of fire. Before the shooting, Sophia had hoped the killer would just focus on her, but he—or she—had shown that they didn't care about collateral damage. It scared the shit out of her. Not that the thought of being killed didn't scare her, too, but she'd never forgive herself if someone died in her stead.

Her mom and Sergei were nowhere to be seen when she walked into the clinic, but Lucas was awake, sitting up, and looking grumpy.

"Should I ask what's wrong with you or should I just assume that you're one of those guys who gets pissy when you're hurt?" she asked, struggling to keep the smile off her lips.

"While I can't say that I enjoy being injured, I like having my charge hurt even less," he grumbled as he started to climb out of the bed.

Sophia hurried forward and planted her hands on his chest. She tried to push him back on the bed, but even hurt, he was as solid and immovable as the stone walls surrounding them. "Nuh uh. Sergei said you needed to take it easy for a few days," she told him sternly.

"He did, and I will—" She let out a disbelieving 'ha!' at that, which he ignored. "—but I can't stay in bed twenty-four hours a day." When she didn't look convinced, he arched a brow. "Unless you want to hold a bedpan for me?" he asked dryly.

Sophia's hands jerked away from him and she stumbled back a step. "Um, no, not really. But you come right back here," she said, hands on her hips as she tried to compose herself again.

He chuckled and got up, moving slowly, which she appreciated. A few minutes later, he was back, grabbing his breakfast and sitting down before she could nag him. The room was silent until the worst of his hunger had been abated. "Are you okay?"

She nodded. "I wasn't hurt too bad, so Sergei was able to fix me up pretty quick." Absently she rubbed at the faint pink mark that was all that remained of the injury. "It's a little tender today, but otherwise, I'm good as new." Then she asked the question she'd been fighting against since it had sunk in that she'd been shot. "Do you think it was the same person who killed Erasmus?" she whispered.

Lucas glanced at the door to ensure it was closed before he shook his head. "I don't know. The location of the book points to Dion or Nick, but yesterday? That was a sniper. We have a few people in the guard that are good enough with a rifle to be called snipers, but Dion and Nick aren't. But there's also the possibility that it was an outsider who shot at us. No one here is hurting for money, and a few could afford to pay for an assassin."

The blood drained from Sophia's face and her fingers trembled. She clenched her hands together to try to stifle the shaking, but it didn't help much. "But why?" she breathed. "Killing Erasmus didn't get them his job. Killing me wouldn't do them any good, either."

"Maybe, but we've just been assuming that your grandfather was killed so someone could take his place. Without knowing who's doing this, we can't do anything but guess as to the why. It could be that someone has a problem with your family. It could be someone who disagrees with how the Athenaeum is being run. It could be personal. There's no way for us to know."

Her eyes closed as his words bounced around in her mind. She didn't realize she was crying until she felt a gentle, calloused thumb brush a tear from her skin. "Sophia," he whispered, waiting until she looked at him. He was kneeling in front of her, his expression understanding, his voice soft. "I know you're scared. I know you're overwhelmed, but I'm not going to let what happened to Erasmus happen to you. We're going to find out who did this, and we're going to stop them."

She wanted to tell him about Seth's visit and the gifts from the patrons, but she couldn't, so stuck with the real question. "How? Lucas, Erasmus died with only one other person knowing it was murder. I've been locked in a closet, scared with fire, and been shot. What's to stop them from stabbing me when I'm alone or hitting me with magic or something?" she asked, desperate for him to tell her something, anything, to ease the fear that threatened to swamp her.

He gave her a half smile, but his heart wasn't in it. "First, you did a damn good job with that shield yesterday. You saved us." She opened her mouth to protest, but he placed his hand over her lips. "I mean it. If you hadn't gotten that shield up, it's entirely likely that one of us would be dead. I'm good, and so is Carla, but snipers aren't a regular part of what we deal with, and we couldn't use most of our powers since there were humans around. So don't discount yourself so quickly. Second, you're going to be careful. You're only going to eat what others are eating or what you prepare yourself. You're going to stay around others and not get into a routine. If you're not predictable, that will make their job harder. You're also not going to leave the Athenaeum until this is settled." She tried to speak again, but he wasn't moving his hand just yet. "They have more options if you're out there, Sophia. We can't risk it. And you're not going to trust anyone but myself and your mother."

Finally, he allowed her to speak, which she did while frowning. "What about Sergei? And Carla? She was shot!"

"What proof do we have that Sergei wasn't involved? He did know about Erasmus, and could have easily slipped him more poison when he was trying to treat him," Lucas countered. "And Carla could have ordered herself shot to take suspicion off herself, whether the sniper succeeded or failed."

Given that Sophia liked both Sergei and Carla, she wanted to argue, but he was right. She slumped and nodded. "Okay."

He brushed his thumb over her cheek before he straightened and moved back to the bed. "Thank you."

A thought entered her mind and made her smile slyly. His new rules might not be all bad. "You know...if I'm safest when not alone, then wouldn't I be safer if I wasn't sleeping alone?" she asked.

He let out a surprised laugh. "I can't argue with that. But you'll have to keep your hands to yourself. I'm still recovering, you know."

She doubted that, but the byplay was taking her mind off things. "Shouldn't you be telling yourself that?" she teased.

"Uh uh. I remember who jumped who," he told her as he laid back down. "Now, I want you to find Steven and get in some more hand to hand practice. Your shield is definitely useful, but I still want you to be able to hurt someone if you're attacked. And I want you to remember something."

"What's that?"

"You're not a guard. No one expects you to be a master with weapons or your fists. If you're attacked and you have to fight back, I want you to fight to break free, then I want you to run like hell. You're new, to both fighting and combat magic. I don't say this to be mean, but you're the least experienced person in the Athenaeum. So if you're attacked, you run. Find me, and if that doesn't work, find Steven or someplace safe and call me."

The fear from earlier returned in a rush. "What if I can't call? What if talking would tell them where I am? What if—"

"Then text me. It doesn't have to be a long message, either. Just text me with a single letter, any letter, and I'll know you need help."

Sophia slowly nodded. "I will." She stood and drew in a slow breath. "Let me know when Sergei gives you the okay to leave the clinic, though, okay?"

"I will," he promised. "He'll probably just check me when he's back, then release me. He's a damn good healer. But in the meantime, be careful."

She only nodded as she walked out of the clinic and to the gym. Every sound made her pause. Every footstep made her stiffen. Every smile turned her way made her wonder if it was masking a murderous intent. The short trip was one of the most nerve-wracking she'd ever had to deal with before, so when she finally reached the gym full of people, her muscles were tense. It took only a moment to spot Steven, and she was relieved he was there to continue her training.

"I am well aware that a punch won't stop a bullet, but I will still sleep easier knowing that you can take care of yourself," he told her.

"So will I," she agreed dryly. "Let me just go change and we can get started."

Steven shook his head. "No need. You won't exactly get a chance to change into workout clothes before a fight. And yes, I'm aware that you're still learning, but it will be good for you to know how it feels to move in a fight dressed in jeans."

Sophia grimaced, but couldn't fault his logic. After an hour she wanted to blame her many screw-ups on the unforgiving denim, but had to admit it was more her preoccupation with the danger constantly surrounding her. She'd missed most of the attacks she'd tried to land and had taken entirely too many for her liking. Steven had pulled his punches, of course, but the ego could bruise just as easily as skin. Still, despite her ineptitude, she'd definitely gotten in a good workout, and was absolutely thrilled when Steven took pity on her.

"I'm going to chalk this up to the jeans and…well, you still got in practice," Steven told her with a faint smile. "Why don't you go get some rest?"

"I might just do that. And thanks, Steven. I'll do better next time."

"I have no doubt."

She was halfway back to her room and already anticipating the sweet relief of a shower when she got a text.

Talos: *Released from the clinic. Meet me in the kitchen.*

She sighed, but tried to console herself. If she was with Lucas, she wouldn't be alone, which was a very good thing right now. She might even be able to talk him into showering with her. So she turned and made her way to the kitchen, just as leery as she'd been on the way to the gym, though she knew she was too tired to be as vigilant as she should be. When she arrived safely, she let out the breath she'd been holding. She managed to smile at Lucas as he made them sandwiches under Agatha's disapproving eye. That woman really didn't like people messing about in her kitchen, even when it was someone she was obviously fond of, like she was with Lucas.

After they ate while making small talk, they retreated to her room. "I know you're used to your room, but Steven worked me hard and I need a shower," she told him. "And since I've got an attached bathroom..."

"I hope you don't mind company. Sergei is a good healer, but no matter how hard you try, only a shower gets rid of all the blood."

The first sentence sent a thrill through her and had her becoming extremely aware of him, but the reminder of the blood had that heat cooling. "I don't mind company," she told him as she kicked her shoes off and tugged the band from her hair, freeing it. She pulled her shirt off and turned to head into the bathroom, but stopped when she noticed he was watching her, and for once it wasn't worry or protectiveness in his gaze. It was lust.

In a rush, the arousal that had begun building at the thought of him joining her in the shower returned. For an instant she worried if he was up to it, but not only was he a gargoyle, he'd been healed by a demigod. She had to trust him to know his body and his limits.

With her eyes on his, she undid the button of her jeans and slid the zipper down, the sound loud in the otherwise silent room. Pushing the denim over her hips, she was unable to break his gaze, and when she straightened, he crossed the room with long, purposeful strides. A hand delved into her hair, tilting her face up as he bent and kissed her. It wasn't the easy kiss of someone who was recovering, but a deep, passionate kiss that made her reach out to steady herself.

He continued to kiss her, his tongue demanding her to respond, to give as much as he took, until she couldn't contain her moan. "In the shower," he demanded quietly against her lips, one hand reaching around her to unhook her bra. When she nodded and leaned back to comply, a finger caught one of the straps, tugging the bra down her arms and off. Her nipples hardened instantly, though the room was far from cold. She expected him to remove her panties next, but he just watched her with intense, pale green eyes as she stepped backward into the bathroom.

When he was no longer in view, she took a deep breath, trying to control herself until they were in the shower. It didn't work. Instead, she started the water so it could heat up while she removed the last of her clothes. When she turned to tell him the water was warm, he was standing in the doorway, completely nude and obviously aroused.

During their one night together she hadn't taken the time to truly enjoy the way he looked or explore his body, but she resolved she was going to now. Though he was in human form, his body was pure muscle, almost as hard as he would be in his gargoyle form. His race might have helped, but this was a man who absolutely worked at keeping himself in prime condition, from his thick biceps, to his defined abs, down to his strong legs. Just the sight of him was enough to quicken her pulse until she could feel it beating between her thighs. Even the faint scars from the bullets and smears of red couldn't detract from how absolutely gorgeous he was.

"In the shower," Lucas repeated, his hands clenched into fists, as though he were fighting himself to keep them off her until they were under the water.

Sophia almost argued. She almost dropped to her knees on the bathmat to see if all of him tasted as good as his mouth. The only thing that stopped her was that she wanted all evidence of the shooting gone from his body.

Stepping under the steaming water, she was surprised when it felt cooler than expected, but there was something about Lucas that made her feel fevered. He followed and shut the door behind him, closing them away from the rest of the world.

When he kissed her, this time it was gentle, and he didn't touch her with anything but his lips. Then, just as she started to sink into it, he shifted her out of the water and urged her to turn around. Confused, she did, and moaned for an entirely different reason when he began to work shampoo into her hair, massaging her scalp.

"I should be taking care of you," she murmured, her voice barely audible above the water.

"I'm fine," he said, pressing a kiss to her shoulder. "But you have been through more shit in two weeks than most people deal with in their entire lives. You deserve a little bit of pampering."

"I don't need pampering." In truth, it was nice, but having him so close but not really touching her was going to drive her crazy.

He didn't answer, just finished washing her hair before guiding her back into the spray. When he picked up the body wash, she decided she wasn't going to be a passive participant any longer. Turning, she held out a hand, cupped and palm up, arching a brow until he smiled and poured some of the soap into it. After squirting some into his other hand, he set the bottle aside.

"You deserve some pampering, too," she told him as she worked up some suds, then placed her hands on the hard planes of his chest. She used this as an opportunity to discover what she'd missed the last time, letting her hands roam, savoring every inch of his skin.

He grinned and ran soapy hands along her sides and hips, but said nothing. Instead, he slowly slid his hands around until they cupped her ass, then sharply pulled her into him until her breasts were crushed against his chest. Her hands were trapped between them, his cock pressing insistently against her stomach, and she arched against him, loving how hard he felt for her.

Her mouth opened to say something teasing, but he caught the words before they could form by kissing her again. The productive part of the shower was apparently over, and she couldn't be happier. Sighing, she worked one hand lower as she kissed him, putting all her recent emotions into it. Her fear for his life. Her gratitude at his help. Her need for someone to make her feel normal. And her growing affection for this man she'd once thought might be a murderer.

Lucas tightened his hands on her when her slick fingers found his cock and wrapped around it. The feel of his skin against her sensitive breasts changed, just for an instant, and she almost smiled when she realized he'd lost control for a second and started to shift. Being able to do that to a man this strong? It was a huge turn on. But she wanted more.

She started to stroke him and he groaned as her hand glided over the hard, silky flesh, his hands tightening on her ass. Tilting her head, she let her lips brush across his chest as she teased him, keeping the touch of her mouth gentle until she reached his nipple. Scraping it with her teeth, he hissed in a breath and bucked against her palm. That was when she decided she wanted to really make him lose control.

Shifting back and slightly to the side so the water hit the front of his body, she continued to stroke him until the soap was washed away, then knelt. The stone floor of the shower was rough on her knees, but she didn't care. Looking up the line of his body, she saw that his eyes had gone stone gray and were filled with heat. Smiling, she kept her eyes locked on his as she ran her tongue around the head of his shaft. One of his hands found her cheek, his touch light against her skin, while the other pressed against the side of the shower. She almost grinned again as her hands came to rest on his hips and she started to play.

Taking her time, she ran her tongue over him, savoring every twitch, every groan, every time the hand on the wall tightened. Then she decided she'd teased him enough and slid her mouth over him. Her name was thick when he breathed it, and she responded by drawing back slowly, sucking hard enough to have her name changing to a low curse. Never before had she been with a man who seemed to enjoy everything she did, and definitely not as much as Lucas did. She loved it. It made her feel powerful and sexy. Humming around him, her head bobbed as she did everything she could to push him to his breaking point. Not just because he'd protected her, not just out of guilt, but because she wanted to see this strong man fall apart because of her. She wanted to make him feel as good as he'd made her feel the other night.

The skin beneath her hands hardened as she pressed forward again, taking his cock as deep as she could. She heard a grinding sound and saw his fingers were actually making shallow gouges in the wall.

Groaning, unprepared for just how turned on him losing control made her, she quickened her pace, stripping away everything from him but pleasure.

His hand released her cheek and instead grabbed her hair, but he didn't hold her in place. He just seemed to need to touch her, to anchor himself. Only a moment later, he stiffened and ground out her name as he came, spilling himself into her mouth. Swallowing him down, she slowed, then when she was sure she'd wrung every drop of pleasure from him she could, drew back, pressing a kiss to his thigh.

Letting go of her hair, he grabbed her hands and pulled her to her feet. Without hesitation, he kissed her deeply, pulling her body flush with his. She was happy for that, as his kiss made her knees weak and she had to cling to him to remain on her feet. She didn't stay like that long, as he turned her away from him, then urged her to bend forward enough to press her hands against the wall. Before she could process what he was doing, he thrust into her, pulling a shocked cry from her lips. He was still hard, and despite the orgasm, still clearly wanting more.

Sophia wasn't about to argue with that.

It was intense and fast, but there was something different about it today than the other night. Before, it had been a lust for momentary pleasure and forgetting. Now, it seemed like a lust for *her*. She wasn't sure how she knew that, or why exactly it made a difference, but it did. It made everything more.

Lucas slammed into her, one hand on her hip, the other braced on the wall beside hers, so his chest pressed against her back. He kissed her shoulder, the tender action at odds with the hard, rapid pace of his hips. And to her shock, the climax built quickly within her. One second she was moaning as he first entered her, and it seemed like only a minute later that she was crying out as she shoved back against him, her body clamping down around him as the release hit her hard. But he wasn't done with her yet.

He pulled out of her and turned her again, reaching for her knee to draw her leg up against his hip. As soon as she was opened to him again, he was sliding back into her. Pinned between him and the wall, steam billowing around them, she could only reach up and drag his head down for another kiss. It wasn't gentle, it wasn't as smooth as their other kisses had been, but it was honest and passionate.

The hand not holding her leg up slid between them and found her clit. The first touch had her gasping. The second stroke made her whimper into their kiss. The third, delivered with more pressure, had her shattering for a second time that night. Her scream was muffled by his mouth at first, until he broke the kiss to groan as the spasming of her sex pulled another climax out of him as well.

His body leaned into hers, but he released her leg so it could slide back down. Breathing wasn't exactly easy with his weight against her, but she didn't care. She wasn't looking forward to the moment when she was empty again.

It came all too soon, and she let her fingers trail down over his cheeks until her arms fell to her sides. To her surprise, he leaned in, giving her a gentle kiss, before pulling her away from the wall. He finished washing her, and if it weren't for the pleased little smile playing about his lips—and wonderfully loose feeling throughout her body—she might have thought she imagined the sexual interlude.

After they got out and dried off, she was prepared for a nice nap, but Lucas killed those dreams, insisting she practice her shield spell and magical punching first. Reluctantly, she gave in, as she was sure she'd need the skills, and soon.

It was bedtime before he relented, and she collapsed in the bed, exhausted. Just before sleep took her, she felt his arms surround her. It was the last pleasant moment she had until morning, her sleep once again plagued by nightmares.

Chapter 38

SOPHIA RECEIVED A RATHER pleasant wake up call the next morning, when the first thing she was aware of was Lucas's mouth sliding down her stomach. After starting her workout for the day early—and much more enjoyably than what she'd receive in the gym—they went to the kitchen for breakfast before they parted ways for a while.

Wanting to get in some more time with her mom while she was in Greece, Sophia accompanied Heather back to her room and helped her carry her bags to the entrance. While she was happy her mom would be safe, she was nervous, too. Her whole life it had been her and her mom. Heather had always been her rock, so saying goodbye during such a difficult time wasn't fun.

"Why can't you get someone to teleport you there?" she asked.

"Because this isn't a time sensitive issue and everyone's still getting back into the swing of things after everything that's happened." Heather smiled. "I'll be back before you know it."

Sophia sighed and nodded. "You'll call when you land in Atlanta, right?" she asked as she gave her mom a tight hug.

Heather laughed. "Of course, Mom," she teased. "I have flown before, you know. And I am the elder of the two of us. I'll be fine." Her humor faded as she drew back and cupped Sophia's cheek. "It's you I'm worried about. All I'll have to deal with are banks and realtors. You're the one who was shot."

Sophia pasted a reassuring smile on her face. "I don't plan on leaving the Athenaeum. I'm sure I'll be just fine." But she was quick to change the subject. Heather had always been really good at catching Sophia in a lie, and she didn't want to give her mom time to employ that particular skill. "You remember what to do with all my stuff, right?"

"Of course. And if I forget anything, it's not like I can't just call you."

"True. Which you should do anyway."

"I absolutely will. But you don't worry about a thing. I'm a grown up. I can handle moving our stuff from the States to here."

"Speaking of moving, you should start doing that or you're going to miss your flight," Ray said as he walked up to them and picked up Heather's bags. Sophia had been told just that morning that he was accompanying Heather, and it had reassured her. Likely, the killer wouldn't bother with going after her mom, but 'just in case' was a thing for a reason.

"Miss your flight? You're not going on the jet?" Sophia asked.

Heather shook her head. "That's just for official business or time-sensitive issues."

"Oh." That had her worrying a little, but it wasn't likely the killer would do anything on a commercial flight. "Yeah, makes sense. Guess I better start thinking about things like that, huh?"

"Probably," Heather said cheerfully. "I'll see you soon, sweetie. Call me if you need anything."

"I will." She shoved her hands in her pockets as she watched Heather and Ray leave and blew out a breath. Uncertain of what to do, she decided to find Lucas, despite the fact that she'd just seen him an hour before. She checked his office and the gym and was nearly to his bedroom when she got a message from Valerie, asking to see her as soon as possible. More curious than concerned, she backtracked and went hunting for Valerie's office, finding it next to the other offices. And like those offices, it had file cabinets and a single desk with two monitors. Valerie was alone, her brow furrowed as she studied something on one of the screens.

"Valerie?"

The woman looked up and smiled tightly. "Sophia. Please, come in. And close the door if you would?"

Sophia frowned, but nodded and did so before sitting in the chair across from Valerie. "Is something wrong?"

"I'm not entirely sure," she admitted. "As you know, I handle most of the financial issues for the Athenaeum. Individuals might have their own financial advisers, but Athenaeum business is mine."

"That's what I understood, yes."

"It means that I'm constantly checking on the various accounts, ensuring nothing looks off. Unusual purchases by Athenaeum members, signs of fraud, things like that."

Sophia frowned harder. "Valerie, I know you don't know me well, but you don't need the build up unless it's necessary to explain whatever you found. It's actually making me a little nervous."

Valerie sighed and picked up a piece of paper, handing it across the desk to Sophia. "I found a transaction—a wire transfer—that processed yesterday," she said, which explained the line that had been highlighted. "Technically, it's from your account, though I know you haven't received that information yet. And as you can see, it's for a substantial amount of money."

Sophia's eyes widened as she found the amount column. She wasn't sure of the exact exchange rate from euros to dollars, but she didn't need to. "Substantial?" she choked out. "You can say that again. Ten million euros?" she asked, looking from the paper to Valerie. "What did they buy?"

"I'm not sure. As I said, it was a wire transfer, not a purchase, so all I have is an account number. I'm trying to track it now, but even for us that's not always an easy thing. Numbered accounts are used by so many people because they are supposed to be fairly anonymous."

"But who did it? You said it was my account, but like you said, I don't know how to access it yet, so who does?" It wasn't likely to be Valerie. If she was responsible, she'd have hidden it and said nothing.

Valerie looked troubled as she shook her head. "I don't know. As you're no doubt aware, we take security very seriously, and that extends to financial matters. For your account? Only you and I should have any sort of access to it. But I'm looking into that as well."

"Is there anyone else helping you?"

Again, she shook her head. "No. Unless you authorize it, I can't go to anyone else. Though Lucas and Peter could be useful. But I'm reluctant—even with your permission—to bring anyone in at the moment."

"No, I get it." Sophia nodded and got to her feet, handing the paper back. "Keep me updated? And let me know if you do need another hand or set of eyes?"

"I will. And I'm sorry, Sophia. I have no idea how this happened."

"You'll figure it out," she said, smiling faintly. She walked on autopilot back to the hall with her bedroom. Ten million euros was a lot of money, and she had a feeling the timing wasn't coincidental. But did it mean that someone had used what was technically her money to hire someone to kill her? Lucas had mentioned that assassins were possible.

Shaking her head, she went to Lucas's room and knocked. To her relief, he was there and answered quickly.

"You okay?" he asked as he invited her into the room and closed the door behind her.

"No. My mom's gone. Ray went with her. And Valerie just found that someone transferred ten million euros from my account to some anonymous account. I think someone used my money to try to kill me."

"Fuck." He guided her to the bed and pushed her onto it before sitting beside her. "Okay, first things first. Ray's good. He may be older than most of the nasaru, but he's still damn good at his job. And it's not likely anyone will go after her, but if they try, he'll keep her safe."

"I know. I'm just worried."

"And I get that. As for the money..." He sighed. "One, we can't confirm anything, not yet. I assume Valerie's investigating?" She nodded. "Money is what she does. As long as magic or actual hacking wasn't involved, she'll figure it out. If magic was involved, we'll still figure it out. It just might take a little longer. And if hacking was? Peter will find it."

"I know," she repeated. "It just freaks me out."

He slid an arm around her shoulders and hugged her to him. "We'll figure it out. And until we do, I'll keep you safe."

She smiled faintly. "Thanks." Resting her head on his shoulder, she asked, "You come up with any ideas on who could be doing this?"

"Nothing new. Dion and Nick are still the most likely ones in my mind. I don't really *want* to suspect either of them, though. Dion's always been a nice guy, very dedicated to his job."

"And Nick?"

He sighed. "Nick and I have always been fairly close, and it's always hard to suspect a friend of something like this."

"I think I mostly don't want to suspect Nick because of Carla," Sophia admitted. "I kind of hated her at first, but she's grown on me."

He gave a small smile. "She's good at that." The smile disappeared. "But if we want to think logically, it's entirely possible they're both working together. Nothing says it's only one person doing this. While it's possible, it would be easier to orchestrate all this if you had multiple people with multiple skills. The guards, for instance, could have done the shooting, but they're not as likely to know about obscure, magical poisons or know the variety of sorcery that might be involved. The magic we learn tends to be more defensive than offensive."

She grimaced. "It's bad enough thinking of a single person, but multiple?" She shakes her head. "It makes me want to run away and let someone else have my job."

He slowly shook his head. "Not possible." After pushing away from the wall, he sat beside her. "I'll be honest. If I had to choose someone, based on the evidence we have now, I'd go with Dion. A lot of people expected him to be Erasmus's successor, he had access to the sixth level, and has the money to have hired an assassin. And as head curator, I don't doubt he has the contacts to find an assassin. Not to mention he probably knows more sorcery than anyone here, now that Erasmus is gone."

"What is he anyway?" she asked, though it was an attempt to distract herself rather than true curiosity. "Shifter like Erasmus?"

"Merfolk," he answered. "Him and Peter both."

Sophia swallowed as the weight on her chest returned and her stomach churned. "It's really hard to think of my cousin deliberately killing his uncle," she said quietly. "Or to think of a nice guy like him doing any of this. But I do see the logic in it. But we can't just accuse him. We need to find proof."

"We do," he agreed. "To start, we need to watch him, but discreetly. I know you don't know him too well, but I've known the man for years. I'll know if he's acting off."

"We also need to search his room. If he's smart, he won't leave anything incriminating just lying around, but he could slip up."

"Hmm. Best way would be if you could distract him—in public, of course, so he can't try anything—while I slip into his room."

Public would be necessary, because the thought of being alone with her cousin now made her shudder. "I doubt that'll be too hard. Everyone knows I'm still learning my job, and the people. I could have him introduce me to any curators I haven't met or something. And if that fails, I doubt anyone would think anything of it if you didn't make it for dinner tonight."

"Good point. Just send me a text either way and we'll go from there. But right now? You're going to the gym. You need to keep up your training with Steven."

Sophia groaned and flopped back. "I'm still sore from my last training session. And I swear I have a perpetual headache from all the magic training."

He chuckled without the least bit of sympathy. "Both will go away with time. And I refuse to lose an aspida because of a lack of training. Just wait until you start getting your formal sorcery training. I've been focusing on quickly teaching you things to keep you alive. An aspida needs to know a hell of a lot more than that."

"Yeah, yeah," she muttered as she got up and went to her room to change into her workout clothes.

It was two hours later when she returned to her room, after a quick stop in the kitchen. Every muscle was stiff and sore. She could barely lift the sandwich she'd snagged, but somehow managed while also stripping on the way to the shower. Lucas had abandoned her to take care of work, but she considered that a blessing right now. The blame for her current physical state was all his. Maybe a little Steven's, but Lucas carried the bulk of the responsibility.

The shower helped, loosening muscles and easing some of the soreness, so by the time she got out, she was only feeling mildly irked at her torturers. After dressing, she went on the hunt for Dion, hoping they could enact the first part of her plan, but since he was in his office, she opted not to chance it and went to the computer room instead. Sure, security was Lucas's area of expertise, but she couldn't always expect him to have the answers. And wasn't the boss supposed to have a working understanding of everything in the Athenaeum, anyway?

"Sophia! My favorite cousin!" Peter said cheerfully the moment she stepped into the room. "How are you feeling? Did Sergei do a good job healing you?" he asked, cheer morphing to concern.

"I'm doing fine," she assured him. "A little freaked out, of course, but fine."

"I think anyone would be freaked out. I'm a little surprised you're out and about."

Sophia shrugged and sat down, drawing a knee to her chest, arms wrapped around it. "I've thought about it," she admitted, "but I'm in the Athenaeum, not out in the world. Not only that, but if I hide in my room, I have nothing to do but think about it."

"Ahh. You're here for a distraction, then?"

"Yes and no. I do want a distraction, but I can't stop trying to fit into my new role just because I had a...bad day."

Peter frowned at her. "I'd say that was more than just a bad day."

"True, but I still can't stop being aspida. Not until I die, anyway."

He sighed and slumped in his chair. "Well, what can I do to help?"

"Teach me about security? Not the guards, but this stuff," she said, waving a hand at his computer.

It took a moment, but he smiled. "I can do that." He reached forward, grabbed the arm of her chair, and pulled her next to him. And he did, slowly, patiently walking her through the basic aspects of Athenaeum security. He was a good teacher, too. She expected her eyes to glaze over, but he explained everything in a way that made sense. He hadn't even begun to scratch the surface, she knew that much, but it still helped.

The security wasn't anything commercially available. It wasn't even anything that the various governments of the world had access to. Mostly because they'd somehow added magic to the programs. Sophia didn't have the slightest clue how, and wasn't going to potentially break her brain trying to figure that out yet. Those programs were in anything electronic that came into the Athenaeum or was used for Athenaeum business.

What she did understand was the various security levels, which ranged from her—who had access to literally everything—to the vetted family members like her mom had been, who needed to have help getting into the Athenaeum and could only visit the top levels of the library. It kind of freaked her out that she could literally access anything on anyone's computer or phone. Or that anyone had that ability. But it did make her wonder about the security logs Lucas had found and the wire transfer. Was the security as good as Peter claimed and the murderer really was either Dion or Nick? Or had someone gotten around the supposedly impenetrable security and deleted or changed an entry? She hesitated to ask before she realized she was expected to ask questions.

Without meaning to, she interrupted him. "You say no one can get in, but how certain are you of that?"

Peter looked mildly taken aback at the interruption, but recovered quickly. "Well, I can't say that it's absolutely, one hundred percent foolproof, because I don't believe in absolutes, but it would take a hell of an effort to get into our system. And for anyone to even make the effort, they'd have to know we were here. So overall, I'd say the chances of anything happening are very, very slim."

"Good. That's good," she murmured, nodding. Very slim wasn't much, but it was an opening.

He jumped back into the ins and outs, and even with his easy teaching style, before too much longer, the words on his screen were blurring from the overload of information and sheer tiredness. And he noticed, giving her a sympathetic smile. "Too much?"

Apologetic, she nodded. "Little bit."

He chuckled. "Not too many people can handle too much technical information at once. You did good, though. By now, most people are snoring in their seats."

"It wasn't that bad," she protested, though she could honestly understand. She liked using computers for research and social media—and streaming movies, of course—but anything more than that went over her head.

"Uh huh," Peter said with a grin. "Go. Recover from the overload. I'll talk to you later."

She smiled. "Thanks. You were a lot of help," she told him before leaving. A quick check of her phone told her it was almost time for dinner. She sighed and sent a text to Lucas, telling him she'd failed to distract Dion. Hopefully, Dion made it to dinner, so Lucas could get the chance to search Dion's room.

Chapter 39

As soon as Lucas received Sophia's text that Dion was at dinner, he moved quickly. Unlike Sophia, he knew every inch of the Athenaeum and went right to Dion's room. The door was unlocked, but it was rare that anyone ever locked them. Doing so would have put a suspicious tag on his forehead. Still, before going in, Lucas muttered a quick spell, surprised when he didn't feel any active magic on the door or the room beyond.

Ensuring no one was around, he slipped into the bedroom and closed the door. It was the first time he'd been in Dion's bedroom, but he couldn't say he was surprised by what he found. The usual furniture was there—including bookshelves—and it was neat as a pin. There were a few artifacts and several dozen books, and that was where Lucas started. Most, he knew, would have gone for the desk, but it was too obvious. Instead, he checked books and behind them, felt on top of shelves and beneath the furniture. Only after searching for hidey holes and coming up empty did he go to the desk. The laptop was closed, and after lifting the lid, he lowered it again since he didn't have the password. Going another route, he checked the books and papers, but they all seemed appropriate for his job. Though he had to admit, he'd never have guessed Dion had a secret interest in video games, much less the online first-person shooters. Still, lots of people played those games, and it could just be Dion's attempt at developing a shared interest with his son.

Then he found the notepad and flipped through it. Frowning, he took a picture before moving the pages back to how they'd been. By that point he'd been there thirty minutes, and decided to leave before he could get caught. He made sure everything was as he'd found it, then he went to Sophia's room to wait. Fortunately, he'd brought his laptop over, because it took almost another half hour before she hurried in and immediately breathed a sigh of relief. "You're okay," she said, slumping back against the door.

"Why wouldn't I be?" he asked with an arched brow as he looked up from his laptop.

She shrugged as she pushed away from the door and joined him on the bed. "I don't know. He could have had some booby traps or something to keep people from snooping."

Lucas wanted to smile. She was worried about him. "No, nothing like that. It was almost boring."

"Almost?"

He made a thoughtful sound and turned the computer so she could see the screen. "For the most part, I didn't find anything. Not that I was expecting to find his evil plans neatly laid out on paper or anything. For that matter, I didn't find anything that was blatantly incriminating. But I did find this," he said with a nod to the screen, which showed the picture he'd taken.

The handwriting was quickly scrawled, the words in Greek, and even after studying it for the past half hour, he wasn't able to make them all out. But four words stood out clearly.

Poison.

Magic.

Hired.

Delphi.

"I thought you said there wasn't anything incriminating," she said quietly.

"Because this isn't, not really," he said, dragging his fingers through his hair. "Yes, it could be notes of what he wanted to do, but it could also be completely innocent."

"He specifically mentioned poison, Delphi, and hiring someone. That sounds pretty incriminating," she argued.

"Or he could be innocent and investigating." They stared at each other for a few seconds before he gave in. "Okay, it looks bad, but it's still not *proof*, and we need proof before we can accuse the head curator of murder and attempted murder."

"You have a point. Feels like we're back to square one. I'm not even sure we ever left."

Lucas closed the laptop and set it on the desk before he laid on his side, facing her. "Ruling things out is still making progress. And we did find something else out, just not in Dion's room."

"We did?"

He nodded. "The bullets Sergei pulled from me weren't from the armory here. It doesn't completely rule out someone here being the shooter, but I'm inclined to think it points to a mercenary of some sort."

"I don't know that I feel any better now," she said blandly.

"It means that if you don't leave the Athenaeum that you're safe from assassins." She didn't look reassured and he ran his hand over her arm. "Look, why don't you just try and sleep and we'll start fresh in the morning?"

Smiling faintly, she nodded and scooted closer until she could rest her cheek against his chest. He wrapped his arms around her and she closed her eyes. "Yeah, that sounds good," she murmured, doubting that she'd be able to get any sleep. Still, she tried, lying there quietly as she heard Lucas's breathing even out as he slid under. For another hour, she did nothing but mull over everything they'd learned—and the questions she still had. The biggest problem she had was simply ignorance. She didn't know this place or its people well enough to do much. Not being a detective didn't help either.

Giving up on sleep, she carefully climbed out of bed, careful not to wake Lucas. She cast the threat and shields spells then made her way back to the secret room at the top of the library. If there was a publicly known spell that could help them figure out who was after her, surely Lucas would know it. But there were plenty of spells he'd never seen, and one of them just might be the answer to their problem.

Once inside the room that felt oddly like a safe haven, she relaxed. She couldn't guarantee no one else in the Athenaeum knew this place existed, but it was doubtful. She grabbed the grimoire and sat down, taking more time and care searching through the book. Once more, she was frustrated by her inability to read most of the spells, but she wouldn't let herself give up. Maybe there was a spell to allow her to easily understand more languages, but she was reluctant to search for one. It felt like cheating, or like it would belittle the time and effort she'd put into learning the languages she already knew. But if things became desperate, she might relent.

There were so many spells in this one book, she doubted that anyone could learn them all in a single lifetime. To be honest, that was a bit of a relief. Someone who knew all these spells—and could perform them—would be extremely powerful and extremely dangerous. In addition to the spells to cause earthquakes and raise the dead she'd found before, she was able to decipher several other terrifying spells. Controlling time—to an extent—controlling minds and emotions, controlling the dead.... A lot of them seemed to control *something*. She didn't even know what all of the things were, like miasma. She did find a spell to absorb knowledge—such as languages—but she flipped past it. However, when she came across one for teleportation, she paused. While she could understand previous aspides not wanting that spell out there, it could be very useful in keeping herself alive until Erasmus's killer was caught. She'd just have to make sure she didn't abuse it. And hope there wasn't a painful downside to it.

According to the grimoire, intent was extra important with this spell, as not focusing could cause the spell to either not work, send her somewhere she didn't want to go, or literally tear her in half. The thought of the latter made her shudder, but she still spent the next hour memorizing the spell and practicing teleporting around the room. She did have a few close calls, though, when her focus wavered. Once she almost teleported *into* a set of shelves, and another time she landed just outside the room, jostling an urn. Luckily, she managed to catch it before it hit the floor. Even better, no one saw her. She was more careful after that.

Tired, as teleportation took a lot more out of her than the other spells she'd learned, she called it for the night but didn't head back to bed. Teleportation could save her life, but it couldn't help her find a killer. As she continued searching, she found a telepathy spell with a lengthy warning that going crazy was a very likely possibility, which was a shame. Telepathy would probably be able to identify the killer, but it would be useless if she was too insane to tell anyone who was guilty. Then there was something about a 'magical language', but she could only read a word here or there talking about it, so that wasn't really all that useful.

Then she came across a set of pages that looked different from the others. They looked important. The paper felt different, thicker, and not the same texture as the rest of the pages. The ink was different, too. The other pages had been written in blue or black ink, but this was a deep red. Dark, but not enough that it could ever be mistaken for black. For an instant, Sophia was afraid the page was written in blood, but convinced herself that blood wouldn't still be red after so long. It wasn't proof, but it helped her focus on what was actually on the pages.

The left page was hard to decipher, since it was in that extremely old version of Greek she wasn't too familiar with. When she managed it, she saw it was a warning, the first line so ominous it left her with a chill that had nothing to do with being a hundred feet underground.

Be cautious and heed this warning well, for the life of every person in the Athenaeum, if not the world, could be at stake.

If you have reached these pages, you are aware that the spells within this book are powerful and, if held by those with darkness and greed in their hearts, dangerous. That danger is minor compared to the devastation that could befall the world if the wrong person gained control of the Athenaeum, of our home. What is to us a place of sanctuary, knowledge, and comfort, could be used to destroy the lives of the people we share this world with. Because of this, we have taken measures to protect the world if the worst should befall us. It pains us to even consider this, but we cannot just protect ourselves and the knowledge within our walls, we must protect the world as well. It is a responsibility we take when we become aspida.

With the help of the gods, we have placed a fail-safe in the Athenaeum, a project which has taken centuries and four aspides. Magic has been imbued into the entire Athenaeum, magic which remains dormant until it is activated by the spell on the following page. It is not a spell to be taken lightly, as it will result in the destruction of everything, and everyone within this cavern, from the labyrinth above to the water beneath.

Nothing will survive.

Not even a scrap will remain after the spell is spoken, which will mean that the work of generations of Zid Nasaru will be lost. Only use this spell if the worst happens and the Athenaeum is invaded with no chance of saving it. Only use it if there is a true risk of our knowledge making it into the hands of those who would abuse it.

It pains me to write this. It pains me to even have to consider the possibility, but as I said, we have a responsibility, and I take that very seriously.

I pray to all the gods that it never becomes necessary to use this magic.

The signature below was impossible to make out, even if Sophia's eyes hadn't grown damp with tears. She crossed her arms on the table and lowered her forehead to them, concentrating on simply breathing until she calmed down. The dedication it had to have taken for these people to basically booby trap their own home, just to protect people.

Not to mention all the aspides who had followed who had learned the spell, just in case. Which meant her grandfather had known it. It was doubtful the rest of the Athenaeum did. For the first time, she truly knew what a terrible burden being in charge could be. Just being the boss was bad enough, but this? It was indescribable.

Lifting her head, Sophia wiped her cheeks and took a deep breath before she looked at the page with the spell. As much as she wanted to pretend like she hadn't found it, she couldn't bring herself to ignore it. She read it through several times, each pass making her feel colder, more hopeless. Finally she decided she was too tired, too emotionally exhausted, to continue, and resolved to spend half an hour, whenever she could, learning the spell. Since it wasn't one she could practice, she had to memorize it perfectly.

When she made it back to her room and slid into bed, she was grateful Lucas was there and still sleeping. She wasn't up for conversation, but pressing against his warm back and holding onto him eased the worst of the chill that threatened to overwhelm her. And when she finally fell asleep, she was lucky enough not to dream.

Chapter 40

WITH THE WAY THINGS had been going since Sophia first learned about the Athenaeum, she expected yet another disaster to occur the next day. When the next three were quiet and calm, she was surprised. For the first day, she was anxious, just waiting for something to happen. She was calmer the second day, and relaxed the third. On top of that, she got quite a bit done. There wasn't any new information on their investigation, but she became more proficient with her spells. It was easier for her to recall the words at a moment's notice and it took less thought to make the magic do what she wanted. The fight training wasn't quite as good, but she was slowly building her endurance, so she wasn't quite as tired or sore after a session with Steven. She even had time to resume her studies on Sanskrit. It pleased her how much she'd remembered from the short amount of time she'd studied the language, though she was far from fluent.

Her nights were spent with Lucas, though he was fully recovered, and her mom was making progress back in the States, so all in all, things were going surprisingly well.

When she woke on the fourth day, she expected another quiet but productive day. She was even optimistic enough to hope for some sort of development on her hunt for Erasmus's killer. Lucas was still asleep, so she slipped out quietly and made her way to the kitchen. It was early, but not so early that Agatha wouldn't already be up and cooking. More importantly, there should already be coffee. Sweet, sweet caffeine.

The lights were off when Sophia reached the kitchen, which surprised her so much she stopped and stared into the empty room. "Agatha?" she called after a moment as she slowly stepped into the kitchen. No answer, though the lights came on. Frowning, she pulled out her phone, but she had been correct in the time. It was after six. Agatha was always in the kitchen by six. Concerned, she called the sweet cook, nerves spiking when the endless ringing turned to a voicemail message.

Shoving her phone back into her pocket, Sophia walked quickly back to her room. Lucas was still asleep, but she didn't hesitate to shake his shoulder to wake him. "Lucas, wake up."

He woke instantly, sitting up in bed. "What?"

"Agatha isn't in the kitchen or answering her phone."

Lucas frowned. "What?"

"It's after six and I went to the kitchen for coffee, but the lights were off and she wasn't there. I tried calling her, but she didn't answer. I know it's probably nothing, but I'm worried."

"It is out of character for her," he admitted as he pushed out of bed and grabbed a shirt, tugging it on. "Let's go check on her," he said, not bothering to put shoes on.

They hurried out of her room and back toward the kitchen. Of course the cook had a room near her 'office'. Lucas rapped firmly on the door, but there was no answer. After they exchanged a look, both thinking the same thing, he slowly opened the door.

Agatha lay sprawled on the floor, her once beautiful eyes fixed blindly on the ceiling.

"Oh god," Sophia gasped, covering her mouth with her hand, her eyes immediately filling with tears. "Agatha," she whispered, as she turned and leaned into Lucas.

He wrapped his arms around her as he stared at Agatha's body, his jaw clenched in anger and grief. "I know," he murmured.

She didn't allow herself to break down, and after a minute she pulled away, quickly wiped her tears away, and pulled out her phone.

"Who are you calling?"

"Sergei. It's obvious she's...but we need to know why."

He nodded. "We do."

It took several rings before a sleepy sounding Sergei answered. "Da?"

"Sergei, it's Sophia." Her gaze slid to Agatha, then quickly away. "I need you to come to Agatha's room."

Just like Lucas had, he woke up quickly. "Why? What's wrong?"

"Just come, please."

"Be right there."

Sophia hung up, then paused and looked back at Agatha. "I don't see any blood or any..." She made a gesture like someone cutting something with a knife.

"Neither do I, but that's not the only option, not with the Arcane."

"No, it's not."

Casting the magic detection spell he'd taught her, she shuddered. "Do you feel that?"

He did the same then, grimly, he nodded. "I do. I didn't think it was a natural death anyway, but now?"

"Why would he—or she—use magic this time? They used poison last time that was essentially untraceable."

"Then they tried shooting you. Maybe they're getting desperate, or they just don't care anymore."

"Neither option makes me feel any better."

Sergei walked in before Lucas could respond and stopped short as he saw the same sight they had. Grief wasn't the first emotion to appear on his face. Anger was. "Who did this?" he asked in a low, dangerous voice.

"We don't know," Lucas said. "We don't even know how."

"I assume that's why I'm here," Sergei answered, all business despite his fury. He strode past them and knelt beside Agatha. After taking a deep breath, he extended his hands over Agatha and they started to gently glow. It took only a minute before he dropped his hands to his thighs and hung his head.

"What is it, Sergei? What'd you find?" Sophia asked quietly.

"It was definitely murder. I recognize the spell." His head lifted and his eyes burned with rage as he looked back to them. "It's forbidden for anyone to teach or learn that spell. I only know it because a healer must. It's a spell that stops the heart."

"Why? Why would anyone do that to Agatha?" Sophia demanded. "She was so sweet. She'd never hurt anyone. Hell, she wasn't even in charge of anything dangerous! All she did was take care of us. All of us."

"I don't know, but you need to find them."

"We will," Lucas promised.

Sergei nodded sharply. "I'll take care of her. But this needs to stop. I'm tired of someone killing my friends."

"So am I," Lucas agreed.

He drew Sophia out of the room and closed the door gently behind them. She was absolutely furious that someone would quietly work on taking out member after member of the Athenaeum. For the first time, she decided to fully embrace her role as aspida. Once again, she yanked her phone out and started tapping quickly, almost violently.

"What are you doing?"

She didn't stop typing, even as she answered. "I'm calling for everyone to gather in the common room. This has to stop. And we can't leave the rest of the Athenaeum in the dark. If they don't know there's a problem, they can't be on their guard, and they need to be."

"They do," he said slowly, "but you have to be careful about what you say. You can't let them know that we know about Erasmus."

That caused her to pause for just a moment. "I know, but there's still the shooting, and Agatha."

"I'd even leave the shooting out. Agatha though...she deserves the truth."

"I can't believe she's gone, but I can't feel bad, not yet. I'm too angry for that," she admitted.

"I get it, I do. I feel the same way, but we have to be smart about this. If we play this the wrong way, more people could end up hurt."

She knew he was right, even though all she wanted to do was yell and confront the killer. "I'll be careful." She finished the message and sent it. Immediately, Lucas's phone dinged and they started for the common room.

They were the first ones there, which didn't surprise Sophia. It was early and most people here tended to wait for a decent hour to crawl out of bed. People started to trickle in, most in pajamas and robes, all bleary-eyed and yawning. A few tried to ask what was going on, but Sophia just told them to wait until everyone was there. It left them looking sleepily baffled—and a few looked annoyed—but the questions ceased.

Lucas leaned in and murmured in her ear. "This is everyone but Sergei, your mother, and Ray."

A flicker of guilt made Sophia's heart clench. She'd been so consumed by righteous fury, she'd forgotten that her mom would have probably gotten the alert as well. She made a mental note to talk to her mom later, but for now, she had a room full of people staring at her, waiting. Her anxiety about being in the spotlight tried to kick in, but Agatha deserved better than her passing this task off to Lucas. Or worse, running and hiding. For that matter, *she* deserved better than running and hiding. She may not understand why she was chosen to lead the Athenaeum, but apparently she was worth choosing and was going to start having more faith in herself.

Squaring her shoulders, Sophia stepped to the front of the room and glanced around. She forced herself to meet gazes without flinching, whether they were confused and sleepy like Nick, or impatient and irritated like Jericho. A few even looked concerned.

"I'm sorry to call you all here so early. I know a lot of you were probably sleeping. Unfortunately, this isn't something that could wait." She took a deep breath, dreading what this would do to the majority of the people here. Part of her wanted to search for the kind, gentle way of breaking the news, but she opted for ripping the proverbial bandaid off. "Agatha has been killed."

Sophia tried to look at everyone she could—as did Lucas—watching for something, anything, that would signal a guilty conscience.

What she saw was pained surprise as a good half of the assembled crowd started to murmur to each other or shout questions at her.

"What do you mean, killed?"

"How?"

"Is this some sort of sick joke?"

She raised her hands and tried to speak over the din, but it took three tries before they calmed enough to hear her. "I know it's a shock—and no, it's not a sick joke," she told them, her voice solemn, her eyes hardening. "I wish it was. Agatha was a sweet woman. She quite literally took care of everyone in the Athenaeum and made sure I felt welcome from the moment I got here. But someone didn't agree. Someone, one of us, decided to take her life—"

Jericho cut her off. "How do you know it was one of us? How do you know it wasn't natural?" he challenged.

She met his gaze, let him see just how supremely pissed she was. "I know it wasn't natural because Sergei has already examined her and determined that she was killed by a spell. I know it was one of us because she was killed in her bedroom. Or are you saying that the guards, the protections the gods put on the Athenaeum, and the physical and magical security on this place isn't good enough?"

Her answer caught him off guard. He nodded once and subsided, his expression shifting to pensive.

"Was it painful?" a woman with brown hair and an Australian accent asked quietly into the pause.

"I don't know. I hope not," Sophia answered, just as quietly. "I know I'm new. I know a lot of you don't have faith in me as aspida—not yet, at least—but I promise you, I'm going to find out who killed Agatha, and why. They took an amazing woman from all of us, and that cannot go unpunished." Sophia's tone softened. "And I know it's hard, but we're going to get through this together, just like we're going to recover from Erasmus's death. But I do ask that if anyone knows anything, no matter how small, please let me or Lucas know," she said, motioning to the head of the nasaru as he stood at attention nearby.

"You said Sergei had already examined her?" Dion asked. When she nodded, he continued solemnly, "I'll meet with him and we'll start preparing her when he's ready."

Sophia wasn't sure she wanted their prime suspect being anywhere near the body of one of his victims, but she could hardly say anything without tipping him off. "Yes, she deserves the best send-off we can give her," is what she said instead. "Again, I'm sorry for waking you all, and please let me know if you can think of anything relevant."

They started to trickle out in pairs and groups, the tears starting to flow now that the initial shock had worn off. Once the room had cleared out, Lucas walked over to her and laid a hand on her shoulder. "You did good."

"Maybe." She looked up at him. "Did you see anything?"

He shook his head. "No, whoever did this is a very good actor."

"That's what I was afraid of."

Chapter 41

AFTER THE LAST PERSON had departed, Lucas left to check the security footage. While they both hoped there would be something there—preferably video of the killer entering Agatha's room—neither would wager money on it. She watched him go, then turned her attention toward the hallway containing Agatha's room. On a mission to discover what had happened, she stalked down the corridor. She wasn't about to disrespect Agatha's memory, so refrained from flinging the door open.

It was empty.

Someone—hopefully Sergei—had already removed Agatha's body. Still, she stared at the floor where Agatha had lain. Anger was washed away by sorrow. There had been too much of it in the weeks she'd been here. All because someone had decided to take the lives of two beloved people. Had tried to take the lives of her, Lucas, and Carla as well. And she still didn't know why. The who mattered, but she needed to understand the why.

Sophia sighed and closed the door behind her. "I'm sorry, Agatha," she murmured to the empty room. "I'm going to find out who did this to you. I won't stop until I find out. This has to end. This *will* end."

Searching Agatha's room felt even more intrusive than when she'd moved into Erasmus's room. It didn't stop her, though. It was doubtful the killer would have left anything major behind, but she'd seen enough TV shows, read enough books to know that criminals always slipped up eventually. All they needed was something to point them in the right direction. Something. Anything. It wasn't enough to say it could be Dion because he fit what they knew. They needed to *know* it was him.

The door opened after she'd been searching for only a few minutes. She jerked around, her pulse quickening, only to stutter, then slow, when Lucas entered the room. "You scared me," she told him.

He closed the door behind him. "Sorry. I didn't want you to be alone for too long, and I thought you would want to know what I saw on the cameras."

She stilled. "What?"

"It's not good," he warned her. "There were blips in the video. The sections that could have helped us were just wiped."

"How? How could someone hack into the security and do that?" she demanded. "I thought this was the best security out there?"

"I don't know," he admitted, running a hand over his scalp. "We've never had a problem before, but we've also not had a murderer in the Athenaeum before."

"Dammit," she whispered. She wanted to give up, to yell, to throw something, but she turned back to Agatha's desk and started to search for even a scrap that would help them. After a moment, she found something that made her frown. "Lucas?"

"What is it?" he asked as he came to stand beside her.

"Would you recognize Agatha's handwriting?" she asked as she brushed a paper aside to reveal the beginnings of a note, one that had only Sophia's name and a mark where it looked like the hand writing it had jerked away.

"I...not sure. It looks like it, but I couldn't tell you for sure," he admitted. "I have no idea why she would write you a letter instead of just talking to you, though."

"I don't know, either. I tried to make it clear that anyone could come and talk to me about anything, but..." She let out a sigh and shook her head. "I'm still new and people still don't trust me."

"They will. Just give them time. Your grandfather was loved, not just respected, so instead of it just being a big change, we're also in mourning."

"I know. I get it, I do. It's just making this whole thing a lot harder than it has to be," she told him, half-falling, half-leaning her shoulder against the wall.

"There's not really any possible way that investigating two murders can be easy, no matter who the victims were."

"I know." Her phone buzzed in her pocket, just as Lucas's chirped. She frowned at him as she pulled out her phone. "It's Peter," she said before skimming the text, which just asked where they were.

"Same."

They exchanged a look before Sophia answered him with their location. "I wonder what he wants," she said as she slid her phone into her pocket. "We should ask him if there's any way for him to trace the blips, too. Just because he's the tech doesn't mean someone else hasn't learned. There are thousands of programmers all over the world. There could be two in the Athenaeum."

"Dion apparently likes video games. Could be he's learned to help bond with Peter," Lucas said quietly.

Her head started to hurt and she rubbed lightly at her temples. "Damn. It just keeps adding up, doesn't it?"

"It does," he agreed.

Peter joined them a few minutes later, eyes rimmed in red, his mohawk limp and disheveled.

"Oh gods, Peter, what's wrong?" Sophia asked as she rushed toward him.

He accepted her hug, holding onto her tightly for only a few seconds before he stepped back. "I..." He stopped, sniffled, and wiped the back of his hand across his nose. A couple of times he started to say something else, paused, and just shook his head. It hung low, as did his shoulders, and Sophia could only think he looked absolutely devastated.

"It's okay. Take your time," she said gently, rubbing a hand over his arm. "We're not going anywhere."

Peter nodded, the movement rapid, jerky. It took him a couple of minutes, tears falling from his eyes. "I think...I think my dad's responsible," he whispered in a voice that was barely audible.

While it was absolutely true Sophia and Lucas suspected Dion, Peter's words were still a shock. She met Lucas's gaze for a moment before he addressed the blue-haired man. "Peter...that's a serious accusation. What makes you say that?" he asked, his voice low and steady rather than the soft, easy tone Sophia had used.

Another sniffle came before Peter looked at Lucas, his eyes sad but fierce. "I know it's serious. Do you think I *want* to be standing here, accusing my own damn father of murder? I feel guilty just thinking it, much less telling someone else." Both hands scrubbed through his hair before his fingers fisted in the sapphire locks and tugged, as though he could pull the treacherous thoughts out by the root. "I don't want to believe it, I don't. I love my dad, but I also loved Agatha." His attention shifted to Sophia. "Like you said, she took care of all of us. I don't think there was anyone here who didn't see her as a daughter or sister or something...which is why I *have* to say something. Even when I'd rather be doing something, anything else."

"It's okay, Peter. If your dad is responsible, you're doing the right thing," Sophia murmured, "but we do need to know why you think this. We can't accuse anyone without proof."

He nodded and took a deep breath, trying to calm himself. "I went to see him this morning, before you told us about...Before you told us. He's been acting...weird. Sort of jumpy. And guilty. I was worried and decided to check on him, thinking he might have been sick or something. I didn't sense anything wrong with him, but I did...there was magic about him. Not like something was cast on him, but like he'd cast something powerful. So when you said Agatha had been killed by magic..." He shook his head dejectedly. "Killing someone would require a strong magic. And with the way he was acting..."

"It does look bad," Sophia agreed with a nod. "It's not definitive proof, though." His eyes widened and he started to protest, but she went on. "That doesn't mean we're not going to look into it. We want to get justice for Agatha just as much as you do. We're going to take care of this."

"But we need you to keep this to yourself until we thoroughly check out your father," Lucas added.

Peter wiped angrily at his wet cheeks and nodded. "I will. I don't want to cause any trouble. And I really don't want it to be him. I hope I'm wrong. I hope the magic was something else, something innocent. Something that makes sense, because him killing Agatha just...doesn't."

"We know you don't. And it'll be okay. You've done the right thing. We're going to take care of it. For now, why don't you go try to relax, maybe get a little more sleep?" Sophia suggested.

"I don't know that I can sleep right now," he admitted as he turned and shuffled robotically out the door.

Once he was gone, the door shut behind him, Sophia sighed. "Well, shit."

"It's not proof," Lucas reminded her.

"No, but who here knows Dion better than his own son? And having cast a powerful spell right after we find out Agatha was killed by one? Come on, Lucas, what are the odds of that being a coincidence?"

"Very slim," he admitted.

"So what's the protocol or whatever for accusing a curator of murder?" Sophia asked tiredly.

"There's not one, but I think we should go talk to him, see if we can sense the same magic Peter did."

It was the best Sophia could come up with, so she nodded. "Let's get it over with." She moved to the door and opened it, surprised to see Peter leaning against the opposite wall, arms folded over his chest, a determined look on his reddened face. "Peter, why are you still here?"

"You're going to confront him, aren't you?" She nodded. "I'm coming with you, then."

She frowned. "I don't know if that's a good idea…" In fact, it could be a disastrous idea.

His arms dropped as he pushed away from the wall and closed the distance between them. "Please, Sophia. I need to be there. I need to hear what he says. I can't just sit back and pretend like nothing's happening. *Please,*" he said, looking pleadingly between them.

"It can't hurt," Lucas said after a long moment.

Sophia would rather Peter not be witness to it, regardless of whether Dion was guilty or innocent, but she couldn't find it in herself to deny him. "Okay, but you need to let us handle it. No one should have to question their own father for murder."

"I promise," Peter told her. "Thank you."

As they began to make their way toward Dion's office, Sophia thought that by the end of the day, he would probably be regretting his request.

Chapter 42

DION WASN'T IN HIS office, which was a surprise since he was a notoriously early riser who got right to work. They opted to check his room before resorting to searching the security feeds. Halfway there, Sophia paused so abruptly Lucas almost ran right into her. Peter had distracted her from her train of thought earlier, but she'd remembered what she and Lucas had been talking about before he arrived.

"What's wrong?" Lucas asked.

Sophia shook her head and turned to Peter. "How familiar is your dad with the security system? Specifically the cameras?"

He blinked, not expecting that question. "I don't know. I mean, he knows how to check the feeds. Why?"

She frowned as she mulled that over, then shook her head and continued walking. Could Dion have misled Peter? Acted more incompetent than he really was in order to be able to operate more freely and without suspicion? Or did he have an accomplice? Lucas had suggested that it wasn't a single person doing all this. Maybe he was right.

They reached the door to Dion's room and Sophia stopped. On impulse, she cast her threat spell, only mildly surprised when it felt like she'd received a jolt. It still wasn't proof, but it certainly meant Dion didn't exactly wish her well.

"Should we knock?" she whispered.

"No," Peter said, pushing in front of her and throwing the door open.

Dion sat at his desk, laptop open, his fingers poised over the keys. When his door hit the wall, he jerked and his head whipped around, clearly startled. His gaze slid over Sophia, then Lucas, before it landed on Peter. Surprise melted into resignation as he rose from his chair. "Is this what it's come to?" he asked quietly in Greek.

Peter responded in kind, fists clenched, his words hot and fast. "Did you think you could get away with it, Dad?"

Lucas laid a hand on Peter's shoulder and drew him back a step while Dion's brow furrowed and magic started to build in the room. "Dion," he began, his expression stern, wary.

Sophia would later hate herself a little because when she felt that build of magic—still such an alien and unfamiliar sensation for her—she froze for a minute. Because of that—and the fact that she didn't hear anyone speak—she was shocked when a blast of magic crashed into Lucas, knocking him off his feet and into her, their bodies bumping Peter. They hit the stone floor with Lucas on top of her, knocking the breath from her body. Peter stumbled back a step, but remained on his feet. As she struggled to fill her lungs, she managed to lift her head so she could see.

Lucas threw his hand out and hissed an unfamiliar word that had a gust of wind hitting Dion hard enough to not just throw him into the wall, but hold him there. He kept his hand raised as he moved off Sophia and to one knee.

Sophia noted that, even with Lucas retaliating, Dion's eyes weren't on him. They were on Peter. His lips moved, but she couldn't hear what he was saying, not over the cry of the wind. Trying to protect herself—and Lucas—she quickly cast her shield spell, relieved when she felt it spring into place on the first try. She was more relieved when fire flared up around them, causing her to scream in surprise at the sudden rush of heat that surrounded them but didn't quite penetrate the shield. It was still terrifying to be surrounded by a wall of flames, and quickly uncomfortable, but their skin was untouched. For now.

Peter yelled, his voice a plea, "Stop this, Dad! We know you killed Agatha. You have to give yourself up!"

Sophia's view was obscured by the flames, but Dion's eyes hardened as he continued to stare at his son. One hand slowly lifted, fighting against the wind Lucas continued to push at him. Sophia felt a spurt of relief that he wasn't pointing toward her or Lucas, but then she realized he was raising his hand toward Peter.

"Peter, look out!" she cried as she struggled to focus past the pain in her chest, past the fear.

Briefly, Peter glanced at her, his eyes filled with heartache, before he turned back to his father. Quietly, he said something and flung a hand toward Dion in a chopping motion. To Sophia's horror, Dion's head snapped to one side at an unnatural angle. The moment it did, the fire extinguished itself with only scorch marks to show it had ever existed. Once it was gone, she could see Dion's eyes were empty, his face frozen in an expression of grief and anger.

Lucas lowered his hand slowly, which allowed Dion's body to ease to the floor, where it crumbled.

"Gods. Oh gods," Sophia whispered, covering her face with her hands. Before Erasmus she'd never seen anyone die. And she'd never seen anyone actively killed before. Neither were memories she wanted to hold on to.

Hands helped her sit up and arms surrounded her. A moment later, a second set joined them.

"He's dead. Oh my god, he's dead," she said quietly, while one pair of arms tightened around her.

"He is," Lucas murmured against her hair, "but we're alive."

Sophia's hands reluctantly lowered and she glanced up, meeting Lucas's gaze for only a moment before her eyes slid to Peter's face. Like her, tears filled his eyes. Like her, he looked horrified and stricken by what had happened. "I'm so sorry, Peter. I never thought..."

"I know," Peter said, leaning back until his butt hit the stone floor, his hands visibly shaking. "I know I said I suspected he killed Agatha, but I don't know that I really believed it." His eyes flicked toward his father's body, but quickly slid away. "Not until he attacked us," he whispered. "I never in my life believed he would attack you. Would attack me."

"Me either. Anyone could see..." Sophia stopped there, unsure if telling him that she believed Dion had loved him would help or just rub salt in the wound. "You should never have had to do that."

"No, you shouldn't have," Lucas agreed, his voice harder than she'd ever heard it. "I am very sorry that your father turned out to be a criminal, though, Peter. And even more sorry that he forced that on you." Curt voice or not, his hand was gentle as he laid it on Peter's shoulder.

"Me too," Peter whispered. He pushed himself to his feet. "I can't stay here. You know where I'll be if you need me for...anything," he said with a tiny wave toward the remains of his father.

"Of course," Sophia said, brushing her tears away. "You just rest and...whatever you need to do. And remember, I'm here if you need me."

He nodded, but didn't say anything else as he left the room.

"Damn him," Sophia murmured as she watched him. "What could possibly have been so important to him that he'd kill Erasmus, kill Agatha, and try to kill us? His *son?*" Anger began to build at the absolutely meaningless deaths. "It's just so stupid!" Her hands slapped against the stone and she shoved herself to her feet, resisting the urge to kick Dion's body. "And we can't even ask him why!" She began to pace the room, but only made it a few steps before Lucas stopped her.

"Sophia, I get it. I do. It was stupid and it was selfish, whatever his reasoning. But we can't dwell on it, either. We have a body here that needs dealt with, and an Athenaeum full of people who are scared and grieving. And that's just the immediate issues."

She took several deep breaths to calm herself before she nodded. He was right. On top of those two main issues, they—or rather, she—would need to find Dion's replacement. "At least...Erasmus's killer was stopped."

"Yes." He hesitated a moment. "I'm not sure we should share that, though."

Frowning, she asked, "Why not?"

"Why put the others through that? What happened today is going to be hard enough. And it's not like he can be punished any more than he already has."

Also true. Something bugged her about that decision, though she couldn't put her finger on it. "Will you call Sergei, get him to take care of the body? I'll call another meeting." She pulled out her phone and winced when she saw she had a text from her mom from earlier.

Mom: *What's going on? Why the meeting?*

Sophia: *Long story. About to call another one. I'll tell you after. I'm OK though. Promise.*

Mom: *You'd better. Love you.*

Sophia: *Love you, too.*

She blew out a breath, not looking forward to that conversation. Putting it out of her mind for the moment, she sent the message which would have everyone gathering in the common room once more. Sliding the phone back into her pocket, she looked at Lucas, who was just hanging up. "Tell me...Am I the worst aspida in the history of the Athenaeum?" she asked with a watery smile.

He chuckled and shook his head. "Not even close. None of this was your fault, after all. I'll wait here for Sergei. You should go. Don't keep them waiting."

She nodded and made her way to the common area. Unlike that morning, people had already started to gather.

Nick approached her, concern written on his features. "Has someone else happened? Is someone else dead? " he asked quietly before she could reach the others.

"I'll explain in a moment, but there...I'll explain in a moment," she told him just as quietly.

He nodded and walked back to Carla, sliding his arm comfortingly around his wife's shoulders.

It only took a few more minutes before it looked like everyone had gathered. She stepped to the front once more. "Is everyone here?"

"Dion's not," a man called out.

"Neither's Peter. Or Sergei."

"Or Lucas."

"I'm aware," Sophia said with a nod. It took a minute for her to gather her strength for what she had to tell them. Unlike when she'd informed them of Agatha's dead only an hour before, she wasn't riding anger, so it was harder. "Agatha's killer has been found."

She expected the immediate shouts, the immediate questions. Who, they wanted to know, and why. Waiting until the bulk of them had gotten their comments out of the way, she continued. "I know this is going to be a shock to everyone, but it was Dion." This time she didn't give people the freedom to call out to her, but lifted a hand, raised her voice, and went on. "I don't know why he did it. I wish I did. Unfortunately, when we went to speak with him, he attacked us and..." She didn't want to tell them that Dion's own son had killed them, so hesitated.

"I killed him."

Several people gasped as they turned to look at Peter, who stood at the end of one of the hallway. He looked even worse than when he'd left Dion's room and his voice was flat, numb, his arms wrapped protectively around himself.

A few people glanced in her direction, seeming to want confirmation. "Yes, it's true. Peter came with us, and when Dion attacked, Peter saved us."

Sophia wasn't surprised when a few people approached Peter, or even when a woman she hadn't yet met wrapped her arms around him, hugging him tight.

"Are you sure it was Dion?"

Sophia turned, expecting it to be Jericho questioning her. To her surprise, it was Steven who looked betrayed.

"As certain as we can be," she admitted. "We were suspicious when we went to speak to him, nothing more. But rather than defend himself, than just talk to us, he attacked us."

Steven nodded and turned, walking slowly out of the room. Sophia felt bad for him. She hadn't known they were so close.

Nick and Carla approached, both looking disturbed by the news. "Did Peter really kill him?" Carla asked.

Sophia nodded. "He did. Dion..." She shook her head. "It was bad. Really bad. Worse than at Delphi," she admitted.

Carla winced sympathetically and nodded. "I'm glad you're okay."

"I know you probably don't want to deal with it right now, but I'm here to help when you're ready to deal with...getting things back to normal," Nick told her.

"I appreciate that. Give me a day or two, though," Sophia told him. "There has been way too much going on since I got here. And I'm not the only one who's going to need to process. Three deaths in such a short period of time is hard under any circumstances. But with one of them being murder and the other self-defense, everyone's going to need...something."

"I understand."

It took time, with people coming up to ask her questions, but eventually she was able to slip away. She found an empty room and called her mom, filling Heather in on everything that had happened. It wasn't a quick conversation, nor a pleasant one. Heather wanted to fly back immediately, but Sophia was able to convince her to stay as long as she needed. She did have to promise to call or text frequently, but that was doable enough. She was sure that the only reason Heather agreed was that the threat had ended.

By the time she was done, Sophia was absolutely exhausted. She contemplated going back to her room, but doubted she'd be able to make it without running into someone. Fortunately, the room she'd chosen was an unused bedroom. Surely it wouldn't hurt if she just laid down for a bit.

She crawled on top of the covers and curled around the pillow, trying desperately to keep the image of Peter magically snapping Dion's neck out of her mind. It didn't work, but within a few minutes, she was asleep.

Normally, being awakened by her phone ringing annoyed Sophia, especially if she'd only been asleep for half an hour. In this case, it was a blessing, since she was caught in a nightmare which replayed and warped the events in Dion's room. She was groggy when she dug her phone out and hit the accept button without looking to see who was calling.

"'lo?"

"Sophia? Where are you?" Lucas asked.

"Um..." She forced her eyes open and looked around. "One of the empty bedrooms. Why?"

"Dion's body is gone. So is Agatha's."

She shot upright. "What? How?"

"We're not sure. They'd both been moved to the clinic. Sergei and Penny were both there. They said they felt a burst of magic before the bodies just disappeared."

For a time, she could only stare at the wall, confusion and anger mingling together within her. "It sounds like you might have been right," she said, her voice quiet, tight, as she fought not to scream. "The only reason I can think of for someone to take those bodies...is if Dion wasn't working alone. And something on him or his body could have proved that."

"I know," he said, sounding as unhappy as she was.

She rubbed a hand over her face as she swung her legs over the edge of the bed. "We need to keep this quiet. I don't want a panic. We'll need to tell Penny and Sergei not to say a word to anyone. But I don't think we can do this with just the two of us. There's too many people, and definitely too much of the Athenaeum that could be hiding the truth."

"I've already told them not to mention it to anyone but the two of us. Sergei's not a problem, and I don't think Penny will say anything. As for the rest...I agree. I'm just not sure yet who we should bring into this."

"Neither am I, but we'll figure it out. For right now..." She let out a little scream of frustration and shoved out of the bed to pace. "We'll have to figure out what to tell people when we don't have a funeral, but I want to try to get things back to normal as soon as possible, outside of our investigation."

"That shouldn't be a problem. I checked, and Agatha wanted cremation and a quiet ceremony. Dion...as a traitor to the Athenaeum, he is essentially shunned in death. We'll get through this, Sophia, but I still want you to be safe. We don't know what Dion's end goal was, or what his partner's goal is. He may back off now that Dion was caught and killed, but he may still want you dead."

A cold shudder ran through her and she nodded. "I know," she whispered. "I'll keep going with the training, but I do need to devote more time to learning how to be aspida. I can't let everything else fall apart while we try to figure out the truth."

"There's nothing wrong with that, and you do need to do that. But if you want to keep up pretenses, you should come to dinner tonight, and tomorrow, we can get started."

Food was the last thing on her mind, and the idea of putting anything in her belly made it roll, but she understood his point. "I'll be there. And Lucas?"

"Yes?"

"Thank you. For everything."

"You're welcome, as long as you be careful," he told her before hanging up.

In the depths of the Athenaeum, in a room people had long forgotten about, a single figure stood in front of a stone slab. On the stone rested the bodies that had been stolen from the clinic.

The figure smiled into the dark and let out a few hissing words. Intense flames, almost white with their heat, erupted from both bodies, turning them to ash in a matter of moments. When the fire died, they stepped forward and ran their fingers through the fine powder that now covered the stone, rubbing it between their fingers. They laughed and looked to the corner, a space where no light could reach, regardless of how brightly lit the room was.

"We're getting closer. They don't know it, but we're closer. Though I think we need to be patient. Let them get comfortable before we step our game up."

They looked toward the doorway, still smiling with sick glee. "This is going to be so much fun."

About The Author

Meg M. Robinson is a fantasy author who lives in north Georgia with her husband, a teenager, and a small menagerie of animals. She's goofy and a little dorky, which greatly amuses her family.

She's obsessed with crows, sea turtles, and houseplants. And, of course, books. When she's not focused on either reading or writing a book, she enjoys playing video games, archery, and baking.

www.megmrobinson.com

Please consider leaving a review for this book. Reviews are extremely important for authors, but especially indie authors like me! Believe me, we appreciate it!